SAVED BY HIS HALO

BRIDGET L. ROSE

Playlist

Always Been You - Shawn Mendes

Eres Mía - Romeo Santos

Like I Can - Sam Smith

Treat You Better - Shawn Mendes

Aleluya - Reik

Broken Home - 5 Seconds of Summer

Potential - Lauv

no lo ves - Grupo Frontera, Ozuna

Stay With Me - Sam Smith

If I Was Your Man - The Vamps

Bésame - Luis Fonsi, Myke Towers

Mercy - Shawn Mendes

Mind Is A Prison - Alec Benjamin

Sola - Luis Fonsi

Last Rodeo - Restless Road

Trigger Warnings

Cheating (Cameron got cheated on by his ex-boyfriend, and both mmc's mothers were cheated on by their husbands), homophobia (from the outside world such as male leads being unable to be seen together in certain countries because of the laws there), vulgar language and two sexually explicit scenes, Formula One crashes that may be scary for some readers, child abandonment and childhood trauma (toxic parental relationships), and dissociation depicted on page as well as panic attacks.

This book is dedicated to everyone who has been told they aren't good enough. A soul as special as yours should never be made to feel like you aren't enough, not when you're so much more than that. You're unique, strong, beautiful, and capable of everything you want to achieve.

Let Cameron remind you of that.
Let Halo prove it to you.

And to everyone who has been with me from the start, since the first book in this series, this one is for you, too. Thank you for allowing me to tell my stories and sticking by my side, always.

Pitstop Series

Team Names

Spark Racing

Disclaimer

There are two chapters in the back of the book taken from The Other Side of Her Storm (Scar and Storm's Novella), but since they are from Cam's and Halo's perspectives of the day they first meet, I have included them for anyone who has not read the novella. If you have read it, feel free to dive right into the book. If you haven't read it, you don't necessarily need to read the chapters to understand the rest of the book, but they are at the back for you to read first in case you want to read about how they first meet each other!

You can also find all the translations in the back of the book.

Happy reading.

Hawke
Hawke
Velocità Rossa
11

Prologue

Cameron

Two Years Ago

Picking up the pieces of a shattered heart is a lot more difficult than people lead you to believe. Especially when you were planning to marry the person and spent almost half a decade with them by your side, talking about your future. Especially when they cheat on you with the one person they always assured you meant nothing to them, that they were no one you had to worry about.

A tear drops down my cheek as I take a sip of my coffee.

Maybe it's wrong to be drinking coffee at one in the morning, but if I don't have a cup, I'll fall asleep, and I'm having a hard time sleeping at the moment. Being in our bed without him brings me too much pain to handle, and even when I finally allow myself to try and sleep, it's always on the couch, far away from his scent. Not that I sleep much or for long because the nightmare of Elijah cheating, the image of them naked in bed with each other, haunts me in my dreams, too.

Although it's completely dark out and I can't see a thing, I stay on my porch and keep my eyes trained on my family's ranch. It's December here in Australia, and I'm enjoying the warmth of the summer temperature even this late at night.

I close my eyes, holding the mug with both of my hands as I listen to the nocturnal wildlife around me make all sorts of noises.

Another tear drips down my cheek.

No part of me understands how he could do this to me, to us. We wanted to get married. We were planning to adopt a child. We wanted *everything* with each other.

Now we have nothing left.

Nothing but pain.

More tears follow, so I cover my face with my hand, sobbing into it.

I've never felt anything like this. I've never felt so betrayed, humiliated, torn into a million pieces, and enraged at the same time.

He sat next to me, his arm wrapped around my shoulders, kissing my temple as he whispered, "It's you and me against the world, Ronnie. You're everything to me. I'll never need more."

My sob turns into an unamused laugh.

He really fooled me with that bullshit.

"Cami?" my sister's voice travels from the front door all the way to where I'm sitting on the wooden bench to the left of it, and I quickly wipe my tears before she appears in front of me.

"Hey, Hazelnut," I reply as she stands in front of me with her arms wrapped around herself. Hazel is only twelve, but we've been through enough in this family for her to often act like she's an adult already. She's certainly had to be with parents like ours. "Why are you awake, honey?"

"I had a feeling you might need me," she replies, and I feel my heart warm as her words sink in.

"Come here," I say and open my arms after placing my cup of coffee to the side.

She studies my face with her brown eyes for a moment, narrowing them as if she knows something's wrong with me.

My heart palpitates in fear because I don't ever want her to be able to pick up on that. My sister shouldn't have to worry about me.

"You've been crying," she points out but also closes the distance between us so she can sit on the bench beside me while I wrap my arms around her.

"I'm having allergies," I lie. My sister snorts because we both know that is the lamest thing I could have said. "Yeah, I've been crying, but it's okay. Even broken hearts mend over time. I just have to be a little more patient with mine while it stitches itself back together." I kiss the top of her head and hold on tighter, feeling a bit of the pressure that was weighing on my chest easing because she's here with me.

She's easing my pain.

"Maybe you can help stitch it together," Hazel says, and I tilt my head down to look at her.

"How?"

She doesn't know Elijah cheated on me. I've kept that secret from my siblings, but she does know that we broke up. Telling both of my sisters that the guy they saw as another older brother would no longer be around destroyed me all over again, but they were kind enough not to ask more questions when they realised I didn't want to talk about it.

"Find something or someone else to fall in love with. A heart can't be broken if it's too busy fluttering in excitement every time you see it or them," my sister, the future poet, says with a gentle tone.

The very thought of falling in love again turns my stomach upside down, but falling in love with some*thing* turns it the right way around again. Hazel has a point, and I squeeze her arm a little as I let my mind wander.

Hazel rearranges next to me until she's hugging me from the side, her head resting on my chest. We don't speak again, but her words swirl around in my head, trying to turn what she said into the solution to my problems.

There's only so much time I have in my life between being an F1 driver, taking care of my family, and trying to spend time with the family I found over the years. It was one of the reasons Elijah said he cheated on me. Because I had no time for him. Because I was always busy working. Because he felt like what I was giving him wasn't enough.

There's nothing like being told you're not good enough right after you catch the man you thought was the love of your life with his hand wrapped around another man's dick.

I suck in a silent but sharp breath to keep the tears away and since her head is on my chest, Hazel notices and holds me tighter.

"You'll be okay, Cami. Elijah was not the man you were meant to spend the rest of your life with. He was a singular chapter in your story, and now you can flip the page and write the next one."

"You really are going to be an author one day, aren't you?" I ask Hazel as I kiss the top of her head again.

"Yup, and I'm going to write about your life. It'll make for a great book."

I tickle her side until she's laughing so hard, I can't help but join her.

She's right.

It's time I write the next chapter of my story.

CHAPTER 1

Cameron

James Landon won the championship last year.

He deserved it, and, as a friend, I was so proud of him for accomplishing the very thing every F1 driver dreams of, but as his teammate and biggest rival? As the person who was fighting him for the title until the second-to-last race?

I was devastated.

Driving for Hawke is the first time in my career when I've tasted race victory on my tongue, and I got greedy for the title, too. I wanted it so badly that looking at James, spending any time with him at all, became an impossible task that I'd avoided to the best of my ability. Well, up until Valentina Romana, one of my best friends in the entire world, told me to get over it because there's always a next season. Another chance to get the title. Considering she's been knocked down far more than I have been in the world of F1, I decided to heed her advice. I let go of my unjustified resentment toward James, and he wasn't mad at me for needing some space either. He simply welcomed me back like a good friend would.

No number of words in the world could have expressed how grateful I was to him for understanding.

I'm having a hard time trying to stay positive like Val told me to be. Part of me thought that Hawke would dominate again this season, but we're far from being at the top. Our car struggles almost every single race weekend, and while James somehow ends up performing better than I do in every race, my car is most often undrivable.

My team is not happy with me, and I can't blame them. I'm not bringing in the results they're expecting of me, the ones I brought in last year, and they're frustrated. It terrifies me because Hawke has a reputation of dropping drivers when they're underperforming, and I'm under pressure to get my shit together so they don't do the same to me.

At thirty-two years old, they probably look at me as more of a burden than a seasoned, experienced driver who could benefit the team.

I'm disposable.

Replaceable.

"Smile, mate. People are watching," James says as he waves to our fans.

We're on the trailer they often put us on during the Drivers' Parade, all twenty of us chatting and admiring the signs fans have made for us to support us. I'm loved by many, hated by others because they think I'm talentless and don't deserve my seat. It doesn't matter how hard I work, how much good I try to do in this sport, it always backfires, and people twist it until they have ammunition to use against me.

To shoot me in the back if they're cowards on the internet, or in the chest if they're brave enough to shit on me to my face.

"Can't a guy be lost in thoughts for a minute? God, can't get a moment's peace," I tell my teammate with a grin, and he rolls his eyes at me before returning the expression.

"Just smile, you wanker," he replies and continues waving at our fans, never taking his blue eyes off them.

Ever since he got married to his wife, Estrella, he's looked more at peace than ever before. Her daughter became his daughter almost instantly because James is a father at his very core, has been since his son Damian was born, and he wasted no time loving Daisy unconditionally. In a way that I wish my father had loved his family instead of his secretary. In a way that a parent who would never leave his family would. In the way that I will love my own children one day. My teammate looks at peace because after thinking he was in love with Val, one of his best friends, for most of his life, Estrella made him realise what true love actually is.

"This heat is excruciating. I feel like someone has made a branding iron shaped like me and is holding it to my skin," Adrian Romana says as he approaches us, pulling at the front of his shirt before moving it back and forth to…air himself out, I think?

I'm not entirely sure what he's doing, but then again, with Adrian, I never know. He's an odd duck, which is one of the many reasons I love him to bits.

"You're so dramatic," James chimes in, shaking his head at his best friend.

"Actually, I think it's a fair response to the blaring heat. If we stand here for much longer, I might melt into a puddle," I say, and James slaps his forehead with the palm of his hand when Adrian smiles brightly at me, content with my response.

"I'm going to find someone else to stand with," James says, pushing away from the railing of the trailer and moving toward Val and Gabriel.

For as long as I can remember, Gabriel Matteo Biancheri has been my best friend and one of my favourite people in the world. He's the one I go to when I feel lost, the one I rely on when times get tough. He's the only person I ever open up to about what happens at home because I don't want to be a burden to anyone else. Any of my friends would be there for me if I asked for their help, for their comfort, but they have their own problems, and I don't want to be the one to pile on.

They rely on me to be the fun, easy-going one.

Not the one that is constantly worrying about his family's well-being, the fate of his career, the happiness of his friends, and the dark void in my stomach growing bigger with every day I feel like a fucking failure in life.

I shake off the deep, dark thoughts, plaster a smile on my face, and turn to the cheering crowd of people.

There's no time to be down. I'm starting from fifth place here in Brazil, and we're expecting rain halfway through the race. My head needs to be ready for the changing track conditions, and I can't linger on whatever darkness is brewing inside of me.

It has started pouring down earlier than we thought it would.

Nachelle Henderson is standing beside me, looking at the radar with me. This is her first season as a reserve driver here at Hawke, something she earned through her hard work, dedication, and drive.

Five years ago, her brother and one of my closest friends, Asher "Halo" Henderson, asked me if there was anything I could do to help her get more sponsors. None of mine were looking for new drivers to sponsor, so I asked Valentina if any of hers would be interested. Being the person she is, she threw everything she had into helping Nachelle.

It was only a matter of time until she made it into F3, then F2, and finally became a reserve driver in F1. She won championships in every other Formula series, and I know that when her time comes to compete in Formula One, she will win a championship here as well.

That is how skilled and talented she is.

"You see this here, Chellie?" I ask, pointing at the monitor. "This is important to keep an eye on because my whole strategy depends on it," I explain before going into more detail about how the radar will determine what tyres we will switch to and when. I know she knows much of this from her days in the other categories, but F1 differs in some ways, so I'm trying to catch her up.

"In the car, I always struggle to determine when it's time to go from wets to intermediates," she says, her hazel eyes full of shame because she's admitting a weakness to me, and that's not an easy thing to do for anyone.

Especially for athletes.

"My team depends on me to tell them, but I'm so scared of making the wrong decision that could cost us a race finish in the points, that I end up staying longer on the wets than I should."

She tugs on the hem of her blue, red, and white Hawke team shirt, the colours complementing her light brown skin. She's a bit taller than me and lean yet muscular, a combination perfect for the world of F1. Her short, dark brown hair is hiding beneath one of the team hats Hawke provided her, and she uses it to hide her expression from me as she looks down at her sneaker-covered feet.

"It comes with experience, Nachelle. You won't get great at everything right away. Some things have taken me years to master, and some I still struggle with to this day," I admit, placing a hand on her shoulder and squeezing it so she looks up at me. "You have to trust your gut. Your initial instinct is most often the right choice, and the overthinking that happens after comes from doubts that try to convince you you were wrong before. You have to find a way to either ignore them or silence them when you're in the car. It's important," I say, a soft smile curling up the corners of my mouth once I'm done talking.

I hope it conveys the kind of comfort my words are meant to give her.

"Thanks, Cameron," she says, and, finally, a small smile appears on her face.

There are thirteen years between us, and it feels that way, too. I feel old next to her. My back is killing me most days, I get tired a lot more easily than she does, and my determination isn't nearly as strong now as it was when I was her age. Mine is weathered, diluted by the rain of failure and disappointment I experienced over the years.

"Anytime, Chellie."

My nickname for her turns her small smile into a full-faced one. It has had that effect since she approached me at the beginning of the season. I think she was seeking a mentor, but it's difficult to mentor someone full-time when you're also racing yourself. I'm not Leonard Tick. He mentored Val while racing for Alfa Adrenalina. The three-time World Champion excels at everything he does, including being the co-owner of a driver academy he built from the ground with Val *and* being the team principal for Grenzenlos.

I don't think that man gets any sleep.

Luckily, Nachelle hasn't officially asked me to be her mentor, and I'm glad she hasn't because, while I will always take the time to answer whatever question she has about Formula One, I don't think I'd even be a good mentor.

"Cameron, time to go," Parker, my performance coach, says, holding the cooling vest I requested earlier because Adrian was right.

The heat is overwhelming.

Parker is tall and muscular with short, blonde hair that is somehow always perfectly styled. Even after a day of us running around, fulfilling all of our responsibilities, they look absolutely flawless, not a hair out of place. I've told them often that I find it incredibly annoying, but they always simply laugh at me.

"Coming," I reply, nudging Chellie with my shoulder one last time before following my performance coach.

It's time to get ready to race in the rain, and I have yet to find a way to stop feeling so bloody nervous.

Everything will be fine, and if my strategy goes well, I could even snatch the win. Protect my seat from being given to someone else.

Someone younger.

Disposable.

Replaceable.

Disposable.

Replaceable.

Disposable.

Replaceable.

The words continue to repeat themselves in my head, and I can't shove them down as easily as I normally do when I catch another glimpse of Nachelle.

They could give her my seat at any moment because I'm not good enough for them, and I wouldn't be able to blame anyone but myself.

I just don't know if I could ever be around her again if she took the spot I worked over a decade to secure.

I hope I'll never have to find out who I'd become if that were to happen.

CHAPTER 2
Halo

It's pouring.

At the beginning of the race, the rain was light enough for the drivers to get the green light and start the race. They were all on wets because water was pooling in parts of the track, but it wasn't nearly as worrisome as the amount of rain currently hitting the track at every corner, every straight.

There are puddles of water that the drivers keep racing through because there isn't even a dry line anymore.

The safety car was deployed two laps ago, ensuring the drivers follow behind it at a safer speed. I have no fucking clue why they haven't red-flagged the session yet, stopping it before another driver crashes. It was terrifying to see one of the Zeitgeist drivers crashing into the wall at the beginning of the race. He's fine, he assured everyone of it over the radio, but it was a bad enough crash that he was taken to the hospital.

"This session has to be red-flagged. My driver and the rest of the grid are in danger." Scarlette Roots, my closest friend for almost a decade, is Valentina Romana's race engineer at Velocità Rossa, and she does not play when it comes to Val's safety.

Scar listens to whoever she's speaking to, while I look at all of the engineers sitting beside me. As the Chief Designer of Velocità Rossa, I'm not involved in the daily trackside operations but I'm in charge of oversight and here for any support they may need. It's up to me to help should any problems come up and check on the designs to make sure they are sturdy.

Which means during the race, I mostly stand by and observe, scan the data that comes in.

It's killing me right now to simply *observe* because if Scar is worried, then I need to be worried.

My eyes shift to the screen where they're showing the drivers at the same moment they pivot to Cameron Kion's car. My heart flutters in the same, stupid way it always does when I get a glimpse of him, and it doesn't even care that I can't see his face. It stumbles and dances anyway. It has been doing the same, irritating thing since I met him five years ago, and the better friends we become, the more I struggle to suppress whatever complicated feelings I have for the Australian. He has this irritating habit of tugging on my weakness, my sister's happiness, and making me like him even more with every second we spend together.

It's why I don't get how his ex could have ever cheated on him.

If Cam was mine, I'd make sure he never, ever had to doubt that I wouldn't want anyone but him. Me. The guy who never wanted to be in a relationship because he didn't want to give his heart to someone. I told Scar the bullshit excuse that I didn't fall in love because I was too busy taking care of my family, but my family doesn't need me to take care of them. They can take care of themselves, which means most days, when I'm not working, I'm spending my time wondering if maybe I haven't been very good at keeping my heart inside my chest, after all.

But all we are for now is friends. Close friends, perhaps, but not more than that.

"I don't care if the stewards aren't willing to call for a red flag right now. If you don't get them off the track soon, someone is going to get seriously injured," Scar says into her headphones' mic, still arguing with the person on the other end of the radio.

"I can't see anything. My car is sliding everywhere," Valentina says over her radio, and my heart drops at the fear in her voice. "Adrian, Gabriel, James, and Cameron are sliding just as much behind me."

I wonder how many more people have to tell the ones in charge that this is dangerous for them to finally listen.

"They're telling me their radars are showing less rain in three laps, so they want to wait it out," Scar explains to Val.

I can hear both sides of their communication, unlike only being able to hear Scarlette's when she argues with who I think are the stewards. One of my headphones is on my ear, the other off, so I can hear better.

"I can barely even see the safety car, Scarlette. This is unsafe!"

My heart is hammering in my chest. This is getting worse by the minute, and nothing is being done to prioritize the drivers' safety. I lift my hand to my mouth because I'm suddenly nauseous and my jaw has a nasty habit of dropping every time I see one of the drivers sliding on the track.

"Someone needs to stop this," I say to myself since no one around me is paying me any attention.

They're all focused on the screens, their gazes stuck to them like glue.

There is an air in the room, one of fear and dread. It sinks its claws into my back until I start sweating anxiously. My hand is still covering my mouth, and it muffles the gasp that escapes me when Adrian slips off the track and into the grass area. He manages to get control of his car again, but when he rejoins the track, he's in last place.

"Fuck," I mumble, but finally, the rain seems to slow down. It's not hitting the track as quickly and with as many drops as it was a lap ago, sending the tiniest bit of relief through my system. My knees buckle, and I settle down in my seat, the one I haven't occupied since the beginning of the race.

I was too nervous to sit still, but now that the rain really is slowing, my heart is settling into a slower rhythm again.

More laps pass, and the rain becomes a trickle. The track is still wet and slippery, but eventually, the safety car leaves, allowing the drivers to get back to racing. Valentina restarts the race without any threat from the men behind her, because she caught them off-guard, and they all chase after her to try and get first place.

The camera focuses on Cam and James battling for fourth, so the screens in the Velocità Rossa garage, in Val's garage, light up with the image of their fight.

I'm on my feet again.

If there was enough space to pace without annoying anyone I work with, I'd be moving up and down in the garage to ease the nerves pushing at my chest until breathing becomes difficult. The track isn't drowning in water anymore, but that doesn't mean battling is safe yet. The stewards haven't even enabled DRS—the drag reduction system—yet, so that the driver who's within a second's distance of the other can get a speed advantage in the designated zones. And they haven't enabled it yet because *it isn't safe yet.*

I can't decide whether to look at the screens or to look at my shoes while Cameron attacks and James defends.

Ten laps before the end of the race, they're still fighting.

The track is slowly drying up, and there is finally a dry racing line for them to take to keep from slipping around the track as much as they were before.

Cam is less than a second behind James now, and the DRS is enabled, which means that when the main straight comes into view, he pulls onto the wetter part of the track to try and overtake his teammate.

That's when the whole world seems to stop breathing.

Cameron gets too close to James, his rear wheel touching James' front wing. Within a second, his tire gets a puncture. Because of the speed he was racing at, he has no time to avoid going onto the grass, his car flipping because of the sheer force and momentum. He slams into the barrier after several 360 flips, finally landing upside down.

My heart stops beating, then drops all the way into my stomach.

"Oh my God."

My hand flies straight back to my mouth.

I notice seven other people in the room doing the same thing, including Scarlette. She looks over her shoulder at me, her blue eyes wide with fear. Mine must mimic hers because she quickly turns back to her screen, hitting her radio button and asking whoever she's talking to if Cameron is okay.

The cameras are no longer showing the crash, which isn't a good sign. They don't show anything when they're not sure if the driver is okay to prevent anyone from seeing something as traumatic as...

No, I won't go there. Cam is okay. He'll be alright. He has to be.

Minutes fly by without any update on Cameron. He doesn't say anything to assure people he's okay, and with every second that passes, I get more and more scared.

"Asher." My sister's voice, her use of my real name instead of my nickname, something she never does, drags me out of my panicked state. I see her approach me with tears in her eyes.

She loves Cameron. Ever since she was little, he was someone she looked up to, so when she joined his team, it was like a dream come true for her. Not to mention, she was in a fever dream for weeks after she heard that he helped her connect with Valentina, who in turn got her new sponsors that pushed her from F4 into F3. Then, when Cam met her, he was always so kind to her, and she was drawn to him even more.

They built a friendship much like the one I built with Scar over the years, and while they haven't been friends for as long, they still care deeply about one another.

"*Todo estará bien*, Nachelle," I assure her and myself in the same breath.

I look at Scar again, hoping she will have an update, but she's still staring at her screens as the stewards call for a red flag. The remaining drivers on the grid drive into the pits, and as soon as she's out of the car, Valentina rushes into her garage and straight toward Scarlette.

"Tell me whatever you know. Tell me he's okay," she says, her voice far more demanding than I've ever heard it, especially while speaking to Scar. It's the fear, the terror, and Scar doesn't fault her for it.

She understands it.

"They got him out of the car and are taking him to the hospital, but Val, his hands—" My best friend cuts off as she looks at her driver with tears slowly spilling into her eyes. "They're taking him in to see what injuries he has exactly, and I'm sorry, I don't know what has been hurt, apart from his hands. I can't give you any reassurance he'll be okay because he wasn't conscious at any stage."

"Asher," my sister repeats, and I hold her closer, my own fear making my heart race so quickly, it may beat out of my chest.

"*Todo estará bien*," I repeat like a broken record.

Everything will be okay.

It has to be.

CHAPTER 3

Cameron

I CAN'T BREATHE PROPERLY. There is a sharp pain in my side whenever I inhale, but it's nothing compared to the excruciating agony in both of my hands.

"Oh my God," I cry out, the pain making my vision blur. It's a relief because I don't want to see what my hands look like.

"Pneumothorax." It's the only word I pick up in the conversation the paramedics are having with each other while rushing me to hospital.

"What does that mean?" I manage to ask, but the words make me cough, which sends a million needles into my chest where they prick me over and over. I scream in pain, but that makes it worse, so I bite down on my tongue to keep from expelling any more sounds.

I'm dying.

It's the only explanation for the amount of suffering I'm experiencing right now. My stomach is twisting, and if there was anything inside of it, it wouldn't be for much longer. Everything in my chest feels like it's on fire, and I'm so scared of whatever is making even breathing this difficult.

"Mr. Kion, you need to stay still. The more you move, the worse it'll get," one of the paramedics says, and if I could, I'd laugh in their face because that's easier said than done when I want to crawl out of my skin.

"I don't want to die," is the last thing I say before everything starts to spin.

My ears are ringing, and my vision isn't just blurring anymore.

It turns black until I see nothing, hear nothing, feel nothing anymore.

CHAPTER 4
Halo

WE'VE BEEN SITTING IN the hospital, waiting for an update on Cam, for the last three hours.

Valentina, Adrian, Gabriel, Leonard, Scarlette, Parker, Nachelle, and I keep staring at the double doors the nurses and doctors use to get to wherever they're going. The white light in this hospital room is giving me a headache, a lovely side effect of having eyes as bright as mine.

"Should we go find someone to talk to?" my sister asks, her leg bouncing up and down because of how nervous she is. I'm surprised she's still sitting since we both have a habit of pacing whenever we're anxious about something.

"Adrian already tried that half an hour ago. They couldn't tell us anything," I remind her, and three seconds later, she jumps out of her seat and starts pacing around the room.

I lean back in my seat, crossing my arms in front of my chest as I watch her walk from left to right and back again.

Scarlette takes Nachelle's seat, and I wrap my arm around her shoulders, pulling her against my side almost instinctively. I know she misses her husband, Storm, right now because he'd give her the comfort she needs, but he stayed with their dogs in Monaco since he's got his own MotoGP race to leave for in a few days. Something I know he probably regrets because when Scar is in distress, there is no place he'd rather be than by her side.

So, I hold her as tightly as possible.

"Val, look," Adrian says and gently smacks her arm repeatedly to get her attention. She has her face in her hands, so it takes her a second to let her eyes adjust to the bright light to look at what he's showing her on his phone.

"Stop it," she blurts out and snatches his phone out of his hands to take a closer look. She hands it over to Gabriel after she's finished admiring what I assume is a picture of some sort, and Gabriel hands it to James, whose bottom lip pushes forward in an adorable pout.

"How has she gotten so much bigger in the last five days?" he asks Adrian, and I notice his eyes have filled with tears.

They must be talking about his newborn daughter.

"I don't know, but I miss her so much," Adrian says while James holds out the phone for me to take. Honored that they want to include me in this whole passing the phone along, sharing this wholesome moment with me, I take it with a small smile.

On the screen, Nevaeh Fuchs-Romana is holding her daughter, who's wearing a romper that says "I love my daddy" on it. Although she's only a couple of months old, she looks like a perfect combination of her mother and father. Her nose and lips are all Nevaeh, and her eyes and hair are all Adrian.

This is most certainly the best way to distract all of us from the uncertainty of what's happening with Cameron.

I hand the phone over to Scar, my attention set on Gabriel. Cam told me once that the two of them have been best friends for over a decade, and that they are as close as two people with such tiring schedules could possibly be. Gabriel has also lost almost every single member of his family except for his aunts and his brother, so I can't imagine the grief currently traveling through his entire body as we wait for an update.

We don't get one for two more hours.

Valentina eventually gets up to get us all some coffee, and I have no idea how any of the F1 drivers are still awake. They must be exhausted. Their emotions have been all over the place since the beginning of their race today, and now they're sitting here, not knowing if one of the people they love most in the world is going to make it.

There's a pit in my stomach, one I haven't been able to get rid of since I saw his car flip all over itself on the track.

The thought of never seeing Cameron's wonderful smile again has a lump forming in my throat, one I can't swallow past. My head is going through all the worst-case scenarios, and no matter how hard I try to think of anything good, the bad dominates my thoughts.

"Try to think of a good memory with him," Scar says, and I look down at her to see that her eyes are unfocused as she stares at the empty, white wall in front of her. "We need to put positivity out into the world. It's the only thing that'll help him," she explains, not looking my way once.

Scarlette might be right. If I keep thinking negatively, if I keep putting that energy out into the universe, it's not going to help him.

I have to think of a nice memory.

So, I close my eyes and lose myself in my favorite one with Cam.

"Why the fuck are we hiking?" I ask Cameron, who doesn't even look like he's broken a sweat. He throws me a wolfish grin over his shoulder, then turns back around to look at where he's putting his feet.

"It's good for Chellie to do something other than work out in a gym for once. Nature is beautiful, why not admire it while you're getting your arse kicked by your workout?" he challenges, still not even a little out of breath.

Nachelle stops at every pretty flower, her phone in her hand. She takes several pictures before she keeps going, the toothiest grin on her face. A grin Cameron put there because, despite not officially becoming her mentor, he's been acting like one since he's met her. He gives her tips, trains with her whenever he's in Moonville, and he's here more and more now that he's broken up with his boyfriend.

Well, now that the asshole cheated on the coolest person I've ever met.

Fucking idiot.

"Plus, it's good for you to get out more. You've been working non-stop for months. You deserve a break," Cam says, his hazel eyes drifting back to me.

He's only five foot nine, but he moves much faster than I do with my significantly longer legs. I blame his muscular thighs. I also blame him for distracting me with his chiseled features, full lips, and curly brown hair.

He's got this smile that could light up any kind of darkness, and when he directs that sunshine my way, I soak it in every time. It's like a healing balm for the soul and a warm hug on a cold day combined.

"Worry less about my taking a break and more about the fact that you're a close second for the championship. You have a lot on your plate and should not be traveling to Moonville as much as you are." Cameron almost misses a step when I'm done talking, and I tilt my head to the side, intrigued by his reaction.

"Yeah, you're right, but I enjoy spending time with you and Nachelle. If that's not okay, you have to tell m—" I cut him off because the mere thought of not seeing him as much sends a wave of protest through me.

"No, it's fine," is the lame shit that leaves my mouth so I can pretend to be unaffected by his words. Cam stops walking, but I keep going, strolling past him and ignoring the bemused look on his face.

I don't want to explain myself or my complicated feelings.

We continue hiking until we reach the top of the mountain—fucking shoot me—and by the time Cameron tells us we've finally made it, I'm completely and utterly out of breath. Nachelle is standing near the edge, sending panic through me.

"Nachelle, da un paso atrás, por favor," I say, and she does as told without even looking at me.

"I was about to tell her to do the same thing. Granted, it wouldn't have been in Spanish," Cameron says as he plops down beside me, holding out his water bottle. I emptied mine about ten minutes ago, so I snatch it from him and take a big sip. He chuckles but doesn't comment on my disheveled state.

"It's a good thing I'm not trying to impress you because this isn't a good look for me," I say and gesture at all of me, every sweaty part.

I take another sip of his water, noticing that he's studying me in a way he's never done before. His eyes travel over my face, along the column of my throat as I swallow, and finally, lower until my heart starts racing for a completely different reason than physical exhaustion.

"I don't know, Halo. I kinda like seeing you so flushed."

Naturally, my cheeks probably go even redder at his compliment, but I don't look away as he makes eye contact with me.

I stop breathing, too scared to move and ruin whatever moment we're having. Because we've never had a moment. Not like this. Things have always been platonic between us, but this doesn't feel the same. This feels intimate, as if I could see every little piece of him by staring into his eyes for long enough.

My heart stutters when his attention drops to my lips, and I can't help looking at his in response.

Anticipation rolls through me, but Nachelle clears her throat beside us, snapping the thread of tension that stretched between us, from my chest to his.

"Can one of you take a picture of me with this stunning view?" she asks, holding out her phone. Cam jumps to his feet before I have the chance to, clearly trying to escape whatever the fuck just happened between us.

I can't even blame him.

If he hadn't, I would have.

And that view my sister was talking about? It is beautiful, but it has nothing on the man who's currently taking pictures of her.

I'm so fucked.

"Mr. Biancheri, I have an update on Mr. Kion's state," a nurse says, forcefully dragging me out of my memory.

The Monegasque jumps to his feet, and I notice his hands are shaking as he approaches the nurse. It takes all of my willpower to stay seated and listen from a distance. The memory lingers in my chest, too, making it difficult to breathe properly.

"Please tell me he's okay," Gabriel says, Valentina appearing behind him and placing a hand on his back to assure him she's there for him.

"Mr. Kion has a punctured lung, most likely caused by the impact of the accident on his chest. His hands are—" The nurse cuts off, looking for the right way to phrase our friend's injury. "He has thirteen broken bones in his left hand, and seven broken ones in his right. His left hand also had two of its six ligaments completely ruptured, so he's had surgery for that as well. He's stable for now and resting."

All seven of us let out a sigh of relief in one way or another, and I notice Nachelle sinking into a squat, covering her face with her hands. I pat Scar's leg once before getting up to wrap my arms around my sister. She's silently sobbing into her hands, and I can't blame her for crying from the sheer amount of relief because tears fill my eyes, too.

I manage to fight them back, but only because if I start crying now, it won't help Nachelle, and I have to make sure she's okay.

My sister will always be my top priority.

I can cry later when I'm all alone in my room, where no one can see just how much Cameron means to me.

So I can hide from my feelings in the way I've always done.

CHAPTER 5

Cameron

WHEN PEOPLE SAY THEIR entire body hurts, most often, they're exaggerating. It's not possible for every piece of your body to ache. There has to be at least one part that doesn't. At least, that's what I believed before.

Now?

Now, I take it all back because, fuck me, my whole body hurts.

I've never experienced so much pain all at once, and as I open my eyes for the first time in I don't know how long, the world seems duller than it ever has before. Part of me knows I'm on a lot of pain medication to help me deal with the amount of pain, and that frightens me even more because if what I'm feeling right now is dulled, I don't want to know how I'll feel when it's not.

The ceiling of my hospital room is the only thing I take in at first because I don't want to look down at myself. I don't want to see what has happened to my hands, to my chest, to whatever other part of me that was injured in the crash.

My head is drowsy, and I don't feel like I'm quite there for several long moments. There are machines beeping from somewhere beside me, but I don't care to find out where. All I want to do is keep looking at the ceiling as I regain full consciousness.

But I don't get to hide for long.

"You know, Doctor Strange is Nevaeh's and my favourite movie. I didn't know it was yours, too," Adrian says, and if I could, I'd smile at his attempt to bring a bit of carefreeness, a bit of lightness, to the situation.

"How bad is it?" I ask instead, hoping he'll make me feel better so I can see for myself what my hands look like.

Although, his Doctor Strange joke isn't giving me much hope.

"You'll heal. The doctors are even convinced that if you do lots of physio, your hands will get back to mostly a hundred percent." I barely keep myself from taking a deep breath of relief because I remember what happened the last time I tried to do so.

Well, I can't *remember*, but right as I inhale, panic moves through me, and I stop myself from expanding my lungs fully.

"What other injuries do I have?" I ask, still not looking at my hands or Adrian yet.

"You have a punctured lung, but it was minimal enough not to need surgery. It'll heal on its own, at least that's what the nurse said." Halo's voice has me dropping my gaze from the ceiling to him, finding his worried yet incredibly handsome face on the left side of my bed. He's holding onto the siderail. His icy-blue eyes are bloodshot, his round lips downturned into a frown.

Finally, I allow myself to take in what my hands look like, and I'm glad when I don't have to see what they look like at all. There are casts on both of my hands, preventing me from seeing the extent of my injury.

"This fucking sucks," I say and let my head drop backward onto my pillow, the motion sending a bolt of pain through me. "How the fuck am I going to hold my dick to pee?" That question gets a laugh out of Adrian.

"Well, you'll have to relearn it for now. You'll also have to figure out a new way to wank," he adds, grimacing a little even though I know that last part was meant to lighten the mood a little.

I can't help the pure sadness and defeat that go through me at the thought of needing someone to do, well, everything for me for however long it takes for my hands to heal enough for me to take care of myself again. Because I'm lucky enough that they *will* heal.

It's just a matter of time.

Hopefully.

"You're not helping," I tell Adrian through gritted teeth, trying to keep from breaking into a panic attack.

The monitor next to my bed beeps faster and faster as my heart rate spikes, and I can't even take a deep breath to calm myself.

Shit.

"Adrian, why don't you go get Val and Gabriel? I'm sure they'd love to know Cam's awake," Halo says, and a moment later, I hear the door to my room close, Adrian's sigh lingering long after he's gone. "Do you need anything?" His question has me lifting my head again, meeting his worried gaze.

"Some water would be nice," I reply, watching him gently push off the siderail and approach the little table they have beside my bed. A cup and a bottle sit there, and Halo pours me some water, then brings over the cup and touches it to my lips.

I take a sip, keeping my eyes trained on him the entire time.

He looks exhausted. There are dark circles underneath his eyes and worry lines etched into the tight lines near his mouth. His hands are shaking like he hasn't gotten much sleep, and guilt runs through me at the thought that I'm responsible for his current state.

Halo is usually a very happy guy who can brighten up your day within minutes of being near you.

He brightens up all of mine.

So being responsible for the pure devastation on his face makes all of my worries about *my* state wash to the back of my mind.

"I'm sorry," I say once he's placed my cup on the table and turned back to me. His hands are back on the siderail, and I notice his knuckles turning his skin above it white because of how hard he's gripping it.

"You almost died, and you're apologising to me?"

A paralysing sort of fear goes through me, and I curse internally because I wish I could take a deep breath. Just one.

Breathing is taken for granted until you're not allowed to do it properly.

"Well, look at you. You look like you haven't slept in months, and, no offense, but it's scaring me a little," I tease, hoping the little smile I muster is enough to show him I'm kidding.

"Are you saying I'm not handsome anymore?" he asks, running a self-conscious hand through his hair to fix it, but there is no need.

His hair looks as flawless as it usually does.

"Only a fool would ever think you're not handsome, no matter how little sleep you've gotten," I say. His cheeks immediately redden, and I can't help but smirk because even while I must look like absolute dog shit, I can still make Asher "Halo" Henderson blush.

And he's my favourite person to make blush.

"I should let you get some sleep. You're all delirious on the drugs they gave you," he says and taps the siderailing with one of his hands, then steps away.

He's halfway across the room when I stop him.

"Halo?" He stops abruptly, turning his head just enough to look at me. "Thank you for being here. Give Chellie a hug from me and tell her I'll be alright." The left side of his mouth pulls upward, but he doesn't mean the half-smile.

He's still too worried.

"I'll tell her. Your sisters have also been in contact with me. I'll let them know, too."

Surprise spreads through my chest like warm liquid, but all I offer him is the tiniest of nods.

It's been days.

Days of me lying in this hospital bed, bored out of my mind while I try to be patient with my body. As soon as my punctured lung is healed enough, I can leave. I can get back to Monaco, to my apartment, where I feel comfortable.

Halo and Nachelle have gone home, and so have Adrian, Leonard, Scarlette, and James. The only two people who stayed are Gabriel and Val, even though I told them to go home since Chase, their dog, probably misses them a lot. Val told me to shut up, that he's enjoying his time with Gabriel's aunts, and I snickered as I sealed my lips shut.

They've come to see me every single day.

But we're all avoiding a conversation I can't avoid for much longer.

A conversation I know my manager, Johanna, has been trying to have with me for days, but I'm not answering my phone.

I don't want to hear the news from her.

I need to hear it from someone I love.

"The doctor said they think you can be released tomorrow," Gabriel says as he walks into the room, Valentina by his side and holding his hand as well as her water.

"Great," I reply and manage a smile even if I don't mean it in the slightest.

While the pain isn't nearly as bad as it was the first few nights, I'm not sleeping well because of it. My hands are killing me. They're swollen, I can see it on my fingers, and itchy at the same time. Every little motion causes me pain, and while the doctor said that's normal, it's not pleasant. Apparently, I also have a bunch of screws in my hands, which is just fantastic.

"How are you doing, mate?" Gabriel asks and places his hand on my shoulder so carefully, I think he's convinced he'd break it if he pressed any harder.

"Better than yesterday. It's starting to feel like I can breathe better without pain," I say, earning a smile from both of them.

They sit down on either side of me, catching me up on what's been happening since they last saw me yesterday, which isn't much at all. They're both sidestepping the topic at hand, my career in F1, and while I appreciate neither of them saying anything, we have to talk about it.

"They've made a decision, haven't they? Announced it to the world already too, I assume." My words have both of their mouths clamping shut, but they don't have to say anything. We've been friends for long enough for me to read them as easily as words on a page. "Fuck," I curse, my head falling backward onto my pillow as tears shoot into my eyes.

"I'm sorry, Cameron. We tried to talk to your team for you, using your email, but even your manager said there is nothing we could do. They have no idea how long you'll be injured for, and they found it easier to simply replace you with Nachelle for the rest of the season," Val explains, and I nod several times as the tears fall from the corner of my eyes.

"What about next season?" I can live with getting replaced for the rest of this season. It's fair. We all have no idea how long it'll take for me to regain enough mobility in my hands to train again, to race again.

But if they kicked me out completely?

Gabriel's face falls, and Val avoids eye contact with me entirely.

Replaceable.

Disposable.

Replaceable.

Disposable.

Replaced.

Disposed.

There is no way I can hide. I can't use my hands to cover my face, so I embrace the tears as they continue to stream down my face. Gabriel is the one who gets up and wipes them away for me, putting his hand back on my shoulder.

"I'm so sorry," he says, and I know he means it.

This isn't how I thought my Formula One career would end. I thought I'd get at least one title. I thought I'd retire when I know my body has reached its limits. It wasn't supposed to end like this. I haven't accomplished anything I desperately wanted to.

A sob jumps free, and I screw my eyes shut because it's the only way I can hide from Gabriel and Val's looks.

Fuck the pain of my injury. This is so much worse.

My hands will heal before the beginning of the next season. I could be ready, especially with my dedication to recovery. *I could be ready.* And yet, they've been looking for a reason to get rid of me for months, and now they finally have a good enough one so people won't hate on them for replacing me.

This accident is the most convenient thing that could have happened to them.

I only wish they wouldn't punish me for giving my life to this sport and almost losing it for them. I wish they didn't rip my heart to shreds after I've just managed to put it back together.

Not all heartbreaks feel the same, and for some reason, this one feels so much worse.

CHAPTER 6
Cameron

Four Months Later

"CHAR, CAN YOU SHIFT it a bit forward?" I ask, gesturing with my right hand to the saddle she's placing on my horse, Willow.

"Do you think it's a good idea to ride Willow while your left hand is still not healed?" my sister asks, but I simply shrug, trying to appear unbothered by the fact that my left hand is just not healing the way it's supposed to.

For the most part, I'm no longer experiencing pain in my right hand, but in my left? Because of the ligaments that ruptured and had to be repaired through surgery, the healing process has taken longer.

"It'll be fine."

My voice and words convey the type of nonchalance I'm not feeling. If I'm being honest, I'm terrified of going for a ride, but I have to do something that makes me happy, and riding my horse usually has that effect. I can't be cooped up in my family's house anymore. I've been stuck here for the past four months.

Charlotte, my eighteen-year-old sister, has been taking care of me, washing my face, brushing my teeth, doing everything for me until I was ready to do it by myself again, so I decided to stay even when I felt better. I stayed because Mum's been gone for months. She's off doing whatever it is she does, and it's not like I can call up Dad and tell him to take care of his daughters.

I don't even have his number anymore, and he wouldn't care.

So, I'm taking care of them as best as I can while recovering myself.

And if I'm being honest, I don't want to be in Monaco right now. The memories of the life I used to live, of the career that was slaughtered days after my injury, haunt me. The fast cars, the fancy restaurants, the elegant city, all of it is a reminder of everything I've lost, and even though my family is there, I found all of them through Formula One.

All of them are still in F1.

It's too painful to look them in the eye at the moment. They all have that pity in their gazes when they look at me, even if they try to hide it, and I can't stand being pitied. Hiding is the only way I can avoid feeling that twinge in my chest from the reminder of everything I've lost.

It's easier to ignore that loss when I have no reminders, and it's hard to find any reminders of the glorious motorsport world when I'm surrounded by hundreds of kilometres of fields, horse shit, and farm animals.

Once Charlotte has fastened my saddle, she steps back and pats Willow on the shoulder.

"If you fall off the saddle because of how bloody stubborn you are, I'm not helping you up," she says, but we both know it's bullshit. She'd be the first to run to my side and help me up if that were to happen.

"Luckily, I have another sister, and she loves me so much, she'd run over hot coals to get to me," I reply, and Charlotte rolls her eyes at me.

"I think you need to watch less reality TV. The drama is getting to your head." I burst into laughter and hardly refrain from telling her I'll never give up watching my reality TV shows.

"Ha, ha. Thanks for your help," is what I say instead, moving toward Willow and placing my right hand on the horn of the saddle and my right foot into the stirrup. "Also, do not tell Parker I did this. They'd kill me." As grateful as I am that they came with me to Australia, they've been restricting my every move for months. I need a second to breathe without feeling like I'm broken.

It takes more effort to lift myself into the saddle than I'd like to admit, but I simply grind my molars together and fight through the discomfort, the pulling sensation, in my right hand. My left one is secure in the brace Parker makes me wear, and I've got it pressed to my chest to keep from accidentally using it out of habit.

"Huh. I didn't think you'd even make it onto Willow," Charlotte says, and I flip her off as I guide my horse into a canter and outside of the stables.

There is nothing but greenery and fields for the first twenty minutes of Willow and me exploring the ranch. My grandfather on my mother's side left this place to us after he passed, but it was never used for cattle or harvesting vegetables or anything of the sort. He had the kind of money that let him run this much land for the sole purpose of having as many animals as possible. When we first inherited the ranch, he had about fifteen horses, twenty sheep, twelve chickens and roosters, eight ducks and thirteen ducklings, and three working dogs.

We have significantly more now, and Charlotte and Hazel spend all day taking care of them when they don't have school. They both love living here, and even though I have hired staff to help out, they genuinely enjoy being around the animals.

My grandfather's sister had a ranch beside ours that she sold after her son and daughter-in-law passed away. She packed up everything, took her grandson, who she took guardianship of, and they moved to some place in the States. Besides their names, Lorena and Aaron Blaze, I know next to nothing about them, except that their ranch is now occupied by the rudest couple in the world. Hazel and Charlotte tell me how often they complain about something happening on our ranch.

Wankers.

"Good girl," I tell Willow when she dips her head to drink water out of the small stream we've walked toward.

I take a deep breath, the scent of freshly cut grass mixed with the scent of rich soil filling my nose. The sun is heating my skin, the February weather here in Australia keeping me warm.

I'm holding Willow's reins with one hand, my left one still pressed against my chest.

It's a nice day, so I decide to jump off the saddle, take her reins, and stroll over the grass with her walking peacefully beside me.

There is nothing special about the ranch except for the fact that it's been in my family's possession for generations. It doesn't even have a name, as far as I know, and there aren't any houses built on it for the people I hired to work here. It could be so much more than it is, but my grandfather never wanted to change its simple ways, so I don't feel right turning it into something he wouldn't have wanted it to become.

My phone rings, but I ignore it like I have for the past three months. I told my friends I need some time to process what has happened, and they've given me the space I requested without questioning me. Well, all but Gabriel and Val, but they're my best friends. Not talking to them does more harm than good for me, and one phone call a week is worth the overthinking, the dull ache in my chest.

Adrian is busy with Nevaeh and their daughter, Leonard and Chiara have been spending the past few months on their private island with their kids, James and Estrella have taken Daisy and Damian to Mexico to spend some time with her family, Scarlette and Storm are enjoying being in the same place for longer than a week because of their differing schedules, and Halo and Nachelle—

Well, I don't think about Halo and Nachelle.

Thinking about Nachelle and her taking my seat brings up so many conflicted feelings inside of me that I'd rather not dissect them. No part of me is ready to look at the pure resentment I feel toward her, unjustified resentment at that, and the pride of her getting a seat she worked so hard for.

It's fucking with my head, making me dizzy the more I think about it, so I suppress it. Bury it as deep as it will go.

And Halo?

I'm ignoring Halo for many reasons. For one, he's Nachelle's brother, and in my efforts to stay away from her, I have to stay away from him. For another, both of them, having entered the world of Formula One, have moved to Monaco, and that's far from Australia. He wouldn't fly all this way to see me, and I'm not ready to return to Europe yet. Lastly, Halo's and my friendship is... complicated.

He looks at me.

I look at him.

He blushes.

My heart flutters.

But it's just that. Nothing more. Because Halo doesn't do relationships, and I'm too distrusting to give myself to someone else after what happened with Elijah.

"Come on," I say to Willow and click my tongue, guiding her to follow me along the path near the woods on the ranch. She loves to trek through there because there are some tree trunks on the ground that she enjoys jumping over.

I get back in the saddle, a little smoother this time, now that I know I *can* do it, leading her into a gallop.

It's peaceful out here.

Riding horseback while the wind blows in my face and hair washes my pain away. I can disappear from the rest of the world for a little while when I'm out here. Surrounded by trees, flowers, and wildlife. Living in perfect harmony with it. I've picked up making perfume out here too, a new hobby to keep me busy.

I can almost convince myself that losing my dream, my seat, was a good thing.

But reality has to come crashing back eventually, and I'm dreading the day that it forces itself back into my life.

Once we reach the open area again, Willow slows down by herself. She brings me all the way back to the stables right as the sun begins to set. I must have been out there for longer than I anticipated. I hurry into the stable, rushing through the routine I go through with Willow every time we come back from a ride.

My hand is aching by the time I'm done, but Willow has lifted my spirits so much, I don't even mind the ache. I press my forehead to hers and close my eyes, taking a moment to simply enjoy the calm in here.

As peaceful as I feel at my family's house, there is always a threat of my mother coming home from wherever it is that she disappeared to and starting a fight out of nowhere. When I'm not home, she's angry with me and thinks I've abandoned our family by moving halfway across the world. When I'm home, she's irritated with me for being in her way.

I'm her oldest child, the one who's taken care of her middle and youngest one, and yet I'm never enough. I have never been enough and I never will be. She treats me like I'm the enemy, projecting what she feels for my father onto me, and it doesn't matter how hard I try to convince her that I'm nothing like him.

She will always continue to alienate me.

It's not my responsibility anymore to fight for a healthy relationship with a woman who so clearly doesn't want me around, even though she depends on me financially and to take care of her children, so there is no use putting so much energy into trying to save what has long been lost.

I give Willow's nose one last stroke before leaving her to eat the fresh hay Charlotte must have put in her stall.

As soon as I step back into the main part of the stable and lift my head, my eyes lock onto his.

For a moment, the world stops moving.

Not the Earth, no.

My world stops spinning, almost sending me off-balance. His eyes are still so blue, like glacier ice, and they're full of the kind of anger I'm too familiar with. It's anger born out of disappointment and maybe even a bit of betrayal. The kind of anger I deserve because I left without saying a single word to him.

"Hi, Halo."

CHAPTER 7

Halo

"It's been four fucking months, and all you give me is 'Hi, Halo'?" I ask the man I want to shake a little right now.

His head drops in defeat, and he rubs the back of his neck as he avoids eye contact. I note that he scrunches his eyebrows together like the motion hurts him. His left hand is still in a brace, not a good sign that his healing journey is going well.

"What do you want me to say?" he asks, tilting his head back again.

He's grown a beard since the last time I saw him, probably because his hands haven't been steady enough for him to bring a razor to his handsome face without the risk of cutting himself several times. Apart from that, Cam actually looks well-rested, almost as if he's at peace here, and it makes me want to scream at him because how dare he? How dare he feel so happy when I've spent the last four months agonizing over how he's doing, whether he will be back, and trying to find a way to make Nachelle feel less guilty about taking his seat.

"How about, 'Sorry I disappeared, Halo. I didn't mean to hurt your feelings or Nachelle's.' Or even better, how about an explanation for once so I can understand why you left? Why you didn't text or call!"

Being this vulnerable terrifies me, but it's easier to ignore that fear while anger is at the wheel.

Genuine surprise crosses his face, and if I wasn't so damn irritated with him, I'd almost find it adorable.

"Asher, I never meant to hurt you. Or Nachelle. I—" He cuts off, and I'm too surprised myself that he used my first name instead of my nickname to say anything. Cam takes a step toward me, and my breathing hitches. "I didn't know my disappearance would hurt you so much that you'd come here, looking all shades of angry."

Maybe I'll strangle him, after all.

"You were my friend. You visited my sister and me countless times in the span of two years, despite your busy schedule as an F1 driver. You were important to me, to us, and you vanished during a time when all I wanted was to be there for you," I explain, waving my hands around in frustration. I never gesture this much, ever, but this man gets under my skin.

"'Were'?"

The word is full of regret, and it makes me realize what I actually just said to him. I laid myself bare even while keeping my most secret feelings hidden behind the walls I so carefully crafted over the years.

"Seriously? That's what you get stuck on, Cam?" I ask, and he takes another step closer to me. There is still too much space between us, too much for me to get a whiff of his cedarwood scent.

"Of course it's what I'm stuck on. You're telling me I *was* your friend, that I *was* important to you. All logic leads toward the conclusion that you no longer think I'm either of those things to you," he explains, his hazel eyes switching between looking from my lips to my eyes.

No words leave me, and he takes my silence as an invitation to close the distance between us enough to make his scent infiltrate my nostrils. My shoulders drop as the tension leaves my body, and he seems to notice because a small smile appears on his face.

"Why are you here, Halo? You didn't fly all this way to yell at me," he points out and tilts his head to the side, inspecting me.

"What if I did?" I challenge, crossing my arms in front of my chest to appear tougher, less affected by his presence.

He takes a step back again, gesturing in a way that says, "Well, go ahead, then." My mouth opens as I attempt to say something, but it clamps shut again because I've already said everything I wanted to say, at least for now.

But Cam's waiting expectantly, so I have to say *something*.

"One text. One single text. That's all it would have taken for me to understand you needed some time. As a friend, how could I fault you for hiding when you were picking up the pieces of a broken heart *and* healing several broken bones? I couldn't, but only after you gave me the decency of a message explaining that. Was that too much to expect?" I ask, uncrossing my arms and shoving my hands into my pockets to keep from waving them around again.

I need to stop.

Cameron shakes his head, his brown, curly hair bouncing with the motion.

"No, Halo, it wasn't too much to expect." He takes a deep breath and lets out a laugh he doesn't mean. "I was a coward. I went into hiding because it allowed me to not address, well, everything." Cameron lets out another, smaller laugh, and I can't help but smile comfortingly because I can see it in his expression.

He's still in pain.

Not physical pain.

No, he's in emotional pain, and from experience, I know it can be so much worse because of how long it lingers.

"I'm sorry. Truly. You deserve a better friend, and so does Chellie. I'm just not ready to be that friend yet." His attention shifts to his left hand, the one that's in a brace, but when he sees me staring at it, he places it behind his back. "I've got more healing to do," he explains, and I realize he doesn't mean physically.

At least not entirely.

He has to heal the emotional wounds he suffered at the same time as the physical ones.

"I get that, but I need your help, Cameron," I admit, and he straightens out his back as he takes in my serious expression.

"You look like you need some food," he says and gestures with his head toward the doors of the stables. "Come on. You can keep yelling at me after you've eaten." This gets a chuckle out of me.

"Sounds like a good plan. I could use more energy to rip you a new one," I reply, and Cameron booms out a laugh that has me grinning so hard, I almost forget why I was upset with him in the first place.

Almost.

Hazel talks without using any punctuation, and I can't stop smiling as I listen to every word. She's got a great sense of humor, and while I only ever met her once, we've been texting a lot since Cameron came back to Australia. She was my only source of information on how he was doing, how his healing process was going. And if Hazel doesn't text me, then it's Charlotte. They both seem to like me enough to want to make sure I continue to stay friends with their brother.

It's more effort than Cameron is currently putting into our relationship.

Friendship.

Into our friendship.

I don't know why his disappearance hurt me so much. We went from seeing each other often to not seeing each other at all. Which is what I convince myself is the reason. My friend vanished. That's it. I sure as fuck will never admit to anyone that I have feelings for him, and not being able to be there for him during his worst times, to not see him when he used to be the best part of my day, hurt me.

I won't even admit it to myself.

"Halo, do you want to see my action figure collection?" Hazel says, and I open my mouth to tell her I'd love to when Cam beats me to it.

"It's late, Hazelnut, and Halo and I have to discuss something important. He's here for another day, you can show him tomorrow," he assures his sister, who mumbles an annoyed "Fine" but smiles at her brother regardless.

She's as bubbly of a person as her brother, and I'm a very big fan of bubbly people. It's why I like Cameron so much. Before his accident, before he lost his seat, he was exactly like Hazel. Cheerful. Happy. Giving off a contagious positive energy.

Charlotte is quieter than her siblings. She seems lost in thought every time I see her, but I can't fault her for it. With her mother being as unreliable and in and out of her life as she is, and her father having disappeared altogether, a lot of responsibility has fallen into her lap. Cam does his best to take care of them for her, but she's strong, independent. If she can do it herself, she will.

Right as we all get up to clear the table, Charlotte puts a hand in front of my plate to stop me.

"Go, talk. I'll take care of the dishes," she says with a small smile. Cameron gets up and kisses her temple before thanking her and gesturing toward the front porch. I nod once, then follow him out there.

We settle down on the bench he has out here, both of us keeping our distance from one another. He's on the far end and so am I, the space between us is like a wall made of bricks.

I lean against the wall of the house, closing my eyes and listening to the crickets chirping. This is my first time being on a ranch, but I can't say I hate it, and I can't say I don't understand why Cam chose to hide out here.

It's calm and peaceful.

Plus, it's the very opposite of the glamorous F1 world.

It makes sense.

"I'm sorry, Halo," Cameron says, and I feel his gaze burning my skin. My cheeks heat because he's looking at me, a nasty habit I wish I could get rid of, so I keep my eyes closed. It's dark enough out here for me to be able to hide my blush, but he has this habit of spotting it anyway when I'm looking directly at him.

"You already said that," I remind him, pressing my lips together to keep from grinning when he lets out a breathless laugh.

"I guess I did, but you deserve to hear it twice, Asher. Take it or leave it. Up to you."

My heart hums when he says my first name again, it hums in satisfaction because it sounds so good falling from his lips. For most of my childhood, I preferred it when my friends called me "Halo." It was a fun, sarcastic nickname I earned for being a little shit to my teacher—because I was *such an angel*—and even though my mother made sure I learned to respect them, I found new ways to be worthy of my nickname.

It became part of who I am.

But when Cameron says my name, it does something to me I don't understand.

"Cam, I don't want your apology. I want my friend back." The admission makes my insides twist into knots, and I barely keep from letting out a hyena-type of laugh because of how vulnerable I'm being. It would be the most unsexy thing I could ever do, so I go back to rolling my lips to keep them shut.

"You came all this way to... spend some time with me?" My head falls forward as I open my eyes, glancing his way to see him still staring at me. I place my elbows on my thighs and lean forward, shaking my head.

"I plead the Fifth," I reply, fixating on my hands. Cam chuckles beside me.

"Don't think that's how it works. You're not under oath. You *can* just lie to me," he says, still snickering to himself. I don't share his amusement.

"No, I can't. I can't lie to the people I care about."

This cuts off his amusement.

There's some rustling, movement that makes the bench shake, and then he's right beside me, sending my heart into a frenzy. His right hand appears on my knee, and I do my best to keep from sucking in a sharp breath because, fuck, he's touching me. It's a light touch, barely there at all, but my heart doesn't know how to keep from thinking this means more than a friend simply comforting another friend.

"Thank you. I didn't realize how much I was missing you until you showed up here, and it means the world to me that you cared enough to travel all the way to Australia to see me. I know it was mostly to yell at me for being a shitty friend, but I don't care. I deserved it, and at least this way *I* get to spend time with *you*," he says, flashing me his bright smile.

It's the most beautiful smile I've ever laid my eyes on.

"As long as no part of you thinks it's creepy or stalkery, then you're welcome," I reply, my attention on his mouth before I force it up to his hazel eyes.

"Well, I didn't, not until you just pointed that out," he says and bursts into laughter. I nudge him in the side, grinning to myself.

Damn him.

One fucking moment in his presence, and I've already forgotten about the rest of the world. He eases all of my worries until they're nothing more than an afterthought.

Cam lets go of my knee, crossing his trained arms in front of his chest to the best of his ability with his hand still in the brace. Looking away is the only thing that keeps me sane because I am weak for trained forearms. Especially when they're tattooed and Cam has a singular tattoo that runs from his upper arm all the way down to his wrist.

It's several butterflies that sit on the flowers he added to the vines he has wrapped around his forearm. The words "Enjoy the butterflies" are written along the vines, too, and there's something so beautiful about it, this isn't the first time I've avoided looking at it. As far as I know, it's his only tattoo, but it's a hell of a kryptonite he unintentionally uses against me.

"Alright, we've procrastinated the conversation on what help you need from me for long enough. Ask me before my generosity runs out. I'm already letting you stay here for free." His grin tells me everything I need to know.

"You're so fucking funny, Cam."

He playfully slaps my arm.

"Spit it out. I don't have all night. I need to get my beauty sleep." I snort.

Yeah, right, as if you need it.

Taking my snort the wrong way, he says, "Okay, that's it. You're sleeping with the sheep tonight." I can't help but burst into laughter.

"Isn't the saying 'sleeping with the wolves'?" He gives me an exasperated expression.

"We don't have bloody wolves here."

"Well, then what have you got?" I ask, and he smiles at me, clearly enjoying this playfulness.

"Dingoes. Several kinds of venomous snakes. Kangaroos. Do you wanna sleep with any of them?"

No, I want to sleep with you.

My cheeks heat all over again because of the direction of my thoughts.

Cam gives me a knowing look, and I blush for an entirely different reason. It has him chuckling.

My chest warms at the thought that when I first saw him, he wasn't in this good of a mood. His deep voice with that beautiful accent of his didn't sound so carefree. He didn't sound and look the way he does now.

Content.

And I'm going to go ahead and take full credit for it.

"Stop avoiding the tough conversation, Halo. Tell me what you need help with," he says as if he wasn't the one to keep distracting me. I take a deep breath for courage, then tell him why I decided to come here in the first place.

"Nachelle needs you."

CHAPTER 8

Cameron

"I don't understand. Why does she need me?" I ask, finding myself inching away from Halo as if it could help me avoid dealing with everything I've been suppressing for a little longer, but his intense gaze keeps me seated.

There is no running anymore. No hiding. He's going to rip me open and lay me bare, and I'm scared it won't only be related to my career. What I told him is true. I missed him. I missed him so much more than I was willing to admit to myself, and it scares me.

It's not a secret I care about him, but the way he's made me feel all night, hell, since he got to the ranch, triggers my trust issues in ways I don't quite understand because we're not a couple. I'm not trusting him with anything, let alone my heart, and yet, I want to run away before he sinks his claws deeper into my chest without even meaning to do so.

"I know she never asked you to become her mentor and you were too busy with your own career to take on such a big role in hers, but—" He cuts off, clearly unsure how to phrase this next part without hurting my feelings. I decide to make it easier for him.

"But now that I don't have a seat in F1 with Hawke anymore and none of the other teams want to give me one, you think I have time to be her mentor."

No part of me means this as an attack on Halo, and I hope I've made my voice monotone enough to convey that message. Lashing out at him won't do a bloody thing. He didn't take my seat. And even though Nachelle did, it isn't her fault either.

"When you say it like that, you make me sound so self-serving, but this isn't just about Nachelle. This is also about you," he explains, and I furrow my brows at him.

"How is becoming her mentor about me?" Again, I don't mean to be irritated with him, but it's getting harder and harder not to misdirect my negative feelings because of how much it hurts me to talk about this. To talk about the sport I gave everything to but wasn't good enough for.

I should really go talk to Val about this.

If anyone understands, it would be the woman who was turned away from Formula One all her life, the one who got more rejections than anyone could keep count of.

"Because I know you want to be back in F1. You weren't ready to leave that world, and it wasn't your time either. You have so much good left to do there, and honestly? This season won't be the same without you driving," he explains, fiddling with his hands. He's nervous. All of this probably makes him as uncomfortable as it makes me. "You were the heart of the grid, Cam, and even if you're not racing, we need you back."

Tears shoot into my eyes at his words, and I look at the roof above us to keep them at bay.

"You're asking too much of me," I say, pressing my tongue to the inside of my cheek. "They kicked me out, and I'm supposed to come back and support the driver they replaced me with? Mentor her?"

Halo wastes no time telling me exactly what he thinks of my question.

"Yes, that's exactly what you're supposed to do because it wouldn't just prove to the world that you're invaluable, but it's also what Nachelle needs. Valentina may have changed a lot of things, but Chellie is still a queer woman of colour. She's going to have triple the amount of expectations on her shoulders. She's going to need a guiding hand, someone who knows what it means to break through the barriers, to stand out in this world."

I study his determined expression, the way his features have never looked more serious than they do right now.

"Why not ask Valentina? She'd know better than anyone."

"Because you also know, Cam. Because you put the entire world on its head when you came out as the first gay man in Formula One history. You started a movement that is still going, a movement that fights for equal opportunities for members of the LGBTQIA+ community. You got so much hate, and you pushed through it all, ignoring every single asshole that told you you didn't belong simply because you didn't conform to the fucking societal standards."

He shifts his whole body my way.

"You're amazing, Cameron. You're a role model. You're the reason why a little kid that feels different because of who they are, who they identify as, who they love, knows that they can still make it."

I watch him carefully, allowing his words to sink in. All my life, I thought the impact a driver can make in Formula One depended on the trophies they won. The titles they earned, but Halo is showing me a completely different side.

There are so many places in the world where it's forbidden to be part of the LGBTQIA+ community. Countries where our rights are getting stripped away by the men in charge. Countries where it's forbidden to love whoever you want. As a driver, I still had to be so careful to hide who I was in those places, but that's why I started that movement in my sport. Because it isn't fair to be punished for simply expressing who you are or loving who you love. It isn't fair to be denied the same opportunities as straight people.

So many of the F1 teams still carry pride flags on their cars to express their commitment to fight for these equal rights.

I've made an impact, such a strong one that the whole world will never forget me.

And I didn't see it. Not until this handsome man in front of me reminded me of what I've accomplished.

My fellow drivers—Val, Gabriel, Adrian, Leonard, James—have felt comfortable to come out as bi or pan too because of the new space I created in our sport.

"This was a hell of a speech to convince me to do this," I reply with a little laugh, and Halo offers me the same stern and determined expression.

"Come back. Please," he says, his voice softer now to reveal the vulnerability in it.

If I didn't know any better, I'd almost think what he truly meant was "Come back to me." But that's absurd. He'd never say that, and I'd never want to hear it.

Would I?

"Can I think about it?" I ask, finally bringing a smile back to his face.

"Take all the time you need because we both know you belong in F1. You belong with the people who love you. You belong with—" He cuts off, and my heart stumbles at the possibility of his next words. "Well, you belong with Hawke, even if they threw you out. You were good there." He leans away from me, his hands moving to his thighs.

"Anyway, I should go to bed. Thanks for letting me stay here," he says and gets up.

"Well, you didn't even book a hotel, so you can thank yourself for showing up here with your suitcase," I reply, but he simply shrugs.

"I'm not spending a cent on a hotel when you've got ten spare bedrooms here."

"It's two."

"Night, Cam. Get some sleep. The best decisions are made *after* a good night of sleep." I smile at the back of his head as he walks away.

"You don't want me to be awake and overthink this." His shoulders shake with a laugh.

"Two things can be true at the same time." He disappears into the house after flashing me a wicked smirk, and I stare down at my left hand in its brace.

"Good night, Asher," I mumble to myself, fully aware he can't hear me.

Parker has been sitting in front of me without saying a single word for the past five minutes since I finished speaking. They look tired from their wild night out, and I'm tempted to ask if they're still a little drunk and therefore don't want to answer my question.

"What do you think I should do?"

I know it isn't exactly an easy question. My head has almost cracked in half while I tried to answer it for myself, but I thought they would have a clear answer ready.

"I'm too hungover for you to pretend you don't know exactly what you have to do," they say and pick up their glass of water, emptying half of it before putting it back on the table.

"Don't pretend this is such an obvious thing, and I'm the only one who can't see it. It's not. My sisters are happy I'm here. I'm finally able to take care of them in the way Mum always judged me for not doing. There are responsibilities here, and I can't leave them to fend for themselves again while I travel the world to be a *mentor*. Not a driver. No. An unpaid mentor," I say and use my index finger to point at the table like it would get my argument across better.

Parker holds up one of their index fingers, then gets up from their chair to walk into the kitchen. A moment later, they walk back into the dining room with their hands on Charlotte's shoulders, guiding her to the seat beside mine. My sister's brows are furrowed in confusion as she glances my way.

"I have no idea what's happening," she admits.

"I'll tell you. Your brother here is worried about leaving you alone at the ranch again while your mother is off being a self-serving asshole." I flash them a scowl, warning them not to say that again. "Oh, please, Cameron. Let's not sugarcoat it. Your mother is vile. Everyone here knows it, and it's time you stop thinking about what she'd say about your life decisions because no matter what you do, she will not approve. So, talk to the person who loves you. Charlotte is an adult and the one who takes care of Hazel when you're not here. This is her decision as well as yours," Parker explains, and I'm about to tell them it's not their place when Charlotte starts smiling, a rare sight these days.

"Finally, someone who doesn't beat around the bush," she says. "Cameron, Mum *is* a self-serving arsehole. She cares about herself and no one else. So, Parker is right. Forget about what she'd say and tell me what it is you want to do. I'll support you no matter what," Char adds and reaches across the table to place her hand in my right one.

"Halo asked me to go mentor his sister, Nachelle."

"This is what this is about?" she asks and lets go of my hand as she leans back in her chair. "Weren't you basically doing that already anyway?"

"No. This would be full-time. I'd travel the world with her, which means I'd have the same schedule as I would if I was still driving," I explain. "Only with no money."

"You can do sponsorships," Parker chimes in at the same time Halo calls out, "We'll pay you." Charlotte snickers.

"He was in the kitchen with me when Parker got me," she says, and I shake my head.

"You might as well join us in the dining room. It's easier than eavesdropping," I tell Halo, who peeks his head through the doorframe with a grin on his face.

"Sorry," is his only excuse before sitting down.

"Are we having an intervention for Cameron?" Hazel says as she appears in the dining room as well, holding one of the books she's reading at the moment.

Fantastic.

"It certainly feels like one," I mutter to myself, but Parker hears me and flashes me their white, straight teeth as they smile.

"This is not an intervention. We're trying to convince Cameron to do what he knows he should do," Charlotte says, surprising me.

"So, you think I should do this?" Her expression softens at my question.

"Of course I do, big brother. I have everything under control here, and we were all expecting you to go back to your life in Monaco eventually. As a matter of fact, I think it'll be good for all of us. Hazel and I have a good rhythm here, and as much as we love having you around, we don't need another adult to look after us. I've got this. So, this decision isn't about us. It's about whether you're going to keep hiding here or if you're going to face what you've been hiding from."

All four of them look at me expectantly, and I almost cower a little under the intensity of their gazes. Halo's words are ringing in my head.

Come back. Please.

Fuck it.

"Okay, I'll do it. I'll mentor Chellie and go back to Monaco. I'll go back to the world of Formula One."

CHAPTER 9
Halo

THERE'S A LOT TO do during the pre-season testing in F1 when you're the Chief Designer. I'm in charge of the test plans, which means I have to make sure that there is an area of the plan to cover every single department and have them get some sort of results to look over. They need to be discussed, and I'm the person who can't fuck up and forget one or more.

One of my favorite things, though, is being in charge of the debriefs with the engineers, Val, and Adrian. They rely on me to tell them the plan and explain the results to them, and it's that trust, the way they know I'm good at my job, that always makes me feel so proud of how far I've come.

Six years ago, I was still working a shitty retail job in Moonville, my hometown. Then, as my sister was advancing in the Formula series, she took me with her, getting me jobs in her team. Which led to me getting an entry-level design engineering job in F1, then becoming a senior engineer, and finally getting to where I am right now. Chief Designer. There are only two people with my position in a team, one who focuses on this season's car and another who focuses on next season's.

I have progressed faster than anyone in my position ever has because of how well I've been doing since I started, but my dream is still to become technical director. Considering I'm already way further than I was expecting to be at my age, I'll enjoy being Chief Designer for a while longer.

There is no rushing because I'm happy where I am.

"Right now, we're here," I say as I point toward one side of the graph included in my slideshow. "And we want to be right here," I go on, pointing to the other side. "Because of that, the aerodynamics team has requested we spend more time focusing on the aerodynamics setup today and see what needs to be changed to improve it," I explain, earning a proud smile from Scar.

Valentina has been listening intently with her arms crossed in front of her chest, not needing to take notes because she retains information better than anyone I've ever met. Adrian, on the other hand, has been furiously scribbling down the entire debrief. Val has shot him several amused glances, but eventually he simply lifted his pinky into the air. From what I've gathered, it's a family inside joke that means "fuck you."

"That's all for today, everyone. Thank you for joining us, and I'll be looking over today's result with the team as we get them in," I assure them, and, as they've done since my first meeting last year, they applaud my presentation.

Pride fills me from top to bottom.

I start packing up my folder and shut my laptop, disconnecting it from the big screen.

"Hey, Halo," Val says as she approaches me, her long, blonde, curly hair swaying from side to side with every step she takes.

"What's up?" I ask, noticing she's rubbing her arm anxiously.

Her wedding and engagement rings are sparkling a little bit extra today, which tells me her husband had them cleaned for her again. It's a habit he's adopted since she mentioned once that her rings have lost a bit of their shine.

It's moments like those between Val and Gabriel when I think maybe I want what they have, after all. Maybe it's not so bad to trust someone with your heart. Maybe, just maybe, they won't break it.

Nah.

Better not.

I can't imagine having to be naked in front of someone in a different way than physically. Being emotionally naked seems so much more vulnerable.

My father surely made my mother regret it, so why would I ever put myself in a position where I'd allow someone to do the same to me?

"Is there any way you could do me a favor? I know I'm not an engineer, but I had an idea. I don't know if it's even allowed, but if it is, maybe it could maximize the settings we've been experimenting with," she says, then places her notebook on the table to show me her idea.

My jaw almost drops to the fucking floor.

"Val, this is good. This is really good. How did you come up with this?" I ask as I lift her notebook up to my face, trying to inspect the information there as well as the drawing she included.

"She's getting too intelligent for her own good. It's going to her head. Yesterday, she was telling me she was the better driver, and while I've always agreed, she's never said it so plainly," Adrian chimes in as he wraps his arm around his sister's shoulders. Val elbows him in the side, and he lets out an *oof.*

"First of all, I was referring to being a better driver in our everyday lives, not in F1, and secondly, I think our race results speak louder than I would have to," she replies, which makes him let out a shocked gasp.

"You see? So conceited," Adrian tells me, pointing at Val over his shoulder with his thumb. I chuckle at their exchange because it's just so very *sibling.*

"Do you mind if I keep this?" I ask Valentina, shaking her notebook a little.

"Sure. If you could have it back to me by tomorrow, I'd be grateful, though. It's where I write down all my ideas," she says, and Adrian playfully rolls his eyes, earning a pinch to his side from Val.

"Nevaeh is going to have a lot of questions if I show up at home with ten new bruises," he says as they walk away, their voices carrying through the room.

"Don't worry. I'll text her that you were being an idiot and she'll know what happened."

They're gone before I can hear the rest of their conversation, but I continue smiling at their banter as I drop into the chair closest to me, studying Val's drawing. I have to get this to the head of the aerodynamics team later, but for now, all my energy has dwindled because I didn't get a chance to have breakfast or my coffee this morning.

I lean back in the chair, watching everyone leave the debrief room. I unbutton my jacket because it's been suffocating me since I put it on. No matter how good I look in a suit, I don't enjoy wearing them. They're restrictive and every time I step outside here in Bahrain, where we're doing the pre-season testing, I start sweating.

A knock on the glass door makes my head shoot up, and my dumb heart starts racing at the sight of Cameron in a white dress shirt and blue dress pants standing on the other side of it. Ignoring it, I wave him inside, welcoming him with a smile.

"I don't think Velocità Rossa is going to be happy to see the enemy in its building," I say as he approaches me with a to-go cup I'm guessing is filled with coffee. In the same hand, his right one, he's holding a white paper bag.

"To be fair, currently, I'm floating around without a team to call my own, so I think they'll let it slide," he says with his big smile, placing down the cup and bag.

"If that isn't for me, you can get out again," I tease, but he keeps his happy expression in place as he pushes both things my way.

"Chellie told me you didn't have time for your—" He cuts off and lets out a nervous laugh. "—*pan con café con leche* this morning."

"*Muy bien*," I praise because, while his Australian accent may have butchered the words, they were right. Plus, I love it when he tries to speak Spanish with me.

One of my biggest insecurities is my own accent when speaking my second mother tongue. While Mami is from the Dominican Republic, Nachelle and I grew up in America, where our father is from. On top of my father insisting on naming me "Asher," he insisted we become fluent in one language before learning another. Mami didn't agree with him on that bullshit, so she spoke Spanish with us anyway, but it didn't come to me as naturally as English. My mother used to tell me it's because I was surrounded by mostly native English speakers who didn't understand Spanish, so while I could speak with her and Nachelle, I couldn't with anyone else. I've also only been to the Dominican Republic three times in my life, and all of those times were when I was younger. I can't remember them well.

It makes me feel so detached from that part of me, from my culture. Nachelle and I've been doing our best to connect with it in our own ways, even asking Mami to teach us more, but I still feel like I don't belong most days. I don't belong with my American side because, while I look like my father with my blue eyes and light skin, I'm not fully American. And I feel like an imposter on my Dominican side because I look and sound American.

It fucks with my head most days.

"Thank you for bringing me breakfast. You didn't have to," I say and take a sip of the coffee before opening the lid to dip the *pan* into it.

"I know, but I wanted to," he replies. "Have to make sure you're taken care of," Cam adds, and I fucking hate that my soul practically sings.

My head is fully aware that he says those things platonically, but my traitorous heart doesn't understand. It's only because I know Cam, because I know the heartbreak he went through, that I'm able to shove down whatever is happening in my chest. His trust has been abused, and you don't get over that by snapping your fingers and willing it away.

He hasn't been in a relationship since Elijah, and there's a reason for it.

"How's your first day as my sister's mentor going?" I ask because he only flew here yesterday from Australia. He had to take care of a few more things before he could join us, but I'm glad he's here.

No, that's an understatement.

I'm *happy* he's here.

"It eased her mind to know I was there to explain things to her after the debrief Hawke had, asking me all the questions she's been wanting to ask someone for days," he explains. "Plus, she's now stuck with my piece of shit race engineer, Cory, so I'm going to have to help her find ways to deal with him until we find a way to convince Hawke to get rid of him." I cock a brow.

"Get rid of him? They didn't for you, why would they for my sister?" I ask, taking another sip of my coffee.

"Well, they were trying to get rid of me, so it makes sense if they were keeping him to make me as unhappy as possible."

Fucking Hawke.

They play with their drivers as if they're worth nothing more than the dirt beneath their shoes. It was one of the reasons I was so worried about Nachelle becoming a reserve driver for them, a full-time driver now, but they had the best offer for her. There's no turning down an F1 team when they're promising you all the right things.

"Their loss," I mumble before biting off another piece of bread. Cameron watches me curiously but doesn't say a word as I enjoy the rest of my breakfast.

"There's something I wanted to ask you," he says and picks up my garbage for me, carrying it all the way to the trash in the corner of the room.

"Are you buttering me up for something?"

I take off my suit jacket, bothered that I'm still so restricted. I fumble with my tie, but I must not have done it properly because it doesn't budge.

"Let me," Cam says as he sits back down in the seat next to mine, reaching out with his right hand to bring it to the knot of my tie.

My breathing hitches, and I stop moving as he places his index finger at the top of it and slowly drags it down.

Oh.

My.

Fuck.

He's not even touching me, but he doesn't have to be for my skin to heat. Shivers run down my spine, and I only barely keep from making a fool of myself by doing something as stupid as whimpering.

He takes his time, lingering even though he doesn't have to, and I realize I've stopped moving to keep from ruining this moment. My heart is hammering in my ears, and I'm practically shaking because of how turned on I am. All because he's close enough for me to smell his warm scent. Feel his breath ghosting my lips.

"There we go," he whispers, and I look at him to see his eyes only half opened as he watches what he's doing to my tie.

To me.

Could it be that he's as affected as I am? That maybe this isn't platonic for him either?

Cameron clears his throat and drops his hand, snapping me out of the moment. I clear my throat, too, bringing his usual smile back to his face.

"There is a dinner party hosted for all of the drivers in Monaco, and I was invited. I'm pretty sure it was a pity invite because of my crash last year, and I don't want to show up there without a date by my side so people can pity me even more."

That gets a laugh out of me.

"You want me as your arm candy so people don't pity you for being single *and* getting kicked out?" He scrunches his nose up in disgust.

"When you say it like that, it sounds even worse."

"*You* said it like that," I argue, still laughing a little.

"I didn't say it like *that*," he argues back, and I raise both my hands to put a stop to this ridiculous line of conversation.

"Okay, you want me to come as your date. That's the bottom line," I summarize.

"I probably should have only said that," he says and bursts into laughter so contagious, I join him. It also helps me dial down the excitement of him asking me out.

Cameron Kion is asking me on a date.

"I'm sorry if this is weird, but all of my other friends are bringing their significant others, so they'll be too busy staring into each other's eyes all lovingly to even notice my presence. I'd be the eleventh wheel, but if you came, my evening would certainly look much brighter," he says, but I don't know what to make of any of this.

"So, are you asking me on a friend date or a real date?"

Maybe it's too forward. Maybe I should have kept my mouth shut.

But there's too much happening inside of me to keep the question bottled up.

Cameron opens his mouth to respond, but then he shuts it again, and a wave of disappointment travels through my chest in response.

"Sorry, that's a silly question. Of course, it's a friend date because I don't have other kinds of dates, and right now, neither do you." I get up from my chair and pick up my suit jacket, slinging it over my shoulder. "I'll be there. Send me the details," I say as I pick up all my shit and walk toward the door.

"Halo, I feel like I've made a mistake somehow. I didn't think you—I mean, we're—" I cut him off because this is pure torture.

"Relax, Cam. You made no mistake. Just wanted to make sure there was no misunderstanding between us." I wink at him to appear more nonchalant, but as I walk out the door, a horrible realization sets in.

I'm disappointed he didn't ask me on a date because, for the first time in my life, the thought of being in a relationship isn't so scary.

The only terrifying part is that I know it's only because I'm picturing being in a relationship with Cameron.

And that's never going to happen.

Chapter 10

Cameron

THANK FUCK YOU DON'T need both hands to play Pickleball.

Gabriel and I have been playing Pickleball for the last two years, and it's something I had to give up for the past four months while my hands healed. My left one may still not be anywhere near a hundred percent, but at least my right one is, and I only need one hand on the racket to hit the balls back to Gabriel.

He's a lot better than I am at this game, but this is one of the few places where I don't feel like I *have* to win. I'm simply enjoying being here, even if I have to ignore the stinging and burning in my left hand every once in a while when I make too abrupt a movement. One might assume I'd gotten better at remembering not to use the hand I'm still struggling with, but, apparently, I haven't.

We hit the ball back and forth, and I'm painfully aware of the people recording us outside of the court. They're trying to get a glimpse at us while I'm trying to simply be with my best friend for the first time in months.

"How's your car feeling?" I ask him because, now that I'm not racing, we get to talk about these things openly. We're taking a quick water break, so we're standing close enough together to keep the crowd of people from hearing what we're discussing.

"It hasn't felt this good in years. I swear, Leonard came in there last season, cleaned up Grenzenlos, and now, I think we could finally be in the run for the championships again," he says with an excited smile.

"That's fantastic, Gabriel."

It's become a habit now to look at my left hand in its brace when I talk or think about F1. A reminder of what it's taken from me and why I was kicked out in the first place. It's a brief thing, nothing more than a glance, but I've noticed I've been doing it more and more.

Being around Nachelle, mentoring her through the pre-season tests, helped me reconnect with the sport, but I've also struggled being in that environment again.

The scent.

The sounds.

The atmosphere in general.

Even if I tried to deny it, I'd be lying if I said I'd be ready to get back in a car right now. I didn't consider that my healing journey would include mental and emotional recovery as well.

"Cameron," Gabriel says, and I realise I've zoned out. He must have said my name a few times because he's shaking my shoulder now, trying to get my attention.

"Sorry. But yeah, like I said, that's great. I'm excited to see you fight for the title again," I reply honestly, but there's concern etched into his features now.

"Mate, if you don't want to talk about it, we don't have to," he assures me, but I step away to make his hand drop from my shoulder, pretending I'm simply putting my bottle away to not offend him.

"That'll be a bit of an impossible topic to avoid considering I came back to mentor a rookie driver," I say with a laugh I don't mean in the slightest.

Gabriel stays silent but looks at me expectantly, and when I straighten out my back again, there is no hiding from his gaze.

"I didn't expect the crash to... haunt me as much as it does," I admit, crossing my arms in front of my chest to close myself off.

"I can see it. Whenever we're talking about the sport, you dissociate. You go somewhere else, and it takes you longer and longer to snap out of it."

A knot forms in my lung, then another seems to form around my heart, squeezing it uncomfortably.

"Can I admit something to you I haven't told anyone else?" It's a silly question. Of course I can. Gabriel would never judge me, and he's always there for me when I need him the most.

"Tell me," he replies, stepping closer to make sure I can talk quietly.

"I don't remember the crash. It was so traumatic, my brain won't allow me to remember what happened. The last thing I can see clearly is trying to overtake James, then...nothing. It's like a black hole in my memory," I explain for the first time.

It's a secret I've been burying deep inside of me, but I made a promise to myself when I got back to Monaco that I'd stop hiding. Not that I could even hide from Gabriel.

"Cameron, I think you should consider trying therapy. It could help you work through it."

I nod several times.

"I've considered it as well, and Parker already compiled a list of therapists for whenever I was ready. Maybe I'm ready now," I say. "But fuck, I don't want to uncover some of the skeletons in my closet because I have a feeling we won't stop after I've dealt with the crash. We'll have to dig into my mother and father, and those are issues I've always done my best to suppress." Gabriel twirls his pickleball racket once, then uses it to point at my chest.

"And you can finally work through what Elijah did to you so you can address what you feel now," he says and attempts to walk away, but I catch him by the elbow to keep him in place.

"What do you mean?"

He smiles, revealing his dimples, and though it's a sad smile, his green-brown eyes fill with a playful glimmer.

"Come on now, mate, we both know you like Halo. You've liked him for a while now, but you don't want to admit it to yourself because you're not ready to trust someone else," he explains, and I drop his arm as I take a step away from him.

"Of course I like Halo. He's my friend." Gabriel shakes his head at me.

"He's more than that. You're both just too afraid to admit it to one another."

My conversation with him from a few days ago resurfaces in my head, but I thought I was the one in the wrong. I thought I made him uncomfortable by accidentally suggesting I was inviting him on a real date when he's told me in the past he doesn't date people.

But would he lie to me?

Did he lie to me?

You don't simply change your mind within a few days, so if Gabriel is right, Halo lied to me about still not wanting a relationship. But I couldn't even be upset with him if that was the case.

I don't know what I want, so I can't expect him to know what he wants either.

"Cameron, stop thinking so hard. The vein in your forehead is pulsing and I'm scared it's going to pop." I smack his stomach, but he's too busy laughing at his own joke to care. He's had this habit for as long as I can remember. Making himself laugh. "Before you overthink everything, go talk to him."

"I can't," I blurt out before he's even done speaking. "How can I talk to him when I have no idea what the fuck I want?"

Gabriel shrugs, and I get the urge to punch him in his pretty face.

"Can't help you if you're being stubborn and oblivious at the same time." He goes back to his side of the court, and I scowl at the back of his head.

I'm not stubborn.

I...I'm still a bit heartbroken. About my career. About Elijah. About leaving my sisters.

Not to mention, my trust issues make me want to crawl under a rock to hide from whoever tries to get close to me romantically. I trust my family and friends not to hurt me in the way Elijah did, a complete betrayal that broke any trust we had, but I don't think I'm ready to allow someone else to have me so fully.

Even if that person is already in my life, making me feel things I never thought I'd feel again.

Maybe it could be different with Halo because we're such good friends already.

Elijah was your friend first, too, my subconscious reminds me, and I'm right back to not knowing what the hell I'm going to do because I sure as fuck can't ask Halo if he wants more if only to tell him, "Well, I can't want more, but thanks for being honest about what you want."

Staying friends with Halo is the safest route to ensure I get to keep him in my life, and I don't want to complicate things while I mentor Nachelle during her first season.

There's too much on the line, and I can't risk losing either one of them for something as unpredictable and often unstable as a romantic relationship.

"You have to be a bit more careful," Parker says as they take my hand out of the brace it's been in since I put it on after my shower this morning. "It's never going to heal if you don't allow it to rest." They may have a point, but all I offer them is an innocent smile that they don't buy.

We go through our exercises, Parker ensuring I go slow and am careful with my hand while also strengthening it and moving it around to get rid of the stiffness in my fingers. We stretch my fingers, then they help me rotate my wrist. I'm biting down on my bottom lip to keep from grunting through the pain.

"You're doing a great job, Cameron. You're regaining full range of motion." I hiss out a breath when Parker stretches my thumb because I'm too paranoid to do it myself. It feels like one wrong move could rupture my ligaments again, rebreak my bones, so they've been helping me more than a physio normally would during PT.

"Maybe, but the discomfort hasn't lessened," I explain, a sweat breaking out across my back as I grind my molars together and finally let out a groan because

Parker isn't letting up, even as they stretch my thumb further than I thought was possible at the moment.

"Because you're out and about riding horses, playing Pickleball," they say, peering up at me through their thick lashes. I burst into laughter.

"I didn't know you knew about the horse riding," I admit, unable to hide from them or lie to them because they clearly have a source of reliable information.

"It's my job to know." Sadness creeps into my chest, but I cover it by keeping a smile plastered on my face.

"It's not anymore, but I appreciate you looking out for me." While I do continue to pay Parker, they could have left me to find a different physiotherapist after I got kicked out. Their job description was performance coach, not full-time physio, and while they are educated and trained in both of those areas, I feel like I'm holding them back by keeping them with me.

"Parker, you should find another job in F1, if that's what you want." They finally release my thumb. If I'd known this conversation would do that, I'd have said it thirty seconds earlier.

"Do you want to get rid of me?" they ask, sliding up the sleeves of their long-sleeved shirt to reveal their trained forearms. Their brown skin is covered in tattoos, most of which are on their arms, and I get stuck on the flowers they have tattooed all over their left arm.

"No."

"Then shut up and let's get back to it." I'm grinning so hard, my cheeks ache.

By the time we're finished with the session, my hand hurts, but it feels like I can move it better than I could this morning. Parker leaves my apartment after we share a beer, and I spend the rest of the evening on the phone with Hazel and Charlotte, checking in on them. Mum hasn't shown her face, which is a big relief because whenever she shows up, shit hits the fan. She yells at my sisters as if they're the ones to blame for our father abandoning our family.

It's always easier to blame other people.

Not that I'm blaming my mother for my father being a lying, cheating, betraying piece of shit, that's all on him. There's no justification for the route he took, no matter how Mum acted in their marriage. Instead of cheating, he should have simply ended their relationship like a mature adult. And he shouldn't have abandoned his family in his attempt to get as far away from Mum as possible, but hey, at least my siblings and I get shitty letters in the mail on our birthdays.

In a way, I'm glad Elijah showed his true colours before we did something as stupid as get married and have babies, because the kind of person he is is not the kind of person I want to raise children with.

Someone who'd destroy his family without even trying something as simple as communication.

CHAPTER 11

Halo

"THANK YOU FOR INVITING me to do this with you. I'm having a great time," Scar says as she picks up another skein of yarn.

"*Arcoíris*, aren't you a bit young to start crocheting?" Storm asks from where he's sitting on the left armchair of the couch where Scarlette and I are currently sitting. He's scowling, but that's nothing new for him.

"You're never too young to pick up crocheting," I argue with a smile he doesn't return. I doubt he would with anyone who isn't Scar, but he especially doesn't with me.

Over the years, his hate for me has gotten a bit better since, obviously, I'm not trying to steal his wife from him, but he's on the fence about me anyway. I, on the other hand, enjoy having him around. Not only can I practice my Spanish with the Puerto Rican, but he also makes me laugh without even meaning to. He's got this dry sense of humor I love.

"Look. I'm currently crocheting Toothless. *¿Eso es muy jevi, no?*" I ask as I lift up the already finished head. His mouth twitches as if he's about to smirk.

"The dragon, huh?" he asks, petting Diablo's head when he approaches him. Scar and Storm have two Bernese Mountain dogs named Jax and Diablo, and they cling to them like glue when they're home.

"Yeah?" I reply, not sure why he looks so amused.

"Why him?" *Shit.*

"No reason." I go back to my crocheting, picking up my crochet hooks.

"Wouldn't be because of a certain Australian whose favorite movie franchise is the one this little guy is from, would it?" I take it all back. I hate Storm. He's an asshole. I'm currently blushing so hard, my head is ringing from the amount of blood that rushed into my cheeks.

"Actually, it's one of my favorites, too, so *vete al carajo*," I tell him, and it's the first time I see and hear him chuckle.

It's irritating how good he looks and sounds while he's chuckling *at me*.

"If this wasn't your house, I'd kick you out," I mutter, which has Scarlette beside me giggling.

"Why don't you bake us something to snack on, husband?" Scar asks sweetly, and Storm, being as wrapped around her finger as he could be, gets up without hesitation to do as she said. He kisses her before leaving the room, and my silly heart cries in envy to have what they have. "Now that he's gone, tell me. Are you crocheting that for Cameron?" she asks, and because I've always found it easy to talk to her, the truth spills free.

"I am, but I'm never going to give it to him. He doesn't even know I crochet, and I'm not in the mood to be judged." Scar looks at me like she knows that last little bit was bullshit. "Fine, I know he wouldn't judge me, but if I give this to him, he might think I like him more than just as a friend, and we've already had a close call the last time we saw each other. I'm not trying to make things more uncomfortable than I know they already will be when we attend the event he invited me to," I explain, fixating on my crocheting to make sure I don't mess up.

Scar is busy making a blanket for Liliana, Elias and Violet's daughter. She's trying her best to make it as pretty as possible for her goddaughter, and it's the cutest thing I've witnessed in a while.

"Sounds complicated," she says with a compassionate look she throws my way.

"It *is* complicated."

We stay silent for a while after that because she doesn't know what to say, and I'm trying to gather courage to admit something to her I've been mulling over since that day in the debrief room.

"Do you think...is it completely stupid of me to want—" Fuck, why is this so difficult?

"To want him?" Scar finishes for me. "As more than a friend and more than a one-time thing like you usually do?"

"Yes." The word bursts out of my mouth without any warning.

"No, Halo, I don't think it's stupid. I think you and Cameron have been dancing around each other's feelings for a long time now, maybe even while he was still with Elijah. He's kept you in this box of friendship because it's where you had to be, where you placed him in return, but that doesn't mean feelings can't grow while you're in there."

I swallow hard as I listen to her, and it's her reassurance that has me breathing a little easier. For days, I've been stuck in my own head, trying to make sense of what I want while also doing my best not to let my past fears cloud those desires.

"But what if he does to me what my father did to my mother?" I ask, my voice barely more than a whisper.

Scar stops mid-movement because I've never told her this part of my family's story. I told her I take care of my family. I told her I don't date because of it. But I never told her the real reason why I've stayed away from romantic relationships.

"When I was twelve, I caught my father having sex with another woman in his car. I'd ridden my bike to his office because it was late and Mami had gotten worried."

The words fall from my lips in a monotone whisper. I'm doing my best to keep the emotion out of it, to pretend it didn't fuck me up as much as it did to see that woman's foot pressed against the window of the back passenger seat and my father's hand against the rear windshield, but it did.

"Months of fighting followed after I told my mother what he'd done. And I did tell her. No matter how he tried to spin the story, what excuses he had, I told her. I had to break my mother's heart, watch it shatter as I spoke words she never wanted to hear. To this day, I'm convinced I heard it break."

I put down my yarn and meet Scar's blue eyes. They're filled with tears, but it isn't pity I see in her expression. No. It's genuine compassion because no child should have to go through something like that.

"Then, he moved out and stopped speaking to me. He claims I betrayed him." It's getting more difficult to keep the tears out of my own eyes. "Nachelle still talks to him, and occasionally Mami does too, but only to discuss important events in our lives. He refuses to take my calls to this day," I explain and go back to crocheting to give my hands something to do, but Scarlette places hers over mine, stopping me.

"I'm so sorry," she says, and I feel a single tear drop down my cheek. "I understand now why you've never been in a relationship. If I went through what you did, I wouldn't want to be in one either," she says, and I know she truly understands because, while it's not the same, she broke off contact with both of her toxic parents.

Her father is the man responsible for the scar that runs from the top of her mouth to the bottom of it, and her mother is responsible for many invisible scars she carries to this day, too.

"But we both know Cameron would never, ever do anything like that, Halo. He's a good person with a good heart, and on top of that, he's got his own experience with cheating. His father also cheated on his mother, and then Elijah cheated on him. If anyone understands the implications of what cheating on someone does to not only the person but also their family, it's him."

I nod as I allow her words to process, and even though it should make me feel better, there is still a massive problem at hand.

"All of that may be true, but you know what's also true?" I ask her as I slip my hands out from under her grasp. "He would never put his heart into the hands of a fuckboy, and unfortunately, that's all I've known how to be."

Nachelle and I live in an apartment a little outside of Monte-Carlo. We have everything we need, and now that she's driving for Hawke, they've even provided her with their newest sports car. Hawke Racing didn't use to be in the sports car business, but they saw how well Spark and Velocità Rossa were doing, so they gave it a shot.

It's magnificent, and it certainly helps us fit into the glamorous world of Monaco, where, whenever you turn your head, you see expensive cars driven by millionaires and billionaires. You see people walking around with five different bags from the most luxurious brands after a day of shopping. Everything about Monaco screams old money, and as someone who is well off enough to live here but most certainly didn't grow up so wealthy, I feel very out of place most days.

This morning, when I went to buy a suit for Cam's event—the dinner party every driver in Monaco has been invited to—the salesperson looked at my shorts, sneakers, and plain t-shirt like I'd personally offended them. I was aware that people always looked pristine here when shopping, but I didn't think my outfit was *that* bad.

I was already in a mood because I couldn't come up with an excuse not to attend the dinner party tomorrow, and then I was thoroughly judged by that asshole, so now I'm about ready to get into bed, scream into my pillow, get some food, and sleep for an hour or two after.

Unfortunately, life is never so kind.

When I get back to our apartment, it's filled with people. Nachelle is standing on our coffee table in the living room, dancing to the music blasting over the speaker.

You've gotta be fucking kidding.

The blood drains out of my face as I take in the crowd of people with some sort of alcohol in the cups in their hands, dancing to the fucking music too.

"Nachelle Esmeralda Acosta-Henderson, just what in the fuck do you think you're doing, throwing a party in the middle of the day? Again?" I ask because this happened once before, only it was at night, and we almost got kicked out of our apartment.

"Well, the landlord said no parties at night, so I thought one in the afternoon would suit him better," she explains, never stopping the sway of her hips. Another woman steps onto the table with her, and Nachelle kisses her without hesitation, the kind of kiss that tells me this isn't the first time they've done that today.

"If we get kicked out, we're not going to find another apartment. We barely found this one," I remind her, but she continues kissing her, waving me away with her hand.

The first time I found my sister throwing a party without telling me, I found it funny. I joined in until we got reprimanded by the landlord.

Today, I'm fucking irritated.

Placing two fingers under my tongue in the way my *papa*, grandfather, taught me, I blow out a breath, making the shrillest whistling sound that has whoever is in charge of the music turning it off.

"Out," I say, pointing toward the door. The expression on my face must speak a thousand words I didn't bother to say because everyone packs up their shit and heads out.

Within two minutes, everyone is gone, the last person walking through the door being the woman my sister just had her mouth on. She waves toward her with a smile, and I notice the redhead blushing before she disappears.

"You were supposed to come home later," Nachelle says as she leans back on our couch, placing one of her arms on the back of it.

"And you weren't supposed to do this again." I shake my head in disappointment at her. "Tell me you locked my bedroom door this time." She digs her hand into her pocket, then throws me the keys.

"I'm not stupid. I learn from my mistakes. Plus, isn't this what I'm supposed to do? At least a little? I'm young. I should be throwing parties and making out with beautiful women. By the way, making her leave was a dick move." She uses her thumb to point at the door, and I run a tired hand across my equally tired face.

"Ever since we moved to Monaco, something's changed. Do you want to tell me what that something is?" I ask, but my sister simply shrugs.

"We moved away from every single one of my friends, and I'm lonely. There's a lot of pressure on my shoulders to be perfect because I'm a woman in F1 and I can be kicked out much more easily than they allowed me in. If I want to let loose every now and then, I think I'm entitled to," she explains, and I appreciate that she's being honest with me instead of shutting me out, leaving me to wonder what the fuck made her throw not one but two parties in the span of five months.

"You are, but not in our apartment. Go to a club. Enjoy yourself there. It's what I used to do in Moonville, what a lot of young people do." Nachelle gets up and tugs her indigo-colored shirt back into place.

"Or, next time, maybe don't come home before you're supposed to." She kisses my cheek before she walks into her bedroom, leaving the apartment a mess.

I'm not her parent. Nachelle is an adult. I won't yell at her or scold her, but fuck, do I want to.

Instead, I text her, telling her that until she cleans up the mess, I won't be making her any *sancocho* because it's her favorite dish I make.

Twenty minutes after I sent that message, I hear her bedroom door opening and another couple of minutes after that, the sound of the vacuum fills the apartment.

A sigh of relief escapes me, but when I think about tomorrow, it's replaced by pure dread.

CHAPTER 12
Cameron

My hands are sweating.

Never in my life have my hands started to sweat because of a date, let alone a *friend* date that's supposed to be entirely platonic.

Yet here I am, standing on the other side of Nachelle and Halo's apartment door with a tulip in my hand because I remembered Halo mentioning they were his favourite a while ago, specifically the yellow ones.

I've never brought a friend a flower before a friend date.

I don't know what the hell I'm doing, but it's too late to turn back. I've already knocked on the bloody door, and there are footsteps coming closer to it.

"Shit, fuck," I mumble to myself because this stupid flower is going to slip out of my hands before I hand it over if I continue to sweat this much.

To my surprise, Nachelle opens the door, and I'm greeted by her hair sticking out all over the place, old pajamas covering her body—well, apart from the very big holes at the shoulder and stomach areas—and her eyes bloodshot from either crying or a lack of sleep. I was expecting her to be as dressed up as Halo and I are for tonight, but clearly, she's not well enough to come with us.

"Chellie, are you okay?" My nerves about tonight vanish, replaced by concern. She looks up at me with irritation.

"It feels like my uterus is having a fucking party and all my other organs joined in, so they're all dancing around down there," she says and walks away, clearly inviting me to come in without saying so.

"Can I bring you anything?" I have two sisters, so I know a little bit about what a person with a period needs during that time of the month.

"How about some scissors to cut this useless organ out of me? Women should only get a uterus if they want to have kids, and I don't, so what's the point?" She drops down on the couch in front of the TV, and I follow because she's still talking to me. "Fucking ridiculous," she mumbles to herself, aggressively yanking her blanket over her body.

I place the tulip on the back of the couch before walking around it and settling on the couch right next to Chellie's head. She shifts back a little to give me more space, and I smile down at her in a comforting manner. At least I hope it's comforting.

"I'm serious. You got everything you need? Pads? Painkillers? Food?" I ask because I notice she's already got her hot water bottle.

"No, I'm good. Thank you," she says, pulling her blanket all the way up to her chin and hugging it to her chest.

"Okay." I place my hand on her forehead, causing her eyes to flutter shut. "If you do need anything else, you can always call me."

"Thanks, Cameron. You're the older brother I always wished I had." A shocked gasp comes from behind me, and I chuckle when she starts grinning. "Relax. I saw you standing there," she tells Halo, her grin widening.

"You're an evil younger sister," he replies, and I nudge Chellie's chin with the backs of my fingers before turning around to look at my date.

And, bloody hell, he looks divine.

Halo's dressed in all black from head to toe, his suit hugging his body wonderfully. He looks even taller than he usually does, and my heart flutters when I take in the way he's placed rings on his fingers, an expensive-looking watch on one wrist, and a single silver necklace around his neck. He's got the top three buttons undone, showing off his tanned skin tone and defined collarbones. His light brown hair sits in perfect waves on his head, and his blue eyes are practically shining with the sunlight filtering into the living room from the big two windows to the left of us.

He smirks as he catches me admiring him, but I'm not even a little sorry because he knew what he was doing with that outfit, those accessories, and his cocky smile.

I'm not strong enough to *keep* from staring.

"You look handsome," is the only thing I manage to say, and it's me who blushes this time. Not him. He looks surer today, more comfortable in his skin around me, and it's by far one of the sexiest things I've ever seen on a man.

"Right back at you, Cam," he says, allowing his gaze to trail down my body appreciatively.

Part of me regrets not having put more effort into my outfit. I'm wearing the most boring black suit and the only splash of colour on me is the pale yellow dress shirt I put on because, well, it's my favourite colour.

It's Halo's too, but I'm going to pretend like he copied me because I'm older.

"Can you two gawk at each other somewhere else? You're blocking my view and my favourite actress just came onto the screen," Chellie says, interrupting our moment.

I let out a nervous laugh and shake my head a little.

"Sorry, Chellie." I step aside and subtly pick up the tulip, Halo following me out of the living room. "I'll have him back around midnight," I assure her as a joke.

"Keep him," she calls back, and I burst into laughter when Halo's face contorts into one of mock hurt.

"Are you looking for a third sister? I don't want this one anymore. She's mean to me," Halo says, but that only makes me laugh harder.

"She loves you more than anything in the world, Asher." For the first time tonight, he finally blushes, and I take that as enough encouragement to hand him the tulip. He takes it from my hand with furrowed brows, clearly confused.

"I only told you this once. How the hell do you remember they're my favourite?" I've surprised him, both of us if I'm being honest.

"Once was enough."

If I'm going to survive this night, I have to figure out a way to a) stop *gawking* at him, as Chellie put it, and b) doing relationship things that could send him the wrong message about what I'm ready for.

Halo deserves better than to be led on just to be let down.

Not that I *could* lead him on, but Gabriel's words have stuck with me, and I don't know anything anymore. I don't know what Halo wants. I don't know what I want.

"You bring all your friend dates flowers, Cam?" Halo asks as he places the tulip in a glass with water in his kitchen, which is right beside the front door.

"Only the ones I'm using as arm candy," I tease, hoping it'll remove a bit of the tension that's settled between us.

Halo's brilliant smile is so bright, it warms my cheeks.

"Fair enough."

He leaves the flower in its glass next to the sink, where a window will let in enough sunlight to keep it happy, then he approaches me, placing one of his big hands on my shoulder in casual affection.

"Then let me show you what this arm candy can do because apart from looking incredible, I can also charm the socks off anyone you want me to impress tonight," he says and opens his front door for me, using one of his hands to gesture for me to go first.

"Oh, trust me, I know you can do more than just charm them."

By the end of the night, at least half a dozen people will be in love with him.

I simply have to do my best not to become one of those people.

An audible gasp leaves Halo when we reach my car. He stops walking as he takes in my new Grenzenlos SW, the glossy black finish with a singular stripe of yellow running through it from the left headlight all the way to the rear.

Leonard got me a fantastic deal on it, and I couldn't say no to the opportunity to drive a Grenzenlos. In F1, they were my second favourite team when I grew up, second only to Hawke, but after what they did with me, they really shouldn't be in first place anymore either.

"Cam, I hope you don't take this the wrong way because I don't mean this literally, but I'd fuck your car," Halo says, and his comment catches me so off-guard, I can't help but burst into laughter.

"Here," I say and throw him the key, which is of course only figuratively since it's keyless go. He catches them with ease.

"You're kidding," he says, staring at the key like it's as expensive as the car itself.

"Nope. It'll give my hand a break. Plus, I like getting chauffeured around," I assure him, making my way to the passenger side.

Dazed, Halo settles down in the driver's seat, his jaw still dragging on the floor. His hands glide over the wheel, the door, the gearshift, and I don't rush him even though we might arrive late.

His amazement is a special brand of beautiful, and I'd never rush this for any reason.

"You okay?" I ask when he studies the display that sits between us and at the front.

"I'm in love, is what I am," he replies, blowing out a breath and placing his hands back on the wheel. "I need to make more money to afford a car like this."

Halo lets the engine roar to life, excitement covering his features.

"I hope you know I'm never giving you your key back," he says as he shifts the car into Drive, getting us out of the underground parking garage of his building.

As excited as he is about driving my new car, he's also incredibly careful and doesn't go faster than the speed limit as we make our way to the dinner venue. It's in Italy, but it's only an hour drive from Monaco.

"You're on the highway, Halo. Hit the gas, feel the speed," I say because he's been driving a hundred and ten kilometres an hour on the left lane and he's allowed to go at least a hundred and thirty which everyone knows means he can go a hundred and forty-five.

Halo lets out a cheer as he goes faster, both of his hands on the steering wheel, the only sign he's still nervous about going faster.

"Atta boy," I say to encourage him, and he bites down hard on his bottom lip to fight back his smile.

I look out my window, trying to wrestle my heart into a normal rhythm.

We don't speak again until we arrive at the venue, and I give Halo instructions on where to go. He drops my car at the valet, both of us getting out almost in synchronization. I wait for him by the steps we have to walk up, cameras already flashing as the paparazzi take pictures of us.

"Nervous?" I ask him as he stops next to me, and he tilts his head down to make sure I'm the only one who hears him.

"I've never taken a bad picture in my life, so, no."

He places his hand on the small of my back to guide me up the stairs, and I curse him internally for the butterflies currently storming through my stomach. As a matter of fact, I blame him for everything I've felt since I picked him up because he's the one who put those things in my head.

Him and Gabriel.

"Take a deep breath, Cam." His words make me realise how tense I've become and how unnatural I'll look in those pictures if I don't loosen up a little. "You're too stiff."

"Remove your hand, and I won't be so *stiff*," I tell him, and he drops his hand with a chuckle.

At least this amuses him.

I plaster on my biggest and brightest smiles, my eyes hurting from the amount of flash these photographers use. Halo casually puts his arms around my shoulders for some of the pictures, and I almost welcome it because he's steadying me.

The media have not been kind to me since I lost my seat. If anything, they've been dragging me through the dirt, saying I had this coming because I was underperforming. They even used the words "waste of a seat" and "talentless" to describe me.

So, being here, somewhere so public, has anxiety infiltrating my system.

What will they say about me?

Will they tear me down even more?

Be surprised I had the courage to show my face after everything?

Not knowing how they're going to spin this makes my stomach twist and turn, but Halo's arm around me settles all of that for a moment.

And this isn't even the hardest part of the evening.

There will be a lot of people here who are going to ask me uncomfortable questions or offer me pity I didn't ask for, and if it wasn't for Halo being my side, I don't think I'd be able to make it through the night.

"Here we go," I whisper as we finally make it inside, a crowd of people already gathered in the space.

"It'll be okay," Halo replies, taking my right hand in his briefly to give it a reassuring squeeze.

And it's the determined expression on his face that convinces me his words are true.

It *will* be okay.

As long as he's by my side.

CHAPTER 13

Halo

IN THE FIVE YEARS I've known Cam, I've never witnessed him appear so out of place in a room full of people. Most often, he befriends whoever he comes across, but tonight, he's avoiding people as if all of them kicked him in the balls in the past.

While he does float around the room, greeting people he knows, he never lingers.

I pluck two champagne glasses from a tray one of the waiters holds out for me, turning to Cameron to hand him one.

"Thanks," he says as he takes it from me, almost downing it in one single gulp.

"Damn," I laugh, handing him my glass as well. "Alcohol isn't going to make any of these people more tolerable, you know?"

"Let me pretend. It makes me feel better," he replies, pulling another laugh out of me.

"Where are our friends? Surely their presence is going to cheer you up," I point out and place both of my hands on his shoulders to guide him through the room.

Deep down, I know I should stop touching him. I've already had my hands on him more often tonight than in the five years of our friendship combined, but I don't want to stop. Not when he melts into my touch every single time.

I subtly shake my head to refocus on the task at hand: finding any of Cam's friends to make him feel more settled at this luxurious event.

Most of the people here at this dinner are strangers to me. They aren't even acquaintances or people I work with. I've never seen any of them, which means while I can pretend to fit in, obviously engineers were not invited to this.

Adrian and Nevaeh are the first ones to appear in my line of sight, the Monegasque's arms firmly wrapped around his wife from behind. His cheek is pressed against the side of her head, and his eyes are closed as they stand with Leonard Tick and his wife, Chiara. They're both scowling, but from what I've gathered over the years, it's the same grumpy exterior Storm has. All four of them are dressed in equally as fancy clothing as Cam and I, but they seem a lot more comfortable in it than I feel.

James Landon and Estrella Cortez-Landon walk toward their group, but I have no idea how they don't trip or stumble over things, considering how they can't take their eyes off each other. James is dressed in a black suit, his pale skin, blonde hair, and blue eyes practically shining in this light. Estrella is in a sage green dress that matches her warm brown skin, dark brown hair, and brown eyes perfectly.

Scar and Storm must not have been invited either, but I'm starting to realize this event is truly only for the drivers and the team principals, as well as the team owners, and perhaps a few other important people.

Valentina and Gabriel are the last couple I notice, the Grenzenlos driver spinning the Velocità Rossa driver once, making her red dress billow out with the movement. There isn't even any music playing, but they seem perfectly content imagining their own melody as they enjoy each other's company.

"Want me to twirl you too?" Cam asks when he notices where my attention is, and I snort.

"First of all, over my dead body. Secondly, I'm taller than you, so I'd be the one who would spin you," I say because it wouldn't make sense the other way around. He'd have to lift his arm way higher but I'd still have to crouch down.

It just wouldn't look elegant.

"Are you attacking my height?" The color drains from my face when he frowns at me in a way he's never done before.

"No, of course not. I just meant—" He nudges me in the side with his elbow as he lets out a laugh.

"I'm fucking with you, Halo. I'm not insecure about my height." He steps in front of me, reaching for my collar to adjust it. "Plus, I like my men taller than me, and being short means most are."

Without another word, he leaves me standing where I am to join his group of friends. I blame both glasses of champagne for his words, but I also can't keep the smile off my face because he was definitely flirting with me.

He *keeps* flirting with me.

The hours drag on and on, speech after speech being given by the people in charge of this event, the team owners, and even one team principal. The dim lighting in this grand room, combined with the same, boring speeches, almost puts me to sleep, and not even the food encourages me to stay awake.

"We're in Italy. Where is all the good food? Why are we being served these tiny portions that couldn't even fill a mouse's stomach?" I ask Cameron when another server places food in front of us with a singular basil leaf on it that's topped with the tiniest sliver of mozzarella and an even smaller slice of tomato.

"I wish I could tell you," he whispers back, shaking his head at the plate, too.

Unfortunately, because he's no longer part of any of the F1 teams, we got seated far away from our friends. Our social batteries are running out faster than ever before, but luckily, Cam eventually has had enough for the both of us.

"Let's go," he says as he leans down, his mouth almost brushing my ear. I feel his breath, and my hands curl into fists because it's all I can do to keep from gasping.

I follow him to each table where our friends are sitting to tell them we're leaving, but they don't appear to judge us. Most of them look ready to head home as well, and equally as bored as Cam and I were throughout the whole dinner.

This time, he doesn't let me drive, and I'm glad because I don't feel like it. I'm tired and hungry, all of my energy having been drained by the most insufferable people.

Oh, yes, I own this car.
Oh, yes, I have three houses spread out all over the world.
Oh, yes, I must show off all the money I have.

I have nothing against people who have a lot of money. On the contrary. My sister is working her way up to being rich, and I'm well off, but it's the way these men are constantly in competition with each other.

They might as well just whip out their dicks and measure, it'd save them a lot of time.

"I'm going to a little pizzeria I know so we can get some real food." Cameron doesn't leave that up for debate. It's a statement because he knows when I get hungry, I get cranky. I don't speak much. But as soon as you put food in me, I'll be dancing in my seat, reborn into my usual happy self.

"Okay," is my only reply.

As we drive, I watch the trees blur past us. We're far enough from a city that the sky clearly reveals all of the beautiful stars there, and the moon is half full, shining light onto the road ahead of us. There are no lights here because we're on a back road, making our way toward what looks like a small village.

"How do you know this place?" I peer over at him, noting that he's only driving with his right hand. His left is still in its brace, and he's keeping it on his lap to prevent himself from using it.

"Because I've been living in Monaco for several years now, and as much as I like the food there, it doesn't compare to a good old Italian stone oven pizza," he explains, looking at me from the corner of his eye.

After that, it's almost like I blink and we're sitting in this small pizzeria, the scent of tomato sauce and oregano filling my nose. We ordered our pizza mere minutes ago, but my stomach is growling as if it couldn't possibly go any longer without eating something.

Cameron plays with the napkins he placed on either side of the table for us, folding it once, twice, three times as he builds a paper plane.

Well, napkin plane, I guess.

He's deep in thought, chewing on his bottom lip like he does when he's concentrating.

When he catches me staring, he lets out a breathless laugh and rubs his nape nervously.

"Sorry," he blurts out.

"For what?" I ask, trying to get a glimpse into his thoughts.

"I'm not good company at the moment. I was thinking about how disastrous tonight was for my career," he says, which catches me by surprise.

"What do you mean?"

Cameron goes back to his napkin, folding another side of it to make the wing of the plane.

"I was hoping anyone, any team principal or owner, would approach me to talk about what happened to me. I was even silly enough to hope that one of them might even be interested in signing me for next year, but they didn't care about me at all."

He adds the finishing touches to his plane, then attempts to throw it my way. It doesn't get far, landing on the table right in front of me. It makes him laugh, but I'm too hung up on his words to join in.

"You were trying to see if you could get back into F1, if they wanted to offer you a seat," I repeat, trying to process this new piece of information.

"How ridiculous of me, don't you think?"

"It's not ridiculous. You deserve to have a seat. Your crash shouldn't have been the reason you got kicked out of Hawke."

He nods in agreement but doesn't respond to me. His hazel eyes skip to something behind me, but I don't have to turn around to know there's nothing there.

Something strange happens after that. He stays silent and his gaze unfocuses. His mind disappears to a place I'll never be able to find him and lead him out of. It's a type of dissociation I've only ever seen on one person.

My grandfather on my father's side.

To this day, I have no idea what happened the day he almost died. He tried to explain it to me, but every time he opened his mouth, he would dissociate, too.

He would get lost in his memories, and there was no pulling him out until he was ready to come back.

So, I wait.

Our pizza gets delivered, but Cameron is still stuck in his memories, so he doesn't realize it. I don't point it out. I don't start eating. I hardly breathe as I wait.

When he comes back into the moment, he looks a bit confused.

"Sorry. What were we talking about?"

Worry has infiltrated every part of my system. Dissociation isn't something to be considered lightly, especially when intertwined with PTSD. Cam has to talk to someone, he has to work through his trauma, otherwise he'll only get more and more dissociative episodes, just like it happened to my grandfather.

"You were telling me about how much you hated the food tonight," I lie because I don't want to trigger him again by bringing up his crash once more.

Cameron, while still unsure, falls into a rant about how much he hated the food, and I listen attentively, smiling at him because he's okay now.

And I'm going to help him find a way to permanently work through what happened the day he almost died.

The day he lost his dream and everything he ever worked for.

CHAPTER 14

Cameron

It's the day of the first race of the season.

Yesterday, during Qualifying, Nachelle did well, given how terrible the Hawke is on the Albert Park Grand Prix Circuit here in Australia. James, being the overachiever he's become, is setting much faster times than Chellie, but a rookie most often will not outperform their teammate, especially if their teammate is James Oliver Landon who's like a lion hunting its prey in his car. It's why racing against him was so difficult. It's why he outperformed me in most races. He's more ruthless on the track, willing to take the kind of risks that make me nervous, and there's no winning against a guy who bends the rules as far as possible to win.

Plus, Hawke thrives on it, so they give him the better, faster, and more reliable car. All of those are facts Nachelle has to swallow before she gets into her car today.

She was upset after Qualifying, despite my reassurance that tenth is a good place. We both know it isn't an ideal position for one of the top cars on the grid to be starting from, but after she was almost one of the five drivers that got kicked out of Q1, barely made it into the top ten in Q2, and then couldn't set a fast enough time in the twelve-minute long Q3 session I think it's a good result.

"Are these nerves ever going to get easier to deal with before a race?" Chellie asks as she shakes out her hands, obviously trying to get rid of her nervous energy.

We're in her private room where her performance coach, Saanvi, helps her get ready for the race. Chellie is wearing my colours, she's driving in my seat, and yet, the thought of her being anxious unsettles me as concern fills my chest.

"Have you never experienced them before a race?" I ask because she's participated in many races in the different Formula Series over the years.

"Not like this. It feels like the whole world is resting on my chest, suffocating me," she explains, stretching out her back with Saanvi's help.

"That's just your ego," her performance coach chimes in, making me laugh.

"I prefer confidence," Chellie replies with a smug smile, but she grimaces a second later when Saanvi presses down on a sore spot on her leg. "*Mierda*."

Once they're done with the stretches, I look at Saanvi and say, "Can you give us a moment?" She offers me a single nod before leaving the room, and Chellie and me, alone.

"Is this the part where you tell me to get over my shit and just go race?" she asks, her racing suit hanging by her hips as she paces around the room.

I've never seen her like this.

"Are you nervous or are you scared?" My question stops her movement so she can turn to me. Chellie crosses her arms in front of her chest and considers me for a moment, her shoulders tensing.

"I'm scared," she admits, her brown eyes dropping to the floor to study the carpet in this room. She uses the toe of her racing shoe to poke at it, taking a deep breath. "This is the first race of the season, and I'm the driver who stole *your* seat. If I don't perform well, people are going to wonder why I deserved it more than you did," she explains, and I realise something I was too busy focusing on my shit to notice.

Ever since I became her mentor a couple of weeks ago, I've been fighting with myself to push aside my own feelings, but that internal battle has taken up so much space inside of me, I forgot about the whole point of this. And the point is to be there for Chellie. To guide her in this vicious space where people bite your head off every chance they get. She's young, inexperienced, and lost in a lot of areas, much like every other rookie who has ever come before her, like me when I started, and no matter how angry I am at Hawke, looking at my hand still in its brace, I know they made the right decision.

I wouldn't have been able to race.

So, it's time I let go of my resentment. It's time I acknowledge that what happened had to happen. It's time I stop blaming the world for a mistake I made during the race.

Most importantly, I have to make sure Chellie knows she's the last person to blame in this situation.

And I won't stand by while she puts herself down because of it.

"People are always going to talk. You should have seen the things they wrote about me online when I stopped performing at a level they expected me to, when I came out as gay, when I wore the ugliest pair of pants," I say, listing three very different things to make sure she understands to what level a person will stoop to shit on people like us. "It doesn't matter what we do, how loved we are by a group of people, or what we've accomplished in the sport these people claim they admire. They will find things to hate about us, and they will dig in their claws and drag them down, hoping it'll leave scars we carry with us forever."

I step toward her and take her hand in mine, giving it a comforting squeeze.

"You are not the reason I lost my seat. I lost it because I crashed and still haven't recovered. And even if my hand had, my mind still hasn't."

I think about dissociating at dinner with Halo a week ago. I think about the worried look on his face. I think about him not mentioning it because he didn't want to risk me getting lost in the black hole where the memory of my crash should be.

"You earned this seat. You worked for it harder than anyone ever had to, similarly to Valentina," I say and offer her a small smile that she returns. She loves Val, and any mention of her name is enough to cheer her up.

My best friend is Chellie's favourite driver.

"You will do your very best this season. You will work hard and the results you get will be just that: results. I have no doubt that they'll be good ones too, and on the days they aren't, we will sit down together and figure out a way to learn from the mistakes. I'm here for you, and I'm not going anywhere," I promise, and she wraps her arms around me, holding me close.

"The whispers and critiques are always going to be worse for me because I'm a woman, aren't they?" I don't have to answer. We both know it's true, but she needs to hear this from someone other than herself.

"They're always going to be worse for people who don't fit the straight, white, rich, male image this sport has revolved around for years." Chellie lets out a crying sound.

"Great, so I'm triple fucked. I'm a woman, half-Latina, and a lesbian. They're going to eat me alive here," she says, and I hold onto her tighter because I'm scared of the world chewing her up and spitting her out by the time we reach the end of the season.

Because she's right.

Nachelle Henderson is going to change the world, and I'm honoured if I can be a part of her story, no matter how small it may be.

"Do you remember what I always say, sweetheart?" I ask, and she starts grinning harder than ever before.

"Fuck 'em all," we say at the same time before she hugs me, and I hug her back as firmly.

The formation lap almost has me biting my nails. Not because I'm anticipating anything bad happening. Usually, nothing happens during the lap that allows the drivers to warm their tyres, charge their batteries, and look at the track conditions. But I'm close to biting my nails because after the formation lap comes the start of the race, and no matter how much faith I have in her, my heart is racing because of how nervous I am.

I realise I'm nervous for all of my friends because the heart racing is followed by sweat collecting at the back of my neck when I see Gabriel's car approaching his spot on the starting grid. Then Val's. Then James'. Then Adrian's.

I take a deep breath to get rid of the pressure building in my head, as if it was about to explode, and it's enough to push the fear of anything happening to them to the deepest and darkest recesses of my mind.

Cory looks over his shoulder at me to scowl, a habit he's had since he became my race engineer three years ago, and I flash him the biggest smile I can muster for the sole purpose to piss him off. His scowl deepens, and he turns back around without saying a word.

Bloody wanker.

As soon as all twenty drivers are back on the grid in their positions, I cross my arms in front of my chest and hold my breath.

The five lights above the drivers' turn on one by one until they're all illuminated. The brief pause where all the drivers wait and wait and wait has me chewing on my bottom lip. They're looking at the lights, all of them ready to press down on the gas and shift into gear, shooting forward to start this race. They can't move. If the other ones are anything like me, they even stop breathing. Anticipation coursing through their bodies until finally, it releases when they're allowed to start.

And when the lights disappear, they can.

Chellie has a great start. She makes up three places within the first lap, sliding into seventh place. James is in third, fighting Gabriel for second. Val is driving away in first, creating enough of a gap to keep Gabriel out of DRS range. Adrian, who started in fourth, is still there, not threatened by any of the other drivers behind him.

The Australian Grand Prix is most often a two-stop race, so the first fifteen laps, before her first stop, Chellie keeps working her way up the grid. She makes it all the way into fifth place, which is brilliant, then gets called in to pit.

Everything goes smoothly, and she's out and back on the grid in eighth place, and it isn't horrible considering the drivers ahead of her have not pitted yet. As soon as they do, she will slide right back into fifth, her hard work having paid off to get her up there where the fastest drivers of all-time are currently battling each other in front.

Gabriel has caught up to Val, and Adrian is chasing James, who was told to back off from going after Gabriel to spare his tyres. I watch them as closely as I watch Chellie, trying to keep up with everything that's happening.

Pride fills my chest as Chellie makes her way back into fifth again, not a single driver behind her fast enough to battle with her for that spot. We're not even halfway through the race and she's already made up five places, and maybe, just maybe, she can even catch Adrian because he's battling with James while Chellie has clean air. It means she's faster and can catch up to them while they're busy attacking and defending against each other.

My eyes are glued to the screens the whole time.

Three laps later, Chellie has caught up to James and Adrian, slipping right into James' DRS without him being able to do anything about it.

His advantage is still being in Adrian's DRS so he doesn't abort fighting him for third but uses the extra speed advantage he gets in the designated areas to keep Chellie behind him. She's been given team orders not to overtake yet because James is still chasing Adrian, but I can see she's biding her time.

Lying in wait, waiting to attack her prey when she knows she can make it stick.

I smile because it's a very James thing to do, and knowing my former teammate, he's not going to like getting challenged by the rookie this way.

Val has kept her first place, her Velocità Rossa fast enough to have created a gap between herself and her husband in his Grenzenlos.

There are a few battles happening lower on the grid as well, but the cameras are on the one for third.

Everyone is watching this scene play out on the track, not sure who is going to come out on top.

Chellie is taking on two World Champions, and there is no way in hell she's going to shy away from a fight just because of their titles.

She didn't make it into Formula One because she was known as the girl who didn't take risks. She made it because she's crafty, fast, and thinks on her feet. Right now, I know she's trying to figure out the best way to overtake both of the drivers in front of her because as soon as she's in the car, she forgets about all of the expectations resting on her shoulders.

She has one goal on her mind, and it's winning, and winning for a rookie doesn't always look the same as it does for seasoned drivers who know they can fight for a championship. Winning can look like overtaking two World Champions and proving to the world that you're worthy of the seat they always said you shouldn't have gotten.

Four more laps pass with the three of them dancing around each other on the track. James makes a move, Adrian defends. Chellie makes a move, James defends.

It's nerve-racking.

My breath hitches when Chellie and James go side by side in the third corner, their wheels so close to touching, my stomach turns upside down.

It almost feels like the moment on a rollercoaster before you descend, my fingers tingling with anticipation and dread in equal measures.

Chellie is ahead as they exit the corner, but James thinks quick on his feet, and within seconds, he's back ahead of her, staying in fourth place. Adrian's had a bit of a chance to breathe, but James doesn't waste any time chasing him down again. Chellie can't stick to James, so she falls backward, having fought well even if she couldn't overtake him yet.

More laps pass, and the second pitstop goes as well for Nachelle as her first one did, which is no surprise to anyone. Hawke is one of the best teams, if not the best, at pitstops, and they currently hold the world record for the fastest pitstop.

Velocità Rossa could never understand because they're the worst more often than not. Missing tyres. Wrong tyres. Can't get the tyres off.

Even though they've won championships, they're a chaotic team, but right about now, I'd give anything to be a part of their little family. A part of any of the other teams, but they don't want me. None of them do.

The rest of the race is uneventful, and by the time the last two laps come around, I've started to feel more at peace than I did at the beginning.

I was scared it would be too difficult to stand here and watch them out of fear something would happen to any of my friends, or because I wouldn't be strong enough to, my past would haunt me, but I did it. I watched the whole race without being triggered by anything, which feels like liquid courage coursing through my veins.

I should have known my own thoughts would jinx this situation.

The Zeitgeist drivers crash into each other, and the sight of their crash doesn't make me dissociate like it usually does when I'm reminded of my crash.

No.

It's so much worse.

Dizziness hits me as my body breaks out in a sweat. A sudden wave of heat hits me, but that isn't even the worst part.

It feels like I'm out of control of my body.

Like I'm back in the car, trapped.

I'm dying.

I can't save myself.

No one is coming to save me.

I'm dying.

This is where I lose my life.

Everything will end.

I'm dying.

My lungs aren't working properly.

Pain surges through my hands.

I'm dying.

And there's no returning from the darkness once it consumes me.

I'll never get to hug the people I love again.

Tears stream down my face before I can stop them.

Chapter 15

Halo

Cameron is nowhere to be found.

I've been looking for him since the race ended and I got released from my responsibilities for the day. We were meant to get a drink while we waited for Nachelle to finish work. It's a plan we made yesterday while we ate dinner at his ranch, where my sister and I have been staying since we arrived in Australia.

I tried to book a hotel, but when Hazel and Charlotte found out, they practically dragged my ass to their place. Nachelle didn't have to be convinced. She heard we'd be near horses and practically sprinted to their truck.

It's not what an F1 driver would usually do, staying at a ranch instead of a glamorous hotel where people wait on you hand and foot, but Nachelle and I feel more comfortable where people *don't* do that. Our parents brought us up wealthy, and I'm guessing my father is still a very rich man. He's the one who sponsored Nachelle. He's the one who, from afar of course, supported her financially while she fought every step of the way to get to where she is today. But all the money in the world couldn't replace the warmth and care of my mami, the way she was at every race and cheered Nachelle on. The way she took days off work, prioritizing her children.

We're at the ages now where she trusts us to handle things on our own, but she'll come visit every now and then. That doesn't mean I can't call her every other day to complain about how much work I have or ask for advice about Nachelle. Sometimes you just need your parent, and I'm lucky enough to have one who loves me more than life itself.

"Have you seen Cameron?" I ask Cory, my sister's piece of shit race engineer.

"He had some sort of breakdown and disappeared like ten minutes ago," he replies with a bored tone, and all the blood rushes out of my face as the information sinks in fully.

"I know you don't like him, but why the fuck couldn't you call someone?" I throw my hands in the air to convey my frustration, but I leave that asshole standing where he is, running to look for Cameron.

There is no one else I can ask to help me because they're all busy with post-race procedures. So, I run around aimlessly. I check the washrooms in the Hawke Racing motorhome, but he isn't there. He isn't in any of the empty rooms. He isn't outside beside the motorhome, in the gaps where drivers walk when they try to hide from the hundreds of cameras. I try to call him, but he doesn't answer his phone.

Of course, he doesn't.

I search for an hour.

No part of me is ready to give up while I'm not sure if he's okay, but this whole finding the needle in a haystack, the crowd of several hundred thousand fans being the haystack and Cam being the needle, seems impossible.

There is no way in hell I'll find him before Nachelle is done, and he's not answering his phone.

Fuck, I hope he's okay.

"Halo?"

His voice has relief flooding through me, and I spin on my heels to see him approaching me with two hot dogs in his right hand, a bucket hat covering his head, and an easy smile on his lips. Part of me is furious that he didn't respond to my calls or messages, but the other part is so relieved to see him here, to see he's okay, that I find myself taking large strides toward him.

Then, I'm hugging him. I wrap my arms around him, pulling him to my chest to feel for myself that he's alright, that Cory is a lying bastard.

It dawns on me too late that we've never hugged like this. Cam and I may be good friends, but we've always kept an invisible barrier between us, limiting physical touch for some reason.

No, not for some reason.

I'm sick and tired of pretending like I don't have feelings for him and that if I were to touch him more, if he were to show me affection in that way, I would fall even harder for him than I already have.

But at this moment, none of that matters.

Nothing matters but making sure he's okay.

"Asher, what's going on?" he asks with his wonderful Australian accent, but he hugs me back, melting against me.

It feels like he needs this hug as much as I do, so maybe Cory wasn't lying, after all.

"Are you okay?" I ask. "Cory said you weren't feeling well, and I've been trying to reach you for an hour. You didn't answer any of my messages or calls, so I assumed the worst," I admit and attempt to pull back, out of the hug, but he holds me close for a moment longer.

"Cory's a dick. Don't listen to what he says," he replies, his cheek resting against my chest. "Halo, your heart is racing."

"I've been worried," I scold.

It's not exactly a lie. I was worried, and my heart was racing because of it, but it's not doing that out of concern anymore. It's doing it because he's running his left hand down my back, and I can hardly keep from shivering. His woody scent fills my nose with every breath I take, and I'm painfully aware of the way our bodies are flush against each other's.

"You worry too much. I'm fine. Look at me," he says and finally steps back, gesturing to all of himself with a giant grin on his face.

If I didn't know him as well as I do, if I was oblivious to his tells, I'd buy his happy exterior. I'd buy this act he's been putting on for years, even more so now after his crash and everything he's going through mentally. But I've studied this man in ways I'm not proud of. I know when he's truly happy, and I know when he's not okay.

He's not okay.

The white part of his eyes is red, and while he tries to hide it by smiling so brightly that it should distract people, it doesn't distract me. He's exhausted. He's probably got a massive headache. And maybe, just maybe, my gut is right when it says he's had a panic attack that was probably triggered by the crash between the Zeitgeist drivers at the end of the race.

I don't know what comes over me, what continues to come over me today, but I reach out and place my hand on the side of his neck, my thumb on his cheek. His smile falters as he takes in the serious look on my face, and I take a step toward him, tilting my head down to keep eye contact with him. He has to look up a little, and I hate how fucking sweet he looks with that stupid bucket hat on and the hot dogs in his hand.

"What happened? Tell me, Cam. Tell me, and I can be there for you. Let me in," I plead softly, carefully, and when he leans his head to the side, into my touch, and closes his eyes, I wish I could hug him again. Kiss him. Reassure him.

"I'm a mess," he says, a singular tear running down from the corner of his eye. It drips onto my thumb, so I wipe it away, offering him a small smile.

"Aren't we all? Doesn't life turn us into messes we spend our lives trying to clean up?" I ask, and his hazel eyes fill with more tears. "Instead of trying so very hard to fix what's broken, why don't we take the shattered pieces and build something new?"

Another tear drips onto my thumb, and I admire him so much for not trying to hold them back. For letting them out and allowing himself to deal with whatever is going on inside of him in the way he needs to.

"If I'd known we'd be discussing existential topics, I wouldn't have gotten us hot dogs. They hardly seem like they'd fit that topic of conversation," he says, and I almost burst into laughter.

"What would fit?" Cameron cocks a brow like he doesn't quite believe I even have to ask that question.

"Ice cream, of course." A little chuckle slips free despite how hard I'm trying to hold it back.

"Of course," I repeat and drop my hand from his face, but he catches it with his left one, surprising me. He wants to hold onto me, and not just that. He's holding onto me with his injured hand, completely ignoring the pain he must feel with the grabbing motion.

"I had a panic attack, I think. I'm not entirely sure. I've never had them before." He's staring down at our intertwined hands, and I rub my thumb along his brace, trying not to hurt him while offering comfort. "I got so dizzy all of a sudden and hot. I started sweating, and this deep-rooted fear sank into my chest until it felt like I was dying. I couldn't come out of it, so I stumbled into the nearest washroom and locked myself into a stall until it passed. After, I walked around aimlessly, trying to figure out what the fuck had just happened."

"I'm surprised you didn't look up your symptoms," I reply to lighten the mood a little, and he cracks a smile because we both know whenever something's wrong, he turns to the internet for answers, no matter how often I tell him that's the dumbest idea if you're looking for reassurance. The search engine is going to convince you that a clogged nose means you're dead in an hour.

"I did. Why do you think I said it was a panic attack?" I slap my forehead with my other hand because Cam hasn't let go of me, and I don't want to be the one to pull away first. "Hey, don't judge me. I would have asked Adrian, Nevaeh, or Scarlette, but they're all busy," he defends, releasing me to poke me in the stomach.

"You could have asked me." The admission hangs in the air for several tense seconds until he says one word. We both know exactly what he means, so there truly is no need to elaborate.

"When?"

I shove my hands into my pockets, trying to close myself off from him the way I've done all my life when people asked me about my childhood trauma, but it's not that easy with Cameron.

He's opened up to me, and who am I not to share my experience with him, especially if it could make him feel less alone during a very lonely moment of his life. He thinks no one understands him, but I do.

I do so damn well.

"About a month after I caught my father fucking his mistress. After he told me he wanted nothing to do with me anymore. After he looked at me, a twelve-year-old boy, and told me I was the worst son God could have ever sent him." I lean back on the balls of my feet and let out a breathless laugh. "I had panic attacks for a year until eventually, they started coming less and less. Then, they disappeared." My shoulders raise in a shrug, and I realize I've been staring at my feet this whole time, avoiding the pity in Cam's eyes.

Except, when I look up, there isn't any pity.

He looks furious.

"If I ever meet your father, I'm going to not very respectfully kick his arse," he says, and I snort in response.

"Trust me, he's not worth it. Bad people are never worth putting energy into, and the sooner you realize that, the sooner you get to put even more energy into the good people," I explain, taking my hands out of my pocket to take one of the hot dogs from him. "What do you say we go to the ranch early and spend some time with the animals? Nachelle can meet us there," I offer, and his face lights up in a real way again.

"I'd love that."

CHAPTER 16

Cameron

Halo and Nachelle prepared a huge thank you meal for Hazel, Charlotte, and I since we've been cooking for them for the past week. They made *quipes*, *locrio de pollo*, and a sweet drink called *avena dominicana* for us to try. It was so good, I asked Halo for a second glass about five minutes after he gave me the first one. He made it with cinnamon, and that's my favourite spice in the world, so to me, it was one of the best drinks I've ever had. I also had way too many *quipes*, but the savory taste of it, the beef inside, was too good to resist.

But perhaps I shouldn't have because now I'm lying on the floor in my living room with my hand on my stomach, contemplating my life choices. There's reggaeton playing over the speakers in the house, and my siblings are dancing with Halo and Chellie while the only part of me I can currently move is my toes. I wiggle them back and forth as I enjoy the rhythm of the music, a smile plastering itself onto my face.

The panic attack earlier caught me off guard. It shook everything inside of me, and I've been questioning what the hell I'm going to do with myself during race weekends, considering how easily I'm triggered, but I'm doing my best to ignore all of that to focus on the happiness currently radiating through my house as if the sun itself is inside of it.

I push up and onto my elbows, watching Charlotte get spun around by Halo while Hazel and Chellie dance together.

"Come on, *viejito,* join us," Halo calls out, and Chellie snorts at her brother. His mischievous grin tells me all I have to know, so I pull out my phone and open the speech option on the internet.

"What does *'viejito'* mean in English?" I ask, watching the thing load because of the shitty connection in my living room.

The translation pops up on my screen, and I let out an audible gasp.

"Who are you calling 'old man'?" I call out to Halo, but he simply shrugs as he keeps guiding Char through the steps. "I'm six years older than you, not sixty."

This makes him laugh, and I take several moments to soak it in because witnessing Halo's laugh is a mesmerizing thing. The way his full lips stretch to reveal his perfect set of teeth. The laugh lines that appear around his eyes. The deep sound of it. He really is breathtaking, and I know I noticed it before. It's not news to me that Halo is handsome, but it's never settled in as hard as it does right now.

"Listen, when I was a kid, my *mama,* my grandmother, used to cook, eat, then dance the night away with my *papa* during our *coros.* And before she danced, she beat all of our asses in dominoes. So maybe you're right. You're not a *viejito.* You're a crybaby."

"You can't possibly be comparing me to your *mama.* I've heard the stories you told. That woman is stronger, fiercer, and cooler than any other person in the world. On top of that, you said she has magical hugs, so truly, you can't compare *me* to her. She's a force to be reckoned with, and I'm just a dude," I say, and it's the way he smiles that makes me smile in return.

He walks toward me after giving Charlotte's arm a gentle squeeze, and I do my best to decipher why his easy-going grin has me wanting to get up and meet him halfway.

Then I remember the way he hugged me earlier, the way he cupped my face, and I suck in a sharp breath because of the way my body thrums with need.

Need for him.

"I can't believe you remember everything I told you about her," he says.

I sit up completely, looking him directly in the eyes when I say, "There isn't a single important detail you've shared with me about your life that I've forgotten."

He looks at me, and I look at him, neither one of us adding anything to my admission, not that I could anyway. I've forgotten how to speak. His gaze has me trapped in its hold, and I feel my heart getting pulled toward him. It's trying to claw its way out of my chest to get to him, completely ignoring its scars and bruises. It only healed the biggest breaks a few months ago, and there are still small ones stitching themselves together at snail pace, so I have no clue why it would want to throw itself out in the open to get trampled on once more.

I tear my attention from Halo as I place a hand on my chest, willing it to stay inside my body.

"Wanna learn how to play dominoes?" Halo asks instead of pointing out the tension between us.

"Depends. Are you incredibly good at it and will wipe the floor with me?" He chuckles, but he starts walking toward his room anyway.

"Guess you'll have to find out the hard way."

He vanishes up the stairs of our old house, the steps creaking a little under his weight. They're so sensitive, even when a bug walks over them they make a sound. Chellie, Hazel, and Charlotte join me in the living room, and we talk about how well Nachelle did in her race today. From what she's told me, she's happy with her result, and that's all that truly matters.

"Okay, so in the Dominican Republic, we play dominoes at almost every gathering, but it's a game that can be played whenever the mood strikes. I remember playing my Tío Luis, sitting on his lap while he had a great time chatting to our family members and sharing a drink with them," Halo explains as he settles down on the ground in the living room, so close to me that our knees brush as he places the dominoes on the low coffee table beside me and in front of him.

I shift around to face it, noticing Chellie clapping her hands together in excitement. My sisters' interest has been piqued, and they're both watching Halo as he spreads out the domino pieces on the table. To explain how the game works, Chellie offers to play a round with Char and Hazel while Halo turns to me. He wiggles his brows, and I press my lips together to keep from grinning like an idiot.

We spend an hour playing.

Once we all understand how it works, we play by ourselves—except my sisters, who play as a team since only four can play at a time. Halo wins every single round, but I'm too busy laughing to mind. He keeps sabotaging me, making it so I can only attach numbers I don't have the dominoes for, and as much as I wish it would irritate me, it mostly amuses me.

By the time we finish another round, I have tears in my eyes from how hard I'm laughing. Halo is lying with his back on the floor, covering his face as he bellows out his own laugh. I shove at him, but that only makes him laugh harder. Somewhere in the back of my mind, I realise all three girls are staring at us with varying degrees of confusion because to them it isn't nearly as funny as it is to us.

But that's the thing about Halo.

He's got this way of making the rest of the world disappear. When he's near me, he takes up so much space in my head, in my chest, in this room, it's impossible to remember bad things even exist, let alone that they have been and are happening to me.

I shove him again, but this time he drops his hand from his face to shove me back, and it has me breaking out into another fit of laughter.

In moments of pure joy like these, I feel invincible.

Like nothing could penetrate through the wall of happiness around me.

It's a childish perception, being invincible, and, in my case, it's a call for something horrible to happen because a second after that realization sinks in, the front door flies open, banging against the wall. The house vibrates because of the forceful action, and I'm on my feet, stepping in front of my sisters and Chellie to protect them without a second thought.

I wish the sight of my mother would make me drop my walls and relief course through me, but it doesn't.

My walls lift even higher.

"Get out," she says as she approaches me, and a bit of surprise filters through the anger, panic, and worry inside of me.

"Hello, Matilda. It's nice to see you as well. Oh, my hands? Yeah, they're fine. Thanks for reaching out after my crash, by the way. It meant the world to know you cared that I almost died."

My mother's hazel eyes, the ones she gave me, are alight with fury because I'm painting her as a monster in front of everyone present, but I don't care. She's trying to throw me out, and I'm not about to leave my sisters alone with her while she's in a rage.

"Get out of my house, Cameron. You've spent enough time here, and I'm tired of trying to avoid you."

Halo's jaw drops to the floor, and I notice he's gotten up too, but instead of stepping in front of his sister, he's almost directly in between the four of us and my mother.

"Well aren't you a fucking delight," he says to Mum, and she turns her furious glare his way. He doesn't crumble under it. Instead, he looks at her with so much distaste, I'd laugh if it wasn't so inappropriate right now.

"Chellie, take Char and Hazel upstairs, please," I whisper to Nachelle, taking advantage of Mum being distracted by Halo. Char is already on her feet, taking Hazel's hand and leading her toward the staircase.

They're used to this by now.

It's happened often enough for them to know I don't want them around while I try to calm Mum.

"Who the hell are you?" my mother asks Halo, but he crosses his arms over his chest, looking like an impenetrable tower of a man.

"I'm the man that's about to haul your ass out of the house if you don't lower your voice and behave like a well-mannered person in front of your son," he warns, taking a step toward her when she tries to get closer to me, cutting her off. She looks up at him, frowning harder than I've ever seen before.

"Oh you must be a new one." She looks him up and down for a second. "You think because you're fucking my son, you have any say in how I get to address him in my home?" Halo's smile is dangerous, a threat in itself.

"Ma'am, I'm not fucking your son, but that doesn't mean I don't care deeply about him. And when I care about someone, there's not much I wouldn't do for them, especially doing said hauling of ass of their mother for being a disrespectful piece of shit."

She sputters some incoherent words, clearly having been caught by surprise that he'd talk back to her instead of doing what every other guest in a house would have done. Roll over and show their belly. No, he fought back, and it's the first time in my life someone's defended me with my mother when she's like this.

I've never been protected before, and in turn, I've never felt so safe with another person.

"Mum, why don't we go sit down, have some tea, and talk about why you're upset with me now," I say because she's more than capable of telling me how much she despises me in a calm voice. I think she's so upset because she came home and wasn't expecting to see my car not in the garage but out in the driveway, informing her I was home.

"No. I want you out of my house, Cameron. You have no business being here. You keep coming back as if you didn't leave like he did, and if you think I'll ever be able to forgive that, then you've got another thing coming, child."

This time, I do laugh.

"You are such a hypocrite, Matilda. Where have you been for the last eight months, huh? Because you haven't been home. You haven't been in this house that *I* pay for with the money I earned at the job you keep guilt-tripping me over. You don't get to kick me out of the house when your name may be on the papers, but you haven't done shit to keep it."

She stalks toward where I'm still standing behind the couch, and Halo attempts to hold her back when she simply shoves him out of the way. She places her bag down on the back of the couch, rips open the zipper, and takes out papers to shove toward me.

"You want to know where I've been? For the last eight months, I've been doing this. I found a way to sell this place without your permission or signature. I found another house in the city that I've already bought, furnished, and gotten ready for Charlotte and Hazel to move in with me. I got a job in the city too, one I've just completed training for. Now, do you have any more questions or can you finally get the hell out?"

Her words process so slowly, it almost seems like she's talking in slow motion as she delivers the killing blow to my chest. I carefully read over the papers she gave me, hoping she's bluffing, but it says it all here on this very official document signed not by one but two lawyers.

"You're selling this place for eleven million dollars?" I ask because it isn't just the house. It's the whole ranch, and it's a large property. The price makes sense, but without my salary from being a Hawke driver who gets paid the big bucks, I can't afford to buy it off her.

"Yes. It's worth this much, according to the property valuer I hired. I could get even more for it, but I don't care how much it is, as long as it's enough to be too expensive for you to buy."

I try not to let her words, the knives she's throwing, go directly into my heart, but they do anyway, making it bleed inside my chest.

"You're a cruel woman," Halo says, and for the first time tonight, since she burst through the door, she smiles.

"Perhaps in the eyes of someone who loves my son and only heard his story, but if you knew mine, I think you wouldn't feel so sure I was the monster," she says, but she's not going to tell her side of the story. She knows it would make her look bad, and I'm in no mood, or mental state, to fight her about *that*. Especially when there's something more important to discuss.

"Where are the animals going to go? My Willow?" Mum knew the question was coming, so she's got an answer at the ready.

"They're included with the ranch."

"I'm going to fight this. I'm going to take this to my lawyers, and they're going to break yours in half. You're not taking this ranch and our animals away from Charlotte, Hazel, and me." I roll the papers before shoving them into my back pocket, walking around the couch to face her. "Have you ever considered what it would do to them if you turned their lives upside down like this? Charlotte graduated from high school less than a year ago, and Hazel's friends are all here."

"Yeah, and she'll make new ones. Charlotte took a gap year to figure out what she wants to do, so she'll go to university in the city. I've thought it all through. The only obstacle is you," she says, pointing at me.

I nod several times, taking subtle deep breaths to keep from screaming, breaking down, or grabbing her shoulders and shaking sense into her.

"Part of me thought you'd be gone for good when you didn't show up after my crash. I thought I was finally rid of you like Dad, but if only I had been so lucky." Shock and anger battle on her features for dominance, but she can't make up her mind, and I don't give her the time to.

I've never been this cruel to her, but she's threatening to take the only place that has ever felt like home from me, the place I come back to at the end of every season, because it's the one place I sleep well every single night. The place I feel connected to nature, my grandparents, my childhood.

"I'm staying here for the night, and so are Nachelle and Halo. In the morning, we have to catch our plane anyway, so we'll be out of your hair," I say because I need to gather my thoughts, contact my lawyers, and speak to Gabriel. All things I'd much rather do where my sisters can't hear me arguing with people or breaking down in sobs.

Both things I wouldn't be proud of.

Taking two steps at a time, I race up the stairs and make my way to Hazel's room where Chellie, Charlotte, and Hazel are. I knock and wait for permission to enter, and once given, I do so without hesitation.

By the way they look at me, I can tell the walls weren't thick enough to keep them from hearing every bit of that conversation.

When Hazel looks at me, tears drop down her cheeks, and a fresh wave of anger for my mother washes through me.

"Why is she doing this?" Hazel asks.

No amount of pain in the world compares to the one I experience when I say, "She's doing it to get back at me." Charlotte's head snaps up, a tear rolling down her cheek, too.

"I think you should go, Cameron."

I take it back.

This... this is the worst pain I've ever felt in my life.

"Char, I—" She cuts me off.

"I've handled Mum in the past, I'll handle her now, but I think you being here only makes her angrier. I need you to please leave."

There's an urgency in her tone that I can't ignore. I do my best to keep my own tears at bay as I walk over to them, place a kiss on each of their heads, and then leave the room again. Halo is standing in the hallway, seeing me at my lowest for the second time today.

He doesn't move to hug me, and I don't go to him either. Right now, what I need is to be alone.

I've got enough to deal with without trying to understand my complicated feelings for him, and I'm too tired of getting my heart broken in every single way to let him in now.

I turn on my heel and walk away, leaving him standing where he is.

CHAPTER 17

Cameron

Halo hasn't reached out to me in days, not once since we got off the aeroplane in Shanghai for the second race of the season. We arrived a few days early, and originally we were going to explore the city, but I've become too good at avoiding people if I don't want to see them.

Not a very flattering personality trait, I know, but it's easy to convince myself the only reason I'm not seeing him, or anyone, is because I'm busy arguing with my lawyers, telling them to find a way to nullify whatever my mother has done.

But they can't.

They haven't found anything.

I'm standing with headphones on my ears, watching Chellie set her times for Q1. The Hawke is thriving on the Shanghai Audi International Circuit. James has been setting laps fast enough to rival the fastest lap ever set on this circuit.

My leg has been restless for days, bouncing up and down. There's a nervous energy working itself through my body, camping out in the nooks and crannies inside me. I've tried distracting myself by making a few perfume bottles with the travel kit I packed when I left the ranch, but it only made me more nervous because I spiraled down all of the worst case scenarios.

What if Hazel and Charlotte blame me forever?

What if Mum sells the ranch to someone who does unspeakable things to the ani-mals and turn our house into a slaughterhouse?

What if I never see Willow again?

What if all my childhood memories drift away as soon as it's been sold?

What if my sisters never want to see me again?

My eyes unfocus as I lose myself in that spiral again, and it takes more effort than I'd like to get out of it, to blink away the thoughts and fixate on the screens again. Chellie easily made it into the top fifteen racers, securing her chance to participate in Q2.

The scent of fuel and rubber is in the air, and I keep my arms crossed in front of my chest as if it would be enough to hold myself together. I used to hug myself as a child when things became overwhelming, but as I grew older, it turned into crossed arms because I can hardly stand here hugging myself whenever I feel buried in worries.

Q2 flies by in a rush of emotions. Val and Adrian are the second fastest on this track in their Velocità Rossas. They're right up there in the positions with James and Chellie, and pride fills me when Chellie finishes Q2 in first place. It doesn't mean she will get pole in Q3, but it's still impressive.

"Cameron?"

My head turns in the direction of where the voice is coming from, and I see a tall woman approaching me. She's got a warm smile on her heart-shaped lips, and her dark brown eyes are welcoming. She's clad in a wine-red pantsuit, complementing her lightly tan skin colour and dark hair. I've never seen her in my life, but she's approaching me as if we're old friends.

"Yeah, that's me," I reply, smiling back at her to be polite. She holds out her hand for me to shake, and I place my palm in hers, her steady grip like a soothing balm to the worries in my chest.

"My name is Munira Said. I'm one of Hawke racing's therapists," she explains, and I momentarily freeze, still holding onto her hand.

"Who told you to approach me?" I ask. I'm not upset, but it's not a coincidence that she's here, talking to me.

"A concerned friend who knows you've been very busy and haven't had the time to look for someone to talk to," she explains, and I nod several times in agreement because whoever sent her my way is right. I have been too busy, and if I'm being honest with myself, I've also been putting it off, too scared to start going to therapy to unravel everything I've built on not dealing with shit for the past thirty-two years.

But I should.

I have to.

I can't keep living with that black hole inside my head where my memories should be just because my trauma pushes it as far down as possible.

"I didn't know Hawke hired therapists," I say because I'm not sure what else to say.

"They hired a group of us, mental coaches, and psychiatrists for the team to make sure anyone who needs help gets it." The surprise must be evident on my face because she lets out a small laugh. "Yeah, I know, it's about time they did."

"Actually, I was more surprised you'd be approaching me if you work for the members of the Hawke team since I no longer am one," I explain. Munira shakes her head a little.

"You are part of Nachelle's team, so you're part of the Hawke team. That means, my services are available to you, and the best part is, it just so happens that I have a spot open during every single race weekend this season."

I can't help it.

I chuckle in response to her words.

"Just so happens?"

"Just so happens," she confirms, and I find myself grinning.

"I think I like you already," I tell her, and she wastes no time holding out her business card with her name and contact information on it.

"Good, then perhaps you will reach out to me and we can schedule our first meeting soon." I carefully place her card in my pocket, giving her a single nod.

"I'll be in touch." We shake hands one last time before she leaves the garage.

Confusion is camping out in my chest. There's only one person I told about wanting to start seeing a therapist, but I have a feeling he isn't the one who sent Munira my way. I haven't even told him about the shit Mum is pulling, so of one of Hawke's team therapists approaching me this soon after what happened at the ranch is either a huge coincidence or more proof that Gabriel wasn't the one who told her to go to me.

I believe in coincidences. I think the universe has a funny way of making things happen the way it wants them to, but something in my gut is telling me this isn't that.

It's telling me I know exactly who's behind this.

Chellie qualified second with James having taken pole, Val in third, Adrian in fourth, Gabriel in sixth, and the rest of the grid following after.

She was so excited about her result, she couldn't stop bouncing up and down in excitement. All of the doubters, the people who wanted to see her fail so early in the season, have no ammunition because she's performing flawlessly.

Better than I did last season.

After she disappeared to do her interviews, I decided to go back to my hotel where I've been sitting on my bed with my phone in my hand for an hour, spinning it around as if that could tell me what to do.

Part of me wants to continue to avoid Halo at all costs. The other wants to talk to him to find out if he was behind Munira approaching me.

I also just want to see him.

It's as if I can't breathe properly when he isn't around anymore, which only adds to my indecisiveness about whether or not I should call him. I didn't mean to get so attached to him, to want to constantly be near him. I didn't mean to put any sort of dependence on him for my happiness, no matter how small.

Most importantly, I didn't mean to develop feelings for a man who doesn't date people because of the trauma of his past.

I stand up and start pacing around my room, longing shooting through me whenever Halo's face appears in my thoughts.

Maybe we could make it work. Maybe he will change his mind about what he wants. Maybe I could learn to let him in.

"I want to marry you, spend the rest of my life with you. I want to raise children with you, Cameron. I want everything with you."

Elijah's words ring in my ears, sending a fresh wave of frustration through me. Frustration, but not heartbreak, not the way it would have months ago.

My emotions are so all over the place that such a little thing feels like the biggest step I've taken on my healing journey. It has hope blooming in my chest, expanding with every breath I take.

I throw my phone on the hotel bed and run my hands over my face, letting out a breathless laugh.

"I don't know what to do," I mumble to myself, my empty room filling with the sound of the words.

Dropping my hands, I stare at where my phone is resting on the throw blanket they put in here. My gaze shifts to my setup where all of the tools for my perfume making are, then I go back to staring at the phone.

The setup. The phone.

A war is waging inside of me.

Call him? Don't call him?

Text him? Don't text him?

I pick up my phone again, unlock it, and stare at his contact for another minute.

"This is ridiculous." My finger taps the call button.

Ring-ring. Ring-ring. Ring-ring.

It rings in time with my heartbeat, only the rhythm of my heart picks up speed the longer he doesn't pick up.

Then...

"Cam." I welcome the sound of his voice as it travels into my ear where the phone is pressed against it.

"Can you come to my hotel?" I don't give him any context or reason why. I give him nothing but that single question.

But he makes my heart leap out of my chest with his response.

"I'll be there in ten."

CHAPTER 18
Halo

My hands are shaking.

I've never been this nervous in my life, but also excited at the same time.

Cameron hasn't reached out to me in days, and I've given him his space in case he needed time to process what his mother is doing, but now he asked me to go to his hotel room. Where it'll be just the two of us.

"Where are you going?" Nachelle asks when I walk back into the bedroom of my hotel room, shoving my phone into my pocket as I reach for my jacket.

"There's something I need to do," I say, slipping my arms through the armholes. Nachelle cocks a brow at me and twists her features into a suspicious expression.

"*¿Algo o alguien?*" she asks, and my cheeks heat in response.

"Shut up," I reply but the smile on my face betrays me. "*Volveré pronto,*" I assure her, even if I have no idea when I'll be back.

"God, I hope not. You and Cameron need to stop fighting whatever is between you two," she says, but I ignore her statement, only throwing an "I love you" over my shoulder before leaving.

Things are not as black and white between Cam and me as they may seem to her. She doesn't know Elijah cheated on him. She doesn't know things are more complicated for me than simply "not finding a person I want to be in a relationship with," as I've repeatedly told her. She doesn't know why we've kept our distance from each other for so long, at least romantically.

The cab ride over, I go through every scenario in my head of what might happen, none of which include Cameron kissing me and telling me he wants to be with me like Nachelle thinks it'll happen.

I'm not a romantic, or at least I've never been a romantic, so it's hard for me to picture anything so... well, *romantic*.

Nothing like that has ever happened to me. No one's ever swept me off my feet by declaring their feelings for me, and it's not about to start with Cameron.

I drop my head against the headrest of the car and close my eyes, scolding myself for being such a fool and rushing toward the man who could possibly be furious with me for asking Munira to go talk to him today. She was the most praised therapist by Hawke's team members, and I wanted to make sure he knew he had the chance to talk to someone about what's going on during the many race weekends we're attending this year. I know he's very busy, so I wanted to make things easier for him.

But now I'm overthinking, and my brain is telling me it's the worst thing I could have possibly done. That I overstepped so far, he'll never forgive me. It doesn't matter if I meant well. If he's upset, he has every right to be.

I'm going to be sick.

The cab stops in front of Cameron's hotel, and I quickly pay before hurrying inside. Cam already gave the person at the reception a heads up that I was coming, so they tell me where to go to get to his room without any trouble.

In front of his door, with my heart in my throat, I knock softly using my knuckles.

The sound of footsteps approaching makes my breathing hitch, and then there he is, standing behind the door wearing a pair of shorts and a T-shirt. His hair is disheveled, as if he's run his hands through it a hundred times, and there's a redness in both of his eyes. He hasn't been sleeping, that much is clear, and I wish I could figure out what the expression on his face means.

"You came," he says as if he can't quite believe it.

"I said I would." He nods, his features pulled into a thoughtful look.

"I know, but you didn't just come. You rushed to be here."

I can't argue with that.

"It sounded like something was wrong," I explain to hide the fact that I simply wanted to see him. "You call, I drop everything to be there for you. That's how it works with me."

Cam steps aside, his hand holding onto the door as he clearly invites me in without saying a word. My feet carry me inside and as soon as the door clicks shut, I spin on my heels to face him again.

"Are you upset with me?" The questions practically bursts out of me. "I'd understand if you were, you know. Upset with me, that is. I should have spoken to you first, but I wanted to show you it could be easy to get help since I know society makes it seem like such a difficult thing to ask for, let alone seek out." I'm rambling, but he's also staying perfectly quiet, which doesn't help because I'm trying to fill the silence between us with my words. "I thought it would help, but I see now that I may have been wrong, and I'm so sorry." The tiniest hint of a smile appears on his face, and yet, no words leave him. "Please say something before I make a fool of myself," I beg, and this time, he fully smiles.

"Before? Then we have to figure out how to time travel to two minutes before you started talking," he teases, and I'm so relieved to see he's not angry, I snort.

"Jerk," I mutter, my grin staying in place even as he approaches me.

"I'm not upset with you at all, Asher." His hands move to my arms and he squeezes them firmly, steadying me.

"God, the way you say my name," I blurt out before I can think better of it, and he tilts his head backward to look up at me.

"How do I say it?" He releases me, and I instantly wish his hands back on my body.

"Like it belongs on your tongue, to be spoken only by your lips."

Cameron takes the smallest step back, obviously taken aback by my words, but I don't want to take them back. Anything I'd say to do so would be a lie, and I'm tired of lying to him about my feelings.

"Hmmm," is his only reply. He places his hand on my chest and drags it across it as he steps further inside his room, leaving my body to overheat with desire.

I need to know why he's touching me like this, but I don't have time to ask the question before he speaks again.

"Stop overthinking about telling Munira to approach me. You did the right thing. I was putting off finding someone to talk to, and I needed that push you gave me, so, if anything, I have to thank you," he says, and I could drop onto the bed beside me in relief.

"If you weren't going to yell at me, why did you call me and tell me to come over?" There's a little chair and desk area near the television in front of the bed where Cameron is sitting now, fumbling with the hem of his shirt.

"I missed you and wanted to spend time with you."

This time, I do sink onto the bed. Cameron's watching me with something akin to fascination, clearly enjoying how flustered I am.

"What does that mean?" I ask, but his gaze drops down to my shoes.

"I don't know," he admits, turning to the desk to avoid my inquiring look. "But I wanted to show you something I've been working on," Cam says, gesturing toward what's on the desk. I do my best to push down the things happening inside of me to concentrate on what he's pointing at.

In front of him are several glass jars, small bottles, and even tinier containers that look like the things we used to have at home to store essential oils for our humidifier. He's also got a funnel, dropper, measuring spoons, and some aluminum on the table.

"Are you making cologne?" I ask because I've seen videos where people made perfume, and their setup looked exactly like his, albeit bigger and with more tools.

"Perfume, actually. It lasts longer than cologne," he corrects. "It's a hobby I picked up because I could do it with one hand, even if it was difficult. On the ranch, I spent my days experimenting with different scents until I found one I think suited me most," he explains and holds up a perfume bottle. "Come here."

His command is soft but firm, and I find myself stepping toward him without hesitation. He takes my arm, twisting it gently until the underside of it faces him. I notice that he's holding me with his left hand, so I stay perfectly still to make sure he doesn't hurt himself, or worse, that I hurt him.

He sprays it once, aiming for the area near my wrist.

"Smell that," he instructs, urging me to lift my wrist to my face. I take a deep breath, his scent filling my nose.

"Smells like you," I say, catching that cedarwood note I love so much.

I go back to sitting on the bed, continuing to smell the spot he sprayed, when he uses the rolls on the chair of the room to get closer to me.

"I also made this," he says and lifts up another bottle. "For you," he adds, but his voice is significantly lower, quieter. I hold out my other wrist, and he sprays that too. I lift it to my nose as well, getting hit by something wonderfully citrusy combined with vanilla and his woody scent.

"How did you come up with this? It's delightful," I say, and he smiles, clearly proud of himself.

"I was combining every note that reminded me of you until—"

He cuts off, lifting my wrist to his nose and inhaling the scent of the perfume. My heart does a backflip and my body tenses as his nose brushes the sensitive skin near the inside of my wrist.

I freeze in place.

Cam lingers.

Goosebumps break out across my skin as a fresh wave of desire, desire for *him*, infiltrates my body.

He looks up at me, his thick lashes framing his hazel eyes. His thumb presses down on the bone in my wrist, the rest of his fingers near my pulse point.

I know he feels my racing heart beneath his fingertips. I know he's aware of how desperately I want him. But there is nothing I can do to stop that. Nothing at all as he holds me in place with those eyes of his locked onto mine.

He's got this way of making time slow down until it feels like it has stopped completely, and right now, it's no different.

We're frozen, him touching me, me watching him touch me.

"Tell me to let go," he says, but his grip tightens like he means the complete opposite.

"No."

His bottom lip slips between his teeth to try and hide his smirk, but I see it clearly enough.

"You're trouble, Asher."

"Never claimed to be anything else," I remind him. He drops my hand, but instead of letting go, he places it on his leg. My fingers instinctively dig into his thick thigh, and he sucks in a sharp breath in response.

"I know, but we both know we wouldn't work because of that. You don't want a relationship, and I'm broken," he says, and I find myself reaching for the bottom of his chair and pulling him toward me until his legs are between mine.

A breath *whooshes* out of him, and he braces himself by placing his hands on my shoulders.

There's no stopping my next words.

No amount of fear could keep them inside.

The anti-relationship Halo I was before Cameron has slowly been chipping away, replaced by a person who wants little more than to be loved the way I know Cam loves.

"What if I did want a relationship?"

With you, I add in my head, refraining from speaking such a bold statement out loud. I might be pining after him and have been doing so for years now, but I won't put my heart out there for him to judge and possibly dismiss.

I'm not brave enough to do that yet.

"Do you?" he asks, his fingers digging into my shoulders.

"Maybe I do."

"Maybe? Or yes?" I groan at his incessant questioning, but I can't fault him for it. He wants to know what's going through my head, why I've pulled him so close and won't remove his hands from my shoulders.

"There's something happening between us, and I don't want to run from it like I have in the past when I've felt something for someone. I want to embrace it, and that scares the shit out of me," I admit, wishing I could take it back when he drops his hands and uses his feet to push back and create some distance between us.

His warmth disappears, leaving me cold and almost shivering on the bed. It occurs to me that it's not cold in the room, but that I'm trembling out of fear, and it's this situation that reminds me why I've never dated.

If only I could turn off my feelings for Cameron as easily as I developed them.

"Do you truly want someone like me, Halo? Someone who doesn't know how to trust anymore? Someone who will need constant reassurance because of his past? Can you look at me and honestly tell me you've thought about what it'd be like to be in a relationship with someone who got cheated on? The patience you'd need while I learn to trust again?"

As much as I'd like to open my mouth and respond, I have no answer that he'll like because I haven't thought about it. Not because I didn't know that's what it'd be like to be with him, but because I don't even know what being in a romantic relationship is like.

How would I begin to understand the emotional, physical, and mental impact a past partner's betrayal would have on a new relationship?

I can't, not without Cameron giving me a chance.

"Plus, I'm dealing with a lot of shit right now, and I don't want to drag you down with me," he says, rolling even further away from me.

The restraint in me snaps and with it breaks the carefully built wall I put around my voice to keep certain thoughts about him, about us, inside.

"Cam, we keep bouncing back to each other. For every step back we take, we take two toward each other, slowly closing the distance between us. We can keep fighting this for a little longer if that's what you need, but eventually, you're going to be as curious as I to know what it would feel like to finally taste you."

I stand up, towering over him for a second before placing my hands back on the armrest of his chair and leaning down until we're at eye-level.

"I'm a man of many strengths, but I'm not strong enough to resist the pull you have on me, not unless you tell me not to come near you." His hand lifts to my chest, and he places it on the spot between my neck and collarbone.

"I want you near me," he whispers, his breath brushing against my lips.

Fuck me.

"Good, because I want you near me, too."

As much as it pains me to break away, to cut this carefully spun tension between us, I have to. I have to do right by him.

"I'll think about what it would mean to be with you, but I need you to decide if you can trust me or not because I can stand here and promise I'll never do to you what Elijah did, what your father did to your mother, what my father did to my mother. But at the end of the day, my words matter less than my actions would, and you have to decide if you're ready to take a chance on me."

This is not where I thought tonight would be going, but I'm glad I finally opened my mouth and told him how I feel, what I want.

Cameron watches me with confusion as I pick up the bottle of perfume he made for me, with the scent that reminds him of me.

"I trust you, Cam, and I hope to fuck you trust me, too."

Because if not, I'm in this alone with my feelings, and I can't think of much that is more frightening than unrequited love.

"I want to," he admits, not moving an inch, even as I make my way toward the door to leave. He's not stopping me, so I know I'm making the right decision.

Space doesn't have to be a bad thing. It can be a very good thing when it makes people realize how desperately they want to be together, and I have faith that Cameron does want to explore whatever is between us.

He called me today.

He missed me.

He wanted to spend time with me.

I'm hoping that once I leave tonight, he'll still feel all of those things for me in the morning.

He'll still want to seek me out to be with me.

And if he doesn't, at least then I'll have my answer.

"Good night, Cam," I say as I open the door.

"Good night, Asher."

I smile the entire way back to my hotel.

CHAPTER 19

Cameron

"THEN WHAT HAPPENED?" ADRIAN asks, on the edge of his seat. He's holding Seraphina, his daughter, as she takes her afternoon nap right there, with her daddy holding onto her and protecting her. He's supporting her head with his hand, cupping it gently as she dozes in the crook of his arms, a sight so beautiful, I have a hard time looking away.

"He left," I say, finishing the story of what happened between Halo and me the day before the race where Nachelle came in third, her first podium of the season. It was one of the proudest moments of my life, almost as if my own sister had won that trophy.

"To grab some champagne to celebrate you two finally admitting to your feelings or..." Adrian trails off, clearly not understanding what I'm telling him.

"No, Adrian, he left to give us some space to think about what any of this means. Some people don't just admit they want each other and then go at it right away, especially when those people have stuff to deal with," I explain, running a hand over my tired face to avoid his inquiring eyes.

"You don't know if you want to give it a shot with him?" Leonard asks, and I look his way with uncertainty lingering inside of me.

"No, that's not the problem. The problem is that I *do*, but I don't know how I'll ever be able to give anyone a hundred percent of me like I did with Elijah. We were going to get married. I was all in, and he broke the part of me that so easily put my trust in the people I loved," I explain, and he nods thoughtfully, leaning back in his chair as he considers my words.

"That's understandable," Storm chimes in, and I can't help but smile at the grump.

"Thanks," I tell him, but he merely nods once before going back to peeling off the label of his beer bottle.

"Cameron, you are by far the kindest person on this planet. Your positivity is a much-needed relief to the pessimism the world harbours in its heart. You have so much love to give, and I've always admired you for giving it away so freely. What makes Halo so different that you're excluding him from that?" Gabriel asks, and it sends such a wave of discomfort through me, I almost tell him to fuck off.

"Oh, you hit a nerve," James chimes in, and I throw my former teammate a surprised look that he chuckles at. "Please, I've known you long enough to notice when you're done with a conversation." He folds his hands together and places them on the table, never taking his blue eyes off me. "You like him. As a friend, you even love him. Why don't you allow yourself to *fall in love* with him, too? Hmm? You're already two-thirds there."

Leonard places a hand on my shoulder in silent support because my mind is spiraling and there's no stopping it now.

I told Halo I want him near me.

I was intoxicated by his touch, his proximity.

I wanted everything he did in that moment.

But as soon as he left my room, it was as if a bucket full of ice and water was dumped over my head, shocking me awake.

Halo's a fantasy. He's what I can no longer want without that strange, foreign part inside of me telling me not to get closer to him. And it isn't a quiet voice. It's loud, screaming at me to get away before something bad happens.

So even though my heart wants him, my head is fighting it with everything it's got.

"Let me hold Seraphina. It'll cheer me up," I say and hold out my hands, wiggling my fingers to make Adrian hand her over to me, but his eyes widen at the same time his lips part.

He doesn't say anything, merely glances at me, then at his daughter, then at me again. His arms tighten as he holds on tighter and lets out a breathless laugh I know he doesn't mean.

"No, thanks," he says, shaking his head at me.

"Adrian, let Cameron hold her," Gabriel tells him, nudging his brother-in-law in the side.

"I think she'll be safer here," Adrian says as he smiles down at Seraphina.

He brushes his nose over hers before leaning back in his chair and looking up to see five sets of eyes on him. I'm pouting, Leonard and Storm are probably scowling, and Gabriel and James wear expressions that speak louder than any words.

"Fucking hell, fine. But if you drop her, Cameron, I'll take you skydiving and shove you out of the plane without a parachute," he warns, so protective of his first child.

"Sounds fair," I say, standing up and reaching out again with my hands, this time wiggling my hands in excitement. Adrian is not impressed, but he gently places Seraphina in my arms. I support her head and hold her close to me, sinking into my chair so slowly. Adrian's face shows approval because of how careful I'm being.

Throughout this whole thing, our newest family member continues to sleep peacefully, her green, blue, brown eyes staying closed. They're exact copies of Adrian and Val's, something so very Romana that no one will ever doubt she belongs in that family. Her blonde hair is just another indicator.

It must be so wonderful not to have a single worry in your life. She doesn't have any experiences that haunt her. Her parents love her more than life, and she receives the same level of love from the rest of us.

Seraphina looks free, careless, and I wish I remembered what that felt like. I wish it would tell me exactly what to do, but instead, I hold her even closer, placing my cheek on her forehead and rocking her from side to side.

"Are you cheered up?" Gabriel asks with a little chuckle, and I nod several times.

"I don't think anything could bother me right now," I reply, my eyes closed as I enjoy this moment with my little niece. Because even though none of us—except Val and Adrian—are bonded by blood, we're family.

"Fantastic, so you don't mind if we ask you why we saw your family's ranch up for sale?" Adrian says, continuing to watch his daughter closely as she sleeps in my arms. He's prepared to catch her, and I almost roll my eyes at his paranoia. I catch myself only because I know if the roles were reversed, I'd be acting the same way as him.

"I didn't sign up to be interrogated today," I remind them all.

"Then why did you come to dinner?" Storm challenges, and it's so out of character for him to talk to me that way that I chuckle despite myself.

"Because I missed all of you dickheads, but maybe I shouldn't have," I say, covering Seraphina's ears right before I swear. Just in case.

"It's no bloody wonder you've been avoiding us all. You're overwhelmed and you refuse to ask for help," Leonard says, and I twist my head to frown at him.

"How would you help me? Hmm? Because last I checked, you weren't in need of a new driver because you have Gabriel and Kyle. None of you can help me with the ranch situation, and the same goes for my sisters hating me right now. My mum has always been a self-serving person, so there's nothing new there for you to help me with either. The only thing I thought you might be able to help me solve is how conflicted I feel about Halo, but you've been unable to do so as well," I rant, but I do it in a calm, steady tone to keep Seraphina from waking up. I might be frustrated, but I won't be the reason this sweet angel wakes up and screams at all of us for being inconsiderate.

"You shouldn't blame us for your mountain of problems," Storm says, and I snort in response.

"Okay, you're too vocal today. I'm not a fan," I tease, grinning to make sure he knows I'm kidding. He merely cocks a brow at me, unimpressed.

"And you're an idiot. Halo has never, ever wanted anything like the relationship he wants with you, Cameron. I've known that man for years. I've watched him have meaningless nights with people left and right, but have you noticed he hasn't been with anyone since your accident?" Storm stops himself and shakes his head. "Of course not. You were too busy avoiding him while he was here, worried out of his mind about you. He didn't eat. He didn't sleep. He didn't look at another person. All that mattered to him was that he didn't know if you were okay, healing, recovering."

My breath catches in my throat as guilt shoots through me.

"The more you push him away because of your past, the more I think Halo deserves better. I know you have shit resting on your shoulders, but do you not see that he would help you carry it in an instant? That he'd be there for you? That he'd give you the space to build trust because that's how desperately he wants to be with you."

Never in the duration that I've known Storm has he spoken *this* much. He usually sits at the table with us, listening to the rest of us chat about whatever we want to. When we ask him questions, he gives us one-word answers, but I can tell he's passionate about this because I'm hurting his friend.

It's not on purpose. I don't mean to hurt Halo by pushing him away, but I have a feeling that's exactly what is happening.

"How do I know I won't get my heart broken again?" My voice is barely more than a whisper.

"You don't, but do you honestly want to spend the rest of your life protecting your heart and never falling in love again?" Gabriel asks, and I hear all of the unspoken words on his tongue too.

I tried it. I tried protecting my heart from ever falling for someone because I was scared I'd lose them like I lost my parents, my grandparents, Maxime. But Val didn't give me a choice, and if Halo is the one for you, he won't either. You'll fall, and the best you can do is embrace it because the harder you try to fight it, the more energy you waste not being with the person you're meant to be with.

Maybe it wouldn't be exactly like that, but my best friend does have a tendency to be incredibly cheesy at times, so I wouldn't put it past him.

"Before Scar, my ex cheated on me, too. Shit like that happens, but as you can see, there are people like my wife out there who would rather step in front of a moving train than hurt someone like that. Halo is another one of those people," Storm says, and I hate that, deep down, I know he's right.

"Alrighty, I think I've had enough of this intervention." I press a kiss on Seraphina's forehead before standing up and handing her over to Adrian again. He grins brightly as he welcomes his daughter back into his arms.

Nevaeh is out with Valentina, Chiara, Estrella, and Scarlette tonight, and I know as much as Adrian misses his wife, he's enjoying every second he gets to spend with Seraphina.

"Why don't we discuss the fact that Velocità Rossa and Grenzenlos are almost equally as fast as Hawke this season?" I ask because every person at this table is passionate about racing, and it's the easiest way to get attention off of me.

"What do you mean 'almost'? We're faster," Adrian says, whispering-screaming to bring his point across more dramatically while also trying not to wake his daughter.

"I think Cameron's right. We are still the fastest car," James replies, taking a sip of his beer.

"Not according to the last two race results," Gabriel adds, all three of them driving for the three different teams.

"Well, this should be fun," I tell Leonard as I flop back against the back of my chair and cross my arms in front of my chest.

"Hundred euros says Adrian will be the first to swear," Leonard says and holds out his hand for me to shake while the three of them keep arguing about their cars' speed and performance on different tracks.

"That's like betting against someone who says the sun will rise tomorrow," I reply, and Leonard starts chuckling beside me, a rarity in itself.

"Fine. Hundred euros says that Seraphina will wake up soon and distract Adrian so much that he forgets what they were talking about." He's still holding out his hand, and I stare at the tattoo there, a necklace wrapping from his index finger all the way down and over his thumb with a charm that says "Mine" hanging from the chain. Apparently, Chiara chose it, and I'm not oblivious. I know he wanted his wife to have a pretty necklace.

"If they end the discussion in any other way, I win," I reply and shake his hand, grinning from ear to ear.

About twenty minutes later, after Leonard started chiming in as the team principal with so much more information—I know the fucker only did it so I wouldn't win the bet—Seraphina wakes up from her nap, stealing Adrian's attention.

"*Bonjour, mon petit ange,*" he says, and when she starts fussing, either needing something changed or some food, he gets up and walks toward the kitchen in James' house, where we all met up today.

Leonard holds out his hand, palm facing up, and I roll my eyes as I dig into my pocket. I pull out my wallet, then the hundred euros I was keeping in there, before slapping it onto his palm.

"Happy?" I sound as irritated as I am. Not at all because this is much too amusing.

"Well, I am a hundred euros richer, so yeah, why not?" he asks, and I burst into laughter because we both know he doesn't need it. He's filthy rich. He bought an island that he gifted to his wife as a wedding present, for fuck's sake.

So, I laugh.

I laugh until my stomach hurts.

Until I realise this moment would only be better if Halo was here with us to enjoy it.

CHAPTER 20

Cameron

"THERE HAS TO BE something, anything, to prevent her from doing this. Keep looking," I tell my lawyer, Aisha. "Please," I add because I'm being rude, and she doesn't deserve that.

"We're working on it, Cameron, but her lawyers have spent the last eight months finding a loophole. It's going to take more than one to fight back," she says, her voice soothing.

"We might not have much more time," I remind her, doing my best to keep the tears at bay. They seem to appear every time now when I talk about the ranch. When I think about neither one of my sisters reaching out to me after Charlotte sent me away.

"I'm working as fast as I can. Have some faith in me," Aisha says and hangs up the phone, leaving me to wrap my hands tightly around my phone to keep from throwing it.

I don't understand how anyone's life could possibly be going so drastically wrong in every aspect of it. The only thing I've got going for me is that Parker assured me I could take my hand out of its brace for the first time today. I'm carrying it with me in case my hand gets tired.

It was a relief to know that, even though I still have some mobility limitations, I'm getting better because as soon as I'm back to a hundred percent, I'm going to tell my manager to fight even harder for me to get another contract. I'll become a reserve driver if that's what it takes, but I want to make my way back into F1. No matter how. No matter from which position I have to start.

But first things first, my hand isn't the only thing that has to heal.

I knock on Munira's office door, waiting for her to tell me to come inside.

"*Enchanté*, Munira," I say with a big grin, hoping it'll make her smile. It does.

"Welcome in, Cameron, take a seat," she says and gestures toward the couch opposite a large chair I think she will occupy soon. I settle down on the couch, taking a deep breath.

"Your hand is not in a brace anymore," Munira says as she takes the seat across from the couch so gracefully, I'm mesmerized by her for a moment.

She looks as elegant today as she did the first day I met her. She's wearing a long dress, and her dark hair flows in perfect waves down her back

"Yeah, we took it off for the first time today. I still have to go to a doctor's appointment after we get back from Suzuka, but I'm excited to see the progress," I admit, wiggling my fingers a little as if to demonstrate what I can do.

"That's great, Cameron." We smile at each other for a moment, but my expression falls first, and I blow out a nervous breath.

"So, how does this work? Do you ask me questions, and I answer them?" This earns me a little laugh from her.

"Kind of, but this is not an interview. I'd like it to be more of a conversation."

"About what?" I ask, scratching my left arm nervously.

"About whatever you'd like to talk about," she replies, picking up a notebook and pen and placing them on her lap.

Silence fills the room for a few seconds while I try to compose my thoughts. They're as all over the place as I am. I open my mouth to start talking about something, anything, but then my brain shuts it down immediately.

What if that's the wrong thing to say? What if she'll be overwhelmed by the amount of shit that's wrong with me? What if I make a fool of myself?

This is so awkward, and the reason why it feels that way is because *I'm* awkward. It's as if this is my first day being around a person and I don't know how to behave.

It's fun to know that I have no idea how to speak to therapists, I guess.

"Take a deep breath, Cameron. Everything is going to be fine," Munira says and puts her notebook aside again. I do as I'm told, and she gives me an encouraging nod. "Very good. I'm going to ask you to try to stay present with me. If you feel yourself spiraling, acknowledge it and try to stay in the moment with me."

"I feel like that's easier said than done. I'm a natural at overthinking," I say with a laugh.

"That's alright. It's many people's nature to overthink, but I'm here to hear all those thoughts and address them with you, if you're comfortable with it," she explains, uncrossing her legs and placing her hands on her thighs. She's creating a more casual space, and I want to hug her for it. First the notebook, now the way she's sitting. It feels like I'm here with a friend.

"I don't know where to start," I admit, lifting one of my legs and placing my ankle on top of the other thigh.

"Why don't we start with something simple? How are you feeling today?"

That's easy enough to answer.

"Good, I guess. My manager is currently asking around to see if any of the teams are looking for a change in their driver line-up next year, negotiating with them for a deal for me. Now that my hand is no longer in a brace, I'm ready to start fighting for a seat again. I'm ready to see what team wants me enough to give me a seat as a driver, not just a reserve driver," I explain.

This is the first time I'm telling anyone about this. Since I only just got my hand out of its brace, it's a new development, so I haven't had a chance to share it with my friends yet. It seems like an easy conversation starter with Munira, though.

"That's great, Cameron. I'm glad you're getting out there, fighting for a seat." It's the genuine tone of her voice that makes me feel like telling her was the right decision. It takes some of the pressure off me to have to know exactly what to say without making an arse of myself. "What about the phone call you had outside my office? You sounded frustrated with the person you were talking to," she points out, and I get a little embarrassed that she heard me.

"I am frustrated. My mother told me a few weeks ago that she'd be selling our family's ranch, and even though we all inherited it when my grandfather passed away, she found some sort of loophole in the will that gives her all the rights. My lawyer hasn't been able to find anything to dispute it, and if she doesn't soon, I'm going to lose the only place that's ever felt like home to me."

The tears reappear, but I manage to swallow them again. It's one thing to cry to myself whenever this wave of emotional pain strikes, but it's another to do it in front of a stranger.

"Did she tell you why she's selling it?" Munira asks, and guilt replaces my sadness.

"No, but I think it's to get back at me. She's blamed me for leaving to chase my career goals since I left all those years ago. It reminded her of how my father left after he cheated on her, and she hasn't been able to see me do anything other than 'start a new life away from my family,' as she put it, since then," I explain, and while her facial expression mostly stays the same, I notice the way her eyebrows twitch as if she wanted to raise them in surprise.

"So, your father abandoned your family, and you went to be a Formula One driver who still had contact with his family and, I'm assuming, supported them emotionally, perhaps even financially?" she asks, and I nod because that's hitting the nail right on the head.

"I've never understood why she was so angry with me. Whenever they needed me, I was there. I tried to be the perfect son, no matter how far away I was. I tried everything, and it was never good enough," I rant, doing my best to avoid eye contact because I'm opening up but one glance at whatever expression she's wearing might be enough to close me again.

"It sounds to me like she's projecting her pain and betrayal onto you because she never got closure from what your father did. She's using you as an outlet for her anger. It's common for parents to use and abuse their children in this way when their significant others hurt them. It's like they see their child as their partner, expecting them to meet their emotional needs their significant others don't care about anymore. They even expect their child to help them raise their younger siblings because they're too busy dealing with their own problems to do so."

I don't know when my mouth fell open, but there is no chance in hell I'll ever be able to close it again. Not when everything Munira just said described what my mother has been doing to me and to our family to a T.

"Fuck, you're good," I blurt out with a breathless laugh, releasing some of the pent-up nervous energy inside of me.

"I am, so you have to believe me when I say this is not your fault. Your mother selling the ranch is not because of you. Her taking her feelings out on you is not your fault either. You didn't do anything wrong."

To hell with keeping the tears at bay. They drop down my cheeks as I pull my knees to my chest on the couch, falling right back into being the teenager I used to be. The one that got so scared whenever his mother was in a bad mood again because it was only a matter of time before she found me and used me as her emotional punching bag. The one who knew when he had to avoid her, keep his mouth shut, and wait until she wasn't so angry anymore to ask her what we would be eating that day. I'm that kid again who needed his mother after his father left, but she was never the same again.

It takes me a while to wrestle back the tears, but once I do, I take the tissue box she's holding out for me, blowing my nose after I've wiped the tears from my eyes.

"You know, usually during my sessions, we start with something smaller, get to know each other first," she says with a small smile that I return.

"Well, I've got a lot I'm dealing with at the moment, so I thought I'd spare us both the boring issues," I joke to bring a bit of humor back into the moment.

"What else are you dealing with?" she says instead of laughing.

"I was cheated on by the man I thought I'd spend the rest of my life with and now I can't tell the man I have feelings for that I have feelings for him. On top of that, every time I see someone crash during a race or someone asks me what happened to me, my hands, I dissociate. I forget where I am, what I was talking about with whoever I'm speaking to, and I fall into a big black hole in my memories that I can't get out of for a while." I rant through the last two big things I'm dealing with, hoping it won't make me dissociate if I don't think about what I'm saying for long before the words come out of my mouth.

"How do you know you're dissociating?" she asks, and my eyes widen before a blush of embarrassment covers my face.

"I looked up my symptoms," I admit in a low voice, hoping there's a way she can't hear me well. But she does.

"Would you mind describing your symptoms to me?" she asks, and I go back to scratching my arm nervously.

"It's never anything bad, I mostly just zone out, I feel disconnected sometimes while it happens. I forget what we were talking about because I got so lost in the emptiness of where the memory of my accident should be." I fumble with my fingers. "I can't remember anything. I remember the first flip of the car, and then nothing."

Munira's gaze is on me, and I finally look up to meet it. I find no pity there, which is a relief. She looks curious and thoughtful, and the dread I felt before showing up today disappears.

"Have you watched any footage of the crash to see if it would jog your memory?" she asks, folding her hands in her lap and crossing her ankles beneath her chair.

"No. I'm scared to. It's not easy watching yourself crash, let alone when that crash cost you your career," I reply.

"That makes sense." Munira picks up her notebook again and jots down some information. "For our next session, if you feel up for it, I'd like to start with a bit of Exposure Therapy. I want us to watch a single crash. Not yours, someone else's. Then, when you're comfortable moving on, I'd like to graduate to watching your crash. There's many other treatments we can try for your childhood trauma as well, but it's going to take time and you have to put in effort as well. You can look into Eye Movement Desensitization and Reprocessing and Cognitive Processing Therapy. Those are two more treatments apart from the Exposure Therapy that I think could be good for you," she says, and I look at the clock on the wall to see, somehow, we've already been talking for almost an hour.

And a part of me that's been blaming itself for years for what my mother has been doing to me, already feels a bit lighter. It's still heavy, of course one session isn't going to be enough to fix years of trauma, but it's a step I've taken today, and I'm so proud of myself.

"As for the man you have feelings for but being unable to tell him because of what your ex-boyfriend did to you," she starts and leans forward, looking directly into my eyes. "Trust is a hard-earned thing that takes time. When trust has been broken in the past, it can feel impossible to give it to another person. It's alright to need time to heal, but if you truly care about this man and he cares about you, isn't that enough for now to allow yourself a chance at happiness? Not everyone will hurt you the way you've been hurt in the past."

Halo's face appears in my head as she says the words, his smile so bright and happy. I think about everything he went through, what he goes through to this day because of his father. I think about bonding with him over the pain we share. I think about what he said to me.

I can stand here and promise I'll never do to you what Elijah did, what your father did to your mother, what my father did to my mother. But at the end of the day, my words matter less than my actions would, and you have to decide if you're ready to take a chance on me.

He asked me to take a chance on him. He asked me to trust him without asking that of me. He bared himself to me, and the least I can do is give us the chance he asked for.

"We can continue this conversation next time. For now, I would like you to write down every single time you get triggered into dissociating because of your crash and bring me the list next time. It'll be a good way for you to keep track and for us to understand exactly what triggers you." She holds out a piece of paper for me with the instructions written on it, and I take it from her with a grateful smile.

"Thank you so much for approaching me, Munira. This is not nearly as terrifying as I thought it would be, even though I bawled my eyes out in front of you," I say and get up. She follows, and I shake her hand like we did the first day we met.

"I'm glad you had a good experience today, and I promise you, the longer we work together, the easier it will be."

I don't doubt her even for a second.

CHAPTER 21

Halo

THE THIRD RACE OF the season is taking place in Japan. The team and I have been making some adjustments over the past few races to the car, and I'm looking at the data and statistics I've been given, satisfied with the results. Val and Adrian are pushing the car to their limits on this track, and they're faster than the rest of the drivers this weekend.

I was watching them closely as they set their times yesterday, Valentina snatching pole for the first time in Suzuka. It was one of her dream races to get pole and to win, but so far she's only achieved one.

Today, we'll see if she can beat her brother and the other eighteen drivers.

Nachelle only qualified eighth, but she wasn't upset anymore when I pointed out to her that James only came in fifth too. Their car is struggling and has been since last year. Everyone blames Cameron for underperforming, but if your car is shit, there is no way you can set the times they're expecting of you. Especially because Hawke prioritizes James.

In Velocità Rossa, they do their best not to have a number one driver because both of them are World Champion drivers. They're both talented and have brought them the kind of results they hadn't seen in years because of Grenzenlos' dominance. They're both invaluable, and there is no way they could ever choose a number one when they're both unstoppable.

And if they did, because of Lorenzo Mattia's—the team principal's—history with Valentina, the way he sees her as his own granddaughter because of his friendship with her grandfather and father, he would choose her as number one. Lorenzo wouldn't be able to do this to another of his friends' grandchildren and children, Adrian, so they don't have a number one.

It works well for them, and not many things do in their team at times, so they won't change the running system.

"*Todavía no me puedo creer que Nachelle sea un piloto de Fórmula Uno*," Mami says from beside me, and I wrap an arm around her shoulders to pull her against my side. I kiss the side of her head, leaning down to do so because my mami is a lot shorter than I am.

"*Yo tampoco*," I admit, smiling when we both see Nachelle appearing on the screen. She's standing on the track with Saanvi, who hands her a bottle of electrolytes. My sister is focused, her mental barriers up, and it's going to stay that way until the end of the race.

"*Se ve tan seria*," Mami adds with a giggle, and I chuckle with her because she's so right.

"*Dramática*," I tease, earning a nudge to the ribs from my mother.

I love being able to speak so much Spanish. No matter how hard Nachelle and I try to use our second mother tongue more, we always end up switching back to English out of habit. It's only when Mami is around that I actually stick to speaking this much Spanish. She also never makes me feel bad for when I slip up and use the wrong terminology or grammar, or when I sound more American than Dominican.

We stay silent while a tall woman with broad shoulders clad in a uniform sings the national anthem. I hold onto my mother because I've missed her so much. No matter how old I am, no matter where in the world I go, a part of me will always miss being her little boy. The days we spent going on adventures. The nights I couldn't sleep and she held me while sharing stories of our family with me. The afternoons we spent together in the backyard, playing soccer.

Damn, I haven't thought about playing soccer in a while...

I was one of the best players in my time at college. My friends and I dominated the world of soccer in the state, but then we grew up. We went our separate ways with different career paths. The people who called me "Halo," who gave me that nickname to begin with, are nothing more than a distant memory now, just like my time as one of the best soccer players in the state. I don't regret the career I chose, no matter how difficult it was to fight my way into it, but I think I've been suppressing any memories of my days in college to keep from thinking about how much I miss it.

Perhaps I can convince Nachelle to go to a soccer game with me soon, help me reconnect with a part of myself I haven't spent any time with in a while.

"*Estoy nerviosa.*" I peer down at my mother, then glance at the screen to see Nachelle pulling on her balaclava and her helmet after.

"She'll do great," I assure her absentmindedly, my attention drifting to the weather radar screens, and even though I'm standing quite far away, I notice a strategist looking at the huge rain cloud approaching the track within the next...I can't see how long.

My heart drops.

Cameron's crash happened when it was pouring rain, and while they've adjusted the rules to make sure what happened that day doesn't happen again, this can't be good for him to witness. If someone crashes, he'll be triggered harder than ever before.

He'll have another panic attack.

My stomach twists into knots.

"Are you okay, *amor*?" Mami asks as I frantically search all my pockets for my phone.

"Yeah, I will be. Give me one moment. I'll be right back." I leave the garage to go to a quieter place, pulling out my phone and opening my chat with Cameron.

We haven't spoken since that night in his hotel room. We haven't addressed anything we said to each other because I wanted to give him space and he wanted me to think about the implications of dating someone who was cheated on, but I'll be fucking damned if I let this man go through another PTSD triggered panic attack on his own.

Me: Hey Cam

Me: I *saw* that it's going to rain soon and I just *wanted* to make sure you know I'm here if you need anything

Me: IF any of this overwhelms you and you need someone by your side text me I'll be there as quickly as my legs can carry me

I send the message before my brain tells me not to. He needs to know I'm there for him because I'm the only one who knows about the panic attack he had. I'm the only one he'll be able to call without having to explain himself. Most of all, I'm hoping that when he's at his lowest, he wants me by his side the way I'd want him by mine.

He doesn't answer right away, so I go back to Mami, placing my arm back around her and pulling her to me. Hers flings around my back, her hand resting on my hip.

We stay like that for a while until it's time for the formation lap and she goes to cover her mouth as she studies the screens closely.

Waiting. Dreading. Anticipating.

My phone vibrates halfway through the lap.

Cameron: Thank you.

It doesn't say anything else, and I'm a little disappointed he's not making some dumb joke like he usually would. I shove my phone back into its pocket right as it rings again.

Cameron: Feeling loosey goosey right now, though, so don't *worry* about me.

A snort leaves me because this is such a Cameron response and it's exactly what I was missing before.

Me: You're so *weird*

Me: Also

Me: Who still texts with periods and commas?

Me: You're such an old man

This time, his response comes quicker.

Cameron: Six years, my handsome man. I'm only six years older than you.

Cameron: As for being *weird*, yes, I am. You still have a crush on me, though.

My cheeks are scorching hot as the fiercest blush ever known to man covers my face.

Cameron's flirting with me. He called me his handsome man.

I shiver, unable to stop the visceral reaction his words have on me, but I also can't be the only one currently losing their composure, so I text him back.

Me: Call me your handsome man again Cameron and I *won't* be responsible for *what* happens between us the next time I see you

I'll put my mouth on him, any part of him that he wants me to, and then I'll put him on his knees and show him just exactly how good those three simple words make me feel.

Cameron: Promises, promises.

There's no time for me to calm my racing heart because all twenty drivers are currently waiting for all the lights to turn off, and I hold my breath with them as their engines roar.

As the lights vanish, all twenty of them shoot ahead.

Nachelle has a horrible start and loses a place, dropping into ninth. Valentina keeps her first place, even with Adrian right behind her, chasing her. Gabriel and Kyle, his teammate, are fighting for third while James loses a place to one of the Spark Racing drivers, Philip.

Everyone is battling each other as the first raindrops fall from the sky.

Every engineer, mechanic, and fan watches their screens and the track even more closely.

This is the first wet race since Cam's accident. We're all a little more nervous than we usually are, or at least it feels that way.

No one overtakes anyone after lap six, when the rain starts pouring down harder. The Velocità Rossas are the first to drive into the pits to change their tires from softs to intermediates for some reason. According to the radar, no matter how brief, it's supposed to come down even harder before easing up again, and if I were to make the decision, I'd have put them on wets.

But that's Velocità Rossa for you. Their strategies make no sense, and I'm pretty sure that part of it is them hoping luck is on their side.

I see Scarlette's hands flying around as she argues with someone into the micro-phone attached to her headphones, and I realize she was not the one who approved the intermediate tires. Lorenzo must have overridden her decision, and when the team principal tells you something, there is not much you can do to change his mind.

"I hope they make a better decision for your sister," Mami says, and I nod several times.

Part of me wishes I hadn't gotten into the career path I have chosen but done what Scarlette is doing just so I could tell my team and driver to put on the tires my gut and the data says is the right decision, even if I would get in trouble. But this way, all I can do is watch helplessly as the Velocità Rossas pit way earlier than the rest and on tires that won't last them.

No one else in the top places pits for three more laps. They're all waiting to see how bad this rain situation will be as the rain cloud moves closer and closer to the track. They're also waiting to see if there will be a safety car, which can save them time during the pitstop since every single car will have to slow down.

Gabriel is currently in first, and I know Leonard is going to make the right decision because he's got the experience. He's smart. He's got amazing instincts.

The Grenzenlos cars pit two laps later, going on wets. Then follow the Hawkes, who do the same thing. Mami sighs in relief, and I place a hand on her shoulder, squeezing it once in comfort and silent agreement because I feel the same.

It isn't just bad strategy to not put a driver on wets when it's raining this much. It's risky. Intermediates are better than slicks, but fuck, they can still cause the drivers to slip more than wets would. Wets have more grip during the rain because of the structure of the tire.

"Valentina just slipped in corner six," my mother says and points at the screen, poking me simultaneously because I wasn't paying attention to her. I was looking at the other screen where they're showing Nachelle going after Gian in eighth place.

They show a replay of Valentina going onto the white line at the side of the track, which is one of the slipperiest parts when it's wet.

"*Coño*," I mumble to myself.

Another three laps pass with heavier rain until finally it eases up again. There's no time to be relieved, no time to acknowledge that maybe Velocità Rossa made the right decision after all, because Adrian slips on the white line, much like his sister did, but he can't get his car under control.

No.

He slips into the grass area, nothing in his way to stop him until he eventually crashes into the barrier.

The red flag is waved almost immediately, an improvement to previous years where they took way too fucking long to respond when a driver was in a dangerous position.

He seems to be doing okay, at least according to his radio messages where he sounds winded but alright, and this time, I sigh in relief.

That relief doesn't last long when I feel my phone vibrate in my pocket.

Cameron: It's happening again.

Cameron: Bathroom.

I sprint out of the garage and to him.

CHAPTER 22

Cameron

THIS WAS BOUND TO happen again.

As soon as I saw the rain falling, I *knew* it would because the odds of an F1 driver crashing out during a wet race are likely.

I should have known not to watch this one, but Munira's words of trying Exposure Therapy rang in my head, so I wanted to try my best to sit through this.

To challenge myself.

But I wasn't ready to watch Adrian crash into the barrier because he's also not a driver I don't know well. He's not someone I saw during race weekends and had occasional driver dinners with. This is Adrian. We were teammates during his first season in Formula One. I took him under my wing and made sure he adjusted well to this change. He's the guy who somehow always found a way to cheer me up when I was down after a race result. He's the one I built a bond with over the years.

Adrian is family.

Watching him crash into the barrier made a wave of panic hit me so hard, I nearly collapsed, and once I knew he was okay, I spiraled into the day I crashed.

Into the emptiness in my mind.

Into the what-ifs.

Into the feelings I felt that day because while I don't remember what happened, I remember being so, so scared I was dying.

Feeling the pain in my hands and lungs.

A wave of dizziness hit me until the whole garage was spinning, and the only thing I could do was text Halo.

I stumbled into the bathroom, I don't know how long ago, dropping to the floor next to the door and pulling my knees to my chest. It feels like I'm going to pass out while simultaneously being too full of panic to actually faint. My head is spinning so hard, I'm nauseous.

Bile rises in the back of my throat, and I'm so hot, I'm sweating.

"Oh my God," I say as I get even more nauseous, covering my mouth as if that would make it any better.

A part of my brain keeps trying to go through the black hole, spin through it in hopes there's a light at the end of the tunnel that leads to the memory of what happened that day. But everything else, every other piece of it is fighting against achieving that very thing, and it's tearing me apart.

Can a brain rip itself to shreds?

A knock on the door pulls me out of the panic, but only so slightly that I fall right back into it without responding to the person asking for permission to enter.

"Cam?" His voice is a soothing balm for my soul, but not even the sound of it can help me right now. I'm humming to keep the nausea at bay, unable to respond.

The door opens carefully anyway. A moment later, I feel his steadying touch on my knees.

"I'm here. You have me for whatever you need," he promises, and I feel my hands start to shake as my breathing picks up pace. Tears trickle down my cheeks, and I'm still so fucking dizzy, I feel my head floating somewhere else, no longer in my body.

Halo's fingers reach out to catch my tears and wipe them away, and I don't know what comes over me, but I throw myself into his arms. He catches me, then rearranges me so I'm hugging his arm to my chest while he uses his free hand to rub up and down on my back. I'm between his legs, and he presses his knees against me to steady me even more.

This is the most vulnerable I've ever been in front of another person, and I don't know why it feels so right that it's Halo.

I wouldn't want anyone else to hold me right now.

I wouldn't want anyone else to rub my back soothingly.

I wouldn't want anyone else to put their cheek on my head as I grip their arm tightly.

I don't *want* anyone else.

More time passes, but I have no sense of it. It could be hours. It could be minutes. It feels like forever, and once I settle, once the nausea leaves and I stop feeling a sense of imminent doom and death, I don't want this moment to end either.

His hand on my back stops moving but only because he places it on my arm instead, trailing it up and down. My head is resting on his chest, and I appreciate him for not making me talk or move. For simply staying in this same position for however long I need to be here. I knew he's patient, but I didn't know just how patient until this very moment.

"You're all sweaty," he says eventually, and I can't help but laugh in response to his playful tone.

"I'm an athlete. We tend to sweat," I reply, remaining in this position for a little longer, even though the worst of it is long over.

"Maybe when you're working out or racing. But right now you have no excuse," he teases, and I laugh again, this time even harder than before.

"Sorry about sweating on you. And I'm sorry for texting you. I—" I cut off, but he finishes the sentence for me.

"You didn't want to be alone," he says, which is *an* answer, and while it may be true, it isn't the reason I texted him.

"No, Asher. I *needed* you," I admit, and it's a hell of a lot easier to be honest when I'm not looking into his icy-blue eyes and have to face the way he tugs at my heart, trying to pull it his way.

"Say it again." His demand is soft but so powerful, there is no resisting it.

Resisting him.

"I needed you."

His hand moves under my chin, and he tilts my head back, making me look at him. He rubs his thumb over my jawline, and I do my best to keep my eyes from fluttering shut. Right now, I can't remember anything that has ever felt this good.

"Say it again," he repeats, his eyes on mine, keeping me in place.

I don't look away as I say, "I need you."

His thumb moves from my jaw to my lips, tracing the shape of them. I shiver in his arms, but he holds me steady with his legs, centring me. His other hand, the one he was using to rub along my back, moves to my hip, and my breathing hitches in response. He notices and presses down on my bottom lip, dragging it down only to release it and watch it bounce back into place.

"Why did you grow out your beard?" he asks, tracing where it has grown on my face with his eyes.

"Needed a change," I explain. "Plus, how handsome do I look?" He tilts his head, and I wish he'd smirk or grin or anything he usually would to break this tension inside my chest. Tension of anticipation.

"Very," he replies. He thinks for a moment before he adds, "You called me handsome before," he whispers, seemingly as affected as I am by what he's doing.

"I also called you mine."

"Hmmm," he agrees, clearly thinking about that message I sent him.

"You liked it," I observe because no matter how much he's in control right now, no matter the fact that I'm putty in his hands, my handsome man is blushing so hard, his cheeks are pink.

"I did. I liked it very much."

He goes back to tracing the line of my jaw, his gaze on my lips. My body doesn't know whether to stop breathing or if I should breathe harder, and my head is spinning again, this time for a completely different reason.

Halo is keeping his distance from me, but I wish he wouldn't. For the first time since we met, the distance we so carefully placed between us is an obstacle I want to overcome, not one I hoped would keep us from making a mistake. Feeling his lips pressed against mine doesn't seem like a mistake anymore. It seems like the best idea I've ever had, but Halo isn't moving. He's not destroying this bloody distance, and as much as I try not to say the words because of how vulnerable they are, they spill out anyway.

"Why aren't you kissing me?"

He leans back a little, but a smile tugs up the corners of his mouth.

"Because the first time we kiss will not be on the floor of a random bathroom in the Hawke Racing motorhome," he replies, slipping his hand into my hair and playing with my curls.

"I didn't know you cared about that stuff. It's so...romantic," I point out with a little smile of my own. "You didn't strike me as a romantic."

"I'm not, but you are, so that's what you deserve." I'd roll my eyes if it didn't make my heart flutter as much as it does.

"Does that mean you'll take me on a nice date?"

"No, but you can take me on a date. Just make sure it's memorable. I've never been on an actual date, so you have to make it epic." His grin is like pure sunshine.

"No pressure then," I reply with a snort.

Halo laughs, throwing his head back to reveal the column of his throat, the way his Adam's apple bops with the movement. It's mesmerizing. I can't look away when he brings his head forward again, revealing his straight set of teeth, full lips pulled into the most wonderful smile, and his eyes sparkling.

"I'm fucking with you. We could go to the grocery store for all I care," he says, and I finally sit so we're facing each other at eye level. I bring my hand to his neck, running my index finger over his pulse point.

"I'll make it special. A first date should be any way, but it being your first date ever means it has to be even more so." I lean forward and press a soft kiss to the area I was just tracing with my finger.

"Cam," he gasps, and I smile as I inhale the very scent I made him. I don't think he noticed, but many of the notes I included in his I also put in mine, the one I wear.

"Thank you for coming to me," I tell him, leaning back, my lips almost brushing his.

"If I get a date with you out of it every time, feel free to call me at every hour of the day." He gets up, holding out his hands for me to help me up, too. In one swift movement, he's got me on my feet, his hands firmly holding mine.

"So, are we really doing this? Are we going on a date?" It feels surreal to even think that mere months ago, I thought Halo would be the last person to be interested in me. I thought I'd never be able to be excited to date again.

Everything's so different now. All because of this tall, gorgeous man in front of me.

"Yes, we are. I'm sorry for any clumsiness or uncertainty on my end. I promise to do my best to figure out how to...do this," he says, letting go of me to rub the back of his neck.

"It'll be fine, Halo. We're going to figure this out together, okay?" He nods, his shoulders falling as he untenses.

"Okay." He takes a step away from me and gives me a singular nod. "Now, come on. We still have the rest of the race to watch."

Halo opens the door for me, and I step through it, trying to dial down my excitement about the fact that he and I are going on a date.

Dread is trying to work its way through me, reminding me of Elijah and everything that happened, but I shove it far down, letting only positive feelings camp out in my chest.

We're going on a date.

He took care of me when I needed him, and it didn't scare him to see me at my worst.

Having panic attacks triggered by my PTSD fucking sucks, but at least it got Halo and me exactly where we are now.

Ready to flip the page and start a new chapter.

With each other.

By the time we return, the race hasn't restarted yet.

Adrian's car is still getting lifted out by a crane as all of the drivers wait for the track to be safe again. The rain has almost stopped completely, which means when they restart the race, they'll be on either intermediates or on mediums or hards to make it to the end of the race. It all depends on how slippery and wet the track is, but considering the sun is shining, I'm guessing it'll dry up fast enough.

Parker is standing off to the side with Saanvi, discussing something about the race, I'm assuming, considering the way my performance coach is flicking their hand toward the screen. I leave them be, even though they came to Suzuka this race weekend to take care of me and my wrist, and I wish I could tell them about what just happened with Halo. But there is no way I can interrupt their conversation when they seem to be enjoying it. They're laughing and Saanvi is playfully touching their arm in a way that tells me she's not interested in being just friends.

Minutes pass, and I switch between watching the screens to looking at where Nachelle is standing, talking with Cory. He's in a mood, like always, and I want to punch him in his stupid face for the way he's treating Chellie. The same way he always treated me.

"Open your eyes and look at the data, Nachelle. I know it's difficult for you to understand, but try a bit harder, would you?" he says loud enough to embarrass her in front of the team, and I take a step toward him, ready to beat him up for his disrespect when Chellie's voice stops me.

"How about you shut the fuck up and do your job, Cory? Hmm? Or is that too much to ask of an insecure little man like you?" Chellie spits back, and I have to slap a hand in front of my mouth to keep from laughing loud enough for him to hear.

Chellie walks past me, and I hold up my hand for her to high-five. She flashes me a proud smile, clearly content with herself.

The race restart happens about eight minutes later, when Adrian's car is finally cleared and the track is safe for all nineteen drivers to make their way onto it with either hard tyres or mediums.

Valentina is starting in first with her husband right behind her in second. Kyle is in third, and James is in fourth. Both Spark drivers are taking up places five and six, and Chellie is in seventh. It's not an ideal position to be for a Hawke driver, according to their high fucking expectations, but given the track conditions and the chaos that happened when Adrian crashed, it's not a bad place to start the race again. She'll overtake the Sparks soon because she's faster, and then she'll be in fifth, right behind her teammate.

Everything will work out for Chellie, she just has to be patient and allow herself time to overtake them instead of rushing into it.

The start is uneventful, despite being a standing start. Most of the drivers keep their positions, and Gabriel, even though hungry for the win, can't keep up with Valentina as she shoots forward, creating a gap big enough to keep her husband out of DRS range.

Chellie overtakes Spencer in sixth three laps after the restart, followed by Philip seven laps after.

James is too far ahead of her, so there is no way she can close the gap in the last twelve laps, not unless James slows down significantly and stops going after Kyle in fourth place.

The camera focuses on Gabriel and Valentina as they go into corner five with their wheels almost touching.

Ever since they got married and Gabriel switched to Grenzenlos because Velocità Rossa wanted Valentina on their team, I've been impressed with their ability to separate work from their personal life. F1 drivers are competitive at their core, but I know Gabriel is genuinely always proud of Val for her performances, even if it means he loses against her again.

Right now, he doesn't care about how proud he'd be if she won. He's trying to take this win for himself, get some points for the championship standings, and I hold my breath as they go wheel to wheel again in corner one when they approach it once more.

Val keeps defending, and eventually, she manages to get him out of her DRS range and keep her first place.

If anyone asked me who I thought the faster driver was, I wouldn't be able to answer the question without hurting my best friend's feelings because I've always thought Val was the greatest driver the world has ever seen.

With every race I watch, every time she outperforms every single other driver, she only solidifies that belief.

Meanwhile, James overtakes Kyle, securing himself third place.

For the next eleven laps, I watch Chellie close the distance between herself and Kyle, but right as she gets into DRS range, they cross the line for the last time, ending the race.

I'm disappointed for her, but she did her best given the situation, and I'm proud of her. As a matter of fact, she's made me so proud during the last few weeks, it brings up that whole feeling like an older brother to her again. I don't know what it is now with Chellie, but considering how often we're together, how much we're working together, it's impossible not to grow closer with someone. Especially with someone who you care about so much.

Valentina, Gabriel, and James bring their cars to the first, second, and third place signs. I stay inside the garage, watching all of it on the screens. Watching her run to her team to hug them and high-five them. Once she's made her round, she turns to see Gabriel behind her. He's still wearing his helmet and so is she, but he grabs her anyway and places his helmet against hers, as if they were kissing. It's a sweet, wholesome sight that makes me so happy to see because those two have been through hell. They deserve any kind of happiness they can get.

After they do their post-race interviews, the three of them disappear into the cool-down room. All of us wait while they take a moment to catch their breath and prepare for the trophy ceremony on the podium. They get to watch clips of the race in that room, and I remember being in there as if it was yesterday.

The glory of winning a race. The excitement of having the whole world watch you excel at something so many people said would never happen. The happiness and pride.

James is the first one to step up onto the podium, followed by Gabriel, and lastly Valentina. My friends take off their caps as they play the Monegasque national anthem for Valentina, then the Italian one for Velocità Rossa. This is a common procedure after someone wins a race, and I miss the days the Australian anthem played to honour me and the country I was racing for.

Once the Italian anthem plays, the entire Velocità Rossa team starts screaming the lyrics from the top of their lungs, one of my favourite sights whenever this special team wins. No one knows how to celebrate like the Italians do.

After the three of them are handed their trophies as well as the member of the Velocità Rossa team they invited up there, they turn to the champagne bottles, picking them up to start spraying them around. Gabriel goes to drench Val in champagne, and James follows suit until both of them are just holding their champagne bottles her way.

I take it all in with a smile and longing, wishing it was still me up there, celebrating my achievements.

CHAPTER 23
Halo

After the race in Japan, Mami came home to Monaco with Nachelle and me. She's taken two weeks off of work to come to the Japanese Grand Prix and spend Easter with us.

It's been almost a week since the race, and my family and I are spending *Semana Santa*, or Good Friday, today, relaxing at home, playing games, and catching up on the months we've been apart. Usually, if we were in the Dominican Republic, we'd be at the beach with the rest of our family, enjoying each other's company. Although I'm not very religious, we'd go to church too, and there are certain rules I follow with Nachelle and Mami, like not eating meat but opting for fish instead.

There is no such thing as the Easter bunny or going on an Easter egg hunt, but because we lived so far away from our family during one of the biggest celebrated religious holidays in my family, she used to give us little presents that made us feel more connected to the relatives we weren't able to be with. Now that we're older, she doesn't do that anymore, but instead, Nachelle and I buy her a present as a way to say thank you for making all of our holidays so special despite missing her family too.

The longer I'm away from my father's toxic influence, the more I realize how much he made Mami give up. He made her move away from her family. He didn't celebrate her holidays with her. He didn't eat traditional Dominican food because he didn't like it.

He made her feel so disconnected from a part of her identity, and as a result, her children had to feel equally disconnected.

It's a good thing I'm no longer speaking to my father because whenever my thoughts go down that path, I want to strangle him for his selfish decisions.

"*Mijo, no se supone que estés trabajando,*" Mami says and runs a hand over my hair before leaning down to press a kiss to the top of my head.

I'm sketching a new design, playing around with the different components of the Formula One car. Part of my job includes sketching new designs, and while most of the other Chief Designers heavily rely on CAD—Computer-Aided Design—most of us start off with the traditional method: pen and paper.

"*No estoy trabajando. Esto es un pasatiempo,*" I reply, but we both know I'm full of shit, so she nudges my chin with the back of her fingers.

"*Mentiroso,*" she says and walks toward where I keep my yarn for my crocheting. She picks up all of the supplies there, including the one I'm still working on for Cam, and carries them over to me. Without hesitation, she snatches the pen and paper from my hand and replaces them with my crochet needles. "*Esto es un pasatiempo,*" she corrects, and I chuckle.

We don't speak again while I simply get to crocheting, doing my best to follow the pattern I found online to make sure Toothless actually does look like him and not a weirdly shaped sheep.

Mami sinks onto the couch beside me, and Nachelle strolls out of her room in her pajamas, lifting her arms above her head as she stretches. It's two o'clock in the afternoon, and this is the first time she's gotten up today, most likely because she only came home late last night.

My sister lifts her fingers to her temples as she stumbles toward the kitchen, Mami and I exchanging a look of amusement.

"*Mi amor, te dejé un poco de café en la cocina,*" Mami says a lot louder than necessary, and I burst into laughter when an evil smile covers her lips.

"Oh my fuck," Nachelle groans, placing her fingers in her ears to keep more sounds out.

"That's what she gets for going out to party while I'm in town," she whispers to me, and I laugh even harder.

"I hate you both," my sister says, grabbing her coffee and going back to her room. She stays there for all of two seconds before coming back out and dropping onto the couch, into Mami's arms.

Our mother hugs her fiercely, kissing her temple over and over until my sister is smiling hard. I watch them for a second, thinking about all the pain that's brought us to this point. Dad might not be speaking to me anymore, but it brought Mami, Nachelle and me that much closer. I know he still contacts Nachelle, he did last weekend to congratulate her on her performance during the Japanese Grand Prix—but I know she doesn't enjoy speaking to him.

She can't forgive him for what he did and how he treated me after, and if Nachelle had to choose, she'd always choose Mami and me.

Never him.

I spend an hour crocheting, finally taking the time to actually finish it instead of staring at it where it was resting on the basket with the rest of my crochet supplies.

With work and traveling the world as well as trying to be the perfect older brother who takes care of his sister, I don't actually have a lot of time for this hobby. Even though I enjoy it a lot.

It lets me turn off my head to concentrate on the pattern.

I raise my wrist to my nose and inhale deeply, wondering if making perfume has the same kind of effect on Cameron as crocheting has on me.

Then I think about that day in the bathroom and the fact that he and I are going on a date soon. I don't know when and neither does he because he's back in Australia, trying to negotiate with his mother to keep her from selling the ranch, but I'm in no rush. When the time is right, we will know. For now, I smile at the plush I crochet, thinking about the way he looked at me. The way he called me his. The way he made me feel without meaning to.

"What are you thinking about?" Mami asks, and I look up at her, realizing I'm smiling from ear to ear.

"Cameron, obviously. Look at his face," Nachelle chimes in. Mami's lips curl into a grin, but she cocks a confused brow.

"Cameron? As in, Cameron Kion, your sister's mentor and your friend?" she asks, and I feel myself smiling even harder.

"Yeah," I reply shamelessly because there's no point denying my feelings.

"The same Cameron I invited over for our *Semana Santa* dinner?" Mami goes on, and surprise makes my smile drop.

"What?"

There's a knock on the front door before she has a chance to answer.

My mother moves, clearly wanting to get up and answer it, but I jump to my feet to beat her to it. No part of me was prepared to introduce him to Mami today, but it also shouldn't be a big deal because we're not actually dating yet.

As of right now, we're just friends.

Friends who have been close and yet so far for so long.

Friends who feel the pull inside each other but have fought it for years.

Friends who don't even know what the other tastes like.

I open the door but instead of inviting him in or greeting him, I step into the hall. Cameron stumbles backward, his smile falling as he tries to catch up on what the fuck is happening.

"What are you doing here?" I ask, taking a moment to appreciate how good he looks.

He styled his hair, his curls more defined today than I've ever seen them. His hazel eyes are glimmering in joy, and his lips look fuller, pinker somehow. He's wearing white, casual straight-leg linen pants and a matching long-sleeve shirt, a combination that would look ridiculous on anyone but him. He's got the top few buttons undone, and I think my mouth waters a little at the sight of him.

"I'm here because I want to be here. Because for the past five days, all I've been thinking about is seeing you. Being near you again. It was highly inappropriate because I certainly shouldn't have any time to think about you, but it's all I did. So, instead of going straight to Saudi Arabia like I'd planned, I came here. I came here and, fuck me, it's one of the best decisions I've made in a while because here you are," he says, using his hand to gesture at all of me. "And you look devastating."

I stare down at my grey sweatpants and black hoodie, not sure what the hell he's talking about.

"I'm in sweatpants," I remind him, tugging on the stretchy fabric. Cameron nods.

"Yeah, I know, but they're grey sweatpants, and have you seen your face and those eyes of yours?" He takes a step toward me, then another, until he's got me trapped between him and the door.

My heartbeat picks up its usual rapid pace as soon as he's close to me and his scent hits my nose. He lifts one of his hands to my chest, looking up at me as he brings his body flush against my chest.

"Did you miss me, Asher?" he asks softly, looking up at me and sending a wave of pleasure through me that's so strong, I almost come in my pants from the sheer feel of his body pressed against mine while he says my name in that way I love.

"Every second," I admit, swallowing hard as he trails his hand upward, cupping my neck.

"Good," he says and smiles, dragging my head down. "Because I know you wanted this to be romantic, but I regretted not kissing you for as long as we've been apart."

He brings his mouth to mine, and my breathing hitches the closer he gets.

This is finally happening.

I've been pining after him for years, always noticing him from afar, wanting him, and now he's finally about to kiss me.

But then the door opens behind me, and Cam has to hold onto me to keep me from falling backward.

"Oh, shit, sorry," Nachelle says. "I didn't know you two weren't fighting but making out." *If only that's what we'd been doing.* "Mami wanted some help with the *bacalao* and the *sopa de mondongo*," she adds with a little chuckle, leaving the door open in clear instruction.

"I don't know what *bacalao* and *sopa de mondongo* is, but I'm curious. Come on. We can't let your mami wait," Cameron says, leaning forward to press the softest kiss to my neck before dragging me inside with him.

My heart is still pounding, but I have no time to linger on it because my full attention is on him as he approaches my mother.

"Dahiana, *es un placer conocerla,*" he says and takes one of her hands in both of his to shake it gently. I'm slack-jawed. "*Tiene dos hijos maravillosos y quiero agradecerle que los haya traído al mundo para que yo pudiera conocerlos.*" I was lying before. Now I'm slack-jawed. As a matter of fact, my jaw could not drop any lower. He throws me a grin over his shoulder and wiggles his brows at me.

"You practiced that on the plane, didn't you?" I ask him as I cross my arms in front of my chest, narrowing my eyes at him.

"Like a million times," he admits and turns back to my mother, finding her smiling.

"First of all, from now on, *en español puedes usar tú conmigo.* And secondly, you greet me with an embrace. You're practically family, Cameron," Mami says and pulls him into a hug that he returns.

The sight warms my chest because I can see how desperately Cam needs this. Both of his parents are, quite frankly, the biggest assholes, and there's nothing like a mother's comforting hug to heal parts of you that you thought could never heal. I think that's why he holds on for longer than a person normally would after meeting someone for the first time.

"Come, come, let's cook," she tells him and gives him one last squeeze before urging him to follow her into the kitchen.

My sister appears by my side, taking my hand in hers. She hasn't done that in years, and I think if my heart experiences one more overwhelming thing today, I might pass out from the sheer amount of emotion running through me at full speed.

"He's good for you," she says, placing her head against my arm. "And you're good for him." Nachelle squeezes my hand and steps away, toward the kitchen.

"He's good for you, too. He's helped you more this season than anyone else has throughout your career," I remind her because I don't appreciate the spotlight she's flashing on my feelings. It makes me want to hide in the shadows. To run.

"Yeah, he is. Mami is right, no matter what title he holds for you, he's practically family. There is nothing he wouldn't do for us, and we feel the same about him. No matter how much you try to hide it, it's obvious." She steps in front of me, a thoughtful expression on her features. "Don't fuck it up."

"Thanks," I say and snort. As if I wasn't worried about fucking things up already. "We should go help them. As much as I love Mami, I'm scared she'll ask him a million questions he may not have the answers to," I admit, and Nachelle bursts into laughter.

"A valid fear, I'm afraid."

We're both laughing as we step into the kitchen, and I can't help but pull my sister against my side again because I hate that she's so grown up. I hate that she's so wise while also not knowing how to deal with the pressure on her shoulders. I hate that she's right about warning me not to fuck up.

Because I could.

I could run when things get too real and break the sweetest man's heart.

CHAPTER 24
Cameron

MY FAMILY DOESN'T HAVE any traditions.

We spent most of my childhood arguing, in chaos, and unprepared for all of the holidays Australia has to offer. My family didn't follow any religion, so things like Easter, as Halo spends it with his family, were never part of our yearly events we partook in. And anyway, the last religion I know my family believed in, my great-grandparents to be exact, didn't have Easter as one of the holidays.

But I'm enjoying learning about all of Halo's family's traditions during this holiday.

Johnny Ventura is playing over the speakers, and I'm watching Halo dancing with his mami. He's spinning her around in the kitchen while they're making the *bacalao*, which I have now realised is salted cod fish.

"Do you want to dance with me?" Nachelle asks, poking my arm. I laugh because I can't help but picture my clumsy self trying to dance to this wonderful music.

"If you want to finish this season with two unbroken feet, I'd advise you not to try and dance with me," I tell Nachelle, but Halo overhears and snickers right before spinning his mother again and going back to stirring the pot while swinging his hips in a way that affects me far more than any other man ever has. I readjust in my seat and look away, catching Nachelle looking at me with a cocked brow.

"Fuck off," I mumble, and she bursts into laughter. I shake my head but grin anyway because I'm genuinely happy.

No matter how fucked up everything is, there's something about being here, around Halo and Nachelle, as well as their mum, that makes joy filter through me.

My lawyer is exploring a route she thinks is promising to stop Mum from being able to sell the ranch. I went to be with Charlotte and Hazel for a few days and, while I think Charlotte still holds some resentment toward me for what's happening, we had a good talk. I think things will go back to normal now.

Actually, I don't know one fucking thing in this wonderful gift called life, or whatever the hell people call it. All I can do is hope.

Hope my relationship with my siblings will heal with time and patience, just like my wrist.

Hope Aisha will find a way to allow Charlotte and Hazel to stay at the ranch, in their lives they don't want to leave.

Hope Mum changes her mind.

"You're lost in your head," Halo points out, placing his hand under my chin to lift it. I look up at him as the tension leaves my body.

"Got a lot on my mind," I reply, and he smiles in response, warming my face with his sunshine.

"Like what?" he asks as he rubs his thumb along my jaw in the same way he did that day he took care of me.

"Like how amazing the food smells. How kind your mum is. How good you look dancing," I say, which is only partially the truth, but I don't want to ruin the lovely time we're having by bringing up the heavy topics of my life.

Today is a good day, and I will do everything I can to make sure it stays a good day.

"Are you watching me sway my hips to the music, *mi luz*?" he asks, and I cock my head to the side, confused.

"*Luz*? As in light?" I ask, and Halo grins sweetly at me.

"You understand more Spanish than I thought you could," he says, but he doesn't tell me why he uses it. Doesn't offer any explanation. Simply walks back into the kitchen to stand with his mother. Nachelle is trying her hardest to snatch a taste of the bacalao while Dahiana swats her hand away.

"*Sigue, y te voy a dar un bofetazo,*" Dahiana says playfully, and I wish I knew what that meant because Chellie bursts into laughter and runs out of the kitchen. Halo is shaking his head, and I find this family moment so beautiful, all I can do is stare and wish my family was like this.

After the best meal of my life, and more *avena* because Halo knows how much I enjoyed it last time, we moved to play a round of dominoes before we settled in front of the television to watch my favorite movie trilogy about dragons. I insisted we watch something else, but Nachelle and Halo love those movies as much as I do, and Dahiana put it on while metaphorically swatting my argument away with her hand. She proceeded to put on the movie and then handed all of us some *habichuelas con dulce*. Parker would be so mad at how much I'm eating today, but what they don't know can't hurt them. Plus, it's a holiday, so I may as well fill my stomach with good food.

Halo and I are as far apart as the room allows, but the distance between us feels palpable, as if I could reach out and touch it.

If only I could.

I'd rip it to shreds.

It's my firm belief that you're never too old to love these movies and get completely swept up in the masterpieces they are, but all I can focus on tonight is how close we keep getting. How close his mouth was to mine. The fact that he's wearing the perfume I made for him.

He smells like him, and a little like me, and I love it.

The possessive part inside me almost groaned when I smelled it on him earlier.

When he catches me looking at him, he blushes and bites his bottom lip, turning back to the television. I find myself smiling because Halo is like no one I've ever met before in my whole life. He's a combination of sweet, kind, driven, hardworking, confident, compassionate, and comfortable in his own skin that I've never encountered in another person. He excites me in ways I've never been excited. He challenges me to become a better version of myself and address things I've hidden from for a long time. He's helping me save myself, my mental health, one small step at a time, and I wish I could describe that to him without overwhelming him with the force of my feelings because I know they're a lot.

Halo's not used to feelings in general, and being met with some as strong as mine without even having been on a date, without having kissed or been intimate in other ways, could scare him.

And I don't want to scare him.

I don't want to give him a reason to run when I think he may be the first person since Elijah that I've felt safe with.

Safe to trust.

Safe to open up to.

Safe to give my heart to.

Panic grips me by the throat because I did trust Elijah. I opened up to him. I gave him my heart. He made me regret it.

Halo is not Elijah, my subconscious reminds me, and one look at him, finding him looking at me with his heart in his eyes, I know it's right.

Elijah most certainly never looked at me like Asher does. He never gave his heart to me the way I think Halo might, and comparing him to the man who hurt me isn't fair to either one of us. Especially when he's never given me a reason to mistrust him.

Nachelle and Dahiana go to bed a little while later, leaving Halo and me alone in the living room. I'm still sitting on the armchair to the right of the couch while he's on the end furthest away from me. We look at each other for a while, neither one of us moving. He's got his bottom lip back between his teeth, and I'm smirking at him because he knows he looks good, sweatpants and all.

"Be honest with me, if my sister and mother weren't in the other room over there, what would you be doing to me right now?" he asks, and I lean back in the armchair, adjusting my position so I'm sitting with my legs spread apart and a single hand on my thigh. I place my chin in the other hand, which I prop up using my elbow on the armrest.

"If they weren't here, Asher, I'd be on my knees in front of you right now." His chest rises and falls faster than it did before, and it would be a lie if I said the mere mental image my words have created didn't have my body reacting in a million ways, one of which I can tell is happening to him as well because those grey sweatpants hide nothing.

"What would you be doing?" I tilt my head to the side and raise a brow.

"Would you like me to describe it in detail even though I can't do anything about it?" I ask, and he stretches out his legs in front of him on the couch, not bothering to hide his erection.

"Please," he says, and I find my own cock growing harder.

Fuck.

"Halo, your family is right through that door. If they hear—" I cut off because we both know I'm right. His head falls against the armrest behind him with a groan, and I do my best to stifle a laugh.

"*Tú me tienes tan loco*, Cameron." He groans again and pulls his legs to his chest, preventing me from seeing the very impressive outline of him. "*¿Qué voy a hacer contigo?*"

"As soon as we're alone, do everything you want to me, my handsome man." He runs a hand over his face and groans again. "But you also wanted to do this right, so we'll do it right. We'll go on a date after we get back from the next race, and afterward, you can have me however you want me."

His head snaps up, and confusion replaces any sign of lust and desire.

"Why after?" I'm a bit taken aback until I realise he hasn't thought about this as much as I have.

"It's not legal for us to go on a date there, Halo. Being gay isn't culturally accepted, and I've had to be very careful whenever I went there, which always included going without any man I was dating at the time." The colour drains from his face.

"Oh," he says, his attention drifting to his hands to study them and process the information I've given him.

"Yeah, so we'll go on a date when we get back to Monaco. Until then, while we're there, we'll have to stay friends."

Silence stretches between us for a moment, until he breaks it again with a question that makes me deflate in my seat.

"How do you do it? How do you exist in a sport where you're in the spotlight and yet have to fight so hard to be accepted the way straight people are?" he asks, and I smile sadly at him because I don't think what I'm about to tell him is the explanation he was looking for.

"Because despite its past, despite still treating minorities as less than, despite still racing in countries that are harmful to these communities, it's always been my dream to become a Formula One World Champion. And I will fight to make a change in this sport until my dying breath, Halo. Because no matter how hard we try, how much progress we make, there are countries electing leadership that take away a woman's right to choose what to do with her body, that take away rights of queer people, that treat people of colour like they don't belong because of their ethnicity. I'm in this sport to change it, not to keep its outdated ways, and as you've pointed out, I've already had a pretty big impact with the movement I started in it. I hope to make a hell of a lot more change happen before I retire for good."

He nods like my words make sense to him, but it's a heavy topic, and we end up falling back into silence. I think about that one country I was describing, and all of the people who are hurting right now because of their leadership. I think about having to be at three races there this year. I think about what the fuck I can do to make a statement because there is no staying silent when so much violence is committed against people based on who they are, where they've come from, how they look, who they love, or what gender they identify as.

"You know, my mami met my father when she was still living in the Dominican Republic. He was there on a trip with his friends, and she told me she fell in love with him almost immediately." I listen closely, but he's not looking at me. His gaze is somewhere far away, mirroring his thoughts. "She moved to his home country a few months later to start a life there with him. Back then, they still sold that place as the land where dreams came true." He lets out a laugh he doesn't mean one bit. "How quickly it turned into a nightmare for a Latina woman who has never done anything wrong in her life. She's worked her ass off, paid her dues, and been the perfect citizen. Now? Now they're threatening to detain her because she's not white and American. They're threatening to deport her, even though she's had the legal right to live there for years."

He shakes his head with anger painting his handsome features. But it's anger that's covering deep-rooted concern for the first woman he has ever loved.

"Every time I get a call from an unknown number, my heart drops into my chest. It could be fucking spam, but I get so scared anyway."

"I can't imagine," I reply, and he rubs his hands over his thighs before he shifts them so his feet are on the ground.

"What a twisted, fucked up world we live in, huh?" he says, and I nod in agreement.

"That's certainly one way to put it." He chuckles as he covers his face with both of his hands. "But hey, at least we get to exist at the same time as Daddy Pedro, and don't you think that's a blessing?" I joke, but he nods in agreement, and we both end up laughing.

We sober up soon, and I find myself getting up because if I spend one more second in his company, I'll do what I was insinuating earlier, which would be so wrong on so many levels. His family is still in the other room and the topic of our conversation was far too heavy to start making out with him.

No matter how he looks at me with those eyes widened and his pupils dilated, like my very presence is a drug he's only too happy to consume. I don't blame him because spending time with him is my favourite type of drug, too.

"Why don't you come to book club night? We're having it in Jeddah this time because everyone will be there, and that way we can still hang out."

He stands up and brings me to the door, holding it open as I walk out and tell him of the plan.

"I'd love that. Which book is it?" I tell him the title and he writes it down on his phone, smiling. "I'll do my best to read the online summary before the meeting."

"That's exactly what I do," I tell him, and then we're laughing again. I don't stop, not until I notice him smiling as he watches me, then reaches out to place his hand on my cheek and neck.

"Thank you for coming tonight. I had a wonderful time," Halo says, and despite all the plans we've made, all the ways I told him I want to do things right, he leans down to bring his mouth to mine. And I smile because it feels so damn right.

But right before his mouth touches mine, a door opens and Chellie screams, "Halo, come quick. Titi Lio gave birth and her wife is on the phone. She has their newborn baby in her arm."

"You better hurry," I say as he drops his hand from my cheek.

"If we get interrupted one more fucking time, my head might explode," he mumbles as he steps back.

"Good night, Asher." A tiny smile works its way back onto his face.

"Good night, *mi luz*."

CHAPTER 25

Cameron

"HAVE YOU HEARD ANYTHING from your manager about potential contracts for next season?" Gabriel asks as we throw a tablecloth over the table we asked the hotel to provide us so we could host the book club meeting in his giant penthouse suite.

"So far, the only team that has negotiated anything was Klein Racing, but they only wanted to offer me the reserve driver position," I reply, fixing the tablecloth on my side. "But the season is still long, and I've got hopes that there will be a team interested in taking me. I have a long history of pretty good results in F1."

"Pretty good?" Leonard interrupts and snorts. "You have a great record. It's not your fault you had a shit car," he defends me, and I turn to see him approaching with several glass bottles filled with water.

"Thanks," I say, trying to fight back very irrational tears. "Hearing this coming from you means a lot to me, Leonard. You're a legend, and I—" He cuts me off.

"If you cry, I'm leaving," he says as he places down the waters. "I'm all for crying to let out overwhelming emotions, but Kieran, Leonora, and Adrian were crying in front of me today, and I don't think I have any energy to comfort another crying person today." I burst into laughter, holding up my hands in mock surrender.

"Fair enough," I say. "I understand why your children might have been crying, but why was Adrian crying?" Leonard faces me, his scowl in place.

"He watched a movie with Seraphina, Kieran, and Leonora and was bawling his eyes out. He said the main characters are now his favourite fictional characters," he explains and rolls his eyes before telling us the name of the movie.

"To be fair, I cried twice when I watched it for the first time," Gabriel chimes in, and even Julián nods in agreement.

"That was a beautiful movie," he agrees, and Leonard slaps his forehead when he hears an "AHA!" come from behind us.

"I told you I wasn't overreacting," Adrian adds as he approaches us with Nevaeh by his side. He's holding Seraphina in his arms, and she's looking up at her daddy with so much love in her eyes, there is no doubt about her being as attached to him as he is to her. Nevaeh is smiling, clearly amused.

"Where were your children while all of this was happening?" I ask James as he joins us with Estrella by his side, too.

"Estrella was testing an upgrade Velocità Rossa made to their new sports car, and they wanted to go for a lap around the Jeddah Corniche Circuit with her." Estrella grins down at her daughter, who's holding her hand with the biggest smile on her face.

"It was awesome," Daisy says to me, and when I look at Damian, an exact copy of James, I notice he's wearing the same smile.

"Mami Estrella drove so fast," he tells me, and I place a hand on his head, ruffling his hair.

It wasn't too long ago that James and Estrella got married to ensure she could keep custody of Daisy. Damian and Daisy didn't get along at the academy Valentina and Leonard built. Now, they're as close as I am with my sisters. Estrella has become Mami Estrella to Damian, and the little man who was abandoned by his biological mother has gone and found himself not one, not two, but three mums who love him and would protect him with their lives. After James agreed that letting Gabriel's aunts, Dominique and Nicolette, adopt his son to give him a stable home life while he continued racing in F1 all those years ago, they have found a balance for him where he gets to spend time with both halves of his family.

His story started off with so much heartbreak, but Damian is now the most loved child in the world.

"I almost had a heart attack, but I'm glad they had fun," James says, but Estrella nudges him in the side.

"I'm a good driver," she says and scowls at him. He places an arm around her, pulling her close until her mouth is close enough to his to kiss.

"You are, but I'd have still preferred it if we'd wrapped them in bubble wrap," he says and kisses her.

"Gross," Damian says, holding out his hand for his sister. "Come on, Daisy, I wanna play Uno."

She places her hand in his and they move toward where Chiara is walking into the suite with Leonora and Kieran. The kids run into the kitchen area of the suite, and Leonard heads that way, mumbling something about fixing them a snack.

Meanwhile, Gabriel and I finish setting up the table, making sure everyone has something to drink and eat while we discuss this month's book. Scarlette and Valentina join us right as we finish setting the table. All of us pull out our copies of the book we read, and my heart aches in my chest when there's no knock on the door. When Halo doesn't show up. I know it's early, he still has five minutes until it's the exact time I told him to meet me at Gabriel and Valentina's hotel suite, but I can't help but wonder if maybe he changed his mind.

Maybe all this interrupting and moments when we get so close but not close enough have made him bored with me. I wouldn't even blame him. This is by far the longest, most torturous foreplay of... well, anyone's life.

"You're turning green," Adrian points out, poking my cheek. "What's wrong?"

"Nothing," I reply and cover my mouth with my hand because this stupid overthinking problem I have is making me sick to my stomach.

Wonderful.

"Tell me. Despite what everyone thinks, I'm actually very good at giving advice," he says, and I offer him the unimpressed expression that statement deserves. "Fine, I'm not that good, but I have a lot of life experience. I may know how to help."

I narrow my eyes at him, but, luckily, Nevaeh saves me.

"You are very wise, *mein Mond,* but maybe I should take this one while you go change Seraphina's diaper," she says and holds out their baby daughter for him to take.

"Again? Sera baby, all you eat is milk from your Mama's boobs. How are you pooping so much?" he asks and laughs, and I can't help but chuckle as he carries her carefully toward their diaper bag, then to the bathroom.

"Alright, talk to me, Cameron. What's wrong?" she asks, sliding her hand onto my shoulder and squeezing it comfortingly.

"Do you think Halo could be bored of me?" I ask, but when her brown eyes fill with confusion, I decide to elaborate. "It's been months of us growing closer without being physical, and I'm starting to wonder if maybe he's sick of waiting."

Understanding dawns on her, and she almost immediately shakes her head, making her brown-blonde hair bounce with the motion. When I look at her like this, wearing a dark orange dress that complements her curvy body and light skin and that absolutely breathtaking personality of hers, it's so very clear to me why Adrian couldn't stay away from her, even when her job forbade them from being together.

Nevaeh is breathtaking, inside and out.

"As someone who had to wait months to be with the man she loved, who constantly got close to him but had to back off every time, finally being with Adrian felt like a relief. We wanted each other so badly, and no amount of waiting dulled that. If anything, we just wanted each other more," she says, and it makes me feel a lot better.

"Yeah, look at James and me," Estrella chimes in, and I meet her brown eyes from across the table. "We spent half a year at each other's throats, then spent our wedding night getting no sleep," she says and winks at me. James, having clearly overheard the whole thing, runs his hand through her dark brown hair, playing with it.

"Leonard and I knew each other for over two decades before he finally made a move," Chiara adds, and I realise they all heard my dilemma.

"And Valentina went and dated another guy," Gabriel says, making his wife gasp.

"Because *you* almost kissed me but then told me we couldn't be anything more than friends," she complains, and all the couples at the table start reminiscing, or arguing playfully, about how they got together.

Scarlette and Julián are the only two staring at each other with smiles, not bothering to argue.

I'm not sure how they met because neither of them has ever told me, but it was something along the lines of them pretending to date so his father helped her get connections in Formula One.

The Puerto Rican is also a successful MotoGP racer who finally got a weekend off at the same time his wife has a race weekend, so he could be there to support her as she helps Valentina potentially snatch the win.

I watch all of my friends, my family, talk to each other while I wait for a knock on the door.

Right as the time changes to six o'clock, there it is, Halo perfectly on time. I get up and out of my seat to walk to the door, but Daisy beats me to it.

"Who is it?" she calls out, not opening the door until she hears Halo's voice.

"*Tu persona favorita*," he replies, and Daisy opens the door, knowing exactly who is waiting on the other side of the door.

"Halo," she says with the biggest smile, and he picks her up, placing her on his hip.

"*¿Cómo estás, margarita?*" he asks her because her name translated into Spanish is *margarita*. He's called her that ever since they met, and I think it's one of the sweetest things.

"*Bien*," is all she replies before hugging him. Halo's eyes catch mine, and he grins as he carries Daisy toward where I'm standing.

"*Hola, mi luz*," he says as he stands in front of me, leaning forward to place a kiss on my cheek in greeting.

"Hey," is my stupid reply.

Halo chuckles as he carries Daisy outside to greet the rest of our friends too. Estrella welcomes him in Spanish, and so do Julián, Scarlette, and Valentina, while the rest of the group does so in English. I know Halo enjoys being able to speak Spanish, especially with Estrella and Julián since it's their mother tongue, and Val and Scar—who learned from her husband and is now fluent—also enjoy practicing their Spanish as much as possible. I merely sit there and try to understand, but it's becoming abundantly clear that I need to become fluent as well. Fluent in Spanish and French since Gabriel, Val, and Adrian are Monegasque, and Nevaeh is now fluent in French as well.

"Now that everyone is here, let's get started," Val says, picking up her book. Out of habit, we all quiet down, paying attention to her. "Welcome back, everyone, to our monthly book club meeting. This month, we read..."

Halo whispers in my ear right as Val keeps talking, saying, "Or pretended to read." I barely keep myself from bursting into laughter. I don't want to be rude to Val, so like we pretended to read, I pretend to listen, but now that Halo is so close to me that I can smell his perfume again, all thoughts leave me.

"Who wants to go first?" Val asks, looking around the table.

Adrian speaks up first.

"I thought the plot twist in this book was *wild*," he says and shakes his head. "I mean, it was her father all along. Who'd have thought?" At least three jaws have dropped around the table, and four sets of eyes have widened.

"Did you actually...read the book?" Gabriel asks his brother-in-law.

"I always read the book," he defends, but that makes almost everyone let out a *pfft* sound. I press my lips together to keep from bursting into laughter. "Okay, fine, I never read the book, but I had to read this one. Turns out I like fantasy books," he says and picks up the book. "And this one was so good," he says, flipping through the pages. "Also, why are you attacking me for actually reading the book. Some people at the table—Cameron—haven't."

"What the fuck are you pulling me under for?" I ask, but Halo chimes in, too.

"Full disclosure, I also haven't, but I'm enjoying being here." He grins, and I find myself placing a hand on his thigh. He covers mine with his briefly, but then picks up the book in front of me and skips through the pages. "I did read that the female main character guts several men on her quest for revenge, so I may have to read this one after all."

As structured as Valentina always attempts to make these meetings, ten minutes in, everyone turns to someone in the group to discuss the book. Adrian and Valentina pull Halo and me into a conversation, giving us a rundown of the events without spoiling it too much. I mean, Adrian already spoiled it, but now that they both know we haven't read it, they're doing their best to keep us in the dark while also discussing it to some extent.

I listen attentively, soaking in the warm feeling this group of people, these wonderful human beings I've met along the way, evoke in me. Because they are my family in every way that counts. Blood is irrelevant when they give me more love than my parents ever did.

Family has always been a strange concept to me. It wasn't unconditional love or warm feelings or anything people tell you it is. It was pain, blame, and guilt, everything always directed at me.

Not with my friends.

With them, the term family has become everything to me. Suddenly, unconditional love made sense. Warmth made sense. Being comforted and always standing by your side made sense. It took me a while to get used to, but through Gabriel and Val's constant downpour of love on me, it eventually sunk in.

As I watch all of their families grow, either through them adopting animals or having babies or finding friends they grow close with, I feel my chest aching with the same longing to expand our little family.

My eyes drift to Halo, and I notice him already looking at me. Daisy is still on his lap, listening to our conversation, and I smile at her before directing the expression Halo's way.

It terrifies me that I can picture this so well. Halo with our kid on his lap, years of marriage in our pocket. I can picture a future with him, and while I know it's not rational and simply my feelings clouding my judgement, I can't stop the visual from taking over.

He fits into our groups so easily, so effortlessly, in the exact same way he fits into my life.

"I'm really happy you're here," I admit, and he picks up my hand, bringing it to his mouth to press a kiss to the back of it. We're in the comfort of Gabriel and Val's private suite, so I get to enjoy him touching me this way without having to worry. I get to enjoy his warmth and scent and steady grip on me. He runs his thumb over the scars on my hand, softly, gently, carefully. Traces them until he must have memorised them.

"Nowhere I'd rather be."

He holds onto my hand for most of the evening.

Chapter 26

Halo

Scarlette and I are working more closely together this weekend. Usually, she's incredible at finding the right setups and making sure that the car is performing at the maximum level for Valentina, but this weekend, she's asked for more of my help than she normally does, so I'm scanning all of the data with her to give my opinion on what the best setup would be for today.

That's what happens when problems arise in performance during Qualifying, and we have to make sure that the race goes better, more smoothly. Valentina has been with us the entire time too, doing her best to give input based on her experience on the track.

"Let's adjust the brake bias, and, Val, I think you should focus on higher wing angles to increase your downforce. I'll also have the mechanics look at the inertia dampers before the race," I say to both of them, Scar nodding along to my words.

"Thanks, Halo," Val says and gives my arm a squeeze. The two women fall into a conversation about the race strategy, and I stand off to the side a little, staring down at my tablet with all of the information lighting up my screen.

I talk to the engineer and mechanics, continuing to solve the crisis one piece at a time. What a lot of people don't realize is how little time we engineers, chief designers, mechanics, and the whole team really have when it comes to fixing an issue during the race weekend. If we're not on top of it, if we aren't lightning fast in our execution of solutions, or even coming up with them in the first place, our driver could be fucked.

They might not be able to start or even if they do, they might have to retire from the race. Maybe they'll only come in last or eleventh, which would be outside of the points. That's not something I can allow to happen to Val.

As things are currently standing, she's in first place in the standings, and I will do everything I can to help her get that championship title, just like for Adrian.

Before we're ready, it's time for Val to drive her car onto the starting grid, where we can continue doing some fine-tuning. Usually, I don't join the team on the grid. It's mostly about keeping the tires warm and doing any last-minute setup changes, which the engineers and mechanics have under control.

Today, I go onto the grid.

It's a mess here. Members of every single team, for every single one of the drivers, are huddled around the cars, and reporters are doing all they can to chase an interview, no matter how brief, with any of the drivers. Celebrities and rich people are enjoying the exclusivity of being here as well, while fans in the grandstands and on the sidelines are waiting patiently for the race to start.

I take a deep breath, inhaling the scent of rubber, oil, and gas, as well as a dozen different perfumes and colognes being carried my way by the wind. The lights at the sides of the track are so bright I almost wish I was wearing sunglasses, and the fans in the stands are cheering every time a driver waves to them.

My eyes drift through the crowd, spotting Nachelle and Cameron standing beside her Hawke, discussing something. He's pointing to her car, then at the car beside hers, Gabriel's. My sister is nodding along to every single one of his words, her arms crossed in front of her chest.

There are no words in the world for how cool she looks with her racing suit hanging down at her waist, her blue fireproofs covering her chest. The lights illuminating the track are making her skin glow where it's not covered by her outfit, and the sheer power my sister has as the second female driver in Formula One, the first lesbian woman of color to get a seat, has me so emotional, tears fill my eyes.

I don't think anyone could be as proud of their sibling as I am of mine.

Then again, no one's sibling is as awesome as mine.

My attention moves to Cameron, and as soon as my gaze latches onto him, he turns his head to look at me too.

I stop breathing the second we make eye contact.

All we get is a moment. A moment of looking, longing, aching. A moment when our attention is undivided, completely zeroed in on the man who affects me more than anyone else ever has.

Both of us linger. We're unable to break away because this tension that always crochets a braided thread between us, from my chest to his, is too strong to resist. It feels too good to ignore.

But we're still surrounded by people and cameras, and we have responsibilities, so he turns away, focusing on Nachelle again as she begins to talk about something else. I study his handsome features for a few more seconds, then go back to work myself.

It's the only thing that can push the thought of Cameron, of us, out of my head long enough to keep my heart from racing.

The minutes fly by, and the rest of the crew and I do our best to finish up the last few tasks before it's time to get off the track. All of the teams rush back to the pitlane. The drivers take their formation lap at the same time, giving us the chance to regroup in our garages before the start of the race.

Tonight, I stay at the pitwall with Scarlette, keeping track of all the data that comes in as soon as Valentina sets the lap times. I have to make sure the solutions I implemented actually work throughout the race, and if any more issues show up, I'm right here to help Scar solve them.

The headphones press down on my ears, keeping out the noise around us for the most part. The roaring of engines is dulled, and so is the chatter of the people around me. I'm in the zone now, watching the data and the cars line back up on the grid.

James is in first.

Nachelle in second.

Gabriel and Adrian are third and fourth.

Valentina is in seventh.

Although they have almost the same exact car, teammates can perform very differently given the setups they are told to use, the parts of the cars not working during some aspect of the weekend, or a million more reasons. Drivers are also a component of the different performance factors that either get them to finish high up on the grid or lower, but for Valentina, this weekend, that wasn't the case. She did everything right. The car simply didn't meet her needs.

Not yet.

But if we did our job well, which I know we did, she'll be fighting her way into the podium places soon.

As soon as all of the drivers are back on the grid in their designated place, their wheels touching the yellow line that they must not cross on the ground, the crowd falls silent. Everyone around me goes silent. We're all waiting for every light to turn on, then vanish as if they hadn't been there in the first place.

One breath.

Two.

Three.

Four.

And five.

A breath for every light, then I hold it completely.

As soon as all the lights turn off, Valentina shoots forward. She overtakes both of the Spark Racing drivers, leaving them behind as she tries to catch her brother off-guard and overtake him in the first corner.

Despite all the issues she had all weekend long, she does exactly that.

Within not even half a lap, Valentina, the absolute boss at starting a race that she is, has overtaken three cars and is now chasing after her husband, who is doing his best to keep her behind him in third place.

But his wife isn't someone who takes it easy on you.

She battles him for four laps, staying in DRS range so that as soon as it's enabled, she gets the speed advantage in the designated zones.

Soon, she's overtaking him.

Valentina slips into third place, and everything I'm seeing on the screen shows that the solutions we've put into place are working. She's fast. She's unstoppable. And if the rest of their strategy works as well as Val's start has gone, then she may just end up taking first place.

"Holy fuck, she's good," I say to Scar, and my best friend grins from ear to ear.

"Understatement of the century," she replies, hitting the radio button to give Val some updates about the time gaps between her and Nachelle as well as her and Gabriel.

I look over my shoulder for a moment to see Julián with his arms crossed in front of his chest in the garage, watching the screens attentively. He catches me staring, and when I wiggle my fingers at him in greeting, he starts scratching his brow with his middle finger.

I burst into laughter.

I focus on the race again, watching Nachelle defending against Valentina as she tries to overtake her in the corner.

The only two women on the track are putting on a hell of a performance, proving to the world that they belong when Val attempts a beautiful move down the inside of Nachelle, but Nachelle defends so well, she stays in second place.

The breath is stuck in my chest again because, on one hand, it's my sister, and I want her to keep her place. On the other, I'm at work, and I can shut off my feelings enough to know Val has to take this second place.

She *will* take second place.

As soon as the next lap rolls around, when Val gets her DRS advantage, she slips past my sister, snatching second place for herself. Nachelle has no time to respond, no speed to hang onto Val and stay in her slipstream or anything of the sort.

Instead, she slows down.

Gabriel overtakes her.

Adrian overtakes her.

Both Spark racing drivers overtake her.

"What the fuck?" I find myself saying, getting closer to the screens as if that would explain a damn thing to me. "What's happening?" I ask Scar, but she's not paying attention to Nachelle. She's talking to Val now, telling her how much of a gap James has created in first place.

My sister keeps dropping places.

I click on the button that lets me hear the commentators, trying to get information on what's happening.

"She seems to be having some sort of engine problem!" one of them screams into their microphone, and the sound is so loud, I contemplate lifting the headphones off my ears.

But I'm distracted by the sight of her maneuvering her car into the run-off area before it turns off completely.

"Nachelle Henderson is out of the race," the other commentator says, and I reach for the button to turn off their talking.

"Fuck," I mumble, and Scar places her hand on my arm in silent comfort while still keeping her eyes on the screens, on Val.

And she's right.

Nachelle might be out of the race, but Val is still fighting for first, and now that the safety car is being deployed, it will take away the gap James worked so hard to create.

Valentina can win this race.

As long as her car doesn't fail her the way Nachelle's did her.

Everyone pits during the safety car, and they all rejoin the track in pretty much the same order as they were in before Nachelle DNFed. The safety car period is brief because my sister was able to get her car to a spot where it didn't endanger the other drivers and the marshals could easily remove it.

James is responsible for the restart, and he's leading the rest of the pack around the track after the safety car leaves. They maintain the same speed, and it's only when James goes faster again, restarting the race, that the rest of the grid is allowed to do the same.

He tried to catch Valentina off-guard, restarting it right after the corner, but it's as if she was anticipating it. She's right behind him on the straight, and for the first time in years, the Velocità Rossa has better straight-line speed. She overtakes him without needing DRS, the rear wing not allowed to open yet since it hasn't been enabled again.

Val makes it stick.

The rest of the race, James tries to catch up to her, but she creates a gap so big, there is no chance he could without another safety car.

They don't pit again either.

The midfield teams are battling each other, and even Gabriel and Adrian almost crash because Adrian is racing a bit riskier today than he normally would, but the first two places don't change.

They stay the same up until Val crosses the line, winning the Grand Prix.

Finally, Scar detaches her eyes from the screens to turn to me and throw her arms around me in a firm hug.

"We did it!" she says, and I can't help hugging her back as fiercely because I need this. My sister's pain has a funny way of infiltrating my chest, too, and as happy as I am that everything we did for Valentina and the car led her to being the one to get first place, I'm disappointed Nachelle couldn't finish the race at all.

I carry that disappointment in my chest as Val comes to hug us and celebrate her win. I carry it while I watch her stand on the podium, the sound of the national anthem of Monaco blaring through the speakers. I carry it while she sprays her champagne, too.

But I push it as far down as I possibly can when I see Nachelle a few hours later, hugging her harder than I have in a while. She doesn't cry, doesn't do anything really, simply hugs me back as my comfort seeps into her.

"Next race will be better," I assure her, and she snorts.

"Cameron already said that," she informs me, and the mention of his name makes my stomach tumble.

"Well, great minds think alike." Nachelle steps back and looks up at me, her eyes glassy with unshed tears.

"You know, Nevaeh taught me a German saying recently. It goes something like, '*Zwei dumme, ein Gedanke*,' which I also think could be applied to this situation," she replies, and I cock a brow at her, smiling.

"What does it mean?" She finally returns the smile.

"Two dummies, one thought." I burst into laughter before attacking her sides, tickling her to get my revenge for that insult. She's laughing and squealing, and once I'm happy with my vengeance, I go straight back to hugging her.

It's as much a comfort to her as it is to me.

CHAPTER 27

Cameron

I'M NOT AS NERVOUS this time as I was the first time I had a session with Munira. Instead of wondering what the fuck I'm going to talk about, I've got my notebook at the ready with every experience that triggered my PTSD and made me either have a panic attack or dissociate.

With my hand out of its brace, the only thing left to heal is my mind if I want to be in a car next season. I have to make sure what triggers me now doesn't trigger me then because I can't be an F1 driver that spirals into a panic attack mid-race because another driver crashes. I have to keep my head in the car with me, not in the memories I cannot conjure.

"Hello, Cameron," Munira says as I step into her office of the day. As we travel around the world, the spaces we have these sessions in will continue to change, but I don't mind it at all. She somehow manages to make all of them comfortable with only her presence.

"Hey, Munira," I reply with a smile. "It's lovely to see you."

"You're in a good mood," she observes, returning my happy expression. "Did something happen to make you... shine this way?" I've never, ever been described as looking like I'm shining, but I'm finding I like it a lot. Especially considering why I'm smiling so brightly.

"Not something. Someone. And I'm taking him on a date in two days, when we get back to Monaco," I explain as I settle onto the chair across from hers.

"That's wonderful, Cameron. I'm happy for you." And her expression is so genuine, my grin only grows. "I had the same expression on my face before I went on a first date with my wife. It's a very good sign," she assures me, and my cheeks start to hurt.

"How long have you been married?"

"Almost a decade," she replies, picking up her notebook and pen before leaning back.

"Then it is a very good sign indeed," I say with a little chuckle.

Munira gives me another moment to stay in my good mood before her expression turns serious. I feel my features dropping, too.

"I'm sorry," she tells me, but I shake my head.

"Don't be. I'm here to grow. I'm here to get back to who I was before the crash." I almost flinch when I realise what I just said. "Well, I know that's not possible. I know what happened will stay with me forever, but you know what I mean." Munira tilts her head as she studies me.

"Pretend I don't know what you mean. What is it you want to accomplish here?" she says as she crosses her legs under her chair, the same way she did the first time we met.

"I want to get back in the car next season. I want to stop getting triggered into panic attacks. I want to remember what happened."

The last admission leaves me on a breath I hadn't noticed I'd been holding. A breath I seem to have been holding since the crash happened. It feels like a relief to say it out loud for the first time, and when Munira nods in approval, I'm proud I managed to get the words out.

"Very good. Having goals is important for your journey, and I'm glad you've been thinking about what you're hoping to get out of these sessions. A lot of people come to me when they're lost and not sure what they want, which is also fine as it is part of their journey with me to answer the question I asked you." Munira taps her notebook with her pen, smiling kindly my way. "You're already a lot further into your healing than you may know, and the hard parts are yet to come, but the hardest is already over with," she assures me.

"What's the hardest part?" I ask, hanging onto her every word.

"Coming to me that first day."

We both fall silent, but she only does because I do. Munira doesn't rush me to find my voice, and I appreciate it. It takes me a little while to swallow the information she's given me, but once I'm ready, I hand her my notebook with all of the things I've written in it.

"I was never that great with homework, but I found myself actually enjoying this task," I admit with a laugh. Munira takes it from me, reading through my words before looking up again.

"So, the crashes are what trigger you the most," she points out, and I nod.

"Watching them, talking about them, any mention of them, if I'm being honest. At first, it was only my crash, but now it's anyone else's, too. It's gotten to the point where I had to tell my friends to refrain from talking about theirs to me," I say, which seems to make sense to her because, again, she offers me a nod.

"I'm assuming last race weekend was tough for you, seeing Adrian—"

She cuts off, but my brain fills in the blank. It fills it in a little too hard because suddenly I'm picturing Adrian in the wall. The panic I felt when I saw him crash out in the rain. It may have been a different track, but my brain easily convinced me it could be the same track. With the samerain drops falling from the sky. With the same atmosphere around us.

"Cameron," Munira says, her voice firm and steady. She must have said my name several times if her tone is anything to go by. It sounds more urgent than it would the first time someone calls your name to get you back into a conversation. "Did you have a panic attack after he crashed?" she asks, and I fold my hands together, staring at my intertwined thumbs.

"I did," I admit. "I had a very bad panic attack."

"I see," she replies, looking down at everything I wrote in the notebook again. "Why didn't you write it in here?" My brows furrow almost instantly.

"I put it in there," I argue, but she turns the notebook to reveal it's *not in there.*

Why didn't I put it in there?

"Were you alone when it happened?" I take my notebook back from her as I try to catch up with her question and figure out why I was so convinced I'd put it in here when I didn't.

"No. Halo was there. He's a friend and he's also the man I'm taking on a date," I explain absentmindedly. "Munira, what's wrong with me? I was so sure I'd put it, and it's not here?" A bit of panic wells up inside of me, but her soft smile confuses me so much, it dies back down before it gets any traction.

"I think your mind was on something else. Someone else, perhaps," she points out, and I go back to the day in the bathroom. The day when Halo and I were so close, I was ready to throw everything, every caution, to the wind.

"Can another person have that much of an effect on someone?" I ask, running a hand through my hair and tugging on the roots a little.

"Of course they can. It's human nature to look for love in some form or another. The pursuit of it can often take over your mind, shift your priorities, and a lot more that we don't have to discuss right now. Bottom line is, I think your feelings for this man are very strong, so you forgot to include the panic attack in your journal. That's not a bad thing, Cameron. Not at all."

"Isn't it?" I blurt out. "My last boyfriend cheated on me after he made plans to spend the rest of his life with me. I gave him everything. I'd have given him a kidney, my heart, anything he asked for," I rant, leaning forward and placing my elbows on my knees. "I loved him *that* much. So irrationally. So wholeheartedly. I trusted him with parts of me I never gave anyone else, and he betrayed that trust. He broke it, and I don't know if I'm capable of giving it to someone else."

Munira opens her mouth to say something, but I notice too late and keep ranting.

"I want to. Don't get me wrong. I want to be able to trust. I want Halo. I want to be able to give myself to him as I've done with my ex in the past. It's just so hard. I saw what my father did to my mother, and they were married for even longer than I was dating Elijah. They had children. So, what if I meet someone, fall in love, start a family with him, and then he does the same thing Elijah did? The same thing Dad did to Mum? How can anyone trust anyone in this cruel world we call romance and love?"

I seal my lips shut, taking a deep breath to settle the turmoil inside of me. Munira waits patiently, making sure I'm really finished talking this time, before she gives me her professional opinion on the situation.

"Putting your trust in someone is taking a leap of faith. That's a fact. They can earn it, sure, but there is no guaranteeing they won't misuse it or abuse it."

"That's not exactly reassuring," I say with a laugh, and she gives me an unimpressed look, clearly not having been done talking. "Sorry," I mutter, deflating a little in my seat.

"Life isn't easy. You know that. And no matter how difficult trusting someone can feel after having experienced such a betrayal, you are capable of it. Evil people are everywhere, so yes, you have to be careful who to trust, but you also cannot close yourself off from that part of your life forever. Otherwise, how will you ever find the good people, the ones who deserve your devotion?" she asks, but it's clear she isn't looking for an answer. I wouldn't have one anyway.

"It'll take effort and time, but if Halo is good for you, if he's a good boyfriend or life partner, he will give you the space to heal the wound Elijah has left. He will be there, reassure you, and prove that he won't do the same thing your ex did."

Boy, she really wasn't lying when she told me we could discuss anything and everything I wanted. This isn't at all the conversation I thought we'd be having when I was on my way here earlier, but I can't say I'm disappointed.

"Halo is amazing. I'm just scared I'll be too needy, require too much reassurance, and that isn't fair to him."

"Cameron, every single person has past experiences that they carry with them into relationships. Some people have it easier because they don't have trauma-inflicted scars on their hearts and heads, but other people have even more prominent ones than you do. I think you have to realise that you're not undesirable because of them. You are not damaged. You're simply learning how to navigate through life now as a new person, not just as someone who has trust issues or PTSD triggered panic attacks but also as someone who is fighting to keep their home. You're very strong, and you deserve to be happy. Allow yourself to chase what brings you joy."

I think about Halo. About getting an F1 seat again. About making sure my sisters stay at the ranch and live the lives they choose, not the one my mother is trying to choose for them.

All of those things would make me very happy, and I will continue to fight for them, like Munira is telling me to do.

"If you'd like, we can continue talking about this, or we can move on to what I'd planned for today," she says when I've been silent for too long.

"Let's move on. I want to try the Exposure Therapy thing you were telling me about. I want to watch a crash and see if I'll react the same as I did when I saw the crash two weeks ago," I explain, and Munira stands up, walking to the desk that's set up at the wall behind her.

She grabs her laptop and places it on the table that's between us, and I suck in a sharp breath when I realise the implications of what is about to happen. I could fall into a panic attack in this session. I could be so vulnerable in front of another person.

"Before we begin, I want to remind you that this is a safe space for you to do whatever you need to do in response to watching the footage. If it gets too much, we will stop and try again next time, okay?" she says, not looking at me as the words spill from her lips because she's focused on pulling up said footage.

"Thank you, Munira."

We don't speak again before she turns the laptop my way, the video of a crash that happened three years ago between Valentina and James illuminating the screen.

At first, as they race down the straight without making any contact, I think I can do this. I think maybe it won't be as bad as last time. There is so much optimism washing through me that I find myself smiling in relief.

But everything changes as soon as they make contact, Val spinning in a circle and James's car flipping once before landing in the barrier.

The panic never creeps up on me. It's never slow, slithering around my throat and squeezing like a snake that hasn't eaten in forever. It's not subtle or merciful. It's a ruthless, vicious creature that slams into my chest, knocking the breath out of me from the sheer impact.

And then I'm spiraling right back down to the tunnel where I hope I'll reach the end of it to get to my memories.

But I never do.

And today is no different.

Chapter 28

Halo

Cameron is picking me up for our first date in less than ten minutes, and I'm putting on yet another shirt. I can't make up my mind on what to wear, but at least I seem to be entertaining Nachelle because every time I walk out of my room, she grins at me like she can see how nervous I am for this first date.

"I don't know what people wear on a first date," I say, pulling on my yellow dress shirt, similar to the one Cameron was wearing the day he took me to the dinner gala with him. If it weren't for Nachelle's amused expression, I'd think *this* was the right choice for sure.

Cam and I both love yellow, so it's by far the best choice of all the other ones I've put on thus far.

Okay, I'm putting too much thought into an outfit when he told me last time, while I was in sweatpants and a hoodie, that I looked amazing. I'm pretty sure I could be naked and he'd tell me I look gorgeous.

The thought makes me blush and smile at the same time.

"Are you done turning your closet into a chaotic mess, or must it mirror your mental state?" Nachelle asks, and I'm so taken aback by her words, my jaw drops a little.

"My mental state is not a chaotic mess," I say, but it's a weak defense.

"When it comes to Cam, yes, it is. Because you have no fucking clue how to do this relationship thing, but you want to try it with him, and yet you have no idea what to wear or how to behave, but also you know what he'd like to see you in, ergo, chaotic mess." It doesn't go past me that she's talking in a messy way to really bring her point across.

"No one likes a smartass," I remind her, but she simply flips the page of her book and shrugs.

"Don't care. I call it like I see it," she says, cocking a brow as she looks at me with a side glance. "Where are you going anyway?" Nachelle asks.

"If I knew that, you think I'd have made such a big deal about what I'm going to wear?"

She puts her book down completely, turns her whole upper body my way, then says, "Yes, I do." I pick up a pillow and hit her legs with it, making her burst into laughter. "No, seriously, though, he's surprising you?" she asks, and I drop onto the couch beside her feet, letting out a deep breath.

"Unfortunately," I reply as I stare up at the ceiling.

"Oh, please, you love surprises. Don't pretend otherwise."

I hit her with the pillow again because there's no point denying it. I do love surprises. I love when the person surprising me knows me so well they come up with something thoughtful that has me on the verge of bawling my eyes out. I may never have been a romantic, but it's different with Cameron. A romantic gesture from that man may be enough to make me fall in love with him.

Because if I'm being honest, I'm already on the verge of it.

Hell, I may already be in love with him, but I know so little about what that feels like. It could be staring me right in the face, shouting at me, "This is what it feels like. You're in love!" and I would still be like, "Are you sure?"

Someone as unused to falling in love as me, someone who's never had anyone fall in love with them, isn't just going to *know* like the movies say. That concept doesn't apply to me, or if it does, then maybe I'm not there yet.

Ugh, why do people do this to themselves? Why do they crave to find someone to spend all their time with? Why do they date and do this whole falling in love thing?

It just seems tiring and confusing and—

My thoughts are interrupted by a knock on the front door. Nachelle laughs at me when I jump off the couch, but I rush to open it for Cameron anyway.

All my previous questions seem to answer themselves at the sight of him.

They do it because the way Cameron is looking at me right now, like he's been waiting to breathe his whole life and I've instilled the breath in him, is the best feeling I've ever felt.

They crave it because they get heady from the very sight of their person.

They date and fall in love because life may be colorful without it, but with it, it's practically glimmering.

He's wearing black dress pants, dressy shoes in the same color, and a white shirt with the top buttons undone to expose his very nice, very trained collarbone and upper chest area. He's got rings on many of his fingers as well as a single necklace around his neck with an angel halo hanging from it.

He's gripping a bouquet of yellow tulips in his hand, holding them out for me to take.

My knees almost give out because of the necklace and the rest of him.

"Ready to go, my handsome man?" he asks as I grab the tulips out of his hand, and I let out a nervous laugh that is a lot more high-pitched than I wish it was. Cameron's eyes go wide in surprise, but there's amusement sparkling in them, too.

"I don't know what the fuck that was," I say and slap a hand over my mouth. "If we could not mention that ever again, I'd be eternally grateful." Cameron lets out a deep, sexy laugh that almost makes the same noise as before escape my lips. He steps toward me and takes my hand, lifting it to his mouth to press a kiss to the back of it. He doesn't linger, but, fuck me, I wish he did.

"Don't worry, Asher, I won't ever mention it." He steps toward me, looking up at me as he inhales subtly, smiling when he notices I'm wearing the perfume he made me again. "I am looking forward to finding out what other noises I can get you to make," he says and my cheeks heat so quickly, I'm sure he notices the blush instantly.

"I'll make all the noises you want me to," I blurt out because it's what I usually would have said if someone flirted with me as openly as Cameron is. I find it a lot more difficult to be that confident person I used to be around Cam right now. He's got this way of tilting my whole world upside down, and no part of me hates being the one to get flustered.

"Oh, I know, Halo. I'm looking forward to it." His hand is still holding mine, so when he tugs on it to get me to follow him, I do so without hesitation. He guides me backward and inside the apartment again where I place down the tulips, then urges me to follow him outside, throwing a brief greeting Nachelle's way.

We take the elevator down to the parking garage, and instead of finding his Grenzenlos sports car like I did only a few weeks ago, we approach a black Kawasaki Ninja 1000sx. There are two helmets on the seat, sitting on top of two leather jackets.

"Since when do you know how to ride a motorcycle?" I ask him, and he lets out a little chuckle I don't return. I can't. I'm too mesmerized to.

"Scarlette and Storm taught me. I went to buy my bike with Leonard, who also got a motorcycle, after I passed my test. The four of us go for rides sometimes," he explains, and I almost call my best friend and ask her why she didn't tell me. Why she didn't prepare me for the sight of Cameron slipping on his leather jacket, a protective layer. He looks sinfully good, and I think I forget how to breathe when he approaches me with a jacket, too. "Turn around," he says softly, and I obey, sliding my arms into the armholes when he holds it out for me.

He lingers, running his hands over the line of my back. I shiver, so he spins me around, reaching for the zipper to slowly drag it up my body. My breathing hitches as I watch him, my stomach twisting as butterflies rearrange my insides with the tornado their frantic flying creates. My heart is pounding in my ears, but the jerk keeps smirking like my very obvious bodily reaction to his proximity, his cedarwood scent, the warmth of his body, is the best thing he's ever witnessed.

"Do you tease all the men you take out on a date this excessively?" I ask when he reaches the top and trails a single finger down the length of my throat.

"I know you won't trust me when I say this, Halo, but I've never treated any man the way I treat you because I've never felt this way about another person before. You pull me toward you with every breath, and as much as I've tried to resist, I can't. So, no, I've never teased a date so much, but it's only because you've been teasing me for as long as I can remember, smiling at me in a way friends don't smile at each other, and I'm only returning the favor now," he explains and brings the finger he was using to run down my throat to my chin, grabbing it with his thumb to tilt my head down. "I hope that's alright with you."

"What if I said I wanted you to stop teasing me and kiss me right here, right now?" He considers me for a moment, and I wish my stomach would stop twisting into knots because of how turned on I am. It's already a pain in the ass that I'm straining against my jeans, desperate to be touched.

"Then I'd tell you I want to wait a little longer until all you can think about is kissing me, tasting me." As if that wasn't the case already.

"You drive me wild, Cam," I admit, and he smiles his bright smile at me.

"I know. That, too, is payback." I chuckle as he releases me and steps away.

Never, ever in my life did being with someone present so many challenges. Usually, it was easy. They wanted me, I was attracted to them, sex. A simple equation, really. No strings attached. One night, move on.

Cameron is far from easy. He makes me work to earn him, and it's one of the many things I like so much about him. He challenges me. He makes me want more than one night. He makes me want to change my perspective on love and being with someone as time turns my hair grey and dents my skin with wrinkles.

Oh my God.

I *am* in love with him.

I'm in love with Cameron Kion, my friend, the man I never thought I could have.

And as he flings his leg over his machine, his helmet secured on his head, I realize that I was right. It wasn't easy to recognize. I had to work for this like I've had to work for every single other step Cam and I have taken toward each other, but the relief of knowing, the joy of figuring out that I really am in love with him, makes it all worth it. *He* makes it worth it.

But fuck, I've never been so scared in my life. I've never given my heart to someone because if no one ever took it from me, they couldn't abuse it. They couldn't shatter it into a million pieces like Elijah did with Cameron. They couldn't break me.

And I didn't give my heart to him.

He stole it from my chest without meaning to, and every part of me hopes he won't ever give it back to me.

Because as terrified as I am, I've never felt more alive than I do right now.

CHAPTER 29

Cameron

Halo's arms are wrapped around me, his chest pressing against my back. He's got his hands on my stomach, and I can't stop smiling because, even if it's a bit awkward because he's taller than I am, I'm enjoying this proximity a lot. The way he absentmindedly runs his thumb over my stomach at red lights. The way he smells like the perfume I made him, like me. The way I never thought I'd be this excited to be on a date again, but here I am, flirting and laughing with the man I haven't stopped thinking about in months.

Years perhaps.

I never cheated on Elijah. Not even emotional. He was all I saw. He was the only one I wanted to be with, even if, from the moment I saw Halo, I recognised just how painfully attractive I found him.

I kept my distance emotionally. I shut down every part of me that saw Halo in any way that wasn't platonic. But now that I'm free to see him however I want to see him, it's so very clear to me that Elijah did me a favour. He broke us apart before I did anything as foolish as marry him. Before any chance I had to be with Halo got washed away.

When it happened, I constantly asked myself why Elijah did it. People always claim that things happen for a reason, but I couldn't think of any to explain my pain.

The reason is currently patting my stomach and pointing at an adorable puppy walking with its owner down the sidewalk.

We stop at yet another red light, and I lean back, placing both my hands on his knees. His helmet touches mine, and I close my eyes because it's soft moments like these that I crave in a relationship. The intimate ones people think are overrated. The ones where I get to feel connected to the person I have feelings for in a way not many people think is important. But I do. I find it's one of the most important things to take a second as often as you can to simply enjoy the gentle touches, the careful lingering, the clumsy and unsure stumble of your heart. Sex offers intimacy that I also crave, but to me, it has nothing on the way it feels when Halo lifts his hands a little to rest them on the upper part of my stomach, his helmet touching mine as he leans his head against mine.

Calm, safe, protected.

He makes me feel all those things and more.

The first stop of our date night, as I've planned it, is a visit to my favourite restaurant. I park my motorcycle instead of handing it to the valet because obviously not every valet can drive a motorcycle. Halo gets off first, allowing me to more easily manoeuvre it into the parking spot. He takes off his helmet as I place the kickstand down, and I watch him readjust his wavy hair until he's sure it looks presentable.

I continue grinning under my helmet, only wrestling it back when I take off my own, fixing my hair too. It amuses Halo.

With a playful roll of my eyes, I grab his hand and lead him to the entrance of the restaurant. The maitre d' guides us to our table, and I pull out Halo's chair for him, watching him blush all over again.

My sweet man so easily blushes when it comes to me.

"Thank you," he says once he's seated and I've pushed the chair in.

"You're welcome," I reply, placing my hand on his shoulder before stepping around his chair and toward my side. I keep my fingers on him for as long as possible before breaking contact, and Halo clears his throat, lifting the menu he was given to hide his face.

"Please don't hide your handsome face from me, Halo. Let me see you," I say, and he drops the menu to show me he's biting his bottom lip.

"I hope you know you're responsible for my massive ego. You keep telling me how attractive I am," he says, placing the menu down completely. I snort at his comment.

"As much as I'd love to take credit, we both know your ego was massive long before we met. A side effect of getting whatever you wanted because of your looks, I'm assuming," I say and cock a brow at him, daring him to tell me I'm wrong.

He doesn't.

"Touché," is his only reply, and I burst into laughter, causing him to join me.

Dinner is wonderful.

After we order, we fall into an easy conversation about my perfume making as well as his crocheting, which I find out is his hobby. Whenever I take a bite, he talks. When he takes one, I talk. We balance each other out, so much so that we sit for a while after we've finished dinner, neither one of us in a rush to finish this conversation we're having.

We've also still got an hour until we have to leave to go to our second location, so I don't tell him to hurry his story along. I simply enjoy hearing it.

"Nachelle was two years old, I believe. I'd only recently found a passion for racing, so my father took me to an IndyCar race. We took Mami and Nachelle with us, and my sister, who'd never shown interest in things like any sort of puzzles, games, balls, dolls, or anything else, did not take her eyes off the track that day. Every time one of the cars raced by, she clapped and squealed, and I remember taking her in my arms to get closer to the track at the fence because her joy brought me joy. I always knew I'd be going into motorsport, but the thought of my sister joining me in that world? It made me truly so happy, I found myself trying to involve Nachelle in everything motorsport-related. Eventually, I even went karting because I knew she'd follow in my footsteps," he explains, and I hang onto every word, trying to get a glimpse into his childhood, to understand how deep his love for his sister and motorsport runs.

"You were never upset that she loved the same thing as you? I know many children don't like to share their passions with their siblings because they want something that is just theirs." I know it's how Hazel feels about her writing, and how Charlotte feels about her swimming.

"No," Halo replies, surprised by his own answer as if he had never considered my perspective, but now that I've pointed it out, he can't quite believe he never felt that way. "I guess I was too happy finding something to bond over with my little sister to mind. With an age gap of more than half a decade, I was scared that we'd never be close. That there'd never be anything to connect us in a way I always hoped I could connect with my sibling. So, I was thrilled when I saw her passion for the very thing I loved with my whole heart."

It will never cease to amaze me how dee ply he cares for his sister. It's the way I love my own siblings, the way Adrian loves Val, and it's something I know I need my partner to understand because when my sisters need me, I will drop anything and everything to get to them. No mountain, valley, or ocean could get in the way of me reaching them.

"What about you? What made you fall in love with Formula One and motorsport?" he asks, dragging me back into the moment, back to our conversation.

"I don't really have a special story. None of my parents liked it, and I have an even bigger age gap with my siblings, so I didn't get to bond with them over it. I started horseback riding when I was younger, but that wasn't fast enough for me, so I switched to racing," I explain with a smile, and he nods along to my words, returning it.

"Perhaps how you got into the sport isn't as important as the story of how you'll get back into it," he says and reaches across the table to run his thumb over the scars on my left hand. His eyes hold mine as he rubs his finger along the visual manifestation of my trauma.

"Maybe," I agree, my head all cloudy from how wonderful his touch feels. "But I still don't have any offer from any team. No prospects for next season," I say and wish I could pull my hand away, to hide the pain, but there's no hiding from Halo. Not when he looks at me and that single gaze makes me want to bare myself to him in every way a person can.

"You'll get an offer," he says with so much optimism, it's hard to argue.

Our gazes are locked on each other's, but the moment breaks the second his phone vibrates with a message. He leans back in his chair, picking it up and placing it back down a second later. It's face down, preventing anyone from seeing any incoming message.

I don't mean to spiral down the path of "Is he hiding something if he puts it that way around?" especially because we're on a first date, hardly an exclusive couple, but it's difficult not to fall into suspicion when Elijah used to do the same thing. He started hiding his messages and turning his phone that way when he began his affair.

Noticing where my attention has drifted, Halo looks at his phone before flipping it so the screen is facing the ceiling.

"Zero, seven, zero, nine," he says, and I raise both eyebrows in confusion. "That's my password. If you'd like, we can also program your fingerprint into it so you can open it that way. Feel free to look through it whenever you need to." My heart stutters because of his words.

"Why would you allow me to do that?" I ask, perplexed.

"Because I have nothing to hide, and I don't mind proving it whenever you need reassurance. I know this isn't about me. It's about what's happened to you in the past, and I want to earn your trust. So remember, zero, seven, zero, nine. It's Nachelle's birthday."

It takes a lot of effort to keep my jaw from dropping because of his willingness to give me reassurance no matter how I need it.

"Thank you," I say, my voice barely more than a whisper. Halo picks up my hand again and drags it across the table, brushing a kiss over one of my scars on my fingers.

"You can always tell me when something I do makes you uncomfortable because of what happened. I'm new to this whole dating thing, so I'm bound to make mistakes, but I'm not unwilling to learn."

"You're doing just fine already, Halo. More than fine, even." I place my hand on his cheek, rubbing my thumb along the apple of his cheek. "Will you let me take you to our second location?" He leans into my touch and smiles happily.

"Yes," he replies, twisting his head to kiss the palm of my hand and make my stomach tumble all over itself.

The football stadium is filled with people tonight. Monaco is playing against Spain, and it seems that every Monegasque sports fan is here to support their team tonight, as well as quite a few people clad in Spain's colours, their faces painted in it as well.

Halo is bouncing on his feet, taking in his surroundings while we make our way to our seats. There are people all around us recognising me, but I don't linger, and they don't ask me for a picture or photograph the way they would if I stayed for longer than a second in the same spot. I have no time to be distracted. My date is currently pointing at the crowd of people on the other side of the stadium that are standing up, holding a huge Monegasque flag.

"It's been forever since I've attended a soccer game." I scrunch my nose in distaste.

"It's football," I correct, but he shakes his head.

"Not where I grew up."

"Yeah, but in every other part of the world, it's football. Even in Spanish you refer to it as *fútbol*," I remind him, and he bursts into laughter.

"Yeah, you've got a point. Fine, it's been forever since I've attended a *football* match," he concedes, and I laugh because I was mostly teasing him.

We take our seats at the very front of the grandstands. Halo is holding a bag of gummy bears we bought outside the stadium for dessert, and he opens it almost as soon as we've settled in the seats. "This is incredible. I've never sat this close to the field," he says and moves to the edge of the seat to get even closer.

The lights are painfully bright as they fill the stadium, illuminating every dark corner. The teams are running around on the field, warming up for the start of the game. Halo watches them with fascination, and I watch him in the same way.

"What are you thinking about?" I ask because I can't help myself. Halo turns his head my way, four different kinds of emotions on his face. Nostalgia, sadness, joy, and excitement.

"I'm thinking about the days I played football. The days people cheered my name. I miss it sometimes. Right now is sometimes," he explains, so I slide my hand onto his thigh in comfort.

"I didn't mean to make you sad. I'm sorry." He doesn't even let me get the apology out before he speaks.

"You didn't. Well, I am a little sad, but it's not your fault. Change is never easy, and playing this game was one of the hardest things I gave up when I graduated and went into F1, but it's worth it. It was something I had to give up to chase my dream," he says and covers my hand with his. His gaze moves back to the field, to the players. "I'm actually a lot happier than I am sad," he admits, chuckling as he turns back to me. "All thanks to you," he adds, his eyes dropping to my lips.

Mine drop to his.

We're locked in a moment of uncertainty, of knowing the crowd around us may be watching us because of who I am and who he is, so neither one of us moves. We can't. What we both want is blocked by what we know we should do: wait until we're alone and in the privacy of his or my home.

But it doesn't stop the need traveling through me. Doesn't stop the pull he has on me.

"Cameron, can we get an autograph," someone asks, and I turn to see a fan standing behind me, holding what appears to be a pen and notebook.

Turning back to Halo, I drop my head forward, but he nudges my chin up with a grin, urging me to get a grip on myself and put on a smile.

I sign a few things, take a few more pictures, and by the time I'm done, there is no time to get back to where we were before because Halo's attention is on the players as they get ready to start the game any second now.

Since I've been watching football since I was a kid, Mum loved it and used to yell at the television when her team was losing, I easily keep up with what's happening, but Halo explains things to me anyway.

It doesn't keep Monaco from losing against Spain. And they lose badly. I've never seen a defence as bad as theirs. Spain is in control of the ball for ninety percent of the match, and while Monaco has some good passes, they mostly stumble through the game as if they had no game strategy at all.

The best part about watching this game is seeing Halo's reactions. He isn't rooting for anyone, so he's mostly just enjoying the entertainment side of the game, talking non-stop to me about what they're doing wrong, what he'd be doing better, the strategy they should have if they wanted to win against Spain.

He continues to talk about the match long after it's over, up until we make it back to my motorcycle. Halo puts his jacket on, still talking, and I think I could listen to him forever because I love the way his face is lighting up. The passion in his voice. The way he can't seem to stop, and I don't want him to.

"Thank you for getting us tickets for tonight. I had a great time," he says before he puts his helmet on. I move toward him to fasten the clasp, even though I know he can do it himself.

"I'm glad," I reply as his hands move to my hips.

A moment of hesitation passes between us because I'm nervous in every way to ask him something I've been thinking about for the last thirty minutes.

"Would you like to come back to my place?" I ask, lifting his visor so I can see his eyes.

"There is nowhere else I'd rather go." A wave of excitement travels through me.

"There is no one else I'd rather take home with me." His eyes flutter shut when my fingers brush the inside of his chin.

He waits patiently for me to finish securing the clasp, then waits even longer until I get ready and position myself on the bike. He goes on the back, wrapping his arms around me.

We don't talk for the whole ride back to my place. He holds onto me, and I drive as safely as possible to make sure he's protected. Gabriel once told me that he was nervous when he took Valentina for some hot laps in the early stages of their relationship. They were filming a video for their fans, and he was so scared anything would happen to her. He was nervous because he was used to driving by himself, never with someone as precious as Val beside him in the car.

That's how I feel about Halo, which is why I go the speed limit, making sure there is no unnecessary risk.

Silence lingers between us after I park my bike in its designated spot in my apartment complex and we take the elevator up to my place. It's not unlike where he lives at all, but my building is older and yet fancier at the same time. I unlock the door for him, holding it open as he enters.

Halo's been here numerous times, so he goes to hang his jacket in the coat closet, then places his shoes neatly in there as well. Once he's done, he walks toward where I've got a speaker placed, and I listen as he connects his phone while I hang up my own jacket.

A minute later, Romeo Santos is playing over my speaker, and although I recognise his voice, I don't recognise the song. I stay by my closet, but Halo lifts his hand, inviting me to join him in the space between my kitchen and living room. It's an open-floor plan, which is why that's the spot in my apartment where we have the most space to dance.

But I don't dance. I'm horrible at it.

I open my mouth to tell him that, but he knows me so well, he senses what I'm about to say before the words even leave me.

"I'll teach you. Now, come here," he instructs, and there's no room to argue.

I approach him slowly, and he meets me halfway, pulling me against his chest. One of his hands moves against mine, lifting our arms up and to the side. His other hand slides onto my upper back, and I instinctively place mine on his arm. One of his legs moves between both of mine, and my breathing hitches a little because of how close his thick thigh is to my groin.

"We're going to bachata, *mi luz*, but we're going to go slow and simple," he says, but I'm not processing much. He's so close. His body is centimetres from mine.

How is anyone meant to be able to think when the person they're attracted to has their hands on their body like this?

"Mhm," is my only reply.

Then, he's moving us. Guiding me through the steps. The way he moves his hips mesmerizes me, enchants me, and I try to keep up with him by simply giving myself over to the rhythm. It seems to be working because Halo lets out an excited laugh.

"You're doing so well," he praises and, bloody hell, I'm a goner.

We go through the steps several more times, his breath and mine becoming one as he presses his forehead to mine. His grip on me is strong and steady, and I'm so painfully aware of his legs still straddling mine.

Nothing's ever felt this intimate before.

When the song comes to an end, he stops dancing, so I do, too. We're both breathing heavily, as if we'd been running instead of dancing slowly, sensually, around my apartment.

"Once we cross this line, there will be no turning back," I remind him, giving him one last chance to turn around and run, if that's what he wants.

If that's what his brain tells him to do.

But instead, Halo says, "Good," and presses his lips against mine.

CHAPTER 30

Halo

I'VE KISSED COUNTLESS PEOPLE.

I've kissed men, women, people of every gender, really.

I've never kissed anyone like Cameron.

His lips are soft, but his kiss is firm, demanding. All it takes is this one kiss, and he's claimed me. Ruined me for others. Shown me what being kissed, truly kissed, actually feels like.

When people say the world vanishes, this is what they mean. Nothing in my head remains except for him. The feel of his mouth gliding over mine. The taste of him, something so very Cam that I have no words to describe it. The scent of him filling my nose.

And when his tongue slips into my mouth to taste me, to explore me, I don't just forget about the rest of the world.

I forget my own name.

My hands are cupping his cheeks, holding him close, but I'm so painfully aware of his hands on my waist. Of his fingers slowly slipping under my shirt. I drop one of my hands to his throat, gently squeezing the sides as I take control of the kiss because I'm hungry for more. I crave a deeper connection with him, as deep as it can go.

Romeo Santos is still playing over the speaker when I guide him toward his bedroom, kissing him until we both have to come up for air. My hands haven't moved from the possessive position on his face and throat, but he doesn't seem to mind because I notice him grinning before I go back to kissing him.

I feel that same grin against my lips.

"Oh fuck," he moans into my mouth when I close the little distance that was still left between our bodies, my hard cock pressing against his stomach because of our height difference. I swallow the sound, my tongue sliding into his mouth and playing with his. Cam digs his fingers into my hips, and I groan as I squeeze either side of his throat a little harder. Not too much to hurt him, just enough to feel his racing pulse beneath my fingers and offer him a promise of what I can do to him if he so chooses.

I nip his bottom lip playfully, feeling the way he's straining against the front of his pants now, too.

"I've wanted to do that since we met six years ago," I admit, kissing him again and moaning when he shifts and my groin ends up rubbing against him.

"It hasn't been six years yet," he reminds me as he trails kisses down my jaw and neck, lifting his fingers to the buttons of my yellow dress shirt.

"Almost," I argue, and he chuckles as he undoes my first button.

"Is kissing me all you wanted to do?" he asks, looking up and into my eyes as he undoes yet another button.

My knees go weak.

"No," I say, sucking in a sharp breath once he's got all my buttons undone and runs his hands over my chest. He takes his time exploring my pecs, my stomach, then traces my V-line all the way to the point where it disappears in my pants.

I whimper because I can't help myself. No part of me can believe Cameron is touching me this way. We were friends. We've always been friends. From the day we met, I thought all we would ever be was friends. But I've never been touched by any of my friends this way.

"What else did you want to do?" he asks, leaning forward to scrape his teeth over my left nipple. My head falls backward as he drags them along the side of my throat, a wave of pleasure rolling through me and settling in my cock.

"I wanted you on your knees. I wanted my cock in your mouth. Your hands on me. I wanted everything you were willing to give me, and I still want the same thing." The admission rushes out of me without any sort of hesitation.

"If I get on my knees for you, Asher, you won't ever want another person's mouth on you. I'll make it so good for you, baby, you'll constantly want more."

I smile at his cocky words because they're so unlike what I would have expected from Cam. He's always confident, sure of himself, but he's never arrogant. He's never this smug. I'm finding I like this side of him as much as I like every single other one he's shown me over the years.

"Cam, I've been pining after you for the last half-decade. You've already ruined me. Might as well make it official in every way possible," I say with a smile that I hope will lighten the heaviness of my words, but he won't have any of it.

His expression turns serious as he stops kissing my chest to look up at me. He studies me for a moment, trying to find an answer to his unspoken question in my face, so I stay perfectly still to let him find it.

He doesn't seem to be able to because he asks it anyway.

"You've really wanted me for that long?" His hazel eyes are full of something I can't decipher, and the previous tension in the room multiplies as we add our feelings to the situation, as if we were adding gasoline to a fire. The resulting smoke sits heavy on my lungs, making breathing more difficult than I'd like to admit.

"You have no idea how often I wanted to tell you. How often I found myself conflicted because I didn't know if what I was feeling was truly what people felt when they wanted to be with another person, but you showed me that that's exactly what it is. I crave you, Cam, and yes, I have been since we met. I want you to belong to me, body, mind, soul, and every other part. I want to belong to you in a way I've never given myself to another."

I take a deep breath as I step back, pulling his hands in mine and pressing soft kisses to his knuckles.

"You think I don't know what it means to be with someone who got cheated on, that the implications haven't dawned on me, but I know, Cam. I saw the way my mother struggled when she first went on dates after what happened with my father. She was seeking reassurance and comfort that the people she went out with couldn't offer her, so I want to be the one to give you whatever you need to help you see you can still trust, no matter how difficult it is. Because if there is one promise I can make you that I'll never break, it's that I will be honest with you if I don't want to be in a relationship anymore. I promise I won't betray you like that."

And it's a promise I say with my whole chest because I mean every word. There is no part of me that will *ever* inflict the kind of pain my mother felt on someone else.

Cam's brows are drawn together and his features have softened. He takes a step toward me again, reaching for my belt. My body responds instantly to his proximity, to the promise of what is to come, and he seems to notice because he drags it out, fumbling with the belt for longer than necessary. He's teasing me, and he knows it.

"From this moment onward, Asher, I belong to you. I'm yours. My trust is yours."

He undoes the button of my pants, and I swallow down the wave of emotion rising in my chest from having someone give themselves to me.

I cup his face again as he slides my zipper down, kissing him until he leans back to say, "May I touch you?"

"Touch me as much as you want to. Do whatever you want to me. I trust you to stop if I tell you to, and I hope you feel the same with me," I reply, so he kisses me one last time before dropping to his knees, keeping eye contact.

There's something very heady about having a man like Cam kneel before me. Worshipping me.

"I trust you. Touch me when you want to." He considers me for a moment, then adds, "I've gotten tested recently, and I'm clear."

"So did I. All clear on my end, too."

As soon as the words are out of my mouth, he's dragging down my boxers and jeans, freeing my hard cock, and I practically moan when the cold air of the room caresses it. My skin is overheating from desire, and the longer Cam teases me, the more I feel like I'm going to combust.

"I know I shouldn't be surprised, but fuck, you're big." He brings a single hand to my dick, rubbing his thumb over the head of it and almost making my knees buckle. He licks his hand once before bringing it back to my erection.

"Why wouldn't you be surprised?" I manage to ask, but my words are breathless. Hardly audible.

"Because of the day you wore those grey sweatpants. I could see—"

He cuts off when a low, long groan leaves me as he runs his hand down the length of my cock. Cam smirks knowingly, but I have to look away because I'm already embarrassingly close to coming, and if I take in his smirk, I might come before he even puts his mouth on me.

"How long has it been since anyone's touched you, my handsome man? Has it been so long that the slightest touch is enough to get you so close?" he asks, but he isn't taunting me. He sounds genuine, so I find myself answering honestly.

"Since before your accident."

He hesitates for a moment, stopping his slow, firm strokes. It's been over half a year now. Seven months. I haven't been with anyone since then because when I saw him crash, when I thought I lost him, a part of me knew deep down if he made it through this, if I got to have another chance at being with him, I'd do nothing to ruin it. And when he disappeared, went into hiding in Australia, I couldn't be with anyone else either. I was constantly thinking about him, worrying about him, and no part of me wanted to attempt to lose myself in another person.

I wanted him and only him.

I still do.

"How long—" He cuts me off before I can finish the question.

"You know how long."

Since Elijah.

"How was I so oblivious to your feelings?" he asks, but I'm not sure if he wants me to answer or if he's simply contemplating out loud. "All this time," he says, so I bring my hand to his chin, cupping it to force his head to tilt back and him to look at me.

"All this time what?"

"All this time I could have had you like this, and I was too stuck in my pain to see the world you would have laid at my feet if only I'd asked for it." He's not wrong, so I don't bother denying it.

"It doesn't matter. Right now, I don't care about the past," I say and place my thumb against his lips, waiting for him to open them before pushing it inside. "I care about what we can build in the future." He sucks on my thumb, and my cock gives an agreeing jerk. "Now be my good boy and put my cock in your mouth, *mi luz*."

He urges me backward until the backs of my legs hit the desk that's standing beside the bed, and my hands move to the edges of it, curling around it for support. Because as soon as Cam's hot and wet mouth wraps around the tip of my dick, my knees buckle. I manage to stay upright because I'm holding onto the desk, but it's a close thing.

"Fuck," I curse through gritted teeth. Cam runs his tongue down the underside of my dick, his fingers digging into my thigh. He runs his tongue back up, swirling it around my tip before taking it into his mouth and sucking hard, his cheeks hollowing out.

A slurping sound fills the room, and I moan even louder than before, doing my best not to fuck into his mouth but give him time to adjust to me at his own speed. No matter how desperate I am to feel what he's doing to my tip on my entire length.

"Mmmmm," Cam moans around me, sucking harder until my head falls backward and my eyes roll into the back of my head.

"Fuck, yes."

He works my cock into his mouth slowly, inch by inch, bobbing up and down. One of my hands lifts to his curly brown hair, tugging on it as if that would make him go any faster. But he doesn't. He drags it out, bringing me to the edge and easing up over and over.

Then he swallows me down completely, gagging around the size of me because I've stretched his mouth as far as it can go, and it's impossible not to imagine doing the same thing to a very different part of his body.

"I'm gonna come," I say and moan, so he leans back, my cock leaving his mouth with a *pop*.

"Not yet, baby," he says and sinks backward onto his heels, reaching for his own shirt's buttons. Frustration bubbles up inside me, so I fist my cock as I watch him intently, waiting for his next move.

Cameron slowly unbuttons his shirt, sliding it off his chest to expose his trained chest. I notice he's added a few more tattoos to it, the butterfly one on his arm is no longer his only one. He's got a Formula One car tattooed on his ribcage, as well as his racing number, thirty-four, on the other one. There are a few more, but all my attention moves to his abs, to the way they flex as he reaches for his pants. The muscles in his arms almost make my mouth water, and I find myself stepping out of my jeans and boxers, where they are at my ankles, at the same time Cameron stands up to take off his.

"*Coño*," I curse when I take in the size of him.

"Do you always swear in Spanish when you see your partner's penis?" he asks with a small laugh, but he doesn't hide. He's standing halfway across the room from me, his hand dropping to his dick to fist it, stroking himself slowly as his eyes drop to my cock.

"Never, but I've also never been with anyone as… thick and long as you," I explain and swallow hard, equal measures of excitement and fear going through me.

Cameron approaches me, letting go of himself to bring his hands to my neck and drag my head down, his lips meeting mine.

This kiss isn't as slow and deliberate as our first one. This one is frantic and desperate, both of us too fucking hard to drag this out any longer.

Even if nothing's ever felt as good as Cameron's hand and mouth on me.

Even if I could spend hours getting edged by him.

Even if the feel of finally taking him in my hand sends pure ecstasy through me.

He strokes me, and I stroke him, our tongues tangling as our hands move faster and faster along each other's lengths. Without ever stopping our kissing, we stumble onto the bed, and he moves on top of me, straddling my hips.

"Shit," Cameron moans when our cocks rub against each other's. I fall backward onto the mattress as I fight not to come already because of how good his hard length feels rubbing against mine.

"Keep going. I want more. I want to come with you rubbing against me," I say, and Cam wastes no time obeying, grinding against me hard and fast.

He's rolling his hips forward, thrusting against me until we're both groaning and moaning, panting each other's names. I look down and between our bodies to watch, but the sight, combined with how good he feels, has an orgasm exploding through me without any warning. Within a second, my balls draw so tight and then all the tension releases again, making me let out a string of curses as I dig my fingers into his muscular biceps, riding out my pleasure while he keeps chasing his.

"That's so fucking hot," he says, and I follow his line of sight to see he's watching me paint my stomach in my own cum.

I'm trembling, shaking from the aftershock of my orgasm, when I reach forward, cupping his balls in my hand. Cameron hisses out a breath, but I kiss him and knead his balls, needing him to cover my stomach in his cum, too.

He gives me what I want almost instantly, his body jerking with the orgasm and his moans muffled in my mouth.

Cam breaks the kiss, but only to look down at the mess we've made on my body. He smiles, and then he runs a single finger through it before placing it in his mouth, tasting the combination of us on his tongue.

If I could, I'd get hard again.

And when he leans forward to kiss me again, sliding his tongue into my mouth to let me taste us, my whole body shivers.

"Let me get a towel to clean you up," he says against my lips, unable to refrain from kissing me as much as possible, as if he wanted to catch up on all the years he didn't.

He leaves the room while I watch his trained ass, and when he returns, he's holding a wet towel in his hands. Without saying a single word, he wipes me clean, his grin remaining in place because he's happy.

I'm happy.

"You look spent," he points out, and I drop backward on the mattress again.

"I feel spent," I admit with a little laugh. All those months of nothing, no touch, and no orgasm given to me by another person, has made this one all the more intense. As if those months of desiring without release have finally left my body.

"That's too bad, handsome, because I'm not done with you yet," Cam says, bringing his hands to both of my wrists and pinning them against the mattress. His body pressing against mine has me biting my lip, holding back a sound of approval.

He kisses me, his naked body fully covering mine, and I spread my legs to press my knees into his sides. I roll my hips, growing hard again from the sheer friction, and Cam bites my bottom lip before making his way down my neck and lingering on my nipple.

"Yes," I moan when he nips it, rolling my hips again.

The sound of my phone ringing pulls us out of the moment, and concern replaces any lust inside of me. It's like getting a bucket of cold water dumped on your head.

"That's Nachelle. I told her to call me in case of an emergency. We need to answer," I tell Cameron, and he's off me and next to my phone so quickly, my head spins.

"Chellie?" he asks as he answers, putting it on speaker so I can hear as well.

"Something's wrong," she cries into the phone, and my senses go on high alert. I'm on my feet, grabbing my boxers, within a breath.

"What happened?" I ask and pull on my underwear. She's breathing heavily into the phone and crying in a way I've never heard before.

"I think my—my ovarian cyst ru—ruptured," she explains, and my heart drops all the way into my feet.

"I'll be right there, Nachelle," I promise her, snatching the phone from Cameron after I've pulled on my jeans. "Ten minutes, tops," I add and she hangs up on me without another word. "Can you drive me?" I ask Cameron, who almost falls over in his rush to put on his pants.

"Of course." He grabs one of his hoodies and throws it my way, then pulls one out of his closet for himself. I notice that the one he's given me is a bit oversized, so I slip it on with ease.

I'm still panicking, but when Cameron takes my hand and leads me to his car, both of us running to get to my sister, I feel like he's sharing the worry with me.

I don't feel alone.

"We're coming, Chellie," Cam mumbles before he lets the car's engine roar to life, and I notice the way he's furrowed his brows in concern.

"She'll be okay," I assure both of us, but he breaks every single speed limit anyway to get to her. He does exactly what I'd do, and it makes me fall even more in love with him.

CHAPTER 31

Cameron

WE FIND CHELLIE ON the floor in the kitchen, lying on her back with blood running down her legs. She's clutching her stomach, crying. Her breathing is choppy, the way a person's breathing turns when they're in so much pain, they can't inhale and exhale properly.

"I can't move," she says, and I rush toward the cabinet where I know they keep their painkillers and such. "I'm in so much pain," she cries, and I notice Halo is beside her now, wiping her tears with his thumb

"Do you think I can pick you up? Your doctor said if it ever ruptured and you were in so much pain, I should take you to the hospital," he says calmly, running a hand over the top of her head.

"I'm so scared," she says, and I rush to get her some water to take the painkiller.

"It'll be alright, Nachelle."

Halo throws me a thankful smile when I hand him the water and painkillers, and he helps his sister to sit up carefully. Chellie takes it, more tears streaming down her face. I can't imagine the pain she's in right now. I've heard a woman comparing this pain to her appendicitis attack, and as someone who's had one of those, I know how fucking awful the pain is. Imagining that on top of the blood she's losing—

Tears fill my eyes at the thought of the agony she's in.

"Can you wait here with her? I need to grab her new pants, underwear, and a pad," Halo explains, and I waste no time settling down beside Chellie and wrapping my arms around her.

"I'm sorry I interrupted date night," she says, and I let out a laugh I don't mean.

"Don't worry about that, sweetheart. We were just watching a movie anyway," I lie, but she snorts because she doesn't believe me, not one bit.

"My brother is wearing your clothes. Doesn't take a genius to put two and two together," she says, and I smile down at her.

"Feeling better?"

"Nope, but I always feel well enough to call out bullshit. My head could be hanging half on my neck, and I'd still tell you that I know you were *not* watching a movie." I can't help it. I burst into laughter.

"No matter what we're doing, Chellie, you're more important. Please don't be sorry," I tell her and run a hand over her forehead.

"That's sweet."

She cries harder again, and I hold onto her until Halo reappears with everything he said he'd bring.

"Okay, Nachelle, I'm going to lift you and bring you to the bathroom," he says, and she's about to protest, probably to tell him she can walk, when he simply lifts her off the ground with ease.

Everything happens in a blur after that. Once he's done helping her change and get cleaned up, which takes a long time because Nachelle is bleeding a lot. It worries me to the point where I'm going so fast, rushing to hospital, that I'm sure I'll have not one but a few tickets in the morning. Halo doesn't say anything, but he's got his hand on my thigh, settling me even though I should be the one to do that to him.

Because of the amount of blood she's losing, they take her immediately, and I hear one of the nurses tell a doctor something about it being a hemorrhaging cyst. My stomach turns upside down in the worst way, making me feel sick.

"Come on," Halo says and takes my hand, guiding me away from where they rushed Chellie through the double doors.

Then, we wait.

A doctor appears just long enough to tell us they've rushed her into surgery to remove the cyst and control the bleeding. From the confident way they were speaking, I'm assuming they do this a lot and Chellie will be fine, but the worry in my chest doesn't leave. It doesn't ease. It won't. Not until I see her out of surgery with her usual cocky smile back on her lips, and that playful gleam in her eyes.

The picture of her lying on the floor with blood running down her legs haunts me, and I hold onto Halo's hand because I know this is so much worse for him because it's his sister. The most important person in the world to him.

Neither one of us speaks, but eventually he gets up to get us both a coffee because it's late and we're drained, but neither one of us is capable of falling asleep in these chairs without knowing how Chellie is doing.

To distract my mind, I look through my emails, scanning through one from my manager that says that Klein Racing has already got two drivers for next season, as well as a reserve driver, which is just another team that doesn't want me.

As disappointed as I am, it has nothing on the amount of pain that goes through me as I read through the email Aisha sent me.

Cameron,

I'm sorry to have to tell you this over email. I tried to reach you by phone call, but there was no answer, so an email will have to do.

There is nothing that can be done to stop your mother from selling the ranch. Because both of your siblings are under twenty-five years of age, the minimum age your grandfather said in his will that they would have to be to make any decisions about the place, their "voting" right on what happens to the ranch goes to your mother. That makes it three against one, and she can do whatever she pleases with it as long as she gives you a share of the profit.

Nothing I've attempted has worked, and I'm all out of options. I'm sorry I can't help you keep your childhood home.

All the hope I had in my chest of making things right with my siblings, of allowing them to stay in the place they grew up, where their lives are, disintegrates into ash right in front of my eyes. Tears fill my eyes and spill down my cheeks before I can stop them.

It's one thing to get another rejection.

It's something else to lose yet another thing I loved so much.

My heart is getting sick and tired of having brief moments of joy, like when I was with Halo earlier and everything suddenly just clicked into place, and then long-lasting periods of agony it has to carry around while I pretend like everything is fine.

Nothing's fine.

I can't keep smiling.

My home is getting taken away from me.

I won't make it back into F1 as more than a mentor to the new talent coming into the sport.

My sisters will hate me forever for this.

I ruined everything.

As if I needed more of a reminder of the mistakes I've made, my left hand starts throbbing from phantom pain, my scars burning.

"She's out of surgery already. Her doctor said everything went well and they removed the cyst and stopped the bleeding. She's sleeping now but will recover fully," Halo explains, but when he notices the way the tears are streaming down my face, his calm expression turns into one of pure concern. "What happened?" he asks and rushes to kneel in front of me, placing down the cups of coffee to rub his hands over my thighs comfortingly.

"Nothing, I'm sorry. I was just concerned for Chellie, and it was hitting me harder than I thought," I say because it isn't a lie. It's just not the truth he was asking me for.

"Cam, come on, tell me. I know you love my sister, but this hurt in your eyes is one of betrayal and guilt, not worry," he says, taking my face in his hands to make me look at him. But I can't tell him. He's just had a chance to breathe again, a second of relief. I don't want to ruin this moment for him.

So, instead of answering, I lean down and kiss him. I kiss him until the ache in my chest dulls a little. I kiss him until my tears stop. I kiss him until I'm sure he's too wrapped up in me to remember what he was asking me.

Because I'm not going to tell him. Not now. When we get a quiet moment and I've had time to figure my shit out, I will. But it's too much. My life is too much, and I can't put more on him.

"You don't have to tell me what's going on, but kissing me isn't going to make me forget what we were talking about, even if it's a close thing," he says and puts his mouth back on mine, lingering because he can. Because he wants to. Because it feels so good. "You know I'm always here for you." And he is. He's always been there when I needed him, when I closed myself off from the rest of the world. It was Halo who pulled me out of the darkness I was in. It was Halo who showed me I was capable of things I didn't think I was anymore.

It's always been Halo.

And I was a fool who didn't see that.

"There's nothing I can do to stop her from selling the ranch. Aisha has no options for me." I don't have to tell him the implications of everything else that comes with that statement, he knows. He knows about my sisters. He knows they don't want to hold me responsible, but there's truth in what I said. Mum is doing this because of me.

"I'm sorry, Cameron," he says, holding onto both of my hands. "I'm so sorry."

There's nothing else to say. There is no magical solution he has for me, and I most certainly don't have one either. Otherwise, I'd have used it already.

My mother finally got her wish.

She broke me in half, all of my childhood trauma leaking out of me to colour the white canvas she's placed beneath me. A painting of her very own making to hang on the walls of her new house.

For years, Gabriel and Adrian have made it a tradition to meet whenever one of them needed to talk or simply wanted to be with the other to silence all of their worries. They're brothers in name, not by blood, but they act as if they'd grown up with each other and spent all of their time bonding as children. So, whenever they need each other, no matter what time of day, they meet to have a hot chocolate and play some cards.

A couple years ago, they invited James for the first time because of what happened between him and his wife while they were faking their relationships.

Now, Gabriel has invited me to be with them.

It's four in the morning and I only just left hospital after Halo and I saw Nachelle sleeping peacefully, recovering from her surgery. He stayed with her, but he wanted me to get some rest.

I texted Gabriel to let him know about what was happening with the ranch since he told me to keep him updated, but I didn't expect him to tell me to get my arse to his house.

I didn't expect a reply at all.

As soon as I get there, right after I ring the doorbell, he welcomes me at the gate of his house and wraps his arms around me in a hug I very much needed.

"I'm glad you came," he says and squeezes me once. "Adrian and James have been bickering like a married couple for the last half an hour, talking about which one of them is better at the card game we're playing," Gabriel adds, stepping back but placing a hand on my shoulder to guide me inside.

"When aren't they bickering like a married couple?" I challenge, and my best friend chuckles.

"Fair point. That's why I'm so glad you're here," he teases as if that was the only reason why.

"Cameron, thank God," Adrian says when we join them on the veranda, where Val and Gabriel have a table at their house. "Who do you think is better at—"

"Let me stop you right there," I interrupt, and he stops talking, his lips parting in surprise. "James," I add, and his jaw drops comically far. It brings back my grin, no matter how wrong it feels to smile at the moment.

"You don't know anything. I don't know why I even asked you," Adrian says and leans back in his chair, crossing his arms in front of his chest. James is laughing so hard, tears are collecting at the corners of his eyes.

"If he had said you, you would have said Cameron knows best," James adds, but he's still laughing, so I'm having a hard time deciphering his words.

"Shut the fuck up," Adrian says as he starts laughing, too, and I watch those two idiots with some of the heaviness on my chest lifting off it.

Once Adrian and James have sobered up, Gabriel and I settle in the seats beside them. I'm next to James, who pats my thigh comfortingly once, while Gabriel sits beside Adrian, who wiggles his brows at his brother-in-law.

None of us speaks about what's happening in my life at first. The three of them simply fill me in on what has been going on with them, with their kids and wives, and I listen attentively while I sort my cards in my hand.

It dawns on me eventually that they're waiting for *me* to be comfortable to poach the subject, so after I take a deep breath, I fill the silence with my words.

"I'm sad," I admit. All three of them look at me as the words leave my mouth. "I'm heartbroken that she's selling the ranch, and there is nothing I can do to stop her."

As soon as I start speaking, the words continue to roll from my tongue. I tell them about my sisters. About how much I'll miss Willow. How disconnected I already feel from my childhood and how much worse it'll get when the ranch is gone. We stop playing as I rant through everything going through my head, and they listen closely because they love me. They want to know what's happening. They care. So, I keep going. I don't worry about telling them everything for the first time in the duration of our friendship. It occurs to me that I tried to shield them all from my childhood trauma for a long time, but I need them, and I can no longer pretend like everything's alright.

"Your mother is a vengeful woman," Adrian points out when I'm done speaking. "Trying to get even with your father by attacking you. What the fuck is wrong with her?" he asks and mumbles a few more not-so-flattering insults about her that I can't even deny.

"I don't have the kind of money she's asking for, and even if I did, she'd never, ever sell the ranch to me." I place my cards on the table, closing my eyes to enjoy the warmth of the spring wind Monaco has to offer.

Adrian and Gabriel exchange a glance, but I have no idea what they're saying to each other.

"What can we do to help?" James asks, bringing my attention to him.

"Your company is comfort enough," I assure him and mean every word.

"Even Adrian's?" James says, but he flinches a second after, yelping in pain. "You wanker," he says and leans down to rub his shin.

"Damn, I'm sorry, James. I've been having these God-awful leg twitches. Did I get you?" he asks, feigning innocence, and I'm covering my mouth to keep from laughing at James' annoyed expression.

"You know what? I've been having those, too," I chime in, kicking my leg diagonally under the table to get Adrian's shin.

"Ow, fuck."

Gabriel almost falls out of his chair from laughter. I join him, and James gets up from the table to protect his legs from any more attacks because he too is laughing.

We're fully grown men acting like a bunch of juvenile idiots, but sometimes, especially when things get so heavy, you have to act a little childish.

Because being an adult sucks.

And every now and then, it's my friends, my family, that remind me that just because I have to be responsible and make sure everyone else is taken care of doesn't mean I don't get to let loose and forget about it all for a moment.

It's why I tell them about Halo and me, too. Why I tell them I've finally allowed myself to be open to the possibility of love, and they couldn't be any prouder of me for being so willing to give my heart to someone else.

To someone much more deserving of it than anyone else I've ever been with.

CHAPTER 32
Halo

NACHELLE BARELY HAD MORE than a week to recover before she had to get back in the car for free practice. She doesn't complain about the discomfort I know she still feels, simply keeps going, doing her job to the best of her abilities.

It's no surprise to me.

Women are expected to move through life without a single complaint about the things that happen to their bodies, and no matter how much of a safe space I give her, the world of Formula One isn't one for her. She can't tell her team she's not feeling well because any sign of weakness will be treated the same way they treated Cameron's. And there is not a chance in hell my sister will let anyone take her seat from her.

We're halfway through the race here in Miami, my mami standing by my side in Adrian's garage, when Nachelle overtakes James, slipping into first place. Her teammate has been struggling all weekend, but even if he wasn't, there would be no stopping my sister as she takes first place for the first time in her Formula One career.

"*Vamos,* Nachelle," Mami says from beside me, clapping her hands together enthusiastically.

She drove here from Moonville since it's not too far, and I'm glad she's here because the excitement I currently feel multiplies by a million with her beside me. Her hands are clasped together, and she's lifted them under her chin to rest it on top of them. Her eyes haven't left the screen, and I feel the nervous energy leaking off her and onto me with every second Nachelle stays in first place.

"Por el amor de Dios, que quede así," Mami says, and I take her hand in mine as we watch my sister complete her first lap ever as the leader of an F1 race.

There are twenty-eight laps left. They've all already pitted, most of the drivers being on hard compound tires now. Val is doing her best in third place, but the Velocità Rossa is not quick on this track. While we may have the speed on straights that we didn't have in previous years, our drivers struggle in the corners. On this particular track, Val and Adrian are also suffering from porpoising, Adrian even more so than Val, which is why I'm on Adrian's side of the garage. His race engineer, Chloe, doesn't need me in the slightest, but if she wants my input, she can have it. I've offered it, but whatever I told her, she already knew, so I just felt like I was mansplaining, and I *hate* that feeling.

So, I stepped back, my tablet near me to keep an eye on the data. Mami is still fevering beside me, and I doubt it's going to change until the end of the race.

James is out of DRS range, but he's staying close to Nachelle. There's no twenty-second gap within ten laps, like James did with the rest of the grid only a few years ago. There's no driving away in first like she's hoping she could. Her teammate is just as fast as her, and he's plotting behind her. My sister is his next target, and if she doesn't defend like her life depends on it, he will take this win from her.

Yesterday, during Qualifying, Nachelle came in close second to James, mere milliseconds between them. No one can deny that she's doing well, better even than Cam did last year, compared to his teammate. Her car is more reliable than his ever was, so comparing them without considering those aspects is wrong, but it's also a fact I know Cameron is probably struggling with.

And yet, he pushes all of that aside to be there for her.

On top of being on the brink of losing his childhood home, his relationship with his sisters, and having already lost his seat, Cameron keeps a smile on his face and helps everyone he can.

It's about time I do something for my boyfriend—a smile covers my face because I like that word a lot more than I ever thought I would—spoil him, take care of him like he took care of me during our date.

With a shake of my head, I refocus on the race, banishing the plans I'm making in my head for my next date with Cameron to the back of my head.

I look at Adrian's data, then at Val's, comparing the two of them.

Beside me, Mami gasps, and I look up to see James attempting an overtake on Nachelle. His front wing is at the height of her rear tire, almost touching. I stop breathing until the end of the corner, where my sister stays ahead, having fended off her teammate.

She stays ahead long enough not to be under threat on the straight, but James is not nearly finished chasing her down.

They battle for several laps.

At one point, James even overtakes Nachelle, and Mami, who never really curses unless she's truly upset, throws out every single Spanish curse word I've ever heard, and then some.

I'd laugh if I wasn't very close to biting my nails.

My head is torn between keeping an eye on my drivers and watching the battle unfold between James and Nachelle.

He's relentless.

I mean, I've watched it in the past, saw what Cameron fought against and all of the other drivers, but witnessing his aggressive driving style being used to fight Nachelle has me breathing a little quicker, shallower.

In every way, James is a more experienced driver. He's done this hundreds of times more than she has. He's raced against drivers with every different style of racing, so he's got answers, a plan, a strategy, for every single one of her moves.

And soon, he's overtaking her, this time moving ahead of her.

Mami is cursing again, and this time, I join her because I'm so frustrated, I could launch my tablet against the wall.

Nachelle is so close to winning the race. All she has to do is get first place back. Part of me wishes I could talk to her because I'd tell her I believe in her, that she can do it, but she has to do this on her own.

My sister doesn't give up. She's fighting James the same way he was fighting her, setting sector times quicker than his to slowly close the distance between them again. She's fearless, and I admire that, but the fact that she isn't wrapped in bubble wrap right now while attempting such a dangerous move makes me want to scold her.

It's part of the job, yeah, I know, but it doesn't change the fact that Nachelle is my little sister, and I would rather chew off my own arm than see any harm come her way.

Watching her car slide beside James' on the straight, the speed advantage of the DRS carrying her forward faster than him, has me covering my mouth in fear. It's all I can do to muffle the sound of shock and worry that leaves me when Nachelle hits his rear tire with hers in the corner, colliding. James' tire blows, and Nachelle is stuck in the wall, not moving.

In terms of a crash, it was a soft one since they were hardly on the gas because of the sharp corner, but that doesn't change the fact that my sister is responsible for this DNF. For her being unable to finish this race and for James limping back to the pits with three tires only.

Hawke is not going to be happy with her.

That was, in plain terms, a rookie mistake, and they don't allow rookies to make these mistakes.

If my sister isn't careful how she handles this post-crash situation, if James also doesn't get to continue this race and she costs them a one-two finish that could have brought them a lot of points, they might replace her with the new reserve driver before she can even blink.

Because that's what Hawke does. They replace without thinking of everything their drivers have done for their team, without considering their accomplishments. This is a bad mistake, but I hope they will be understanding of it, not punish her more than this DNF already will.

I keep one of my eyes on my phone screen, waiting for Cam to text me in case he needs me, but no message ever comes through. My head battles between feeling relieved and wondering if he's having a panic attack and simply not telling me.

There's no time to linger on it with everything that's happening right now.

"*Mi amor*," Mami says, pulling at the sleeve of my arm to get my attention.

"*Ella esta bien*, Mami, *no te preocupes*," I assure her, but she tilts her head and frowns at me.

"What does this mean for her?" she asks, and it's clear that her concern isn't because she crashed out of the race.

It's because Mami also knows how Hawke treats its drivers. Well, every driver except James. He's their golden boy, their project, and they invested so much time and money into him that he's now winning them championships. He can do no wrong. But every second driver of the team can. It's as if all of their lenience is given to James, with none left anymore for any of his teammates.

"It's only one mistake, no matter how bad it is, it's only one. She's done well so far in the other races, well enough so they can't say anything." I don't know if that's true at all, but there is no point in being honest. Sometimes, a lie like this is necessary to ease the worry for Mami.

"Okay," she replies and nods, which tells me I made the right choice.

Now, it's a matter of waiting and hearing what they say to Nachelle.

After the race, Valentina having taken the win after everything that happened, and James only coming in fifteenth, I walk toward Hawke Racing's motorhome. Nachelle is already standing outside arguing with Cameron about something.

"How can you be so optimistic? Look at what they did to you!" Nachelle says loud enough for me to hear even as I rush to get to them.

"You're not me, Chellie. You are not unworthy of the seat like I was. I didn't belong in Hawke. I didn't belong in F1. You do. You worked so hard for your seat, and they won't take it from you because of one mistake."

If it was any other team, none of us would be so paranoid, but we've seen what Hawke can do. One mistake was enough to demote Henri Allard a few years back. They kicked out Cameron because of his injury with no chance to return. They dispose of their drivers like they do trash, and my sister is well aware of it.

Formula One is a glamorous, beautiful world with fast cars, expensive tastes, and a community of people who are passionate about the sport. It's wonderful in so many ways, but this, this fear my sister has, is the dark part of it no one can deny.

The drivers are a key component of the sport, but reporters, teams, and even some "fans" use them as puppets in whatever game they're playing.

"You don't know that. I fucked up big time. I cost James and me the race. When I walked past the team principal, she gave me a sad look because she knows she won't be able to protect me from the wrath of the team owner and every investor," she says, and Cameron falls silent when I approach them to place a hand on Nachelle's arm.

"Yelling at Cam won't help you, Nachelle," I say softly, but I should have kept my mouth shut altogether because she slaps my hand away and takes a step back.

Cameron is the one to step toward her, grabbing her arms to make sure she looks at him instead of trying to avoid hearing what others have to say and listening to her intrusive thoughts.

"Every driver makes a mistake eventually. Some even make hundreds. Hawke decided to let you and James race, which always comes with a side of risk. If they weren't prepared for this outcome, they wouldn't have allowed it. If you want to blame yourself, you're also going to have to blame them."

He releases her in case she wants to leave, but she doesn't. There is a reason why Nachelle wanted Cam as her mentor. She listens to him. She trusts him. She looks up to him and values his opinions.

"You can be hard on yourself all you want, and while I do agree that we should learn from our mistakes, beating yourself up over all of this won't change the outcome. All you can do now is look over the footage and make sure you don't do what you did today again," he goes on, and Nachelle nods several times, allowing his words to sink in.

She stays silent for a moment, but then she looks up at Cam and me, shaking her head and sighing.

"Nothing is going to ease my mind, so I think I'm going to go take a shower and hope it'll wash away the tension in my body," my sister says and gives me one brief hug before strolling into the motorhome, going to do exactly what she said she would.

Cameron runs a hand over his handsome face, and I let out a small laugh because, fuck, what a horrible situation for every party involved. When I'm close enough, he turns to me, sliding his hands onto my chest and up my neck. My heart does its usual tumbling and racing because he's close and touching me, and I can't help but smile as I lean down to bring my lips to his. My hands lift to his cheeks, cupping them softly as I deepen the kiss.

I don't care if people in this sport who have an old mindset stare or disapprove, not that there are many people here anyway. But we are in a country where people in general don't approve of our relationship, and have gone as far as electing leadership to make sure we get our rights taken away.

So, I kiss Cameron harder. I kiss him until we're both breathless because I need this to reassure myself he's okay, and he needs it because he's frustrated and doesn't know how to fix anything that's happening.

"Are you okay?" I ask him, caressing his cheeks. His eyes flutter shut, and Cam lets out a little laugh I know he doesn't mean.

"Yeah, the crash didn't trigger me, which made me very happy, but it didn't last long because as soon as I saw Chellie, the relief was replaced by needing to comfort her. But she pretty much turned down any attempts at it, so now I just feel like an arse."

"You're a good friend and an even better mentor, Cam. You did everything you could to ease her worries in an impossible situation," I assure him, and his tensed shoulders fall as he lets my words fill him with relief.

"Careful, Asher, you're starting to make me really happy. Soon, I'll have big feelings for you, and then what?" Cam asks with a little teasing grin, but my expression is as serious as it gets while I hold onto his face, ensuring he looks at me while I voice words that scare me to death.

"Then we'll finally be on the same wavelength." His mouth falls open like he wants to respond, but I'm terrified of the answer, so I kiss him again.

"Let me answer," he says between kisses, but I keep kissing him, making him chuckle.

"I'm taking you out on a date tonight. Meet me in the lobby of your hotel at eight o'clock," I instruct when I pull back, Cam's hands on my wrists to hold onto me.

"Where are we going?"

"Somewhere to take your mind off everything," I reply, rubbing both my thumbs over his cheeks one last time before stepping back and spinning around to get back to my mother.

Cam's voice stops me.

"We *are* on the same wavelength, my Halo. I'm sorry it took me so long to get here with you, but we are now."

I throw him a grin over my shoulder, then smile to myself as I hurry to get everything ready for our date.

CHAPTER 33

Cameron

CHARLOTTE AND HAZEL HAVEN'T returned any of my calls, and I don't blame them. Any moment now, Mum could be telling them she won. That she's selling the ranch. If she hasn't already.

All of those thoughts, all that negativity brewing inside of me, is pushed to the furthest corners of my mind the second Halo steps into the lobby of my hotel with yellow tulips in his hand. A smile that is completely out of my control covers my face, and I let it because I meant what I said to him earlier.

He makes me so happy.

"Hi, *mi luz*," he says as he approaches, placing the softest kiss on my lips.

"Hey, handsome," I reply as he hands me the tulips.

"I know they're my favourite and you've told me you don't have a favourite flower, but I thought maybe this could be...ours," he explains, but he seems unsure, and his next words only confirm it. "I'm sorry if that's lame. Maybe I shouldn't have done this. You're much better at this stuff than I am and—" I interrupt his rant by kissing him.

"These are wonderful, Asher. I'd love it if this was ours, our thing." He's got this uncertain smile on his face, and a blush follows it right after.

I love it when he blushes.

It's as if he's painting his face in his feelings, joy and love, and it's so special because this specific blush is one he only wears around me.

"So I did well already?"

"You're perfect, baby. Everything you've ever done for me has been perfect. You are a lot better at this than you may think," I assure him, and he takes my hand with a satisfied grin.

"Perfect, huh? You're making all these compliments go straight to my head," he replies, and I slip my hand into his, letting him guide me outside.

There's a rental car parked near the valet, clearly waiting for us while he went inside to pick me up like the gentleman he is. My heart warms at the thought, and I look up at Halo, studying the sharp cut of his jaw, his wavy brown hair, his icy-blue eyes, and his full lips, admiring every single one of his features.

He doesn't seem to notice because he's too busy smiling at the valet who's handing him back his key, and I wonder, truly wonder, how I could have possibly been so oblivious to this wonderful man for so long. I know we were friends and he had this whole no-dating thing going on, but he was always different with me. He never sought any sort of brief relationship like he did with people in the past. For as long as I can remember, Halo has done everything in his power to keep me around.

I rub my thumb over the back of his hand, holding on tighter. If he notices, he does me the favour of not mentioning it.

Once we're in the car, we fall into an easy conversation about how his mother is doing and what we're going to do once we get back to Monaco. But there is something else I need to discuss with him that I've been putting off for a few days now.

"Will you come with me to Australia? I want to spend a few more days on the ranch before Mum sells it," I explain, feeling my heart thudding in my ears. Not because I think he won't come. I'm starting to realise Halo would do just about anything for me, but I'm nervous to go home, to have to face that loss and heartache.

In my session with Munira yesterday, I didn't even mention the ranch or that my only hope of keeping it has been flushed down the drain. We didn't have time for it, I tell myself, because it's easier to say than to admit I'm not ready to address the mountain of grief that comes with losing the only place I ever felt tethered to. A place I could keep coming back to, no matter what happened. A place that became so much more after my crash when I lost my biggest dream.

"Cam, wherever you need me, I will go."

Such simple words, but they're not so simple after all, are they? Because they carry a weight in them that hits me square in the chest, a weight I don't shake.

"You terrify me in the best and worst way, Halo. I need you to know that," I say and take his hand from my thigh to pull it to my mouth and place a kiss on the back of it.

"Why?"

"Because I've never felt this way about someone. Because I've felt less for Elijah, and it still hurt me so much when he cheated, when I walked in on him with another man. I cannot fathom the power you have over me, my Halo, and that? That terrifies me."

He's said all sorts of wonderful things to me already.

He told me how he felt without speaking the words, and I didn't have to hear them to know what I mean to him.

It's time I offered him a glimpse inside my head and heart.

I got close earlier, but he was walking away and it was a coward's way to tell him how I feel. This is as brave as I'm able to be with my heart screaming in fear.

"Fuck am I glad I'm not the only one who feels this strongly," is the first thing he replies before letting out a genuine, breathless laugh of relief. "Oh man, you have no idea how happy I am that I have the same kind of grip on you as you have on me, *mi luz*." Despite the heaviness of this subject, I start grinning because how the fuck could I not?

My Halo has this way of always uplifting a situation, whether he means to or not.

"We'll figure this out, Cam. You and me. We will learn how to trust each other, and we will learn how not to let our past experiences influence the happiness we create together. As long as we're patient and understanding, communicate to the best of our abilities, I don't see why we wouldn't be able to make this work," he assures me, pulling my hand to his face so I cup his cheek. He then slides his hand on top of mine, keeping it there as he continues to watch the road. "Also, if I ever stumble across your ex, I'm going to very disrespectfully punch him in the dick."

I can't help myself. I burst into laughter, which brings the most wonderful smile to his face, lighting up his blue eyes.

"I'll film it," I reply, and then he's laughing too, the sound of our joy filling the car with the utmost ease.

"What the hell are you all doing here?" Halo asks Valentina, Gabriel, Adrian, Nevaeh, Seraphina—well, perhaps not the baby, but she's also here—Leonard, Chiara, Leonora, Kieran, Damian, Daisy—again probably not the children because they're busy talking to each other about who knows what—James, Estrella, Scarlette, Storm, Nachelle, and Dahiana.

"It's your fault. You told me about your plans, and I accidentally blurted them out to Adrian, who texted the whole group chat about it." Chellie's words only make Halo turn a darker shade of red, and I place a hand on his back to ease his anger.

"Welcome to my big, messy yet beautiful family. They know hardly any boundaries, but they will protect you with their lives," I say because even though Scarlette is Halo's best friend and he's known her and Storm far longer than I have, they've become my family, too. Plus, Halo is not around the other members as much, so he's not used to them doing pretty much everything together.

"This was supposed to be a special date, just you and me," he whispers to me as Adrian blabs on about how his company is a blessing and Halo should consider himself lucky that he graced us with his presence. I know he's joking, but my handsome man gives me an unimpressed look.

"It *is* special. Having them here doesn't ruin anything. Actually, I think it does the opposite," I say and kiss his cheek, taking his hand in mine to lead him to where Nevaeh is standing with Seraphina in her arms. "Hi, sweetheart," I say and attempt to take the baby from Nevaeh's arms when Adrian looks like he's been punched in the stomach. "I thought we've gone over this." He grimaces, letting out a fake laugh.

"Sorry, reflex," he says, but he watches me and Halo closely as I take Seraphina in my arms.

"*Mein Mond*, would you stop that," Nevaeh says to Adrian, but he shakes his head. "Fine then," she says and grabs his face in her hands, pulling it down so her lips meet his. As she anticipated, the world fades away for him, and he melts into the kiss, smiling against her lips.

"She's so adorable," Halo says, running a careful finger over her blonde hair. Seraphina is fast asleep with a pair of headphones on her ears to protect them from the loud noises around us.

From what I've gathered, we're at an amusement park of some sort. There are children running around, parents chasing after them, couples in love pointing at the different rides they want to go on, and friends who are having fun simply being in each other's company. The warm summer wind brushes over the bare skin of my arm as I look at the rainbow of colours illuminating the amusement park from the different lights.

"Can I hold her?" Halo asks, and I look down at Seraphina with a smile.

"I think Adrian's head would explode if someone else held his *petit ange*," I whisper, but he hears us anyway and stops kissing Nevaeh long enough to take Seraphina from me. He gently places her inside her stroller, content she's no longer in danger of being dropped. He's grinning, though, and I can't fault him in the least. If I was a father, if I had a little angel to protect, I'd be the same way.

"Uncle Cameron," Damian says, and I look down my side right before he wraps his arms around my hips. He's grown so much, and I'm not in the least bit surprised that he's already *this* tall because his father is over two metres tall. Okay, he's not actually, but for someone as short as me, it sure seems that way.

"What's up, little man?" I ask, and he waves his hand to make me lean down so he can whisper in my ear.

"Will you sneak me onto the adult rides? Dad said no, but I know you're cool," he says, and I burst into laughter, getting his father's attention. He scowls in that way he does when Damian misbehaves, but within a second, it turns into a smile as he puts his hands under his son's armpits and lifts him away from me.

I'm laughing when he tells Damian, "You're being very naughty. Don't make me tell Estrella to yell at you again." Estrella, having overheard him, slaps his arm.

"I've never yelled at him!"

And yet, he's been teasing her about it since they met because Estrella used to be Damian's instructor at Val and Leonard's academy. She reprimanded the kid for pulling Daisy's hair, and James got upset with her for it.

"Sure you haven't," James replies and throws her a playful look.

"*Arcoíris*, I know you're not the biggest fan of rollercoasters, so I thought maybe we could go play at the arcade instead," Storm tells Scar, who breaks out in the biggest grin because of his thoughtfulness.

"*Vamos*," she says and pulls him behind her, and the man who never smiles wears the most brilliant one on his face as he follows behind his wife.

Leonard and Chiara are leading Leonora and Kieran toward where their children are pointing to, and Gabriel and Val throw me a knowing look when Halo takes my hand, lacing his fingers through mine.

I'm too happy to prevent my face from revealing that fact.

"I guess you're right. It's nice to have them here," Halo says and brings me to where Chellie and Dahiana are standing, getting some cotton candy from one of the trucks.

"Plus, they're so busy with each other, they'll be doing their own thing anyway," I assure him right before we stop in front of his family.

"Um, excuse me, Mami and I are having date night. Go away," Chellie says and *shoos* us away, making Halo burst into laughter.

"Okay, okay," he says and lifts his hands in surrender. "I was just trying to be polite."

"Well, be polite somewhere else, *hermanito*. Perhaps while you help your boyfriend onto the rollercoaster. The old man will need the assistance," she teases me, and I let my jaw drop in mock offense. It doesn't last long because Dahiana gasps and swats her daughter's arm, saying something in Spanish that's way too fast for me to understand.

"Come on. Mami can scold Nachelle without us here," Halo says and pulls me away, toward the first rollercoaster we'll ride tonight. "My sister can be so mean. You're obviously not too old for these rides," he says as we line up. "You might be too short for some of them, though." I do my best not to burst into laughter.

"What if you're too tall for this ride?" I counter, and he grins. "I guess you'd have to bend over a little."

"You'd like that, huh?" he fires back, sending heat straight into my cheeks. I'm blushing, and it only gets worse when I look at him and he's smirking down at me, telling me I understood the dirty message perfectly well.

I clear my throat, but it's useless.

My body is on fire with lust, and he knows it.

CHAPTER 34

Cameron

CHASING ADRENALINE HIGHS IS a hobby for Formula One drivers. Some of us do it by partaking in other motorsport activities in our free time, going skydiving, getting a motorcycle like me, or in a hundred other ways. I think we're partially addicted to it, and especially now that I'm not racing anymore, I don't get to chase that high anymore.

Today is as close as I've come to how I feel when I'm racing in months. Every day that I'm home, I'm training in my simulator now that my hand isn't bothering me anymore. I'm working out with Parker. I'm on top of things in case any of the teams want to give me a chance, one last one, but so far, I still have only received rejections or ridiculous offers that I simply couldn't accept.

Halo takes my mind off all of it. We go from one ride to another, then grab a little bite to eat. Our friends are somewhere around us, but we're not paying attention to them.

He's lost in me, and I'm lost in him, just like it's supposed to be on a date.

"Let's go on this one," Halo says, taking my hand once more and guiding me toward where people have lined up to go for a ride on the high altitude carousel swing.

"You want to be that high up, just the two of us sitting next to each other, nowhere to run?" I ask with a teasing smile, and Halo furrows his brows at me.

"What have we been doing all night if not that?" he challenges, but it's not the same thing. The other things were hardly what I'd consider romantic. This seems a lot more romantic and intimate. Even if we're going to be swung around in the air.

"Oh, good, you're here. Mami refuses to go up with me on that thing," Chellie says as she joins us, and I look behind her to see Dahiana has sat down at a table with Leonard and Chiara, who are making sure their children are eating something.

"Give me a second," Halo says and presses his mouth to mine, going to check on his mother. Which gives me the perfect opportunity.

"When we're up there, do me a favour and take a picture of Halo and I, okay?" Not only do I want to take pictures of the memories we create, but I want to gift him that picture framed one day soon, whenever we celebrate a first.

Because I want to celebrate a first with him.

I want to celebrate all of our firsts one day.

"Sure thing. Give me your phone," she says and holds out her hand, wiggling her fingers demandingly. "I have my clumsy phases, and I'm not risking dropping my own phone," she explains when I hand mine over with a confused expression.

"Fair enough," I reply right as Halo joins us again, his hand moving straight back against mine before he laces his fingers through mine.

He smiles at both of us as we all wait for our turn.

We don't have to wait long for our turn. Soon, we're sitting on one of the benches, Chellie in the one in front of ours, and Halo holds onto the railing. Usually, I've only seen these things have single seats, but I like that we're sitting together, that he's so close to me.

As soon as we're lifted into the air, Halo smiles brightly, and I can't help but use my fingers to tilt his head my way, kissing his smile.

Up here, there is nothing that can hurt us.

Up here, we're invincible.

Up here, what we have is immortal.

The carousel picks up speed and we break apart, but we don't look away from each other. There's nothing and no one else you want to look at the moment you realise you're in love with someone.

So, I don't look away from him.

Not for a long time.

Halo and I stumble through the door of my hotel room, his mouth on mine.

Adrenaline is still pumping through our veins, and it's multiplied by the need we feel for each other. I want to take my time undressing him, but simultaneously, I just want to rip his clothes off, have his naked body pressed against mine again.

"What do you want?" I say after he breaks the kiss to fumble with my belt, opening it and pulling it out of the belt holes in my jeans.

"I want your ass, Cam."

A shiver of pleasure rolls down my spine at the same time all the blood in my body rushes south, hardening my cock until it strains painfully against my jeans. His eyes, which were already on my groin, take in the way my body reacts to his words, making him pull his bottom lip between his teeth. Without thinking, I lean forward, kissing him to make him release his bottom lip only to pull it between my own teeth, biting down on it.

A groan rumbles from his chest, and he deepens the kiss, forgetting about undressing me as he cups my face in his hands. His mouth glides over mine, his tongue slipping inside when I part my lips for him. There is need and lust, and then there's whatever I feel for Halo.

Something stronger and more consuming.

"Is that something you want, too?" he asks, breathless against my lips, so I grab his hand to guide it to my hard cock.

"You saw that I did. Now you can feel it, too. I want that more than anything else right now," I admit and moan against his mouth when he palms me through my jeans, firm and just how I like it.

"Then get yourself ready for me." He kisses me one more time before stepping away, moving towards the bed in my room as he reaches for the hem of his shirt, pulling it over his head.

With my heart racing, I disappear into the bathroom, closing the door and leaning against it as a bright smile covers my face. I'm nervous as if this were my first time, which it feels like a little considering I haven't been with anyone like this since Elijah, but it isn't a bad kind of nervous. It's anticipation filling me from top to bottom, and I'm shaking because of how desperately I want this.

Once I'm ready, I slip out of the bathroom completely naked, finding Halo sitting on the bed still wearing his jeans but nothing covering the top half of his mesmerizing body. It hurts me how beautiful he is, and it hurts me even more that he looks at me, gloriously naked, like I'm the most attractive person he's ever laid his eyes on.

Then he says, "I could spend a lifetime looking at you, Cameron, studying every inch of you, and never getting my fill. You are breathtaking in the most literal of senses because I physically can't breathe when I look at you," and stands, moving toward me to bring his hands to my neck. His icy-blue eyes are on mine the entire time, even as I try to slow my racing heartbeat.

"Says you, who looks like he's been carved to perfection by the goddess of nature." It's such an underwhelming thing to say after what he's just told me, but it feels wrong to leave this one-sided.

"Get on the bed for me, *mi luz*, on your back. I'm going to show you just how perfectly made for you I was." He nips at my bottom lip before smacking my butt once to gesture for me to get on the bed.

I notice he's found the bottle of lube and box of condoms I brought for tonight, placing them on the mattress for easier access. I lick my lips as my whole body thrums with need, and Halo appears behind me, trailing his hands down my arms while his lips press a soft kiss to the side of my head.

"Nervous?" he asks, but he bends down a little to bring his touch to my stomach, dragging his hands lower painfully slowly.

"In the best of ways," I admit as a smile works its way onto my lips. Halo runs his fingers over my abdomen, but he doesn't go lower. Doesn't go where I want him to touch me most. "Halo," I say or whimper would be the more accurate description.

"Beg, Cam. Let me hear it. Let me hear every little thing you want me to do to you," he says, his voice low and demanding in my ear before he nips the lobe, sending goosebumps trailing down my arms.

"Take me in your hand. Please, baby," I beg, and he wastes no time wrapping his big hand around me and giving me a firm stroke that has my head falling backward against his shoulder. "Fuck, yes. Like that, please."

Halo strokes me again, faster and harder, until I'm bending over at the waist, my hands grabbing the sheets on the bed. His body is curled around mine, his impressive, hard length pushing against my naked backside, and I wish his clothes away. Wish it was filling me while he stroked me. Wish for a lot of things I can't say out loud because I'm moaning. I'm rolling my hips to fuck into his hand and chase my pleasure because it feels so good. He feels so good because he knows exactly how to touch me. How to fuck me.

"Halo, I want to come with you deep inside me while I look at your handsome face," I say, doing my best to voice whatever I desire as he requested. It's easier than I thought it would be.

It's never been this easy with anyone.

He grinds against me, and there is something so sexy about me being naked while he's still wearing jeans that turns me on even more. The way the rough fabric of his jeans feels as he rubs his erection against my butt, moaning when the pressure is just right.

"Get on your back," he says after kissing my neck and rubbing his thumb in circles around my tip until my eyes rolled into the back of my head.

My body is weak with pleasure coursing through me, but I manage to get on the mattress, on my back. Halo stands at the edge of the mattress, smiling as he takes in the sight of my naked body on display for him. I'm not the type of man to get shy, especially not when I stroke my cock and he starts blushing so hard, it tells me just how much he wants me.

Almost as much as I want him.

"Hurry, please," I beg because I can't stand waiting anymore.

Halo reaches for his pants, dragging them down to let me see the way his hard cock presses against his boxers.

Fuck, he's big, and it's been so long since I've been with anyone, and—

"I know you specialise in overthinking," he starts as he pulls his boxers down, freeing his cock. "But I'll make you feel good, I promise. We'll make it fit." His words are followed by his hands sliding onto my thighs before he spreads me open, his gaze lingering on me. "You'll get used to me, *mi luz*."

He seals his promise with a kiss that has his dick rubbing against mine in the most delicious way. I moan into his mouth, enjoy the friction, but it isn't nearly enough, and he knows it. It's why he reaches for the condoms and slides one down his impressive length with a thoughtful look on his face. It's why he puts an equal amount of care into picking up the lube and dripping some of it on his cock first, then letting it coat me. He works the lube into me and around me with his fingers for a moment until I'm practically shaking because of how turned on I am.

"Fuck, you're so tight, Cam," he says and pushes another finger into me, making my back arch off the bed a little.

"Shit."

A moan leaves me, so loud and unrestrained that Halo keeps stroking his fingers inside me, rubbing against that wonderful spot that sends pleasure rolling through every piece of me. When I can no longer wait, when all patience has left me, I lean forward and pull his mouth onto mine. It brings his naked body flush against me, his cock pushing against me, slightly into me, until I'm shivering beneath him.

"Please," I beg against his lips, and then he's pressing into me, his head fully inside of me. I moan and so does he, but it's not enough. I need more.

"Slowly, Cam. I don't want to hurt you," he says, his arms shaking where he holds himself up on either side of me. I grab his face, making him look down at me instead of at where we're both connected now.

"You're not hurting me, my Halo. Please, I need all of you." And though I beg, though he pushes inside of me more, he takes his time loosening me up even more. He goes slow and gently, even while he goes deeper, and I'm writhing beneath him, desperate. Wanting.

Then he's finally all the way inside of me, both of us sighing and moaning.

"You're so perfect," I say as he shakes on top of me, taking his face in my hands again. His icy-blue eyes are on me, and I smile at him because his brows are creased in concentration while he fights to stay still, to keep from coming already. "You feel perfect. Look perfect. Are perfect," I say and lift off the mattress to kiss him, feeling him grin against my lips. His hand slips between us, wrapping around my cock until I'm moaning again.

"That's you, Cameron. You're perfect. You're everything to me," he says and slips out to drive back inside of me, soft and slow but hitting that spot again, making my whole body fill with pleasure.

After applying a bit more lube, Halo goes faster. Harder. He's steady, trying to make me come as quickly as possible because I know he's close. It's been long for him, but it's been even longer for me, and the way he's fucking me, the way his strokes are combined with his hand working my cock, I'm a mess underneath him. I'm calling out his name, scratching at his back, spreading my legs wider so he goes deeper all while trying to meet the movement of both his hand and dick.

I'm so full, so hard, so ready that my orgasm takes over quickly, his mouth finding mine again as my balls draw tighter and I spill all over my stomach. Two strokes, and he's there with me, filling the condom as he stays inside of me and his whole body shakes wonderfully from the orgasm. I feel him pulsing, feel as he comes, and it spikes my pleasure higher, dragging out my orgasm until there is nothing left inside me.

Halo grins down at me and kisses me again before disappearing in the bathroom to take care of the condom. When he returns, dropping onto the bed beside me, I drape my body across his, enjoying the way he wraps me up in his arms and holds me close.

We talk about everything that comes to mind. About life, about how far I've come in my healing journey, about his family, then mine. We talk about deep topics and light topics, before he slides down my body and takes me in his mouth, starting all over again, while I keep the grin firmly placed on my face because I've never been this happy in my life.

How could I not be?

The man I love is worshipping me, and I waste no time returning the favor.

CHAPTER 35
Halo

HAZEL AND CHARLOTTE HAVE barely spoken five words to Cameron since we arrived at the ranch yesterday. They haven't been avoiding him, but they haven't sought him out either, and he's giving them the space they so obviously desire.

Charlotte told me that a few buyers came by over the last few days, but that their mother got an offer so irresistible, all of the contracts have been signed already.

The ranch will no longer belong to the Kion family in two weeks' time.

When I told Cameron, tears appeared in his eyes, but he swallowed them back and led me to the stables where his horse, Willow, greeted him excitedly. She's completely brown with two patches of white to break up the color, one on her chest, the other on her forehead and muzzle. Her mane is an even darker brown than her body, both it and her tail well-kept, revealing how taken care of she is here.

It's been several minutes since we got to the stable, but I'm giving Cameron as much time as he needs with Willow. He's not only losing the ranch, he's also losing her, and no matter how much he pleaded with his mother, she wouldn't let him take her anywhere else. On paper, Willow belongs to her because she adopted her, so there is nothing, no amount of money, that convinced Cam's evil mother to let him take Willow.

"Should we go for a ride?" Cameron asks, tilting his head my way. He's got a brown cowboy hat on his head, and, though he shaved weeks ago, he's been growing out his stubble again. I've never been more attracted to him than I am right now.

This whole cowboy look suits him.

"I'd love to," I reply, readjusting my own cowboy hat. He gave it to me in the house, but I've felt silly ever since I put it on.

"Let me," Cam says as he approaches, lifting it off my head and putting it back on the proper way. "There you go, handsome."

He doesn't kiss me, doesn't take my hand, doesn't do anything he normally would now that we're dating. We're both very big fans of physical touch to convey our emotions, but I know Cam also loves acts of service. He loves taking care of people, and he's doing that right now. He takes care of everything so that I only need to get my ass into the saddle behind him. My boyfriend—I grin every time I think or say that word—holds out his hand for me, and I take it before putting my foot in the stirrup, then slinging my other leg over Willow's back.

Soon, we're off riding across the fields and fields of land the ranch is made up of. Cam shows me all the different animals that live here, introduces me to some of the people working here, and the places that harbor his childhood memories.

"Right there is where my grandmother taught me how to chop wood," he says and points to a stump of wood the size of a small inflatable pool. "She was the coolest woman I'd ever met, but then Val walked into my life, and now she holds that title."

"I think your grandmother would approve of that," I say and rub a comforting hand down his arm.

We keep going, keep riding, the cool winter air repelled by our jackets. It's only about sixty degrees Fahrenheit here in winter, but the wind has got a bite to it that had Cam pulling a spare jacket from his closet and wrapping me up in it.

"Here is where my grandfather taught me to ride a horse," he goes on, bringing us close to the stables where we took Willow out from.

"Did you fall off at any time?" I ask, and he tilts his head to show me a proud smile. It's the first time he smiled since we got here, but it fades away, taking with it his bright light, the one he constantly shines my way to illuminate my life.

"Never fell off. I was too skilled of a rider from the moment I sat on a horse for the first time." His arrogant words don't carry that cocky kick to them that they would if he wasn't so sad.

"Your grandfather must have been proud," I say as Cam guides Willow into a slow trot.

"He was a difficult man to impress," is all Cameron replies before we fall silent, continuing our ride around this huge ranch.

There are fences, trees, shrubs and bushes, animals, miles of green grass, everything one might expect to see at a ranch. There is a serenity to this place, a calmness that makes me understand why Cam went here to hide in the first place. Why he keeps coming back here. Why this feels like the place he belongs most. In a world full of adrenaline, risk, screaming fans, loud engines, this is the one place where everything stops. Everything quiets. You can actually hear your own thoughts out here, connect with nature, and realize that maybe all of your problems aren't as bad as they seem because you get to be alive. You were given the gift of life, and you get to spend it here or wherever you feel so at peace.

Eventually, Cam stops at a part of the ranch where we're surrounded by trees, almost like a forest area of it, and he takes Willow's reins into his hand, simply walking alongside us. He's taking in everything for the last time, and I stay perfectly silent as he does. I run my hands over Willow's mane, watching Cameron come to terms with everything he's about to lose.

I wish there was more I could do.

I wish I didn't have to feel so useless.

But I don't have the kind of money his mother is demanding, and there is no way I could ever get it in such a short amount of time.

All I can do is be there for him and hope it's enough.

Cameron walks back to the house without saying another word to me. He takes care of Willow while I pet the other horses in the stable. I don't know their names, but I refrain from asking because once he's done, once he's sure Willow is okay in her area, he walks toward me with tears in his eyes. He doesn't let them drop, won't allow himself to, but he hugs me hard. He's taking the comfort he needs from me, and I'm only too willing to give it to him.

"What else can I do, *mi luz*?" I ask, but he shakes his head.

"I don't feel like *luz* right now. I feel like *oscuridad*," he replies, and I'm so impressed with his knowledge of the word that I step back and let out a breathless laugh.

"How do you know what darkness is in Spanish?"

"I looked it up in case I wanted to make a joke one day, but I guess it works in this context, too."

A sad laugh escapes him, so I press my forehead to his, closing my eyes.

"I'm sorry." It's all I can think of saying because nothing else seems right.

"I'm sorry, too. You didn't sign up to have a boyfriend whose life constantly throws curveballs at him," he replies, but I brush my nose against his.

"Actually, I did. I signed up to have you, and that includes all curveballs." Finally, he brushes his lips against mine, and I love that he lingers for a while because kissing Cameron is by far one of my favorite things in the world.

He gives me one more firm kiss before he steps back, taking my hand in his to lead me out of the barn.

"You know what I could go for right now? A warm cup of coffee."

"And a side of me with it?" I ask, making him turn his head just enough to show me his smirk. "I'll take that as a yes."

Excitement moves through me as we step inside the house, but it dies as soon as I see Storm standing with Matilda. He's signing some sort of paperwork, scowling as always.

"*¿Qué estás haciendo,* Julián?" I never, ever use his real name, only ever his nickname because that's simply how things have been since I met him in Moonville, but it's his actual name now that gets his attention.

"*Estoy engañando a esta malvada mujer.*" I almost smile.

Matilda throws me an irritated look, Cam too, before looking at Storm as he signs the papers.

"How do you know each other?" she asks, stepping back now that she's been caught by surprise.

"Well, Mrs. Kion, your son and his boyfriend are actually two of my closest friends, and you've been fucking with one of them for too long. Now, I have signed all of these papers and so have you. The money is already being transferred into your bank account, and I am holding the deed to the ranch in my hand, which means this place now belongs to *me*, and the first thing I'm going to do is gift it to your son."

Cameron doesn't move. He doesn't say anything. He simply stares at Storm like he must be joking, but even though he's always serious, I've never seen him *that* serious.

"Well, actually, the first thing I'm going to do is throw you out of *his* house, with Cameron's permission, of course," he says and turns to Cameron, who still hasn't found his voice.

He doesn't throw out his mother, but he doesn't have to.

She makes the choice for him.

Without saying a word, she grabs her bag and jacket, then storms out of the house, not even bothering to confront any of us. Storm collects the contract he signed calmly, sliding the papers into an envelope before turning to both of us.

Cam and I haven't moved. We've simply been watching him because what the fuck just happened.

"I think we both need an explanation," I say, and Cam nods, the first sign of life he's offered in minutes.

Storm looks from Cam to me, then leans against the edge of the dining table and crosses his arms in front of his chest.

"We all pitched in. Gabriel and Valentina, Chiara and Leonard, Nevaeh and Adrian, James and Estrella, Scar and I, and Nachelle. Every single one of us gave about one million, pooled it together, and bought the ranch. Now, I had to be the one to do this whole process because your mother didn't know me and couldn't recognize me from your life in F1 because I'm not known in that world. She had no idea who I am, so there was no suspicion, and she sold it to me as soon as she saw how much I—we—offered.

"Since she wanted to sell quickly, she didn't second-guess it. She didn't look into me. Nothing at all to stop her from signing these papers, sealing the fate of the ranch. It's yours, Cam. Well, yours and Hazel's and Charlotte's. We will change the ownership to the three of you."

"I need to sit down," Cam says, but he squats down and puts his head in his hands. "Everything is spinning," he adds, and I lean down to rub his back.

"Why didn't you say anything? Why didn't any of you?" I ask a stoic Storm, who hasn't moved an inch. He's simply watching us.

"Because as long as the papers were not signed, there was a risk we couldn't pull this off, and we all agreed we didn't want to give Cameron false hope if we couldn't make this work," he explains and pushes off the table to grab my boyfriend by his arms and help him up. "I'm sorry you had to go through this, but we were working on it for a long time. None of us was ever going to allow her to take this place from you and your sisters," he says, his soft side coming to the surface. He usually reserves it for Scar, but it's clear he cares about Cam. That he wants to comfort him.

"Thank you so much." Cameron wraps his arms around Storm, who hugs him back briefly, just a quick squeeze.

"Don't thank me. This was all Valentina's idea."

Of course it was.

That woman is truly something else in the best way possible.

Tears of relief for Cameron fill my eyes, but I swallow them back when the sound of Hazel's voice fills the kitchen.

"Did it work?" she asks, covering her mouth once she's done speaking. Storm and Cam both turn to her, and more surprise fills my man's eyes.

"You were in on it?" he asks, and Charlotte appears next to her sister.

"Of course we were. Why do you think we've been avoiding you? Because we can't keep a secret from you," she says, and the relief that hits Cameron fills the whole room. He's by his sisters' sides a moment later, wrapping them in a big hug.

"I thought you were mad at me," he says, but Hazel shakes her head immediately.

"We weren't. We had to process what was happening at first, but we quickly realized none of this was your doing, Cami. It was Mum's. I'm sorry we've been so quiet with you, but you know how I get. Once I start talking to you, I don't stop," Hazel explains, but Cameron doesn't care about what happened between them before.

All he cares about is that he's not losing them. He's not losing the ranch. He's not losing anything he loves so dearly.

"*Gracias, pana,*" I tell Storm when he steps beside me.

"You can thank me by making your famous *bistec encebollado.*"

"Deal," I reply and nudge him with my shoulder.

He nudges me back, but both of our gazes are trained on Cameron and his sisters while they continue to hug. Cam keeps soaking in the waves of relief hitting him, and Hazel and Charlotte are both smiling at their big brother as he cries, letting out everything he was trying so hard to hold back.

There's so much left to discuss, so much Cam still has to figure out with his sisters, like how we're going to make sure Hazel gets to decide whether to stay with Charlotte or go with her mother to the city, but for now, he can breathe. For now, he can be relieved.

And whatever stupid feeling I have in my gut that our troubles are far from over can shut the fuck up and let us enjoy this moment.

Tomorrow, I can figure out why the more I try to silence it, the heavier the pit in my stomach gets.

CHAPTER 36

Cameron

Mum has conceded.

After the months of fighting, plotting, scheming, she has conceded. She's allowing Hazel to stay with Charlotte at the ranch while she moves into the city. My sisters have been taking care of themselves for so long, have found a routine that works for them, so they were ecstatic to hear they'd get to go back to how things were before.

My mother has been radio silent ever since, and I have no intention of trying to heal whatever has been broken in our relationship. She will never stop blaming me for what my father has done. She will never stop seeing me as the cause of all her problems. And I'm sick and tired of being her punching bag.

There are too many more important things happening in my life that I'd much rather focus on.

After her DNF in Miami, Chellie only came fifteenth in Imola and ninth in Barcelona, two race finishes that are not nearly good enough for Hawke Racing. She's been feeling down ever since, and no matter how often I try to tell her that it's not her, that there's something wrong with her car, and Cory is most certainly not offering her the best race strategies, she doesn't believe me. She blames herself. Which doesn't surprise me in the least because Hawke has a way of making you think their mistakes are your own.

The fans talking badly about you most certainly doesn't help. All of Nachelle's fears have come true, and there is nothing I can do to ease her worries.

"Come on, Cam," Halo says, pulling me back to reality and with him.

The last six weeks with him have been pure bliss. In all the chaos, he's my very own halo, shielding me from anything that can truly, irreversibly hurt me. We spend our days simply being with each other, going on dates or having them at home. At night, we lose ourselves in one another for as long as we want. I know these phases come to an end eventually, that darkness usually finds a way to seep into the light, but I'm not letting that thought taint what we have right now. We're happy, and I won't overthink and ruin that happiness with what-if scenarios.

When Halo smiles at me, it's so hard to remember any and every intrusive thought.

Today is the annual Racing Stars Football Cup hosted at the Stade Louis II Stadium here in Monaco. Every current driver, as well as former ones like me, were invited to partake in this charity match. With a bit of convincing and donating, they even allowed Halo to take part in it, and my man has been bouncing in place for the past twenty-four hours, since I told him.

"It's so nice they let you two be on a team together. It'll allow me to beat your asses more efficiently with Valentina by my side," Chellie says as she skips past us, running toward one of my favourite people in the world. She flings her arm around Val's shoulders, and the Monegasque smiles brightly at the Dominican. They're both dressed in football attire, right down to the cleats, the same outfit Halo and I are wearing, only they're clad in white and we're in black.

This is the first time since Storm bought the ranch in all of my family's names that I'm this close to Val. I tried to see her during all of the race weekends since, tried to speak to her when we were both in Monaco, but she's been so busy, we haven't had time. I haven't had the chance to thank her to her face yet.

Halo squeezes my hand and releases it, urging me to go to her. So I do. I close the distance between Val and me, wrapping her up in the biggest hug.

"I think if I'm meant to guess who it is, you have to cover my eyes because this tattoo is a dead giveaway," she says and points to the butterflies and the words "Enjoy the butterflies" engraved in my arm.

"This is a thank you, Val. I've already thanked everyone else, but not you." I kiss the side of her head, and she melts into the embrace.

"You're welcome."

From the day I met her, I knew she'd touch many lives in the best way possible. She gave Leonard a purpose in F1 after his championship-winning days were over. She offered Scarlette the chance to live her dream as a race engineer. She loves Gabriel in the way he's always longed to be loved. She protects her brother. She took Nevaeh in and befriended her when she had no one. She helped Estrella get back into a racecar when she thought she'd never be able to again.

The list goes on and on, and I doubt she'll ever stop being who she is and changing others' lives for the better.

"You're something quite remarkable, Valentina Romana," I say, but I hear a grunt of disapproval. I look up to see Gabriel frowning at me, arms crossed in front of his chest. "Bloody hell, sorry. Romana-Biancheri," I correct, and he gives a single approving nod before turning away and getting ready for the football match. I roll my eyes as Val steps out of the hug to spin around and grin at me.

"You know he hates it when people don't use my full name. Especially because he's always referred to as Gabriel Romana-Biancheri." From what he's told me, he took Val's last name because it's only fair they both have the exact same last names, that on paper it shows that he belongs to her equally as much as she belongs to him.

One day, when I finally marry, my man will have my last name and I will have his.

My eyes drift to Halo where he's standing with Adrian, Gabriel, James, and Leonard, laughing about something Adrian said.

When I marry *him*.

"Welcome, everybody, to the annual Racing Stars Football Cup," the hostess of the charity event says with a thick French accent. "Players, please start warming up so we can start the match soon," she adds, and Valentina winks at me before jogging away, joining Chellie. Gabriel looks after her, longing in his eyes. He's on my team, so I approach him.

"Let's go," he says, and we head toward the rest of our team to talk strategy.

Then, we're warming up. Halo, who watches me struggle for all of three seconds before he laughs, helps me with my form, making sure I don't make a fool of myself during the game. I'd be offended if I wasn't in such desperate need for assistance. I've seen clips of my friends during the matches in the previous years, clips of them falling, missing the ball, missing the goal by a kilometre. Because of them, I avoided taking part in this match for as long as I did, but I wanted to be with Halo today. I may fall on my face, but at least I've made him happy.

Football is definitely not my sport. The more we practise, the more Halo's hair stands in every direction from how often he's running his hands through it in frustration.

"Just pass the ball to me whenever you can, okay? I will stay close to you," he says, kissing my cheek to make sure I know he's not upset about this and also that I shouldn't feel bad about my lack of football skills.

"Sounds like a plan," I reply, and soon we're ushered to our side of the football field after they flipped a coin.

Halo nods his head in the direction he wants me to go, and I allow myself a moment to admire his trained body in that outfit. The way his shorts are hugging his thighs and butt. The way his shirt stretches across his muscular back. The way his socks are wrapped around his trained calves. He's fixed his wavy hair, all the strands sitting perfectly on his head again.

I follow him, and we stick together for the duration of the match.

It's a wonder I manage to pass the ball at all, considering how much I'm laughing, not just at myself, but at most of my fellow F1 drivers. Nachelle, Valentina, Halo, Adrian, and, for some reason, Leonard—I guess the reason being him excelling at everything he does—are doing well, but Gabriel is a mess, James is clumsy, and the rest of them are simply trying to enjoy it.

Our team does a lot of defending and not a lot of attacking. The other team is in control of the ball ninety percent of the time, and I'm stumbling my way through the match, trying to keep up with Halo. Even though he covers me most of the time so I don't make a fool of myself.

The fans are cheering in the stands as we keep running around on the field, sweating our arses off in an attempt to defend against the other team.

Halo is magnificent.

I met him long after he stopped playing football, so I never got to see him partake in a game or show off his skills, but fuck me, he's good. Whenever we're told to take a quick break while the teams switch out players, he dribbles the ball, doing some tricks with his feet that always make my jaw drop to the floor. But no matter how good he is, it doesn't make up for how bad the rest of our team is, including me.

Val and Nachelle's team beat us by far more goals than I'd care to admit, but they deserve it. They played much better than we did.

Sweaty and exhausted, I move toward where some of the fans are in the grandstands, signing the things they hold out for me.

"Cameron! Can we take a picture?" someone asks, and I move over to them. Then another fan asks, and another, and I only get pulled away when Halo reminds me that we still have to attend the dinner tonight that they've started hosting after the match.

"I hope you'll get another seat soon," a fan with a thick Spanish accent says, but I don't get a chance to reply. Not that I would know what to say.

Halo pulls me with him toward the lockers, but he pulls me down an empty corridor instead, trapping me against the wall by placing both of his hands on either side of me. I lift mine under his shirt, smiling up at him.

"Take a shower with me. Get wet and slippery with me," he says before bringing his mouth down to mine, just shy of a kiss.

"Why? So you can tease me in there like you're teasing me out here?" I challenge, leaning forward to kiss him, but he leans back before our mouths make contact.

"Yes. Let me spend the next twenty minutes teasing you." More like edging. He finally kisses me before I can answer, and my whole body loosens up as I trail my hands down his abs.

"Okay," I hear myself saying because he's so convincing, I'm not even thinking about every other person that'll be in that locker room. I'm not thinking about anything but getting his hands on me.

We break apart when my phone rings, and he pulls it out, handing it to me with a smile.

"Take it. I'll wait for you in the locker room," he says and gives me one last kiss before walking away.

My manager's name illuminates my screen, and I hit answer with my eyebrows furrowed.

"Milena? What's wrong?" She knows I have the football match today, so I'm surprised she's calling me, worried even.

"We got a good offer from one of the teams, Cameron. A really good offer," she says, and hope explodes inside of me, filling me from top to bottom.

"That's incredible! Which team is it?"

The silence that stretches between us for the five longest seconds of my life is answer enough for me.

"Hawke Racing wants you to take your seat back. They want you to replace Nachelle."

No.

Oh my God.

My knees give out, and I slide down the wall, dropping to the floor.

This is by far the worst possible seat I could have been given an offer for. I would have taken a seat in Aerodinámica, the slowest team on the grid. I would have taken any other seat, but *this one? I can't.*

Can I?

"She took it from you first, Cameron," my manager says as if she could hear the battle happening inside my chest.

"I'm going to have to call you back." I hang up without giving her a chance to say anything else.

My stomach is rolling as I drop my head in my hands and do my best to keep from throwing up everything inside of me.

What the hell am I going to do?

CHAPTER 37
Halo

Monaco is one of my favorite races of the season.

Usually, it's one of the more uneventful ones because overtaking here is a pain in the ass, so Qualifying is often seen as the more important part of the weekend, unlike the other races. But even if you do well in it, even if you get pole, you still have to bring it home. You still have to get your car through all seventy-five laps. Your strategy still has to be better than your rivals'.

Valentina got pole yesterday.

Ever since she started racing in F1, she has won every single Monaco Grand Prix. It's almost like magic the way she somehow always excels on this track. People have titled her the Queen of the Monaco Circuit, and I would tend to agree because during no other Grand Prix weekend have I ever seen her this calm, confident, and collected. She's so sure, the feelings rub off on every member of her team until we're all standing in her garage with not a single worry on our minds.

Adrian is the opposite.

He's a nervous wreck because he wants the win. He qualified second, and he finally wants to end his sister's winning streak to win his home race.

All twenty drivers are currently waiting for the warm-up lap on the track, and I'm standing with one of the mechanics on Val's team, asking her about the part we fixed earlier ahead of the race.

Our conversation is interrupted by a message lighting up my screen.

A message from Cameron.

"I'm sorry, Fio, I have to take a look at this," I say and excuse myself because for the past few days, Cam has been avoiding me. Ever since the day of the charity football match, he's been acting weird, and I tried to ask him what was wrong, if it was the phone call, but he just shook his head.

He didn't say anything.

He simply went to shower on his own, mumbling an apology and saying he's not in the right headspace, which is completely fine. He had more than just the right to change his mind about wanting to have sex then and there. I merely wish he'd have told me what was wrong.

Mi Luz: There's something I need to discuss with you later.

He didn't provide any other information, and, though this is my first time in a serious relationship, even I can tell this is *not* a good sign.

Me: What's *wrong*?

He makes me wait a full minute for his response.

Mi Luz: It's best *we* discuss this face-to-face.

Mi Luz: I'm sorry I'm being so vague, but I've been a coward these last few days, and this way you can hold me responsible and demand *we* talk about why I've been so distant.

At least he sees it, too.

Me: Okay baby

He doesn't respond again, and I don't blame him either. Whatever it is that's on his mind, it's clearly bothering him to the point where he's retreated into himself, his favorite method of avoiding his feelings when he's not ready to address them.

My mind is stuck on Cameron, going through every scenario of what he wants to discuss with me later when the cars get the go-ahead to take their formation lap.

I can't tell anymore why my heart is racing. Is it Cameron? Is it the race? Fuck if I know. All I can do is throw myself into the data I keep getting on my screen, keeping an eye on Adrian and Val's cars' performances. They've been quick all weekend, but that doesn't mean that the two Hawkes behind them won't be able to overtake them if anything as unpredictable as a red flag happens.

This year, the stewards have also added a new rule that states you have to pit twice. If you don't, you get a thirty-second penalty.

It's an attempt to make the race more interesting since a lot can go wrong in those pitstops. Cars can pit when they're in first place, and all it takes for them to lose that spot to the person behind them is a red flag or a safety car. Formula One is an unpredictable sport. Even when you think everything is said and done, there's one car that shocks everyone.

At least, that's how it has been since I was a kid.

The start goes as most people expected, as Val hoped it would. Because the distance between the first corner and the starting line is so short, Adrian doesn't have much time to gain an advantage over his sister, especially because her reaction time is much better than his. She stays in first place, but he's on her tail, keeping a short gap. James is in third, but he doesn't stick to them because he's busy fending off Nachelle.

All through the first pitstop, most of the drivers stay in the places they were in from the start of the race. Nothing changes.

Adrian pits before Val to attempt an undercut, but she has too much grip left in her tire and sets lap times that allow her to keep her first place after she comes out of the pit lane again with fresh tires.

Everything on my end looks great for both of them with only small adjustments that need to be made by Chloe and Scarlette.

My eyes keep drifting to the battle between Nachelle and James, but it's clear that my sister has been told to back off to manage her tires because she's keeping a steady gap of a little over a second to James, who is currently doing his best to chase down Adrian. A team's priority is always going to be to beat the other teams first and then to let their own drivers fight it out. The only exception is when the other teams are too far in front, then they're allowed to battle.

If I'm being honest with myself, I don't want Nachelle to fight James. Hawke already seems pissed at her, and I don't want anything to happen, accidentally or on purpose, that could make them want to kick her out.

She's a rookie who's made rookie mistakes, but they have no patience for it.

The rest of the race is as uneventful as the first half of it. There are no red flags, and the safety cars don't really impact the order of the drivers. All in all, it's one of the least exciting races we've had this year, but I'm relieved Nachelle comes in fourth. Val won yet again, and Adrian, as upset as he might be, loves his sister enough to be happy for her. And I'm glad the race didn't emotionally drain me because what happens after is so much worse.

I make my way outside with the rest of Val and Adrian's teams, with the Hawke team also here to celebrate James getting third place.

That's when I overhear two mechanics discussing something. I hear the worst *chisme*, as Mami would call it, in the entire world.

"Did you hear Cameron's been offered Nachelle's seat for the rest of the season?"

My heart drops all the way to the floor, along with my stomach and every other organ.

"Yeah, I heard the same thing, but apparently, he hasn't made a decision yet. I wonder what's taking him so long. It can't be because he's her mentor and dating her brother. No driver would put that before their career, especially a career like Cameron's, where he constantly had to prove himself and show that he belongs in the sport."

My head is spinning as everything suddenly makes sense.

Why he wants to talk to me.

Why he's been avoiding me.

Why he's been acting so fucking strange.

He's been offered Nachelle's seat and he's been keeping it secret from me for *days.*

A sense of betrayal fills me as I drown out the rest of the world, my heart racing because of how sick I suddenly feel.

Then, all I feel is anger.

CHAPTER 38

Cameron

HALO TOLD ME TO meet him at my place, and since I've given him a key a few weeks ago, I'm not surprised to see him standing against the back of my couch with his arms crossed in front of his chest. I am surprised to see his anger, though, but then it dawns on me.

"You know."

It's not a question because it's clear as day.

For days, I've been torturing myself, not knowing whether to tell him or simply turn down the offer and pretend I never got it in the first place. Because I will turn it down. I won't steal Chellie's seat from her, no matter our past. It was different when she took my seat. I wouldn't have been ready to start the season, so she took what was there to claim. What I couldn't claim myself. This? Taking that seat from her when she hasn't had any time to prove herself would be vile, and I can't do that to someone who feels like a sibling to me.

"Yeah, I fucking know." He pushes off the back of the sofa and takes a step toward me. "You know, I thought cheating would be the worst betrayal a partner could do, but this also feels pretty horrific to me, Cameron. Maybe even more so than cheating would because at least if you'd cheated, you would have only hurt me and not my sister," he says, and I bite my tongue to keep from snapping back at him because I know he's disappointed and angry.

He's lashing out because I kept this from him, and he has every right. If someone was threatening to steal one of my siblings' dreams, especially if it was Halo, I'd be furious. I'd be furious with him, and I'd be furious with myself for letting someone like that come close to me and my family.

So, I understand him. I understand him so much that I'm incapable of being angry with him for his words, no matter how much they sting.

"I'm not taking her seat," I say and lift my hands in surrender. Surprise flickers across his features, but his anger is too strong. It replaces it within a second.

"If you really aren't, why have you kept this from me for so long? Why did you risk that I'd overhear what was going on? You know how quickly rumours spread in our world," he says and points at my chest in frustration.

"Because I was scared that no matter what I said or how I told you, we'd end up here, in this position where you had to fight between wanting what's best for your sister, protecting her, and also wanting me to have the one thing I've been fighting for, for months. The reason why I've started seeing Munira. The reason I was so relieved when I could use my hands without pain again. The reason I've been training as hard as I have."

Halo looks at me as if I'd slapped him in the face. In all of his anger, he hadn't considered my side of it, but now that I've pointed it out to him, his face falls in defeat. If I'd told him, he would have immediately had this battle. This sense of betrayal he has from overhearing about my contract offer from someone else shielded him from this internal battle.

"Is that really why you kept it from me? Or were you hoping I'd hear it from someone else because things have gotten too real for you and the thing you're actually terrified of is giving your heart to me? Putting that trust in me after Elijah broke it?" he asks, crossing his arms in front of his chest again to close himself off from me.

"That's not fair," I mumble, but I can't deny it either because maybe there's some truth to that. Even though I wanted to protect us from pain, maybe I was expecting this pain to find us anyway, and I wanted it to happen sooner rather than later.

Because later, I'd be even more attached than I already am.

"Why?" Halo challenges, his blue eyes filling with tears when mine do the same.

"I texted you that I needed to discuss something with you. It was this. I wanted to tell you today," I defend, but he shakes his head at me.

"Today is five days after you found out about the offer. Five. Days. You've been hiding this from me for five days by *avoiding* me. How do you think that made me feel, Cam? You went into hiding again, only this time you were right in front of my face. Then I find out about you not telling me about the seat. What the hell am I supposed to think?"

He takes a step back and runs his hands through his hair.

"Did you honestly, with all of that in mind, expect me to think you weren't taking that offer? Did you honestly think I wouldn't feel so betrayed? This is my sister we're talking about. I'd kill to protect her from pain."

I step toward him, but he puts his hands up, puts up his boundaries, so I stop approaching him. The rejection stings, but not as much as the guilt currently camping inside my chest.

"I'm sorry," I say as a tear drops down. "I should have told you immediately because you're right. This doesn't only affect me, and I should have discussed it with you. But you also can't tell me that no matter what scenario or how I would have told you, you would have believed me if I said I wouldn't take the offer."

"Well, now we'll never know, will we? You made that decision for me, and I never get to prove otherwise to you," he says, going back to the couch to lean against it again. He drops his face in his hands, then runs them through his hair. I notice how red the white of his eyes has gotten from his unshed tears, which makes another of mine drip down.

"I needed a second to be ready to give up my dream. Can you at least understand that?"

He studies me for a long moment, but I can see he's still hurting. I can see no matter what I say now, he's right. I waited too long. I was a coward for too long.

"If you'd come to me, if you'd trusted that my feelings for you would be strong enough, I'd have told you that we should talk to Nachelle. She was scared this would happen in some form or another since the beginning of the season, but she would have also understood because it's so similar to what they did to you. She may have even given you her approval, but again, you didn't give either of us the opportunity to talk this through. You retreated into yourself and made a decision you thought was best for everyone. Tell me if I'm wrong, but I thought being in a romantic relationship with someone meant that big life decisions like those are discussed together, or am I simply a stop along the way, Cameron? Does it not matter what I think of your future and the opportunities you are given?" he asks, and a wave of panic hits me so hard, I almost bend over at the waist.

"Asher, you're not a stop along the way. You are the destination. You are the finish line, the very thing I'm racing toward with everything I've got." More tears fall down his face, and this time when I approach him, he places his hands on my hips, which I take as permission to place mine on his cheeks. "You are the high I feel after winning a race. The calm I feel after everything quiets down again. Your opinion matters to me, but having an opinion on this that doesn't hurt either Chellie or me is impossible," I say, and his fingers dig into my hips, just shy of painful.

"I don't care. You should have told me. I shouldn't have overheard it from someone else who just wanted to spread gossip." His voice is so soft, so full of the pain and betrayal he feels, I'm not even surprised when he gets up and walks away from me, into my kitchen.

"You're right. I should have. I'm so sorry that I didn't," I say as I follow him.

"But I understand your side too, Cam. And now I'm just fucking confused because I'm angry, but I don't want to be angry. You've been through so much, so of course getting offered that seat isn't something you can easily turn down. Or even if you could, how were you supposed to tell me when this is about my sister? I'm so mad at you for keeping this from me for so long," he explains, and his frustration fills the room. "I don't know how to deal with any of this."

He fills a glass with water, then takes a long sip.

"The question is, will you ever be able to forgive me, or was this too much of a betrayal of trust?" If he can't forgive me, if everything is ruined, it will be my fault.

I will be the one to have caused all this pain, not him. It'll be on me. I'll have broken both our hearts.

His eyes lift to meet mine, and a moment of complete silence passes between us. My heart is in my throat, its fearful pounding so loud, it rings in my ears. Halo looks so torn, I've never seen him this bent out of shape, and I wish I could hide the frown on my face, hide the guilt and pain, but I've always been more on the emotional side.

"How does this work? Am I allowed to leave and take a couple days to sort through my feelings, or does that mean we're broken up? Because I don't want to break up, I just need a moment."

"You can take all the moments you need. Partners fight. They go their separate ways for a few days to cool off. That doesn't mean we have to break up," I promise him, and he nods, clearly relieved.

"Okay. Okay, I think I need some time then. This is all too fresh, and I need to sort out my feelings," he explains, and he walks around my kitchen island to place his hands on my cheeks. My heart hurts because he's still wearing the perfume I make him. He smells like me. "I'll be back."

He seals that promise with a kiss, but it's so brief, so very reserved, I'm scared that even when he comes back, it'll be to tell me we're over.

Leonard, James, Adrian, and Gabriel haven't asked me why I requested all of them to meet me for a beer and a round of cards. They simply appeared at Gabriel's house and have been talking about everything and nothing for the past hour.

It's only when Gabriel gives me *that* look, the one that says, "Come on, mate, I know you want to tell us what happened," that I finally tell them everything from start to finish. I tell them about the seat at Hawke Racing, which they have apparently all heard about already, and then I admit to them that I didn't open up to Halo about what was going on. Adrian is the only one with a visceral reaction, grimacing at me in a way that shows his disapproval.

"Oh, mate, you fucked up royally," he says once I'm done talking, and I almost appreciate the way he doesn't sugarcoat it the way I know Gabriel or James would.

"Yeah, I know," I reply.

"Like truly fucked up. I didn't use to be an expert on love, but even I knew open communication about what you're feeling and all the happenings in your life was the most important thing to earn and keep trust."

"Respectfully, Adrian, put a bloody sock in it. You're not helping," Leonard says, making his jaw drop to the floor. He's never, ever spoken to Adrian like that, which is why I almost burst into laughter at the sheer shock this table feels in response.

"Actually, Adrian's right. There's no point denying it. I fucked up. And I may have just ruined the best thing to have ever happened to me."

"Nonsense. You made a mistake. If he loves you, truly loves you, he'll want to work this out. Considering he so desperately wanted to make sure he could take some time without you thinking he wants to break up shows that he wants to be with you. He merely needs a bit of time to understand his feelings," Leonard says as he regards the hand Gabriel has just dealt.

"Couples fight all the time. Only yesterday, Estrella and I had a huge disagreement over where we wanted to go on vacation," James chimes in, and I look his way to see he's offering me a comforting smile.

"How did that fight end?" Adrian asks with a grin because he knows how in love James is with his wife. He knows he's wrapped around her finger.

"It ended with me telling her we'll go to both places, then apologising for starting the argument...with my mouth," he says as he considers Adrian, then shifts his gaze to me.

"Maybe you can make it up to Halo that way as well," he suggests, and even though I let out a breathless laugh, I shake my head.

"Not sure he wants that or anything else from me right now," I reply, picking up my own cards. Leonard, who is sitting beside me, places a comforting hand on my shoulder.

"Don't worry, Cameron. Everything will work out the way it is meant to, and I don't only mean you and Halo. I also mean your future in F1. Hawke lost their chance with you, but that doesn't mean one of the other teams doesn't want you." He squeezes my shoulder once, then goes back to his cards.

"I hope you're right."

But for now, I soak in my family's comfort, soak in the sounds of their laughter, until my heart feels a little lighter.

CHAPTER 39

Halo

It's been twenty-four hours.

Twenty-four hours of misery.

I didn't sleep a wink last night, and Nachelle has spent all day trying to get me to open up about what's bothering me, but I can't. I can't tell her what's wrong. If I tell her what's wrong, then I'll have to tell her what happened. I'd have to tell her Hawke is looking to get rid of her.

"Scarlette," Nachelle says while the four of us—Scarlette, Storm, Nachelle and I—are sitting in a circle crocheting. My sister invited the two of them over when she realized she needed back-up to get me to open up, but neither of them has tried to make me talk yet. "Beautiful Scarlette," Nachelle adds, buttering her up. Being the sunshine of a person Scar is, she smiles brightly at my sister's way of addressing her. Storm, on the other hand, glowers at Nachelle. "Could you please make Halo open his mouth? I hate it when he gives me the silent treatment," she says to my best friend.

Scar turns to me, tilting her chin down to look up at me and blink rapidly.

"No," I say because I know what she wants.

"Just talk, Halo. We all know you want to, and we're here to listen," Storm chimes in, and I look up at him to see his two differently-colored eyes scanning my face.

"Since when are you keen on hearing me talk?" I ask, holding my crochet needles tightly in my hand while I follow the pattern I downloaded for Toothless's head. It's the last part of him before I'm finally done and can give it to Cam.

"Since I can see how badly you need to get whatever is bothering you off your chest," he says, and for once, he actually stops scowling to offer me the tiniest sliver of a smile.

My attention shifts to Nachelle, who is watching me closely, eager for me to open up.

I do so with a heavy heart.

"Cameron was offered your seat at Hawke for the rest of the season, and he kept that information from me. I only found out because I overheard some mechanics talking about it, and we had a huge fight after, one where I walked out because I needed some time," I explain, never looking away from Nachelle so I can see how she feels about everything I've just said.

She furrows her brows and pulls her legs under her butt on the couch, staring down at the space between us. Her eyes dart from left to right as she processes the information, then she brings her gaze to mine to show me the tears in her eyes. Her chest rises and falls more quickly, and I put down my needles to grab her hand in mine.

"They want to get rid of me?" she asks, and I bite down on my bottom lip to keep from answering because she knows. It's not a question that needs answering. "But it's only been eight races, and I did well. Mostly," she defends, fighting back her tears to keep them from dropping.

In my peripheral, I see Scar covering her mouth, and Storm putting his hand on her knee.

"Fucking Hawke," she mumbles and rubs her hands over her face, letting out a breathless laugh. "Wait, you're not seriously upset with Cameron for this, are you?" my sister asks, grabbing my arm a little harder than necessary.

"Aren't you? He was offered your seat, and he hasn't said a single thing to you," I reply, but Nachelle leans away from me and shakes her head.

"He's not taking it," she says, so sure of her words, there is no room to make her believe the opposite.

"How do you know that?" I ask. Her brown eyes meet mine.

"Because I know Cameron. I know who he is deep inside, and he would never take it, not even if I told him he could. It may be his dream to get back into F1, and it may have taken him a few days to come to the conclusion I'm so certain of, but I knew that's where we'd end up. Because I know *him*," she explains, making me feel like the biggest fucking idiot.

"You're right. He told me he isn't taking it," I admit, and she nods repeatedly.

"Damn fool, that man," Storm mumbles, and Nachelle and I both turn our heads in time to see Scar swat his arm.

"Don't say that," she says, but he merely shrugs.

"Either way, they're planning to get rid of Nachelle, and even if he doesn't sign the contract, they'll continue to get rid of her. The best plan isn't to find a way for Nachelle to keep the seat, it's to find her a new one at a different team. Then, while Cameron gets the Hawke one, he can continue looking for a different one too."

My sister looks impressed by Storm's evil mastermind-level plan, but I'm not so convinced that's the right path. It would be an ideal outcome, but it would never unfold that way. Not with only nineteen other seats available in Formula One, and several of them already having been taken. Plus, a lot of the teams that *are* available to sign a new driver for next season have already either given Cameron a contract with a shit deal or no contract at all.

"Let's put a pin in that because I don't hate the idea, but most importantly, Halo—" My sister cuts off to turn to me and grab me by the shoulders. "I love you. You're an amazing older brother who always looks out for me, and I understand your frustration with Cameron for not opening up about the offer, but you can't forget people need time to say no to something as big as that. They need to be uninfluenced by someone like you who's so close to the situation. To top it all off, he didn't want to burden you with this information, and most likely, he wasn't even allowed to talk about the offer. So, stop being an idiot and go get your man," Nachelle says, but I lean away, my back touching the armrest of the couch.

"It's not so simple," I reply, tilting my head back to stare at the ceiling.

"Why not?" Scar asks, her voice soft and gentle.

"Yeah, why the fuck not?" Nachelle adds, her voice much less soft and gentle.

"Because he isn't just my boyfriend who didn't talk to me about a big life decision. He's also my friend who disappeared once already, and this felt a lot like it, him distancing himself when things got tough," I explain, but I can hear how irrational that argument sounds from miles away. It's not the same situation, and I can't compare them.

"Do you love him?" Scar asks, and I close my eyes. I haven't admitted this out loud, and no part of me is planning to tell anyone else before I tell Cameron how I feel.

"Of course he does. That's why he's so upset. He loves him, and he's scared Cameron doesn't love him in the same way. It's why him not confiding in Halo is hitting him so hard, because Halo would have confided in Cam if it was the other way around," Storm says, and I look at him, almost falling off the sofa, because who the hell is this man and what has he done to the true Julián "Storm" Alvarez?

Storm is right. Everyone in this fucking room is right about my fears and my commitment issues and everything else keeping me from going to Cameron right now.

This is such a dumb fight. If I were a better person, I'd have understood him immediately. I would have stopped being angry the second he said he's not taking Nachelle's seat, but Storm is right. I'm terrified Cam doesn't love me as much as I love him, doesn't love me period, and the mere possibility of that has me wanting to run as far away from him as possible.

"Relationships are so hard," I mumble, rubbing my temples with both my index fingers.

"Sometimes, other times they're as easy as breathing," Nachelle says, a faraway look entering her eyes.

"And just how would you know that? You've never been in a relationship that lasted longer than five minutes," I say, but my sister simply shrugs.

"Not because I don't want to be. The women I've been with simply have never understood my lifestyle. Or they wanted me to make them famous, which I only did one time," she says with a grin, but I know my sister. I know she's looking for love in a way I never did, and all she's ever gotten in return was... nothing.

Love can be cruel like that.

But it hasn't been to me. It's been kind. It has somehow infected the man I was in love with for years, convinced him loving me was a good idea, and I'm not about to throw that away.

He didn't betray me. I know that now. He didn't break any trust. He simply needed time to process yet another curveball life threw at him, and instead of giving him the space to do so, I pushed him away. I made him think he was responsible for the shit Hawke was pulling.

I stare down at the almost finished crochet Toothless and pick up my crocheting needles to add the finishing touches. Scar, Storm, and Nachelle are all looking at me, I feel their gazes burning my skin, but I have no time to waste.

Once I'm done, I jump off the couch, placing a single kiss on Nachelle's head, before grabbing my jacket, keys, and shoes.

Then, I make my way to the man I love, hoping he won't hate me for asking for time to process this.

Hoping that when I tell him I love him, he will say it back.

Chapter 40

Cameron

"Anything trigger you recently?" Munira asks, scrolling through the videos on her tablet.

"Nothing at all. I haven't had a panic attack either, which is a relief," I say, and she looks up at me, narrowing her eyes like she doesn't quite believe me, but once she sees the sincerity in my expression, she raises her eyebrows in surprise.

"None?"

"None," I affirm, my voice as monotone as it's been all day.

We started our session a few minutes ago, simply catching up on how I've been doing. Part of me considered cancelling our session today because I didn't feel mentally prepared to watch another clip of a crash and potentially have a panic attack, even if that hasn't happened in the last two sessions we've had. But with the way I'm feeling about Halo and our whole situation, I'm a lot more susceptible to a panic attack than I was when we were happy.

"Do you think you'd be ready to take a look at your own crash today then? You've been making a lot of progress, but this decision is still up to you," she says and watches my reaction in the way she always does when we're about to take another step in my mental health journey.

"I don't think I'll ever be ready, but I would like to try," I say because it's the most truthful answer I could give her.

Munira considers me, then goes back to scrolling through the files.

A wave of anxiety hits me because of what we're about to do, what I'm about to see. No matter how hard I've tried to remember, there is still a black hole in my memories where the crash should be. Nothing we've done has brought it back yet, and I'm scared to see what actually happened. At least once I do, I can stop coming up with every single scenario, every single possibility, and stop breaking my head over the what-ifs. I can find peace in knowing exactly what happened, which is the only thing encouraging me that this is the right decision.

Part of me wishes Halo could be here to hold my hand through it, but I know there are simply some things in life one has to do on their own.

This is one of them.

"Ready?" she asks, and all I manage to do in return is nod.

She flips her tablet around, pressing play so I can see the video. My heart stops beating.

It's raining on the screen. At the point of my crash, it was falling at a much slower pace and the track was far drier than it had been on previous laps, but it was so fucking slippery anyway. I was battling James. I almost had him right before I crashed, I remember that.

But what I don't remember is how close I got to him.

I don't remember my rear tyre touching his front wing because I slipped on the track.

I don't remember getting a puncture.

Something deep down inside me remembers what happens next, though. The way it felt to fly and then hit the barriers at such high speed, I'm lucky to be alive.

The closer I look, the more I realise what saved me.

What protected me from certain death.

I'm alive because of my halo. Because of the addition they made to the car years ago.

I was saved by my halo.

"Oh my God," I whisper to myself when the clip continues, images of my car upside down, hanging half in the barrier, filling the screen.

The clip replays in slow motion this time.

Maybe I was passed out, maybe I was conscious, I still can't recall, but I was dangling there for a very long time. The marshals ran to get to me. They were working as quickly as they could to get me out of the car, out of the horrible position I was in, but it took time. It took so long, I'm swallowing hard because I can see myself now. I see myself unconscious, hanging there in the car while marshals and now paramedics went to check on me, but I was unresponsive.

No part of me moved.

When they lifted me out of the car, I was a lifeless body.

Fear takes over every part of me.

The clip continues up until they carry me into the ambulance, then the screen freezes, but I don't move. I'm spiraling down the dark tunnel, trying to find my memories, trying to reach the light, and this time, I do.

I remember the scent of rubber. I remember my fuel tank leaking onto me. I remember the pain in my hands, the sheer agony I was in.

All of it comes back to me.

Every sensation.

Every emotion.

Every single piece of the crash.

My skin lights on fire before sweat collects at my nape. Everything starts to spin, and so does my stomach, until I feel so sick, I have to cover my mouth. I barely register Munira holding out a trash can for me, barely manage to grab it before I'm throwing up everything inside me, which isn't a lot since I haven't been eating.

It's as if my body is rejecting the memories because it's spent so long repressing them to protect myself. But there is no more hiding.

Panic has its claws sunken into me, and I try to stop my spinning ahead, but it's useless. My panic attack keeps pulling me deeper as I recall every little detail about that day. The way it felt to be in the air right before the impact. The fear and dread I carried in my chest moments before my hands were crushed and my lung was punctured. The fans gasping. My engine shrieking. My seatbelt pushing against my racing suit, trapping me. The fucking pain.

I spiral further and further down my panic attack, unable to stop it.

"It's okay. Don't fight it. You have to go through it," Munira says, her voice distant.

So, I do.

I allow myself to fall as far as possible, until there is no further to go. My memories overwhelm me, and the pain I felt that day seems just as horrible as it felt back then, my hands pulsing and aching from phantom pain.

The only way out is through.

Eventually, once the events of the past go back to the corner of my mind where they belong, my head finally stops spinning. The nausea subsides. The panic attack slowly eases away, and I put the trash can on the floor, letting out a *hmpf* because I need a toothbrush and I need it as soon as possible.

I should probably be embarrassed because of what just happened and because I did it in front of Munira, but all I feel is free. Relieved.

She doesn't rush me to find the ground beneath my feet again. Doesn't rush me to sort through how I'm feeling. We simply sit here in silence as I come to terms with the fact that yes, I crashed. Yes, I would have lost my life if it wasn't for my halo. Yes, that was a terrifying crash. But I *am* alive. I've recovered. My hands are fine. My breathing doesn't pain me anymore.

What happened that day on the track is going to stay with me for the rest of my life, but it's no longer going to haunt me the way it did. I won't have to spiral down *that* dark tunnel anymore because now I know.

I remember.

"Thank you," is the first thing that comes out of my mouth when I'm ready to speak.

"For what?" Munira asks softly.

"For helping me. For being patient with me for the past couple of months. For everything," I explain, but she smiles at me, tilting her head to the side a little.

"They do pay me to, you know?" I let out a laugh, making her smile even harder.

"Yeah, I guess you're right, but still...thank you."

"You're very welcome." Munira stands up and walks to the desk situated behind her, opening one of the drawers and pulling out a new toothbrush and a tube of toothpaste.

"Here," she says and hands both to me.

"You are an absolute treasure," I say and take them. "I'll be right back," I add with a laugh, earning another smile from Munira.

"Take your time. I'll be here."

After my session with Munira, I go to my favourite café to grab a coffee and something to fill my empty stomach with. My apartment is near an overlooking point of the sea, so I settle down on a bench with my drink and food, watching the water move. The yachts in the harbour. The people walking on the beach.

This is one of my favourite spots in Monaco because of how quiet it is. When silence is as rare as it is in the life of a Formula One driver, a person constantly surrounded by their teams, fans, family, strangers, and more people, you seek it out as much as you can. And silence is exactly what I need at the moment.

Well, silence with Halo. That's what I need, but as long as he needs time to figure out his feelings, I'll keep from messaging him. From telling him how much I miss him, even though it's only been twenty-four bloody hours. From sharing what happened during my session today.

Instead, I simply sip my coffee and take a bite of my sandwich.

Milena, my manager, was not happy when I told her I didn't want to sign the contract, but she's gone back to inquiring if there is another seat available for me to take. I knew it was the right decision, but I'm not hopeful that I'll be able to get back into F1. *Ever.*

Maybe it was never my destiny, or whatever people believe in, to win a championship. Maybe I was always meant to be the one to come second, third, fourth, or wherever I landed. Maybe I simply wasn't good enough. Not everyone deserves a seat in Formula One. That's common knowledge. You have to earn your spot. Some drivers, like Nachelle, Val, and Leonard, had to do more than just earn it. They had to fight a world of discrimination that I didn't have to go through because I only came out to the world after I got a seat.

So, no, F1 isn't fair. Some drivers have bought their way into the sport. Others have made a million mistakes and get to keep it. And a few of them don't even want to be in the sport anymore but their teams and families make them think it's the best decision to stay. I know Kyle Hughes from Grenzenlos is one of those few.

Every driver has a different story, a different mark they leave on our sport.

I've left mine, and if my happy smile and fight for equality of queer people is the only thing I leave behind, then that's okay for me.

Once I finish my coffee and sandwich, I do my best to find the strength to get up and leave this safe place. I have a million things I have to do today, and Charlotte and Hazel are waiting for me to call them, too, but I'm stuck on this bench.

Stuck in my head.

And because it's not in a bad way, because I'm not spiralling but simply enjoying being by myself, I allow myself to linger.

I haven't felt this good about myself in months, and that's with the guilt still nesting inside of me because of keeping the offer of the Hawke seat from Halo and Nachelle.

Calling Chellie is another thing I have to do today. I want to explain, and hope, once she hears my apology, she'll forgive me for keeping this from her. Once she hears it was never my intention to get an offer from Hawke, that I never would have taken it, that I didn't betray her as a friend or a mentor, she may not even be angry.

Fuck, at this point I don't know if I'm lying to myself or being realistic.

A sigh slips past my lips as I stand up, taking one more look at the sea before turning.

My heart stops beating at the sight of him.

He looks like he's gotten the same amount of sleep I have: none. His blue eyes are filled with the kind of agony and yearning I feel deep inside of me, and my shoulders drop in relief when I see the tulips resting in his hand.

"My Halo," I say, taking a step toward him.

"*Mi luz*," he replies, not moving a centimetre.

That's okay. We have a lot to talk about, and I have all the time in the world to fight for the man I love.

CHAPTER 41
Halo

FROM THE MOMENT I met Cameron, I felt a pull toward him. Stronger than anything I have ever felt with a person. It's almost as if a part of me, my soul perhaps, tethered itself to his, and it has stayed there all this time. Through the years of friendship. While he was in love with another man and very much ready to spend the rest of his life with him. And as much as I thought he'd never be with me, never want anything of the sort with me, here he is. Standing across from me with his heart in his eyes. The heart that belongs to me.

Mine aches for him.

For the friend I could always go to for anything, who protected me and defended me even when I was in the wrong.

For the person who let me teach him about my culture, the part of me I always felt so disconnected from.

For the man who taught me how good it feels to be in love.

He stopped moving toward me when he realized I wasn't closing the distance between us, and there's uncertainty in his features now. At first, after he spotted me and the tulips, he looked so hopeful, but there's something in my face that made him hesitate. He's giving me the distance I don't want, the distance I asked for when I was overwhelmed, and I don't know why I'm not opening my mouth to tell him everything's alright.

That's all I want to tell him.

I open my mouth, but it falls shut again, my feelings wrapping around my throat and squeezing.

But when I spot the fear inside him reflected in his eyes, the grip loosens again, and the words fall from my lips with the utmost ease.

"I love you, Cameron."

He takes a step back, clearly surprised.

"No one has ever made me feel the way you do, *mi luz*. You've caught me from endlessly spiraling through this life on my own, looking for the other part of my soul. I thought I was meant to be alone to protect myself, I thought I was supposed to walk through this existence alone. But I'd much rather spend it being in love with you. Taking care of you. Being there for you. Getting loved by you in turn." I close the distance between us, placing the tulips and my bag on the bench to the left of us to grab his face in both of my hands. His eyes flutter shut and he tilts his head to the side, leaning into my touch.

"I'm so sorry I was so angry, that I asked for distance. It was so stupid because I didn't want to be apart from you. I just wanted to understand how I was feeling, and I realized I should have been there for you instead. This was a shit position you were thrown in, and I made it ten times worse by blaming you for needing time. I'm so sorry," I say, but Cam shakes his head, lifting his fingers to snake them around my wrists.

"No, I should have been better at communicating what was going on because you're right. This didn't just affect you and me. It affected Chellie too, and we both love her and want the best for her. So, I should have told you as soon as it happened. I should have listened to your opinion. I shouldn't have hidden this, and I'm sorry I did, Asher." I drop my forehead to his, leaning down to do so, and he meets me halfway, his grip on me tightening.

"Please believe me when I say I never, ever wanted to hurt you or betray you," he begs, and I bite down on my bottom lip, chewing on it.

"I believe you." His shoulders fall in relief, and I feel the tension slipping out of my body in turn. "I'm sorry about comparing this to the thing we're both most afraid of," I add, but he shakes his head, his nose brushing against mine with the action.

"Don't be. Without any context from me, having to overhear it from strangers, how does it not compare? Trust is such a fragile thing for people like us, and any threat to it, no matter how big or small, is easily seen as the very tool to break that trust. I don't fault you for that."

We fall into a brief silence after that because he's right. Trust is fragile for us. I doubt it's going to change anytime soon, but what will change is both of us realizing that putting trust in each other isn't a mistake. It isn't going to lead to the pain our mothers felt, the one Cam felt after Elijah. Not to mention, we seem to be pretty good at this communication thing when both of us are ready to talk about what is bothering us. We're fighting for each other, and it's the best feeling in the world to have someone put as much effort into a relationship with you as you're putting into your relationship with them.

"Is this how all fights go? You take a day to cool off and then come back to each other to apologize?" I ask, but Cameron lets out a watery laugh, clearly fighting his tears.

"No. Sometimes, it's way worse. Some people even break up for a little before they find their way back to each other," he replies, and I furrow my brows.

"But I didn't want that. I wanted some time for myself, but I always knew I wanted to come back to you. I'll always come back to you because it's you, Cam," I say, my thumbs rubbing over his defined cheekbones. "It's always been you."

"It's always been you for me, too, Halo, even when I was too oblivious to see it. Even when you were right in front of me." I let out a little chuckle because he *was* oblivious. Then again, I was in denial, so I guess fair's fair.

"I'm glad we got our first fight out of the way, though, because if this is how all of them go, I'm ready for whatever the world throws at us," he says, stepping on his tiptoes a little to bring his mouth to mine.

It's a kiss of forgiveness. A kiss of reassurance. A kiss of belonging.

It's the kiss to end all kisses, pure desperation, desire, and love woven into it.

When Cameron's lips meet mine, I forget the fact that I bared my heart and he hasn't said anything in return because he's showing me. He's letting me taste his feelings as he slips his tongue into my mouth. But even though I can hear them as loudly as words this way, he still pulls back to tell me the one thing I wanted to hear most.

"I'm in love with you, my Halo." He kisses me briefly, then goes on. "You saved me in every way I needed to be saved. You taught me that it's okay to be scared of letting you in because you're you, and you've given me a safe place to love, to be myself, to explore parts of me I never have before. With you, I'm never scared I'll turn around and catch you breaking my heart in the same way it has before because I know who you are deep inside. I know what it means for you to even put *your* trust in *me,* and I've never wanted to be so worthy of someone's heart than I do of yours."

No part of me knows how to react to his words. Turns out, telling Cameron I'm in love with him was far easier than hearing he loves me back. Even if it's exactly what I was hoping for. Even if hearing it fills my heart with so much joy, it feels like it's going to burst any second.

I've never been loved like this. Maybe that's why I'm having a hard time believing it to be true, letting it settle inside of me as a truth, not of something I thought was an impossibility.

"I think I'm going to need to hear you tell me you love me several more times before it sinks in fully," I admit, letting out a breathless laugh when he starts smiling his famous smile at me. The one that's as bright as a light, illuminating the dark with its rays.

"I'll say it as often as you need me to. I'll write it on your skin so you can look at it whenever you doubt my feelings. I'll kiss you until you believe it with your whole heart, my handsome man." I let him finish speaking before dipping my head again to put my lips on his.

Neither one of us breaks it for a long time. We can't. We've missed each other, missed how the other person tastes, for almost a week now. We've said all there was to be said, and I'm finding that no words of reassurance compare to this kiss. To the way he *shows* me that we're going to be alright now, that one single fight isn't enough to break us apart. I know people wouldn't understand why I'm almost glad this happened, but I am. I'm glad I know we can be upset with each other for a day without it causing our relationship to fall apart. I'm glad I know that we can talk through these things. I'm glad things happened the way they did because now I feel even closer to him than I did before.

So, I kiss him harder. Longer. Slipping my tongue back inside his mouth to taste him. To taste something that is purely Cameron mixed with the coffee he must have been drinking before. He groans, and I damn near whimper when his hands slide under my shirt, trailing over my lower abdomen, then tracing the waistband of my pants.

I suck in a sharp breath as my body tenses. Cameron, knowing my body inside out, steps into me, kissing me harder as he pushes his hard body against me.

"A kiss is all it takes to get you this worked up, baby?" he asks, his hand slipping into my hair before he tugs on the strands, making me grit my teeth.

"Only when it's you kissing me," I reply, my grip on his neck tightening as I use every bit of self-control not to go back to kissing him. Because if I do, I won't stop, not until we both get what we need, and even if there isn't a single person in sight, this is hardly the place to do that. "Take me back to your place," I whisper, my lips a mere inch from his.

"To do what?" he teases, smiling like he knows exactly what I'm going to do with him but he wants me to say it out loud.

"To catch up on the week we haven't really seen each other. To strip you naked and lick every inch of your body until you're quivering and begging me to give you what you need. To sink so deep inside you, you'll know how every inch of me feels about you," I say, and he bites down on his bottom lip, letting out the sweetest *hmmm* sound I've ever heard.

"We better hurry home then," he says as his fingers slip through mine. He attempts to walk away but I pull him back to me, placing my forehead against his one last time.

"Tell me again." Cam needs no elaboration.

"I love you." I smile from ear to ear.

"Again."

"I love you, my Halo."

My grin is bright and happy, and I hand him the tulips and pull what I've crochet for him out of my bag to hand him both.

"Did you make this?" he asks, studying the little figure.

"Maybe," I say and blush, but he smiles so brightly as tears fill his eyes again that I go straight back to kissing him.

"Thank you," he mumbles against my lips, but I simply keep kissing him.

Until we're both perfectly out of breath.

CHAPTER 42

Cameron

The Canadian, Austrian, and British Grands Prix have passed since Halo found out about my offer from Hawke. In those three races, Nachelle has proven to the team that replacing her is by far the most foolish thing they could do because she scored third, second, and third again. She's been performing so well, I haven't heard anything from any team, no gossip, that they're trying to find another driver to replace her.

None since me.

Chellie has shown nothing but confidence since finding out about their plans, the ones they were making behind her back, and I couldn't be prouder of her for knowing her worth. For showing them. Because even if they do replace her, she's made her mark. She's shown what she's capable of, and the other teams have taken note.

They won't forget her name, ever.

I haven't gotten any offers since then from any other teams, but a strange sort of peace has filled my chest over the past seven weeks. A peace I found after my session with Munira, where I remembered my crash. We've had several more since then, and every time we do more Exposure Therapy, the better I feel.

And when I look at Halo, I'm happy.

He's busy working right now, and I just wished Nachelle luck for Qualifying, so I'm standing there like an idiot, doing absolutely nothing. There is no times being set yet, and I most certainly don't feel like talking to fucking Cory, who looks like the stick up his arse is bothering him more than usually today.

Dickhead.

My phone vibrates, pulling me out of my thoughts and back into reality. As soon as I see Leonard's name on the screen, I furrow my brows while picking up his call.

"Hey, mate. What's going on?" I ask, but he gives me the most cryptic answer.

"Grenzenlos motorhome. Two minutes. Don't be late." He hangs up without saying another word.

"A text message would have sufficed, you grumpy old man," I mumble to my phone, even if he can't hear me anymore.

This is not the first time in the duration of our friendship that he's demanded my presence. Usually, it's to discuss something relating to an event he's hosting about things I know more about or to ask me for advice on which charity he should support next. Once, he even asked me to help him with something regarding his and Val's academy.

So, I get my arse to the Grenzenlos motorhome where Leonard is already waiting outside for me. He's dressed in the light blue shirt of the Grenzenlos team, the colour perfectly complementing his dark, tattooed skin. His short curls have grown out a little since the last time I saw him a few weeks ago, and he's got a bit of a stubble going on that makes him even more handsome than he already is. It should be criminal to be this effortlessly attractive, especially while he's scowling like it's been raining for seven months without end.

"Hi," I say with a grin, but he merely tilts his head to gesture for me to follow him. "So secretive today," I mumble with a laugh.

He doesn't respond, but I see his shoulders shake as if he was chuckling, which can't be. I've tried to make him laugh many times, but it's like he's reserved them all for Chiara and his children—and yes, I'm including Adrian when I say his children.

Once we're in what appears to be a makeshift office for him this weekend, he pats the back of the chair on one side of the desk, then takes the seat on the other. For a long moment, he merely sits there, one hand by his lip as he squeezes his bottom one, considering me. I narrow my eyes, but the smile on my lips gives away how amused I am.

"Are you ready?" he asks, and I tilt my head, confused.

"Ready for what?" Another little laugh leaves me, but he's as stoic as always.

"To get back in the car." My smile falls. Even more confusion fills me from top to bottom, but this time, I'm unable to speak because of how perplexed I am.

"I'm not following, Leonard. What are you saying?"

"Well, I'm not saying anything. I'm asking you a question. Are you ready to get back in the car?" he asks, his voice so firm and steady, I'm no longer hesitating.

No longer incapable of answering.

"Yes. I'm ready to get back in the car." Leonard nods as he looks down, scanning the papers in front of him before sliding them across the desk toward me.

"Good because I'd like you to take over for Kyle during some of the free practise sessions that remain for the rest of the season," he explains, and a wave of disappointment hits me, one that doesn't last very long because his next words bring back so much hope, it nearly knocks me out of the chair. "Initially, I was going to give him the chance to sign again for next year, but he's decided to retire. Since I'm not the kind of person to throw a driver out before they're ready or before they have a contract with another team, I couldn't offer the second seat at Grenzenlos to you before. Now I can."

He picks up a pen and uses it to point at the paperwork he handed me, something I've now realised is a contract for next year. A contract for the second Grenzenlos seat. A contract to get back into F1 the way I've wanted to come back this entire time.

Leonard is a great team principal. His unwillingness to kick Kyle out of the team shows that. He waited for him to be ready, and now that he is, he's giving me the seat. No one else.

"Why didn't you go through my manager to give me this offer?" I ask, but Leonard leans back in his chair to give me the tiniest sliver of a smile.

"Because you're family, and I wanted to watch you bawl your eyes out when I told you you could race for me, if that's what you wanted," he says, and I burst into laughter, but that laugh only brings back the tears.

"Gabriel will be my teammate?" I ask because that's an added bonus. Teammates spend so much time together, and being able to do so with my best friend while we race alongside one another would make me even happier. Yes, we're going to fight and butt heads, but we'll also get to spend more time together, and like Leonard said, we're family. And you can never spend enough time with the family you chose, especially when your lives are so busy.

"Yes, he will be your teammate. You get to bring Parker with you as well, I know it's important to you that they're included. You can also choose your own race engineer because I want you to have someone you can have a good relationship with, not another Cory situation," he goes on, and I think I might be dreaming because this can't be true. It's too perfect to be. "Your signing bonus, pay, everything is in there. Take your time to read it. I've also sent a copy to your manager for her to look over." *This man.*

I get up and walk around the desk to throw my arms around him. Expecting me to, he stands up so he can return my hug properly.

"I can't thank you enough," I say, but Leonard shakes his head.

"This isn't anything to thank me for. You have the talent. You have the dedication. You have what it takes. I simply want to give you a car equal to your teammate's and faster than everyone else's that will allow you to finally get that championship title you've been working toward for the past ten years," he says, and I squeeze him even tighter because this embrace is the only thing assuring me this isn't a dream.

"If I cry on your team shirt, will you take back the contract?" I ask when the tears return and I'm unable to stop them this time.

"Probably." I instantly pull back, and he lets out a deep laugh that surprises me so much, it shocks my whole system. "Okay, that was it, Cameron. You can go now. I have to get back to my team to make sure everything goes smoothly during Qualifying," he says and squeezes my arm, picking up the contract again to hand it to me. He's making sure I don't forget it, but there is no way I could forget the key that unlocks the door to my dream.

Once Leonard has left the room, I take a moment to soak in this information. I take my time reading the contract. I cry. I laugh. I smile. I was so at peace with never being able to get back into F1 as a driver, but now that I'm given another chance, there is nothing stopping me from taking this one last chance at a championship.

And there's only one person I want to share this joy with.

I'm running as fast as my feet can carry me. I'm running until my lungs are burning. I'm running to get to the man I love. He's standing next to Scarlette, discussing something regarding the times Val's already setting for Qualifying now, but when he sees me, sees the expression I'm wearing, he excuses himself to rush over to me.

I don't care who sees. I don't care what they'll say. I simply kiss him when he's close enough. I kiss him because I'm so happy, it feels like I'm about to burst, and he's the tape keeping me together.

"What happened?" he asks, but he's smiling and grabbing my face with both of his hands, the way he always is. Steadying me. Holding me in place.

"Leonard has offered me the second seat at Grenzenlos for the next two years," I whisper to make sure he's the only one who hears.

His eyes widen and his lips part in surprise as he freezes in place from shock. Then, he's laughing in that way people do when something good happens but they can't quite believe it.

"I thought Kyle—" I cut him off because I'm feeling too bubbly.

"He's retiring. His seat is available for the taking, and I'm going to sign the contract once my manager has looked over it too." Halo lets out a little chuckle.

"Well, we both know Milena is going to have some notes to get you the best possible deal," he replies, and I shake my head because he's just so perfect. I'm still in disbelief that he's mine, that he constantly smells like me, that he's everything I thought I'd never have again.

"I love you so much." Halo grins as he leans down to place the softest kiss on my lips.

"I love you, *mi luz*." Then, he's kissing me again, disbelief fading into more joy.

The pieces of me that broke when I lost my seat, when I crashed, when my father abandoned his family, when my mother shattered the person I used to be with every interaction, are finally finding their matching parts as Halo's and my life intertwine themselves more and more with each other.

We get to be broken together, spending the rest of our lives using the pieces of ourselves to make one beautiful puzzle that is our lives.

Epilogue

Halo

SEVEN MONTHS LATER

Cameron flew with Mami, Chellie, and me to Santiago de los Caballeros in the Dominican Republic for *Carnaval Dominicano* because my family lives in Sabana Iglesia. When I saw Mama and Mapa yesterday for the first time in years, I almost broke into tears, especially because Papa started tearing up and if that man cries, then you cry. Other than Mama, he's the toughest person I've ever met, so seeing his eyes fill with tears when he hugged Nachelle made me feel like I was a kid again, the one he showed how to cook during our *coros*. The one he held in his arms when I cried after accidentally hurting myself.

Chellie never got to be around our big family. She was born so many years after me, and Mami and Dad never went here again. My stupid father wanted us to celebrate all the American holidays, be in that country for all of them, but he never put the same effort into the holidays that were important for Mami. For his children to feel connected to the other part of their family.

I still hate him for it.

I'll always hate him for disconnecting us as much as he did.

Because of Cameron, I don't feel so disconnected anymore. He allows me to embrace my culture. He helps me feel connected to it in every way possible. He flies here with my family so we can see the rest of them, be with them for one of the biggest celebrations in our culture. He's picked up Spanish just so I can speak more Spanish at home. He's letting me teach him about my food so I can share that part of my culture with him. He dances with me in the kitchen, the rhythm of the music my family always listened to flowing through my veins.

Today is Independence Day, which means that the biggest celebrations are happening today. In Santiago, right in the city, people will dress up in costumes, especially like *Diablos Cojuelos*, carrying inflated cow bladders in their hands that they whip around as they walk through the crowds. People will wear folkloric dresses—off-the-shoulder ones with layered ruffles that are the color of the Dominican flag—and dance choreographed dances.

It's a celebration of our culture and traditions.

"I think Chellie is never leaving," Cam tells me as he drops down on the sofa in my grandparents' small living room, right beside me.

"Why would you think that?" I ask with a laugh. His hand moves onto my thigh and he leans over to press his lips to my neck.

"Because she's getting all of the attention here. Everyone is doting on her," he replies, lifting his lips long enough off my neck to say the words, then goes straight back to kissing me until my body hums happily.

"Not all the attention. I have yours," I remind him while he scrapes his teeth along my throat.

"Of course you do. You'll always get my attention. You're too handsome not to," he says, his voice teasing to let me know my looks are not the reason why he's always going to give me attention. Well, at least not the main or only one.

"I'm also your fiancé." He doesn't need the reminder, but after I say it, he slides his hand onto mine, onto the engagement ring he put on my finger not even a week ago.

He proposed to me and said, "I know this may be far earlier than I'm supposed to do this, but I don't want to wait. We've known each other for years and have been dating for almost one of them. Plus, it just feels right, don't you think? It feels like we're meant to be together."

I furrowed my brows, but he got on one knee before I could ask what he meant.

Then he added, "People throw around the term 'love of my life' so easily nowadays, but I've never used it. To me, those words should only ever leave you if you're a million percent sure you won't ever regret them, if doubts don't plague your mind as you voice the words. With that being said, Asher "Halo" Henderson, you're the love of my life. Will you marry me?"

Without a second of hesitation, without a single doubt, I told him, "Yes, I will."

Not a moment since he slipped that ring on my finger, gave me one to slip onto his in return, have I regretted my answer. Because he is right. It does feel like we're meant to be. It feels like we were always meant to end up together. He's the love of my life.

"Practically my husband," he says, moving his lips to my jaw to trail kisses to my mouth. I shiver visibly, making him smile against my skin. "You like that, baby? You like it when I call you my husband?" I dig my nails into my thigh right as his lips brush mine.

"A lot." So much so that I don't know why I ever thought I didn't want this.

"We should probably get ready to go. Your mama and papa sent me in here to make sure you're ready, not to make out with you," he says, but he kisses me as soon as he's done speaking. I chuckle against his lips, but I kiss him back harder, too. Needing more of him.

"I knew they should have sent me," Nachelle says, her voice breaking Cam and me apart. Next thing I know, she flings a pillow at my head. "Let's go," she says and walks out of the room, leaving me to roll my eyes and Cam to laugh.

"Let's go," he repeats, patting my thigh and getting up.

"I need a minute," I reply and lean back on the couch, covering myself with a pillow.

"Good God, Asher," he says with a laugh, making me grin, too.

We drive into Santiago to witness the people dressed up in their costumes and others dancing along to the music they're playing over the speakers. I hear some merengue and notice a few women in their dresses moving with the rhythm, and Cam lets out an excited laugh as he takes everything in. I think he falls in love with this side of my family's culture. Well, even more so than he already did with every piece of it I shared with him in the past.

I fall in love with my culture when I take in all of the people. The passion they have for this day. The *Diablos Cojuelos* are everything I thought they'd be with their terrifying masks covering their face and the inflated cow bladders hanging from where they have them at their hips. Some even have whips in their hands that they use to make a whipping sound.

The people are brimming with joy, and I find myself smiling the whole time.

Mama and Papa are walking with Nachelle, and Mami has her arm slipped through mine as we watch the various performances, Cam's hand slipping into mine as he stands beside me and grins from ear to ear.

There are so manye masks people are wearing that are colorful. I was expecting to see all of this because of the stories Mami, Mama, and Papa used to tell me, and it's wonderful.

At some point, I pull my mami to dance merengue with me, and Nachelle steps toward Cameron to dance with him as Mama and Papa do the same. We're laughing and having the time of our lives, staying far back as to not get hit by the whips or bladders the *Diablos Cojuelos* are known to hit people with as they walk by them.

Eventually, Mami dances with Nachelle, and I pull my fiancé into my arms as the music changes to bachata. Mama and Papa continue dancing with each other, not a care in the world, and I smile at them before bringing my full attention to Cam.

He's gotten incredibly good at dancing, and he knows it, so he sways his hips with confidence, letting me guide him.

The parade continues for hours, but Mama and Papa promised they'd host our family, and I can tell they're both getting anxious to get home and go back to preparing the food.

"We will come back again," Cam says when I linger, taking in the masked people, the ones clad in the dresses, those that are wearing costumes, and others with face paint covering their features.

"I'd like that," I reply, finally tearing my eyes off the parade and bringing my gaze to his hazel ones.

At home, a lot of my family members have already invited themselves into the house, mostly my grandparents' other children, and they're in the kitchen eating some of the food Mama and Papa made this morning.

My grandparents go overboard. There are *bandera dominicana, tostones, empanadas, chimichurris, yaniqueques, quipes,* and so much more.

Some of my cousins have put up speakers to let more music flow through them, and I notice Cameron standing with them, chatting to them about something. Considering I'm pretty sure Higuel and Abnar don't know that much English, my fiancé must be speaking to them in Spanish, and I have this urge to get closer and hear how he's doing.

Then again, it's Cameron. He's so confident even when he isn't fluent in a language, and when he makes a mistake, mispronounces something or uses the wrong conjugation by accident, he corrects himself without tripping over himself.

"*Ven aquí, mi amor. Necesito ayuda,*" Mama says, taking my hand and leading me into the kitchen where the mountains of food are.

My family is talking and laughing, the house filling with the sounds of their voices in the most beautifully chaotic way.

Nostalgia has wrapped around me like a blanket, and I soak it all in because I didn't realize just how much I missed it, all of them, until all of their voices and laughter combine in my ears, making my heart beat a little more evenly.

By the time dinner is wrapping up, Papa pulls me toward the table where my cousins are playing a round of dominoes. Cam appears by my side almost immediately after I sit down, and I place an arm around his waist while he wraps his around my shoulders.

"I don't think it'll be a good look if I beat your family members in dominoes, but I really want to play. And win," he adds the last two words after a bit of hesitation, and I can't help but burst into laughter.

"How about we play together? Then they can be mad at me if we win," I suggest, and Cam looks down at me with his bright smile.

"So, this is what you were describing when you were telling me about the *coros* your family used to have when you were a kid?" he asks and runs a gentle hand over my hair.

"Yes, this is exactly that."

"It's incredible. It feels like home," he says, but he gets distracted by us getting our dominoes.

I agree with him. This does feel like home, especially because he's here. He's completing my family, and there is nothing else I need in the world.

Just my family, him, and all of our dreams that are coming true.

Cameron

MY HEADPHONES ARE A steady weight on my head and ears as I sit in the corner of my garage before my race, watching my engineers and mechanics run around for the last-minute tasks that have to be done for the car. I'm moving my upper body from side to side as I listen to some music to calm my nerves.

We're two races away from the end of the season. I've got a twenty-five-point lead over Gabriel in second place in the championship standings.

I'm starting from pole and he's starting from third place, so as long as I finish anywhere above him, I'm going to go home a World Champion today. My last chance at a championship before I retire and move to live on the ranch with Halo for a while.

Leonard promised me the fastest car on the track when I signed with him two years ago, and that's exactly what he gave me. He gave me a car equally as fast as Gabriel's too. No bullshit prioritising Gabriel the way Hawke used to do with James and me. No. I got a fair shot, and now I'm about to take the title home.

This is the closest I've ever been to winning a championship. The closest I ever will get.

My eyes drop to the ring wrapped around my ring finger, and I think about my husband. I think about him fevering in Adrian's garage while we wait for the start of the race.

I think about what he said to me this morning.

Today is your day, mi luz. *No one can take this away from you. This title belongs to you.*

My eyes fall shut as his voice replays over and over in my mind.

This title belongs to me.

No one can take it away from me.

Today is my day.

Over and over until it's time for me to get into the car. Parker hands me everything I need, and my gaze lingers on the halo made up of tulips drawn onto the top of my helmet. I've been wearing this symbol for the past two years to have my Halo in the car with me.

After slipping on my balaclava, I bring the helmet down over my head, taking another second to inhale deeply and get rid of all of this nervous energy inside of me. I haven't had a panic attack in almost a year, but that doesn't mean I won't be able to have one now, when it feels like the fate of the world is resting on my shoulders.

And while it isn't actually, today isn't just about winning. It's about proving everyone who said I didn't belong in this sport wrong. It's about showing I deserved the seat Leonard gave me. It's about knowing for myself that I was worthy of everything I achieved here.

All of the pain, struggle, hurt, and heartbreak will be worth it when I cross the finish line a winner today.

It feels strange to be in the car for the second-to-last-time. I'm not ready to say goodbye, and at the same time, I know it's time. I know this is it for me in the world of F1.

And I'm going to go out with a bang.

I drive my car onto the grid so we can go through every single pre-race procedure. My team goes to work on the car again while I stand with the rest of the drivers to listen to the national anthem of Brazil.

Everyone is silent today.

Val and Adrian have been struggling all weekend with their cars, so they're not happy at the moment. Gabriel isn't speaking to me much today because we both know what's on the line. James has a lot on his mind, and Chellie is focused. Not a single one of my family members is in the mood to chit-chat, and I can't blame them because neither am I. This is the track where I almost lost my life, and this year, it could be the one where I win the title.

I have a job to do.

By the time the anthem is over, I make my way through the crowd of people currently on the grid. I'm on a mission to get to my car where Parker is standing, waiting for me.

"You look like you're about to throw up, you're *that* green in the face," they inform me, and I glare at them.

"Do you think that's helping?" I ask, but they merely shrug with a smile.

"Helps me." I bite down on my cheek to keep from smiling at them.

Soon, it's time to get into the car. Everything feels so rushed today, but that only means I get to chase my title sooner. As long as I don't jump the start, I'll be fine. I'll get my first and last championship. This one is reserved for me, and me alone.

"Did they fix the diffuser?" I ask Parker, and they give me a confident nod.

"Yup. You shouldn't have any problems with it anymore."

"That's good. I remember what happened last year during the British Grand Prix to James when he was headed straight into Chapel and his diffuser blew." That day scared all of us because his engine also ended up catching fire, and it was pouring rain.

The only upside was that we got to see a rainbow every time we drove by the finish line when the other side of the storm appeared and the clouds slowly started to disappear. It's almost like we could see the inside of the rainbow.

Parker and I don't speak anymore.

They usher me into the car, and I obey, slipping into my seat. I place my seatbelt on, then run a single hand over my halo, the very thing that saved my life over three years ago.

Before I'm ready, it's time for the formation lap. Since I got pole yesterday, I'm the one to lead us around the track for it. I look in my mirrors to see Chellie in second place in her Hawke Racing car.

After Hawke completely changed their leadership, things changed very quickly, and she is in a much better place with the team now. She pushed through the difficult times.

I had never been so proud of anyone in my life. I blame Chellie joining them for their changes for the better, even if she denies it.

After bringing my car back to its designated spot on the starting grid, I wait for everyone else to follow suit.

The lights appear once everyone is there.

One by one, they turn on, but today there is no period between all of them being on and turning off, where we have to wait. No. Today it's an immediate thing. Almost as soon as the last light illuminates its box, they all disappear again.

My reaction time is luckily fast enough to keep Chellie behind me, but she's fighting off a determined Gabriel. All I can do is push to make sure I have enough of a distance from him if he manages to take second place.

Because if he does, he *will* be hunting me down.

"Rae, tell me the gap between me and Gabriel," I say after hitting my radio button, taking my car into the second corner of the track for the third time today.

"He's three-point-nine seconds behind. He's in Nachelle's DRS range and is trying to overtake her. As soon as they enable it, he should be able to," she informs me, which only makes me push harder.

Chellie keeps Gabriel behind her far longer than anyone was expecting. Her Hawke has a lot more straight speed on this track than Grenzenlos thought her car would have, more than she showed they were capable of during practise and Qualifying. She keeps him behind her almost until it's time for our pitstops.

Brazil is most often a two-stopper. We start on soft, then switch to mediums, then go back to softs. It's exactly what my team and I do. Nothing spectacular happens during the first pitstop, but the second one is trickier. We stopped right after Gabriel pitted in an attempt to undercut me, but my team reacted quickly enough to make sure he didn't close the gap between us with his newer and fresher tyres.

But once both of us have stopped, once there is nothing in the way anymore, we're free to race.

And Gabriel wastes no time closing the gap between us as quickly as possible.

"Time?" I ask Rae.

"Zero-point-nine," she replies, and I curse because I can see how close he is. I can see that if I'm not careful, he's going to overtake me.

It's moments like these when it's easiest to make mistakes. If the pressure gets to me, I'll make reckless mistakes that could cost me the win today. The title.

I take a deep breath to calm myself right before taking another corner, feeling the G-force press down on my body even more. My neck feels so sore from getting yanked around as much as it does in an F1 car, but I bite through the pain and keep pushing.

Gabriel and I cross the line head-to-head. We move into the first corner again, but I brake later than him, making sure I'll stay ahead of him as we exit it.

I do.

I let out a breath, but my relief doesn't last long because when we get back to the finish line, he's trying to overtake me again.

Somehow, I manage to defend for the second time.

"How are his tyres?" I ask when we're about ten laps from the end of the race.

"His front ones are degrading faster than his rear ones."

"What does that mean?" I ask because I need a more concrete answer. I need to know if he'll have to stop attacking me soon or if he can keep this up for the rest of the race.

"It means focus on your race. Keep doing what you're doing. He's putting pressure on you, so you need to focus on yourself."

There is no arguing with Raelynn when she's got this tone in her voice, so I clamp my mouth shut. I don't speak to her again. She doesn't speak to me.

Gabriel continues fighting me for first place, and I have no fucking clue how his tyres don't give up on him when we reach lap fifty-five of fifty-seven.

It's impossible.

Even my tyres are starting to give up on me.

"Fucking hell, Gabriel," I mumble to myself because this man is proving to me and the rest of the world why he's a multiple-time Formula One World Champion, and there is nothing I can do but hang on for dear life and fight with every bit of strength I have left.

"Last lap, Cameron. You can push more now," Rae informs me, and she doesn't have to tell me twice. If my tyres are still okay for me to squeeze every last bit of performance out of them without blowing, then I'll do exactly that.

Sweat is dripping down my body as I make my way around the track for the last time in Brazil.

Ever.

Gabriel attempts another overtake three corners before the end of the race, and I curse because he got so close, I could practically feel his front tyre touching mine.

But it doesn't.

And that was the last attempt he could make.

I cross the finish line as a champion.

I cross the finish line with my dream becoming a reality.

I cross the finish line knowing I was worth everything, every opportunity and investment anyone's ever made in me.

I'm screaming beneath my helmet, barely registering Rae telling me that I'm the champion. That I've done it. That the title is mine.

I barely register anything at all during my cool-down lap as I wave to my fans. Gabriel pulls his car beside mine so we can celebrate together, and he even gives me a thumbs up I know pains him to give because I've taken what we both wanted.

My whole body is shaking when I drive my car to the first place sign. I can't help but sit there, ripping my gloves off and staring at the scars marring the skin on my hands.

This almost didn't happen, but I was given another shot at life, and I made something of it.

I won.

I married.

I reached my dream.

I'm going to be a father one day and have an even bigger family.

Halo's face is the thing that gets me moving out of my car. I rip off my helmet, running straight into his arms. He catches me, the impact not even making him take a step back because he was expecting the force of my hug.

I barely move back, barely have time to prepare for the kiss he plants on my lips.

It's too brief, too short, but the rest of my team picks me up and lifts me in the air to celebrate me before I can get more of my husband.

At least I think it's my team.

But when I look down, I see Adrian, James, Gabriel, Chellie, and Val lifting me up, celebrating me. The tears drip down my cheeks because they love me so much, and I love them so much.

They drop me back on my feet only to hug me and tell me how proud they are of me, and when Leonard appears beside me, I cry even harder.

He gives me a proud smile, placing his hands on both of my shoulders as he looks me in the eye.

"You did it, you remarkable driver. You won, and I'm so proud of you."

"It wouldn't have happened without you giving me another chance, Leonard," I remind him. He simply shrugs, and I hug him, fully crying on his team shirt this time. I'm retiring anyway. It's not like he can kick me out for doing it, not like he could two years ago.

Every single one of my family members has post-race responsibilities, so they don't linger, but the love of my life does. He's waiting for me to go back to him, and I do. I move back into his arms, kissing him again because this is my moment.

But it's only my moment because he's here with me, too.

"Never thought I'd have a Formula One World Champion husband," Halo mumbles when I go back to hugging him, smelling the perfume I will continue to make him for the rest of my life.

"Never thought I'd be one." Halo leans back to take my face in his hands.

"I always knew you would be champion," he replies, and I shake my head, dropping my forehead against his chest. "And I'm so glad you're mine, too."

"I'll be yours until the universe ceases to exist, my Halo."

"Good, because that's how long I'll belong to you, too."

And we have the rest of our time to give life to those words.

The End

Translations

Todo estará bien.
-
Everything will be alright.

Nachelle, da un paso atrás, por favor.
-
Nachelle, please take a step back.

pan con café con leche
-
bread with coffee and milk

Muy bien - Very good

Arcoíris - Rainbow

Mierda - Shit

¿Algo o alguien? - Something or someone?

Volveré pronto - I'll be back soon

Bonjour, mon petit ange
-
Good morning, my little angel

Enchanté - Nice to meet you

Todavía no me puedo creer que Nachelle sea un
piloto de Fórmula Uno
-
I still can't believe Nachelle is a Formula One driver

Se ve tan seria - She looks very serious

Dramática - She's dramatic

Estoy nerviosa - I'm nervous

Translations

Amor - Love

Coño - Fuck

Mijo, no se supone que estés trabajando
-
My son, you're not supposed to be working

No estoy trabajando. Esto es un pasatiempo.
-
I'm not working. This is a pastime.

Mentiroso - Liar

Mi amor, te dejé un poco de café en la cocina.
-
My love, I left you a bit of coffee in the kitchen.

Dahiana, es un placer conocerla.
-
Dahiana, it's a pleasure to meet you.

Tiene dos hijos maravillosos y quiero agradecerle que los
haya traído al mundo para que yo pudiera conocerlos.
-
You have two incredible children, and I want to thank you
for bringing them into the world so I could meet them.

En español puedes usar tú conmigo.
-
In Spanish, you can use "you" with me

mi luz - my light

Sigue, y te voy a dar un bofetazo
-
Keep going, and I'll slap you

Translations

Tú me tienes tan loco, Cameron.
-
You drive me crazy, Cameron.

mein Mond - my moon

Tu persona favorita - Your favorite person

¿Cómo estás, margarita? - How are you, daisy?

Bien - Good

Hola, mi luz - Hello, my light

Vamos - Let's go

Por el amor de Dios, que quede así.
-
For God's sake, let it stay like this

Ella esta bien, Mami, no te preocupes.
-
She's fine, Mami, don't worry.

Hermanito - brother
¿Qué estás haciendo, Julián?
-
What are you doing, Julián?

Estoy engañando a esta malvada mujer.
-
I'm deceiving this wicked woman.

Gracias, pana - Thank you, friend

Ven aquí, mi amor. Necesito ayuda.
-
Come here, my love. I need help.

The following are the chapters from *The Other Side of Her Storm*, where Halo and Cameron meet for the first time.

Halo

Making it into the world of Formula One to become a technical director is a hell of a lot harder than I was expecting it to be. I've been applying for low-level engineer positions for over a year now, trying to get one foot in the door, but so far all I've gotten is rejections.

"You're not qualified."

"We have already filled the position."

"We're not looking for people in engineering at the moment."

It's honestly one of the most exhausting things, and even worse, I'm not getting any internships either. So, I'm stuck at this fucking retail job in Moonville, wasting my time somewhere that won't get me to where I want to be.

It makes me worry about the day my sister fights for her spot in F1. With Valentina Romana becoming the first female F1 driver, the chances of my sister getting a spot one day have multiplied by a million, but I don't know if that will be enough for the sport to start inviting more women. She's currently in F4, fighting every single race to work her way into F3 or F2, whichever would be willing to give her a chance.

"Halo, are you okay?" Scarlette asks, and I drape an arm across her shoulders to hug her to my side.

"When have I ever not been?" I challenge with a smirk I don't mean in the slightest.

"Let's see. When Leonard Tick left Grenzenlos you frowned for a week straight and hardly spoke to anyone. When your favorite toothpaste company went out of business and you had to find a new one, you disappeared for three days, not telling anyone where you were going. And a year ago, when you tore your second favorite jacket, you all but had a funeral for it." I step away to give her the shocked look that rant deserves.

"Those were all valid reactions," I reply and point my index finger at her, bringing the sweetest smile to her face.

"I never said they weren't. We were talking about when you weren't okay in the past," she defends with a shrug of her shoulders, but I simply roll my eyes at her before wrapping her in another side hug, this time keeping her there.

A few years ago, around the time I kissed her to make Storm jealous, I realized I could fall for this woman. This ray of sunshine that could turn all of my bad days into good ones. The one that inspired so much joy inside of me. We have a million things in common, and she has the biggest heart of anyone I've ever met. And if she hadn't been so in love with Storm, I could have fallen in love with her. Not in the joking way I always said I was. In the way that I've never *let* myself fall for anyone.

It's a good thing I have full control over my emotions and shut that down before I got my heart broken.

Plus, Scar might just be my best friend in this whole world, even if I'm not hers.

I'm used to being the fun one that never gets asked to stick around. It's why none of my relationships ever worked out and I decided that instead of attempting to find myself a partner that may just leave me when times got tough, I wouldn't try being in a relationship at all.

You can't get your heart broken if you never give it to someone who could trample on it.

Fuck, my thoughts are way too deep today.

I shudder and shake out my limbs, inevitably shaking Scar too. She laughs, a melodic sound that travels through her husband's garage. It calls his attention to her, and he lifts his head from where he's standing next to one of his mechanics who is talking to him about something related to his bike.

"Touching my wife again, Henderson?" he says from all the way across the room without having to raise his voice. The deep sound simply travels through the room effortlessly, the warning as clear in his tone as it is on his features.

"What are you going to do about it?" I challenge because I love fucking with that grumpy man.

Up until he starts storming toward me, which is when I drop my arm and raise my hands in mock surrender. He stops and turns on his heel, not even enjoying getting what he wanted. No. For him it's enough that I'm scared and no longer touching his wife.

"So possessive," I say to Scar and click my tongue, chuckling.

"Yeah, but possessive Julián is sexy. He's always broody, but when it comes to someone being too close to me?" She fans herself with her hand, and I burst into laughter, rolling my lips to hold back more when I see several of the mechanics turn my way. "Oh, also, I should let you know that there will be a Formula 1 driver here later."

My interest is piqued immediately.

"Who?"

"Cameron Kion." My jaw drops all the way to the floor.

"Shut up," I reply, grabbing her arm as if that would tether me to reality because this simply can't be real.

Cameron Kion is my second favorite F1 driver of all time.

He's never won a race before, but he's the fun and easy-going type of person that brings so much light to the sport. No matter what car he's in, he always gives everything he's got. When Adrian Romana went into the sport, he was a hell of a mentor to him. He never speaks badly about the rest of the drivers, instead, he finds a way to joke about the things that clearly piss him off. From what I've heard of him, he also takes care of his family ever since his father abandoned his family, and to top it all off, he was the first F1 driver to come out as gay.

From what Scar has told me, he's not the only queer driver now.

Valentina Romana has told me personally that she's pan, Adrian Romana has flirted more with Storm than his own wife even has, Leonard Tick, although mostly private, has recently shared a lot about being queer in the world of F1 on top of also being the first black driver, and Gabriel Biancheri, according to Scar, very much agrees with his girlfriend that it wouldn't matter to him what gender Valentina identifies as.

He loves her for who she is, not because of her gender.

A man after my own heart.

James Landon, although he hasn't ever discussed his sexuality to me or Scar, gives me the type of vibe that he's very much part of our community as well.

"He'll be here in about half an hour so, please, prepare yourself," Scar says, twisting her arm to get out of my grasp only to put her hand on my arm instead and give it a gentle but warning squeeze.

Okay.

Get my shit together.

I can do that.

Totally.

It's not like I'm about to meet an F1 legend. Someone who's gotten that status simply by having a huge impact on the sport without even winning a race or a championship in his years there.

No.

It'll be fine.

Oh my God, I'm sweating.

The next half hour passes agonizingly slowly, probably because I'm staring at the time on Scar's screen.

But when he finally walks into the room, my breath catches in my throat.

Cameron Kion is about five foot nine, lean but muscular as fuck, especially his thighs, and chiseled beyond anything I've ever seen. He's got curly brown hair and hazel eyes as well as the biggest and brightest smile I've ever seen on a person.

As soon as he approaches, I feel my heart flutter in a way that I don't ever want to fucking dissect because, well, it's never done that before.

I'll simply blame the fact that he's a celebrity.

"Cameron, it's wonderful to see you," Scar says and hugs him, a hug he returns so fully, I'm a little jealous.

I think a hug like that would heal a lot of parts of me that have been broken for far too long.

His gaze shifts to where I'm standing, and he furrows his brows as he studies my expression, the one I currently have no control over.

"Who is pretty boy and why is he looking at me like I'm his savior?" Cameron asks Scar with his thick Australian accent, and a blush immediately heats up my skin. I barely keep the nervous giggle inside because he just called me "pretty boy."

This is not "getting my shit together" at all.

"Cameron, that's Asher 'Halo' Henderson. Halo, this is Cameron," Scar says, turning to me to widen her eyes at me as a way to tell me to unfreeze.

"Nice to meet you, Halo," Cameron says as he extends his hand to me.

"Yeah, nice to meet you, too," I reply and shake his hand, trying not to slap myself for that lame response.

"Is he okay?" Cameron whispers to Scar when I haven't stopped shaking his hand for longer than necessary.

"I'm not sure. He's usually more unaffected and confident than this," Scar whispers back, and I finally manage to release Cameron's hand. A nervous laugh slips past my lips, and I slap a hand in front of my mouth because *what the hell is happening to me?*

Cameron chuckles and places a hand on my shoulder, squeezing it as a way of comfort. What it does is make more embarrassment heat up my cheeks.

Fuck me.

"It's okay to be starstruck. It happened to me the first time I met Fiona Wise." Scar's head snaps toward Cameron at his words.

"No way. You met basketball legend Fiona Wise? In person? No one ever hears anything from her anymore since she's retired."

The two of them fall into a casual conversation about that Fiona lady, and I do my best not to gape at Cameron, but it's so hard not to. On top of being my second favorite F1 driver, he's even better looking in person than he is on a screen, a fact I'm having a very hard time processing at the moment.

Especially because I can't keep from studying his strong, muscular neck, the way his Adam's apple bops as he speaks, and how his full lips shape words.

He has a boyfriend.

He has a boyfriend.

He has a boyfriend.

The mantra is meant to help me stop ogling him, but the only thing that really helps is when Scar tells us the race is starting soon and the three of us turn to her screens as Storm lets his engine roar to life.

It's time for the sighting lap.

Cameron

I've never attended a MotoGP race before. This specific Grand Prix fell on a weekend when I didn't have to race myself and in my home country, so I had to come to see Scarlette and support her and her husband.

We met a year ago during a particularly wild party Leonard Tick hosted to celebrate his wife's gallery opening, her second location in England. He invited Storm and Scarlette, and I spent the night talking to her about Formula One. She wanted to become a race engineer in the sport we both love, and knowing she's finally getting her chance, especially working with one of my favorite people, makes me a very happy man.

She deserves all the success in the world, and if I'd had the power to—meaning I could fire my useless race engineer who hates my guts—I would have hired her on the spot.

"Can I ask you a question?"

A smile tugs at the right side of my mouth.

"Found your voice, have you?" I ask Halo, turning my head to grin at him and find his cheeks still wonderfully red. I don't think that man has stopped blushing since he shook my hand for too long.

"Listen, man, you're super famous, and I admire you a lot, so if I'm a bit awkward, you can only blame yourself," he replies, finally gathering a bit of that confidence Scarlette was talking about before.

"A bit?" I tease him, and he blushes even harder, his face turning an even darker shade of red. "I'm kidding. Ask your question. I'm curious now."

Halo chews on his ridiculously full bottom lip for a second, trying to build up the courage to ask me whatever it is that's weighing on his chest. He's significantly taller than me, so I have to tilt my head back to look into those icy-blue eyes of his. He's also wearing a white polo shirt that complements his tanned skin, and his brown hair sits in messy curls on his head.

"My sister is currently in F4, and she's working her way up into the next categories, but it's really difficult to find sponsors. Do you have any tips or..." Halo trails off, and I cross my arms in front of my chest as I raise my brows at him.

"We know each other for five minutes and you're already asking me for favors?" His eyes widen and his lips part as regret consumes his features.

"No, that's not—I didn't mean—You're just so—" I cut him off.

"I'm messing with you. If we're going to become friends, you're going to have to learn my sense of humor," I say, which seems to settle him a little because his shoulders drop in relief. "What's her name?"

"Nachelle Henderson," he replies and pulls out his phone to show me a picture of her in her racing gear.

"I've heard of her. An up-and-coming driver with a bright future." Halo's eyes soften immensely at my words, and I can tell that he loves his sister. So much so that he'd ask a guy he barely had the confidence to greet for any tips on how to get her further in her career.

It's sweet.

"I'll see if any of my sponsors are looking for new talent to support," I promise him and mean it because F1 is in dire need of more women, and if there is anything I can do to help that happen faster, I will.

Silence stretches between us, and we both shift our attention to the screens again just in time to see Julián leading the rest of the grid into the warm-up lap. He's starting from pole with Viktor right behind him. From what I've gathered from reading up on this season, those two have been fighting each other for first place since the beginning.

Scarlette is working hard, looking at three different screens in front of her at the same time while Storm makes his way across the track, warming his tires.

It's nice to be on this side of it. There is a nervousness weighing on my chest, but it's nothing compared to the one I feel when I'm in the car, getting ready to race.

A lot of people assume that just because it's my job and I do it twenty-plus times a year it would get any easier, but I always get nervous. No matter how long I've been driving, I feel my chest get tight with anticipation and fear.

I'm sure it's the same for Storm, even if he looks calm and collected from this perspective.

The twenty-two riders line up on the grid in their designated spots again, and I find myself holding my breath when all the lights turn on above them.

I wonder if Elijah feels this way before my races, and the thought of my boyfriend has me smiling so hard, my cheeks hurt. I try to get it under control because I notice Halo giving me a confused look, and I don't particularly feel like telling him I'm grinning like an idiot because I've never been this in love before.

Once the lights disappear, Storm and the rest of the riders shoot forward, starting the race. He stays ahead throughout the first three laps, and I find myself relaxing a little when he creates a small gap between himself and Viktor, who seems only too eager to find ways to stick to Storm so he doesn't race away in front.

I'd have expected MotoGP to be a lot more different from Formula One than it actually is.

"Tell me something, Halo. What is it that you do?" I ask when the riders have made their way around the Philip Island Grand Prix Circuit for the fifth time.

"I'm currently working in retail, but it's only until I find a place in F1. I want to become a technical director, so there are a lot of steps I still have to take before I'm even qualified enough to reach that position," he explains, surprising me.

"You're also trying to make it into F1, but you asked me for help for your sister before asking for yourself?" Halo doesn't look at me as I ask the question. He merely shrugs like it's the most natural thing to put others' needs before your own.

"She means more to me than any job in F1 ever would," he says, and I suddenly understand him better than I've ever understood a stranger this quickly.

"I get that. I'd give my life for my siblings. For me, protecting them comes above everything else," I reply and turn my head enough to see him smiling. "What?"

"Nothing. I just wouldn't have expected you to be the one to do the protecting considering you're an F1 driver that puts his life at risk every time he sits in that car. Seems a bit ironic, don't you think?" he asks, so I cross my arms in front of my chest and turn fully to him.

"I do what I do to pay for my siblings to have the best life they could have. I can buy them everything they want and ask for, which isn't a lot because my siblings don't like asking for things. If risking my life means they get to have a good one, then I'll risk my life. Simple as that." Halo nods thoughtfully, clearly agreeing with me.

"So you understand why I asked for my sister and not myself."

It takes everything I've got to fight my smile because I get now what he was trying to do.

"Well played," I say, and Halo grins, winking at me before turning his head back to the screens.

My gaze lingers on him for another long moment, but he doesn't call me out on it. He lets me study him before I turn away, too, focusing entirely on the race.

It's a brutal one.

Storm is fighting Viktor at every turn starting lap seven. They swap positions several times until finally, Viktor makes it stick. He races away, creating a gap of a little over a second over Storm, who is fighting to get back first place.

I'm glued to the screen, chanting for Storm to get Viktor again, but it's not working.

When they cross the line, Storm is in second place. Viktor takes first, closing the gap that the Puerto Rican has done his best to widen, even if it's only by a little.

Scarlette's head drops in defeat, and I know she's as disappointed as her husband is right now.

As disappointed as I am most days when I cross the finish line not a winner. It's a pain that never gets easier.

The following pages are a teaser from Nachelle's book which will be releasing in 2026. The art work you are about to see has not be revealed yet, so I ask you not to share it with anyone. It is for your eyes only.

-Bridget

Chapter One

Nachelle

AUSTRALIA IS ONE OF my favorite races of the season.

This is only the third Grand Prix of the year, but I've already won one and came second in another, the best start I've ever had. Since I switched from Hawke Racing to Spark Racing—after Hawke tried to replace me with Cameron Kion, my brother's husband and my former mentor—I've been working my way to the top with my new team.

My teammate, Dakila Bautista, is my biggest competition so far, but Formula One legend Valentina Romana, who's racing for Velocità Rossa for the ninth year in a row, is a close third in the standings.

We have the whole season for the rest of the drivers and teams to catch up, but, as of right now, I feel good.

I feel confident.

Today is race day. I'm currently standing with all twenty drivers on the grid as we respectfully listen to the national anthem of Australia. The sun is blaring down on us, which is why Dakila has opened up one of the umbrellas our team gave us, offering us both shade. I bump his shoulder with mine halfway through the anthem, and he nudges me back. I suppress a smile, but he snickers beside me, earning us a warning look from James Landon. The Brit used to be my teammate at Hawke, but now he's sort of become the dad of the grid. I think it's because he has two kids at home, Daisy and Damian, as well as two cats, so he's always in Dad Mode these days.

I find it extremely entertaining to watch him try to keep all the rookies and younger drivers in check while they swarm to him because of his knowledge and experience in the sport.

Plus, who doesn't want an F1 World Champion as their mentor?

"He should really pull that stick out of his ass," Dakila says as we head toward where our cars are in their designated spots on the grid.

"It's not a stick. It's gotta be at least pole sized by now," I reply, making my teammate burst into laughter.

A few people around us turn their heads, watching us with confused looks. Dakila and I get that a lot. We're unlike most teammates. Instead of pretending to be friends, we actually are friends, and we spend most of our time together, laughing about what the other person says, because of how alike our senses of humor are. Of course we fight when something happens between us on the track, a crash or a disagreement, but, for some reason, we never stay mad at each other for long.

I'm grateful for it because Formula One can be a very lonely sport. When I joined, everyone had already found their people in here. Valentina and Adrian siblings and as close as they could be, and she's married to Gabriel Biancheri, the number one driver of the Grenzenlos team. James has been best friends with all of them for years and years, and Cameron left the sport a year ago, which left me on the outside. I tried to befriend the other drivers, but they weren't interested in being friends with me.

No one until Dakila.

"Safe race," he says and holds out his hand for me to do the handshake we came up with for luck before every race.

"Safe race," I echo, then we both walk away, finding our cars and our teams.

"Feel ready?" Saanvi, my performance coach, asks as soon as she meets me at the car. She's clad in the orange colors of Spark Racing, which make her brown eyes glow wonderfully. Her long, dark hair is woven into a braid, preventing it from hiding her sharp facial features and warm smile.

Saanvi and I have been working together for years. She's seen me at my lowest, and I was there for her when she left her husband because of how emotionally abusive he was. We're bonded in a way not many drivers and performance coaches are, and I wouldn't have it any other way.

"About as ready as one might feel before they bungee jump," I reply, but she merely shakes her head at me because I tell her the same thing every single time.

It's a wonder she keeps asking me how I'm feeling anyway.

"Can you come up with something new? I'm getting tired of the same answer every race weekend," she says, feigning annoyance, but her smile betrays her words, no matter how much she tries to hide it.

"I'll try to think of something more irritating next time," I tease, and Saanvi playfully frowns at me before handing me my earplugs for my radio.

After I slide them into my ears, I grab my balaclava out of her hand. It's raven-black, and, with my hair braided out of my face, it easily slips onto my head. Next, Saanvi hands me my helmet, and I place my forehead to the front of it as I take a deep breath.

Por el amor de las carreras.

Por la gloria de ganar.

I repeat the same words over and over in my head, breathing deeply and steadily to get in the zone. It's dangerous for an F1 driver to be anything but focused because, at times, we drive at over three hundred and fifty kilometers per hour. There is no room for mistakes, for thinking about anything other than the track, the drivers behind and in front of you, and everything else we have to do while we're racing.

It's too dangerous for us to be distracted.

Once I feel ready, I lean back and study my helmet. It's indigo-colored with swirls of white and blue mixed into the design. There are some logos from my sponsors integrated as well as a Hispaniolan boa. Asher, my brother that everyone—including myself—has adapted to calling Halo for his "angelic" nature, told me about the time one of those snakes scared the shit out of him when he visited our family in the Dominican Republic. It became so much of an inside joke between us that I decided to weave it into my helmet design.

This way, my brother is always with me in the car, even as he does his job as the Technical Director for my team's biggest rival: Velocità Rossa.

Saanvi nods at me once I've got the helmet on, and I nod back, taking one last deep breath to settle the nerves in my chest before I make my way into the car.

With my helmet secured using the HANS device—technology developed to make sure my shoulders and head are firmly set in place to keep from being jerked around—I secure my seatbelt too, protecting me even further.

"Radio check, Nachelle," my race engineer says, and I press down on my radio button on my steering wheel to answer.

"Hear you loud and clear, Zuri," I reply, and, while I can't see her, I know she's currently nodding repeatedly while looking at every single screen in front of her.

There are a few more pre-race procedures we work through while we wait for the light to turn on, signaling the start of the formation lap where all twenty drivers get to warm up our tires, charge our batteries, and get one last look at the track conditions before the start of the race. It also allows all of the teams to clear the grid after they were working on our cars during the pre-race procedures.

I'm starting from pole position with Dakila in second, Valentina in third, James in fourth, Gabriel in fifth, and Adrian in sixth, followed by the rest of the grid. My two biggest rivals this season are right behind me, and there is not a doubt in my mind that they will throw everything they have at me as soon as this race begins.

My heart lurches in fear in my chest, thudding so hard against my ribcage that I have to adjust in my seat a little to find a more comfortable position.

Then it's time for the formation lap. I lead the rest of the pack across the track at a much slower pace than we usually drive during the race. Checking my mirrors, I notice Dakila swerving side to side to get some heat into his tires, but Valentina doesn't bother with any of that. Her Velocità Rossa is a frightening sight, a lion on its hunt in my mirrors, and I have to look away to stop feeling so intimidated.

It's difficult not to get intimidated by the coolest person the world of Formula One has ever seen when she's also the best racer it has ever had.

We line up on the grid again once we get back to the starting line, all of us making sure we don't cross that yellow line on the track since we could get harsh penalties for improper starting positions. Zuri is quiet in my ears, which means there is nothing on her end that she needs to inform me about, and I'm quiet too because everything, so far, is as expected. No rain, no issues with the car that I can feel, nothing at all to prevent me from snatching this win for myself.

There are five red lights right above us on the grid that turn on one by one with a second between them. Then, as soon as they're all illuminated, there is a delay in them turning off again, telling us to start the race. None of us know how long it will take because it's always random, so we have to be ready, fingers above the buttons on the steering wheel and feet ready to press down on the gas pedal.

All five lights turn on.

Less than two seconds later, they vanish.

My reaction time is so good, I make it through the first corner without a single overtake attempt from Dakila or anyone else behind me. However, when I check my mirrors I realize my reaction time wasn't the only thing that allowed me to have this easy of a start.

No.

Valentina overtook Dakila, and I watch in my mirrors as my teammate tries to get his second place back.

I have to focus back on the track in front of me for the next corner, but I hear it.

I hear them crash moments before I see yellow flags being waved at the sides of the track, telling us to slow down.

"Zuri, what happened?" I ask as I hit my radio button.

"Dakila drove into the back of Valentina's car. Both are out of the race. Valentina was on the radio, saying she's fine and cursing out Dakila, and he mumbled something about how sorry he was, but I think he got the wind knocked out of him because he was breathing quite heavily."

They'll have to take him to the paramedics at least, maybe even the hospital for a check up, to make sure nothing is seriously wrong.

Fuck!

That was way too damn careless of him. My heart is still racing from the sheer fear shooting through my system, and it doesn't ease when I see the red flags being waved.

This is going to be a long race if within the first lap we already have a red flag.

If Dakila is fine, I might strangle him later for scaring the shit out of me.

I shake my head as I drive my car into the pits, lining up at the beginning of it as is done during a red flag.

After parking my car, I stay seated for a moment, my eyes closed as I try to process everything. All of the pressure to get a good result for the team is now on me. There is no room for error.

But I've got this.

I open my eyes as determination sets in.

Today's trophy is mine.

Acknowledgements

Since this is the last book in *The Pitstop Series*, it is only right that these acknowledgments are fully and wholly directed at every single person who has been with me throughout this journey. Words will never be able to express how grateful I am to each and every single one of you for sticking with me, reading eleven books about this characters (11!!!) and watching me grow as a writer in the meantime. Thank you for your patience, for your kind words, for all of the love you have constantly thrown my way in support.

My goal with this series was to ensure people could feel represented and seen, and every single time one of you has reached out to tell me that is exactly how it made you feel, it kept me going. Thank you for that. Thank you for reminding me why I started pursuing this career to begin with, no matter how hard it may get at times. It is *you* who makes it all worth it.

I love you all, and I promise this is not the last time that we will see these characters. Not even close. *The Pitstop Series* is my home. These characters are my family. I will always come back to them.

Plus, there are plenty of them who have yet to get their story told.

Lastly, the biggest thank you needs to go to my sister, who has been on this journey with me since we edited *Rush: Part One*. She's the person who wiped my tears more often than not, the person who helped me out of the dark when things looked very bleak, and who was always patient with me and my wild ideas. Without her, this series would not exist.

And again, thank you to each and every single one of you. You mean the world to me, and I hope Halo and Cam's book was the perfect end to this series for you as it was for me.

2026 is going to be filled with many new and exciting things, and I cannot wait to share them with you.

All my love,

Bridget

About the Author

Bridget L. Rose is a queer author currently located in Toronto, Canada. She was born in Germany and is half-Italian and half-German. During her teenage years, she was fortunate to live in Singapore and the USA as well.

Bridget fell in love with books from a young age, and soon discovered her passion for writing as well. Over the past two years, Bridget has written and self-published ten books. She writes contemporary romances, most of them set in the world of Formula One, as well as cowboy and tennis romances.

In her books she aims to be inclusive because of her own experiences of being queer and living with mental illnesses. Even nowadays, people still make assumptions and use stereotypes about queer people as well as people with mental illnesses, which she experiences daily as well. Bridget is passionate about changing the narratives on these subjects, especially in the romance market.

When Bridget is not busy writing, she loves to read and spend time with her family, including her two furry children JJ and Diego.

Books by Bridget L. Rose

The Pitstop Series

Jump-Start

The Last Championship (Novella)

The Inside of a Rainbow

The Other Sider Of Her Storm

Rush: Part One & Two

Chase: Part One & Two

Reserved

Diffuse

Straight to the Chapel

A Romana Christmas

Silver Creek Ranch Series

From Angels to Devils Series

To Pluto & Back

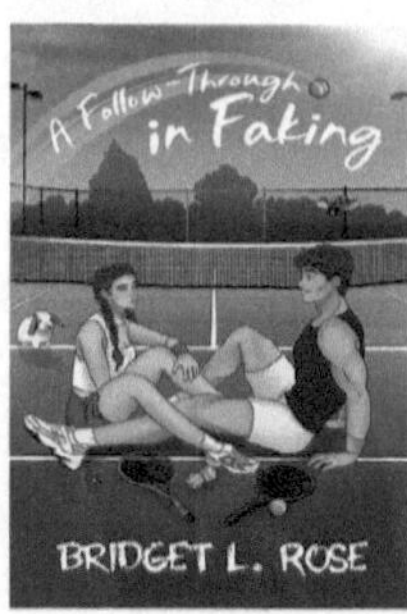

From Devils to Angels